Robin Hood's
DAWN

BOOK I
THE ROBIN HOOD TRILOGY

The Robin Hood Trilogy, Book 1: Robin Hood's Dawn
Second Edition: Copyright © 2019 Olivia Longueville and J. C. Plummer
First Edition: Copyright © 2017 Olivia Longueville and J. C. Plummer
Trade paper ISBN-13:   978-1-947878-05-1
Kindle ISBN-13:   978-1-947878-01-3
EPUB ISBN-13:   978-1-947878-02-0
Audible ISBN-13:   978-1-947878-04-4

This work includes both fictional and historical persons and events. The historical events follow the timeline of history. Our representations of real historical persons abide by the known facts of their lives. However, the passage of so many centuries has obscured much about these historical figures; therefore, the dialogue, opinions, and personalities of these long-dead people are the products of the authors' imagination.

Likewise, the fictional characters and events are the products of the authors' imagination, and any resemblance to actual persons, living or dead, or actual events, is purely coincidental.

The characters described in the Robin Hood ballads can be found in numerous fictional stories which have been written over the course of centuries. These characters are in the public domain. The authors have created their own original versions of these well-known characters, and any resemblance to actual persons, living or dead, is purely coincidental.

Cover design: Damonza.com
Interior design and formatting: Damonza.com

AngevinWorld.com

*For my parents who are always
so supportive and interested
in the work I do as a writer.*
— Olivia

*For Lesley H.
in heartfelt appreciation
for her support and encouragement.*
— J. C.

Notes on the second edition: The Prologue has been slightly altered, and the original Chapter 1 (the 1159 siege of Toulouse) has been removed. To read the original Prologue and Chapter 1, and to enjoy bonus material relating to this book, go to our website:

https://www.angevinworld.com/robin-hood-trilogy/rhd-bonus-material/

Acknowledgments:

Many thanks to our pre-readers and editors. In alphabetical order: Anne, Armand, George, Kathleen, Kevin, Nadezda, and Nathalie

Contents

WILLIAM THE CONQUEROR'S
DESCENDANTS

King William I (King of England, 1066-1087)
married Matilda of Flanders

Children (partial list):
Robert II (Duke of Normandy, 1087-1106)
William II "Rufus" (King of England, 1087-1100)
Henry I (King of England, 1100-1135)
Adela of Normandy

Henry I (King of England, 1100-1135)
married Matilda of Scotland

Children:
Matilda
William Adelin (d. 1120)

Adela of Normandy
married Stephen II, Count of Blois

Children (partial list):
Theobald (Count of Champagne & Blois)
* Stephen of Blois
(King of England, 1135-1154)

Matilda married
Geoffrey V, Count of Anjou

Children:
Henry II (King of England,
1154-1189)
Geoffrey, Count of Nantes
William FitzEmpress

---

* Stephen of Blois (King of
England, 1135-1154)
married Matilda of Boulogne

Children (partial list):
Eustace (d. 1153)
* William (Count of
Boulogne & Mortain,
Earl of Surrey, d. 1159)

Theobald (Count of Blois
& Champagne) married
Matilda of Carinthia

Children (partial list):
Henry I of Champagne
* Adela of Champagne

Henry II (King of England, 1154-1189)
married * Eleanor of Aquitaine

Children:
William (b. 1153 - d. 1156)
Henry the Young King (b. 1155 - d. 1183)
Matilda (b. 1156 - d. 1189)
* Richard (b. 1157 - d. 1199)
Geoffrey (b. 1158 - d. 1186)
Eleanor (b. 1162 - d. 1214)
Joan (b. 1165 - d. 1199)
* John (b. 1166 - d. 1216)

---

* Adela of Champagne
(Queen of France, 1164-1180, d. 1206)
married Louis VII, King of France

Child:
* Philippe II (King of France, 1180-1223)

* Historical figures who appear in
The Robin Hood Trilogy

FICTIONAL FAMILIES IN THE
ROBIN HOOD TRILOGY

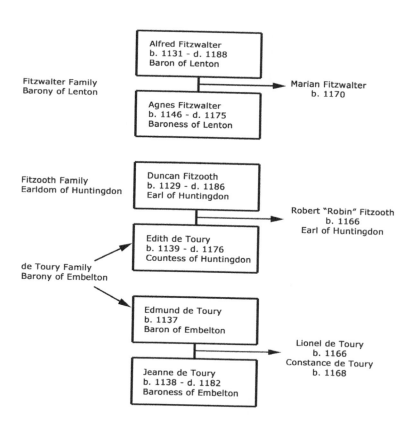

Fitzwalter Family
Barony of Lenton

Alfred Fitzwalter
b. 1131 - d. 1188
Baron of Lenton

Marian Fitzwalter
b. 1170

Agnes Fitzwalter
b. 1146 - d. 1175
Baroness of Lenton

Fitzooth Family
Earldom of Huntingdon

Duncan Fitzooth
b. 1129 - d. 1186
Earl of Huntingdon

Robert "Robin" Fitzooth
b. 1166
Earl of Huntingdon

Edith de Toury
b. 1139 - d. 1176
Countess of Huntingdon

de Toury Family
Barony of Embelton

Edmund de Toury
b. 1137
Baron of Embelton

Lionel de Toury
b. 1166
Constance de Toury
b. 1168

Jeanne de Toury
b. 1138 - d. 1182
Baroness of Embelton

PROLOGUE
THE BLOOD OF THE CONQUEROR

25 October 1154, Dover, Kent, England

"My son, the blood of the Conqueror courses through your body."

Stephen of Blois, King of England, Count of Boulogne, and grandson of William the Conqueror, was dying. Lying on a narrow bed in the Dover Priory, he had already received the last rites, and he was desperate to set his affairs in order.

He clutched the hand of his only remaining son, William, gripping it tightly as another spasm of pain overwhelmed him.

William, the Earl of Surrey, was attractive and intelligent, but he was only seventeen, and Stephen had begged God for just a few more years. That was all he needed to put into place his scheme to ensure that William, not Henry Plantagenet, ascended to the throne.

After years of civil war between Stephen and his cousin, Matilda, Stephen had reluctantly signed a treaty acknowledging Matilda's son, Henry, as his heir and successor. It had been the same type of stalling tactic he had used twenty years earlier when he had

1

agreed to recognize Matilda's claim to the throne, only to seize it for himself as soon as her father died.

And now, eleven months after signing this treaty, he lay dying. He closed his eyes and implored God for just two more years. Perhaps one more year would be sufficient. Another wave of torment engulfed his body and forced him to concede that he would be fortunate to survive the coming night.

Stephen grimaced as he struggled to endure his suffering. Opening his eyes to gaze at his son, who was sitting on the edge of his bed, he demanded, "Summon Huntingdon." He was eager to confer with his most loyal and trustworthy earl.

Duncan Fitzooth, a young, strikingly tall man with wheat colored hair and pale blue eyes approached and genuflected to the king.

Stephen frowned in confusion and looked back at William, who explained, "Father, Huntingdon died months ago. This is his son, Duncan, the new Earl of Huntingdon."

Movement at the periphery of the chamber alerted Stephen to the presence of other men. "Who else is here?" he quietly asked.

Before William could answer, Duncan boldly replied, "Sire, I have brought two of my most trusted vassals: Alfred Fitzwalter, Baron of Lenton, and Hugh FitzCurzon, Baron of Gisborne."

Two men in their twenties stepped forward and briefly dropped to one knee as they performed obeisance to the king. The barons were a study in contrasts: the fair-haired Lenton was graceful and impeccably groomed, while Gisborne was brawny, his wavy black hair disheveled and unfashionably long.

The king began coughing and retching, and when he tasted blood, he swallowed and murmured, "My son, it is over there on the table. Do you see it?"

Prince William leaned away from his father, peering into the dimly lit space. "Yes, Father, I see it."

"Bring it here," the king commanded hoarsely.

The prince dutifully rose to retrieve the artifact, and he held it in front of his father.

With pronounced effort, Stephen lifted his head and reverently pressed his lips against the object. "William, I give you this as my heir and successor. It is a blessed talisman and a symbol of all that I cherish. When the time is right, consider it your key to the kingdom. It belonged to the Conqueror. You bear his name, and your body houses his illustrious blood."

"It is heavy," William observed.

The king nodded. "The guardian of this sacred object will have to bear the weight of a kingdom." He paused to gather his strength. "Give Huntingdon the documents I showed you yesterday."

William promptly obeyed, and Duncan commenced shuffling through the pieces of parchment.

Stephen hastened to explain, his voice ragged and his breathing tortured gasps, as a shroud of mortality descended upon him. "The first is my new will, designating William as successor. It has been signed, and all the official seals are there. The second is a list of loyal vassals; nobles who have sworn fealty to me, and who are ready to support William over Henry. They will provide funds and men-at-arms in order to ensure that William, not Henry, becomes king."

Stephen groaned, incapable of further speech. Nevertheless, relief inundated him. He had made his deathbed proclamations, and he had great faith in the Fitzooth family. After all, it was his benevolence which had bestowed vast wealth and a lofty title upon Duncan's father. He closed his eyes as the chamber became unbearably bright.

"Father?"

Alfred realized that King Stephen had entered into his final rest, and he gently addressed the youthful William. "Sire, he is gone."

At first, William froze as he stared at the lifeless body of his father. Then, he stood and resolutely faced the Earl of Huntingdon. "You must immediately implement Father's plan. It is imperative that I secure the throne before news of Father's death reaches Henry in Normandy."

"*Sire,*" Duncan's voice was dripping with unmistakable contempt. "I've already sent word to Normandy that Stephen was dying. Henry is my liege lord, not you."

William paled as he sputtered, "But…you swore allegiance to my father. My father bestowed the Earldom of Huntingdon on your father."

"King Henry is willing to overlook your role in this plot; you are just a boy and a pawn in your father's schemes. But if you pursue the throne, your name will be added to this list of traitors."

A heavy silence fell upon the room until William ripped his dagger from its sheath and abruptly slashed his palm as the other men gaped at him. He calmly held the talisman of the Conqueror in his bloodied hand and raised it aloft as he declared, "By the blood of the Conqueror, I curse the three of you! Your treachery is your ruin, and as your true liege lord, I claim dominion over you and your children. Even if I must haunt you from beyond the grave, I promise that you and your children will suffer for what you have done to me!"

Alfred and Hugh uneasily crossed themselves while Duncan sneered, "A blood curse? Only weak-minded peasants believe such superstitions. Take heed of my warning—pursue the throne and die a traitor's death, or swear fealty to Henry and live." With that, the three men hastily left the death chamber.

Chapter 1
Kings and Queens

1 May 1188, Huntingdon Castle, Huntingdonshire, England

A lone man stood apart from the crowd and gazed at his target as he hastily wiped a bead of sweat rolling down his temple. The woman he loved was counting on him, and he could not, would not, disappoint her on this special day.

Behind him, a throng of spectators murmured. All eyes were on the young man, his wheat-colored hair slightly ruffled by a soft breeze, and his pale blue eyes intently focused on half a dozen bags of grain stacked in the distance and covered by a white cloth. His goal was the red circle emblazoned on the fabric. The problem was not the target, even though the distance would have discouraged most archers. The complicating factor was the large wagon wheel held aloft by two anxious peasants at the midpoint between him and the target. To win, his arrow would have to pass through the axle hole of the wheel before landing in the middle of the red circle.

He slowly raised his bow, and everyone hushed. Drawing the bowstring, he was just about to release his arrow when the jittery men dropped the wheel and lurched backwards.

Robert "Robin" Fitzooth, the Earl of Huntingdon, lowered his bow and groaned in frustration. He yelled at them, "Do *not* move. You are in no danger."

They hesitantly picked up the wheel and returned to their previous position.

Before he could take aim again, a warm hand landed on his shoulder. His uncle, Edmund de Toury, the Baron of Embelton, quietly spoke to Robin. "My son, are you certain you can do this?"

Robin huffed in aggravation. "Of course, I can do this. But they must hold still."

Edmund nodded in understanding and signaled to someone in the audience. To Robin's surprise, Edmund was joined by Alfred Fitzwalter, Baron of Lenton, and the two barons strolled across the meadow to where the frightened peasants were clutching the wheel. Edmund and Alfred were in their fifties and attired in refined, conservatively styled bliauts which distinguished them as wealthy, yet unpretentious, nobles. After a few words with the peasants, the two older men took the wheel themselves and held it up for Robin.

Robin contemplated these men whom he had known and loved all his life, and their faith in his skill helped him relax. He took a deep breath to steady himself, and any remaining doubts fled his mind as he lifted his bow once more. At that moment, the world around him faded away. The only objects that existed were his nocked arrow, the hole at the center of the wheel, and the splotch of red beyond.

He drew his bowstring, and an extraordinary sense of rightness and completeness settled over him. He would never be able to adequately explain it to another individual, but there was always a moment when he just *knew* that the arrow was perfectly aligned. Robin released the arrow and watched as it soared swifter than any bird, passing through the hole of the wagon wheel and piercing the red circle.

The people of Huntingdon cheered wildly: whistling, whooping, and applauding.

Alfred and Edmund set the wheel down and promptly rejoined him, slapping him on the back and congratulating him on his impressive feat and his victory in the archery competition, which earned him the coveted title, King of Mayday. Now it was time for him to select his queen.

Robin affably accepted their kind words and then surveyed the crowd, seeking the one person whose favor he desired most. Lady Marian of Lenton was a magnificent creature of remarkable beauty and grace. Her pale blonde hair glistened in the sunshine, and her green eyes were alight with a mixture of pride and mischief. She was resplendent in her emerald bliaut with its trumpet-shaped sleeves elegantly cascading to the ground and a shimmering belt woven with gold and silver threads loosely encircling her slender waist.

Marian's gaze locked with Robin's, and he beamed exultantly. Marching until he stood in front of her, Robin extended his hand to the side, his eyes never straying from hers. His loyal servant and best friend, Much, took Robin's bow and exchanged it for a crown of flowers, which Robin placed upon her head.

Reluctantly looking away from this woman who had utterly bewitched him, he raised his voice and addressed the gathering, "As champion of the archery competition and King of Mayday, I claim the right to choose my queen. I have chosen Lady Marian Fitzwalter. As Queen of Mayday, Lady Marian will lead us to the castle bailey, where I have arranged for a feast." Pumping his fist in the air, Robin joyously shouted, "Let us bring in the May!"

The crowd cheered again, only now they were waving flowering boughs and greenery which had been collected from the neighboring woods at daybreak. Robin bowed before his queen and gestured for her to lead the Mayday parade. Alfred and Edmund also bowed to the newly crowned queen. Queen Marian was still smiling playfully as she put her hand on King Robin's arm, and they led the festive procession to the castle.

Soon they were seated at a trestle table which was elevated above the others in the courtyard of the castle. Robin and Marian, as King and Queen of Mayday, sat at the midpoint of the table. Marian's father, Alfred, sat next to her, while Edmund de Toury was on the other side of Robin. Edmund was the brother of Robin's mother, who had died twelve years ago, when Robin was only ten years old.

The feast was abuzz with the happy sounds of laughter and conversation as musicians played their instruments. Overhead, there were enough clouds to mute the heat of the bright, late spring sun but not so many as to threaten rain.

Alfred was filled with both joy and sorrow on this day. His precious daughter, the only child of his marriage to survive infancy, was rapidly approaching the eighteenth anniversary of her birth, and it was time to let her go. Truth be told, she was past the age when most girls of her rank married and left home. His musings were disrupted by the boy who had stolen his daughter's heart. Of course, Robin was no longer a boy, but to Alfred he would forever be the tow-headed, blue-eyed son of his life-long friend and liege lord, Duncan Fitzooth. With Duncan's death, Alfred had become Robin's vassal, and he was proud of this honorable, compassionate man who loved his daughter.

Robin tilted forward in his seat and summoned Alfred. "Lord Lenton, whose idea was it to let Marian read the story of Odysseus? Don't you realize that such tales will encourage her to think up these absurd schemes?"

Marian was grinning mischievously as she reminded Robin, "You are fortunate that I could not locate any 'axe rings' such as those described in the story of the archery contest that Penelope devised for the men competing for her hand in marriage. However, I consider 'axle ring' to be a suitable substitution."

Alfred chuckled. "You should thank me that it was just *one* wagon wheel. Marian had originally wanted to line up twelve wagon wheels, in keeping with the spirit of the legend. I explained to her the difficulty in finding that many wheels which could be spared from the wagons."

"I could have *easily* prevailed over such a challenge, but you are right; the wagons need their wheels," Robin confidently asserted.

Edmund joined in the merriment. "I am just happy that Robin was not required to go to war for twenty years first. Although, if I remember correctly, Odysseus was not at war the entire time that he was away from Penelope."

"Robin has already been away at war," grumbled Marian. "The seven years that he was gone felt like twenty to me."

Alfred gently chided his daughter. "Marian, my dear, Robin did not go away to war; his father sent him to the court at Poitiers to further his education in the arts. Besides, you were only nine years old when he left. I do not remember you pining for him."

"Father did not foresee that I would end up learning the art of war from Prince Richard," Robin disclosed.

Edmund reminisced, "Duncan was quite distressed when he realized that his son and heir had been taken under the wing of King Henry's least favorite son. It was a rare misstep for Duncan; he was always so eager to please Henry."

"It has been nearly two years since I returned to England," declared Robin. "Let us all look forward, not back, for I believe that our best days are yet to come." He grasped Marian's hand, squeezing it softly and regarding her tenderly.

Edmund and Alfred murmured in agreement, and Alfred recognized that the moment he had dreaded was upon him. He stiffly rose and motioned for the musicians to put down their instruments. The crowd quieted and attentively turned to the head table.

"Today—" Alfred was embarrassed as his voice broke with emotion. He cleared his throat and started again. "Today, I am making an important proclamation. I have consented to a betrothal between my daughter, Lady Marian Fitzwalter, and Robin Fitzooth, Earl of Huntingdon. Over the next three Sundays, the priest will announce their betrothal in Huntingdon's church. Then, during the coming months, this will be repeated for three Sundays in Lenton, Locksley, and Embelton. Assuming that there are no objections, the wedding will take place at Michaelmas, following the harvest."

Robin then jumped to his feet, and with great enthusiasm, he lifted his goblet high. "Lords and ladies, people of Huntingdon, let us toast Lady Marian Fitzwalter, the future Countess of Huntingdon!"

Everyone stood and joined in the toast. Lady Marian, Queen of Mayday, blushed with pleasure, tears of joy shining in her eyes. All her dreams were coming true, and she knew that her life with Robin would be abounding with love and happiness.

June 1188, A Royal Estate, Paris

"This plan will make your son the wealthiest, most powerful man in all of Christendom." Ambroise de Limours, Count de Montlhéry, spoke in a calm, authoritative voice filled with conviction. His steady, unflinching stare bore into the uneasy eyes of the woman whom he had been faithfully serving for over twenty years. He did not need to glance at her son, Philippe, to know that the King of France was fully supportive of his strategy.

The three conspirators were meeting in a sumptuous apartment in the palatial estate of the dowager queen, Adela of Champagne, who was restlessly fiddling with the lace edging of her sleeve. Adela's hand stilled, and she found herself descending into the shadows of Ambroise's penetrating scrutiny. She had known this man all of her adult life; yet, she had never been able to reconcile her confident reliance on his wisdom with the disquiet that he often inspired in her heart.

"Your Grace, we have discussed our plan on many occasions. The first phase has already been implemented. The time has come to finish what we have started. There is no going back." Ambroise's voice was insistent, and his gaze unnerved her.

Consciously breaking the hypnotic spell that Ambroise frequently used to manipulate her, Adela abruptly rose and walked to one of the windows that brightened her luxurious personal chambers. Outside, the summer sun caressed the bountiful flowers of her lavish garden. A fountain cheerfully gurgled, and she could detect a faint rainbow where the sun's rays kissed the spray of the water. The vibrant splendor of her garden seemed to accentuate the darkness that had shrouded her life in the years since she had decided to fund Ambroise's audacious scheme.

Now in her forties, the queen still possessed an uncommon beauty. Although her delicate, flawless features and golden hair had entranced even the pious King Louis VII, Adela recognized that it was not her appearance that had motivated the king to make her his queen. She had been Louis' third wife, and as a descendent of William the Conqueror and a member of the formidable Blois-Champagne family, Adela had brought both wealth and valuable political alliances to the marriage.

Nevertheless, it was Adela's success in giving birth to the long-awaited and much desired heir to the Capetian throne of France that had been her greatest triumph. She knew that the birth of Philippe was the real source of the power that she continued to wield, even twenty-three years after delivering the child whose nickname, 'God-given,' represented not only the answered prayers of an aging king but also the prospect of significant influence for his young mother.

She looked away from her perfect garden to behold her perfect son. He had all the ingenuity, strength, and energy that his father had lacked. Philippe was truly a son of the House of Blois, and the blood of William the Conqueror was strong in his youthful, handsome body.

Adela's only desire as she faced the autumn of her life was to ensure his success. Yet, the price of her ambitions was becoming more than she could bear. Gold, silver, gems—she was happy to sacrifice such things to help her son achieve the glory that he so richly deserved, but the selling of her soul had begun to weigh heavily upon her slender shoulders.

Sliding her eyes to Ambroise, she contemplated his many years of loyal service to her. He was shrewd, resolute, and completely devoted to her and her son. For twenty years, ever since her coronation, this man had diligently assisted her in navigating the treacherous pathways and perilous tempests of the French court. She would have never attained this degree of influence without his guidance and cunning.

He has made me the queen that I am today, for better and for worse, she reflected thoughtfully as she wandered to a nearby table and lightly stroked a lovely length of blue silk embroidered with fleur-de-lis designs in gold thread.

Ambroise's strategy to elevate her son, a ruthless scheme that had been so easy to discuss in the abstract, was no longer idle talk and speculation. The complicated plot to acquire vast wealth and power for her dear Philippe was progressing as intended, and real people were paying the ultimate price for her son's glorious future.

She had eagerly anticipated the rewards of their success: generations would know her as the woman who gave birth to the most magnificent king to ever rule France. *Nay!* To ever rule France *and* England. History might remember Charlemagne, but only as a precursor to the brilliance of *her* son. People will always remember William the Conqueror, but now he will be known as her son's ancestor. Such glory and majesty were within her son's grasp.

If only this grand plan had not overshadowed her life, her heart, and her very soul in ways she had never foreseen.

"Your Grace?" Ambroise interrupted Adela's somber musings and refocused her on the issue at hand. She returned to sit in her elegant chair and briefly searched her mind for what he had been saying before her attention had drifted. *There is no going back.*

Faltering, Adela replied with a nervousness that was uncharacteristic for this intelligent, poised, and eloquent woman. "It is difficult; I had not expected to feel this way…I am disturbed by the *lethal* aspects of your strategy."

Ambroise nearly rolled his eyes in exasperation. A stately, middle-aged man, Montlhéry was surprised by her hesitation; it was not her usual nature. He silently cursed women and their emotional, irrational approach to life.

Fortunately, her son, Philippe, was a gifted, bold, and fearless leader. He was prepared to execute the elaborate scheme that Montlhéry had so meticulously devised. He would not let Adela hinder them.

Philippe reached out to his mother, and his long, slender fingers gently cradled her small, dainty hands. "Mère, we are building an empire. The House of Capet will rule all the lands from the Pyrenees to the border we share with the Holy Roman Empire, and we will govern these lands without interference from vassals whose wealth and power rival our own. Ambroise will take the throne of England as my vassal, and he will have a Capetian queen of our choosing. We will control England, just as the Angevins have controlled duchies such as Normandy and Aquitaine. This plan enables us to defeat our enemies with a minimum cost to us in terms of treasury and men-at-arms."

"But is this plan honorable? Must we kill so many?" hissed a visibly agitated Adela as she pulled her hands from Philippe's affectionate grasp.

Montlhéry decided it was high time for him to take charge of this conversation and lead Adela through the thorny moral conflicts that were plaguing her. He was well-practiced at guiding the queen to the appropriate conclusion. "Your Grace, there are five men who must die for our plan to succeed; two have already left this world under circumstances that have been widely accepted as either natural or accidental. The other three will meet similar fates. Is that really so many?"

"These are not ordinary men; you are talking about killing

the entire male line of the English royal family." Adela's voice was increasingly shrill.

"That is correct," intoned Montlhéry. "The same family who stole the throne of England after the death of your uncle, King Stephen."

Philippe's anger was rising. "And, Mère, consider the tragic fate of your cousin, William. Henry Plantagenet stole his birthright, and William will be avenged by Ambroise's ascension to the English throne."

Adela covered her face with her hands, but Montlhéry and Philippe could still hear her muffled words. "When Henry the Younger sickened and died, I told myself that it was perhaps not the result of Ambroise's plot, but the type of stomach ailment that might take the life of any man." She reached for a square of cloth lying on an adjacent table and dabbed at the tears rolling down her cheeks. "But then, I was there, at the tournament, and Prince Geoffrey's death…"

"Maman," Philippe tenderly addressed his mother. "Geoffrey was my friend, and I am sorry that you were there when the horses trampled him." The king paused and leveled a disgruntled scowl towards the older man. "I have ordered Ambroise to avoid violent deaths in the future. The remaining fatalities will be like Henry the Younger's—a sudden stomach complaint, an easy death."

Philippe placed his fingertips under Adela's chin and tilted her face so that they were gazing into each other's eyes. "Geoffrey was my friend," he repeated. "Yet, I was strong enough to let go of him for the greater good of France. Ambroise has a plan which requires that a handful of men die. If we rely on traditional warfare, hundreds of men, possibly thousands, will die, our treasury will be bankrupted, and we might not prevail. Therefore, which strategy is more honorable? A few men die, or a thousand die, and we risk losing everything. Do you want France to be ruled by the Angevins?"

At this, Adela leapt to her feet and swore, "Never will I allow those vile Plantagenets to take France."

The two men also rose.

A distraught Adela stalked to the door where she lingered and looked back at her son and her advisor. "I have only one request. I do not wish to have any further involvement with this scheme. Take what you need from my accounts. Philippe is a grown man, and he is king. The two of you will proceed—do whatever you must to ensure that you are successful, but never again will I discuss this plan with either of you."

They bowed to the queen as she abruptly exited, and Philippe sighed loudly. "What a relief. We can more easily implement our strategy if we no longer need to involve her."

Montlhéry flashed a fond smile at the young king. "Women are, at best, creatures of emotion who do not understand the hard choices required of men."

Philippe concurred, "That is true. Let us concentrate on the next steps we must take."

The two men strode to a table where a large map had been unrolled, its edges secured by small marble sculptures from the queen's extensive collection of art.

The King of France launched a review of the strategy that would make him the most powerful man in Christendom. He had no doubt that Ambroise's scheme would deliver on its ambitious promises. He spoke briskly as he pointed decisively to a spot on the map. "My first move will be to take Châteauroux in Berry and several neighboring baronial castles. That will be sufficient to lure Henry away from England. Once he is here, I will keep him occupied for some time with a series of trifling incidents."

"Sire, if I may ask, how long will you be able to keep him away from England?" Montlhéry was carefully studying the map of France.

Philippe shrugged nonchalantly. "As long as necessary for you to accomplish the goals I have set for you. I will alternate between minor skirmishes along the border and useless peace conferences. In his old age, Henry has become quite susceptible to such meaningless gestures. We meet, discuss our differences, argue about the Vexin and Prince Richard's betrothal to my sister, come to an agreement, and then retire to our respective sides of the border. This is followed by another conflict and misunderstanding. If it appears as though he is tiring of my game, I will deliberately stir up tensions between Henry and Prince Richard. As you can see, toying with Henry is not difficult. It is actually quite diverting."

A thought occurred to Montlhéry. "Are there feasts at these conferences? I could send my apothecary to help season Henry's food."

Philippe countered sharply, "Nothing must happen to any of the Plantagenets when I am present. This is vitally important. If even a whiff of scandal or blame is attached to me, I will hang you, and your accomplices, and no amount of pleading from my mother will save you. The name 'Ambroise' might mean 'immortal,' but I assure you that you are not."

A chagrined Montlhéry reluctantly acquiesced and moved to examine a map of England laid out on a separate table.

Philippe joined him at the other table, and his astute, piercing eyes assessed the older man. "You will need to establish control over at least one fortified city. This will serve as our base of operations in England. You will need loyal men-at-arms in place. It is also imperative that you find a way to build your own treasury. My mother and I cannot afford to fund every aspect of this scheme. How will you achieve this? Your success in managing this part of the plan is crucial. You must prove to me that you are capable of ruling England as my vassal."

A nearly imperceptible flash of irritation passed over Montlhéry's expression, but years of regulating his emotions allowed him to force a smile that did not reach his eyes. "As soon as Henry leaves England, I will easily accomplish all that you expect of me. I will also win the trust of the youngest Plantagenet, John Lackland, while you are busy manipulating Henry and Richard."

Philippe maintained his unwavering scrutiny of Montlhéry. Like Queen Adela, he recognized the sinister facets of Ambroise's character. Unlike his mother, he had no ethical qualms about using the man's evil nature to achieve his unprecedented conquest of the Angevin Empire and England. He pressed Montlhéry for a more detailed answer. "What, exactly, is your strategy? How will you gain control of a fortified city? Secure the trust of John Lackland?"

Montlhéry smirked, and his eyes lit with merriment. "Sire, this is where Alaric de Montabard will find his purpose."

Philippe grinned at the mention of Alaric, and the tension in the chamber dissolved. "I had forgotten about the existence of the shadowy Alaric."

Montlhéry dipped his head in a polite nod. "As you know, the name 'Alaric' means 'ruler,' and this will be his mission: to rule an English fortified city."

Uncertainty flickered across Philippe's face. "One of my courtiers cannot just march into England and assume control over a city."

Dismissing his king's worries, an unperturbed Montlhéry explained, "True. However, Alaric has recently acquired the title, Baron de Argentan, a barony in the heart of Normandy. This will provide us entrée into the English royal court, which will lead to the attainment of our goals in England."

"A Norman barony? Ingenious. How did you arrange that?" Philippe was both pleased and intrigued by this unanticipated revelation.

Montlhéry jauntily answered, "It was simple: a baron with an aging, unwed daughter and no living sons, a quick wedding, followed by an outbreak of plague–"

"Let me speculate," interrupted Philippe, "the plague only struck the old baron and his newly married daughter?"

"The spread of such disease is a mystery, Sire." Montlhéry's matter-of-fact response was belied by a wicked glimmer in his eyes.

Philippe grinned knowingly. "Go, my friend. We have a kingdom to conquer."

July 1188, the White Tower, London, England

Alaric de Montabard, Baron de Argentan, was calmly sitting in an elaborately carved chair in the White Tower, awaiting his audience with Prince John. In his early fifties, Argentan's close-cropped hair was transitioning from grey to white, but his trim, athletic build revealed him to be a man of action and vigor. His dark clothing was made of the finest quality fabrics, but the style was austere and lacked any ornamentation.

With a critical eye, Baron de Argentan watched the captain of his guard, Sir Guy FitzCurzon of Gisborne, anxiously drag his hand through his thick, chestnut colored hair as he stalked from one side of the chamber to the other, only to turn and march back to where he had started.

Argentan wondered if the knight truly appreciated just how fortunate he was to have risen to the position of his captain. After all, Guy had been born to the widow of Hugh of Gisborne after Duncan Fitzooth had killed Hugh in a duel. Several years later, the impoverished widow and her young son had left England and returned to France where Count de Montlhéry had kindly taken them under his wing. In return, he enjoyed the services of a beautiful mistress who had been grateful that her fatherless boy was given the opportunity to become the count's squire, receiving his training and education courtesy of the count's benevolence.

Guy closely resembled his mother, with his dark hair and angular features, and although Gisborne had become an obedient and skilled knight, Argentan wished his captain was more cunning. It was the weakness of his mind that caused him to behave in such an agitated manner at a moment like this. His occasional battles with his conscience were also a problem. A moral compass was very inconvenient for a man in Gisborne's position. It was a regrettable inheritance from his mother, the older man mused.

"Gisborne, enough." barked Argentan in French.

Guy stopped and lifted his apprehensive pale blue eyes to those of the baron. "Yes, my lord?"

A sneering Argentan mocked, "Until you learn to control yourself, you will disclose what you are thinking and feeling to everyone around you. Here you are, panicking like a virgin facing the marriage bed. Be a man, and stand still."

Gisborne's eyes narrowed at the insult, but he submissively moved to a spot behind Argentan, where he resisted the impulse to fidget.

Finally, the door opened, and a chamberlain officiously announced the arrival of Prince John. At twenty-two, he was the youngest child of King Henry and Queen Eleanor. Although short and thickly built, John's handsome face was undoubtedly a legacy from his father. His auburn hair was fastidiously styled, and his opulent clothing sparkled with small jewels that were sewn into the fabric.

Argentan stood and joined Guy as the two men briefly dropped to one knee to give the prince proper obeisance.

John theatrically paraded across the chamber and settled into the ornate chair which Argentan had just vacated. Unfortunately, the large chair merely emphasized the prince's short stature. He exuberantly exclaimed, "I am pleased to see you, Alaric. You may sit in my presence." John imperiously flicked his wrist in the direction of a nearby bench, and Argentan obediently sat while Gisborne lingered in the background.

"Alaric, you have been here a fortnight, but I have not yet seen you at court. You must make an appearance," urged the prince.

Argentan solemnly professed, "Sire, I am a modest man. I do not seek the notice of others. I am content to remain in the shadows, lit only by the reflected glory of truly great men, such as yourself." He paused for effect, and a look of profound sorrow darkened his countenance. "I am also in mourning. My baroness tragically passed away from plague earlier this year, along with her father. God-rest-their-souls."

Argentan and Gisborne bowed their heads and reverently crossed themselves.

John insisted, "That is why you must come to court; the many grand entertainments scheduled for the next fortnight will raise your spirits. I have arranged for these diversions to pass the time while Father is in Normandy battling Philippe." His brow creased with uncertainty. "Tell me again the reason why Father sent you."

"Sire, King Henry did not speak to me personally. One of his stewards informed me that, because so many advisors were traveling with the king, you were left with administrative duties that are clearly too mundane for someone with your abilities and intellect. Therefore, I was sent here to serve you as a trusted vassal."

Prince John was evidently becoming bored with the conversation, so Argentan hurriedly proposed, "Let us focus on *you*, and how I might serve you best. That is the reason why I am here: to be a footstool for your royal feet, to support you, humbly and loyally. I have also brought you a gift. Knowing that you are a connoisseur of jewelry, I would like to give you these trinkets from my dear, departed wife's collection."

Upon hearing those words, Guy immediately retrieved a small wooden chest. Kneeling at John's feet, he opened it, revealing that it was filled to capacity with exquisite gem-encrusted rings, brooches, and necklaces. Gisborne then repositioned the lid and set the box on the floor beside the prince before rising and returning to his place behind Argentan.

The prince's eyes widened in surprise and gleamed with avaricious satisfaction.

Argentan continued, "I have many managerial skills. I can serve you as an administrator, which frees you to devote your time to more important pursuits. I am not interested in attaining fame at court. Enhancing your glory will be my only purpose as I enter the twilight of my life. Perhaps a post away from London? One that enables me to demonstrate my value to you? Something along the lines of a sheriff?"

"Hmmm," the prince pondered. "There are several posts that are vacant at this time. I recently heard something about the need for a sheriff in Northampton."

Argentan's dark eyes twinkled with amusement as he suggested, "Did you say Nottingham, Sire?"

A blush pinked John's skin as the embarrassed prince scolded, "You must listen more attentively. That's what I said: Nottingham." Abruptly, he frowned. "That is very far from court. It is in the wilds of Sherwood Forest. You would not want that." The prince became distracted by a small stain on his sleeve and tried to brush it away.

Argentan leaned forward and declared, "Sire, I accept your generous offer. I am honored to serve you as Sheriff of Nottingham. I will gladly dwell in the shadows of Sherwood Forest, and I will work tirelessly to prove myself worthy of your benevolence and glorious royal patronage."

"What?" the prince's befuddled gaze darted to the baron.

"I promise, Sire, you will not regret appointing me Sheriff of Nottingham." Argentan rose and went down on one knee in front of the prince. Gisborne echoed the movements of his master.

The prince swiftly recovered from his confusion and stood. In an exaggerated gesture, he waved his hand over the two and pronounced, "It is with the greatest of confidence that I send you to this important post. I will have my steward make the necessary arrangements. But now I must leave you; there is a backgammon tournament beginning presently." The prince held his hand out, palm up, with an air of expectation.

Guy was momentarily confounded, but then comprehension dawned, and he dutifully picked up the chest of jewelry and put it in John's outstretched hand. The prince possessively hugged it to his side before pivoting and dramatically exiting the chamber without a glance back. As soon as the door shut, Gisborne exhaled loudly in relief.

Reverting to French, Argentan gleefully proclaimed, "That was almost too easy. Everything is falling into place, Gisborne. At the appalling pace of the English court, it will probably require another month before we arrive in Nottingham, but that will be perfect timing for us."

Gisborne scowled. "I don't understand. Count de Montlhéry–"

Argentan's features contorted in rage, and he slapped Guy hard across the face, causing him to rock back on his heels from the force of the blow.

"Fool!" the baron snarled menacingly. "Do not *ever* utter that name again. While we are here in England, our success demands the utmost secrecy. We are from Normandy, not the French court."

"My lord, I apologize." Guy massaged his cheek and meekly pledged, "You can rely on my discretion. How will you carry out the plan so far from London?" He trailed off, his mind sifting through what little he knew about their mission. "Why are we here in England? Why Nottingham? What is the plan?"

Argentan was satisfied that Gisborne appreciated the need for prudence, so he moderated his tone and smugly answered, "Although I do not owe you any explanations, I am feeling charitable today; perhaps it is my joy in discovering that Prince John is everything I had hoped for in a royal patron: vain, inattentive, and easily manipulated." Sobering, he divulged, "We are in England to amass as much wealth and power as possible. I have selected Nottingham as the ideal fortified city for our purposes. The area surrounding the city is rich in resources. It is like a ripe apple ready to be plucked, crushed, and pressed for cider."

The baron assessed Gisborne with disdain. "However, you lack the intelligence to grasp the genius of King Philippe's strategy. Therefore, I will not reveal it to you. Your duty is to obey me, and if you serve me well, then your reward will be a share in the riches that I will accumulate. You might even receive a barony for your service. But never forget: your future depends on *my* success—but surely that comes as no surprise."

Observing Gisborne's face tense with resentment, Argentan decided to give his captain an additional incentive. "There is something else that I should tell you about Nottingham: the Earl of Huntingdon spends most of his time in a neighboring village."

Guy's irritation over Argentan's dismissive insults instantly flamed into a zealous determination to destroy the son of Duncan Fitzooth. "Will you allow me to avenge my father by killing him?"

"I might grant you the privilege of taking his life and ending the Fitzooth family forever, but first you must prove yourself to me." Argentan was pleased to see his captain's eyes burning with hatred. Hate was such a useful emotion, and there was nothing like the hunger for revenge to turn a man's blood to ice and his mind to murder.

The lengthening shadows of impending nightfall alerted Argentan to the late hour, and he commanded, "Come, Gisborne, we must return to our quarters before the courtiers arrive for the evening festivities."

"With your permission, I would like to stay and watch the entertainment," Guy requested hopefully.

Argentan directed a withering glare at him. "We are not here for your pleasure. We do not want to become known to anyone at the English court until the time is right." He paused. "And that means you will forgo entanglements with wealthy widows and comely servants who catch your eye. Your insatiable lust for female companionship will be your downfall, Gisborne. Mark my words:

someday one of these pretty vipers will poison your future with her venom."

As Argentan sauntered to the door, Guy rolled his eyes at the familiar rebuke. Women often flocked to the tall, handsome knight whose aloofness and dangerous reputation seemed to arouse their curiosity and excite their passions. Sighing in disappointment, he resolved to amuse himself with thoughts of torturing and slowly killing the Earl of Huntingdon, whose father had murdered his father and ruined his beloved mother's life by making her a widow at the mercy of the diabolical Count de Montlhéry.

CHAPTER 2
THE EARL OF HUNTINGDON

22 August 1188, Locksley Cemetery, Nottinghamshire

obin was deep in thought as he examined two stones in the ground. One was weathered and becoming difficult to read, while the other was a more recent addition to the graveyard near the Locksley church.

The harvest was underway, and the distant sounds of peasants at work created a muted clamor of shouts and creaking carts. Flies were buzzing in the warm August air, and birds chirped from their perches in the large trees which lined one side of the cemetery. He remained adrift in his reverie until he recognized the whispery rhythm of familiar footfalls approaching him from behind.

"Robin, I knew that I would find you here," Lady Marian of Lenton's dulcet voice was a welcome respite from his melancholy musings.

"It was two years ago, today," he replied, his eyes still trained on the grave markers.

"That is why I knew you would be here."

Robin smiled to himself. In the two years since his return to England, she had come to know him well.

"Are you still mourning his loss?" she inquired.

Robin studied the ground at his feet as he carefully considered his response. "That is not exactly my sentiment at this moment. It is more a profound sense of frustration that we never had the opportunity to resolve our differences. I have many questions that will forever remain unanswered."

Marian sympathetically reached out and took his hand.

He finally raised his eyes to hers and gave her a wan smile, hiding the fact that his heart leapt at her touch, and that every part of him: mind, body, and soul, came alive in her presence. Robin gazed into her green eyes and contemplated how they reminded him of the great forest that surrounded Locksley and covered most of the shire. Just as travelers frequently lost their way in the thick foliage of the greenwood, he often became lost in the sublime tenderness and beauty of her eyes.

She interrupted his brief enchantment and cautiously asked, "What of your mother, Lady Edith?"

Robin frowned as he regarded the weathered stone. "I remember with anger how Father kept me from her when she grew sick. Another missed opportunity to bid a loved one farewell."

Marian squeezed his hand, and the lament in her voice was an echo of anguish for her own long-dead mother. "I wish that I had known her. Even in Lenton, there are many older servants and peasants who still talk about her compassionate and charitable nature. And they tell the story of how a baron's daughter from the far north captured the heart of the mighty Earl of Huntingdon."

A playful gleam shone in Robin's eyes as he teased, "I owe my very existence to your father. If not for the friendship between him and Uncle Edmund, I doubt that my parents would have ever met. Your father is now responsible for the betrothal of a second Earl of Huntingdon. Perhaps he should provide matchmaking services to other noble families."

Marian giggled merrily at such a ridiculous suggestion, and Robin was so entranced by the musical sound of her laughter that he impulsively pulled her into his arms, kissing her gently as he resisted the urge to ravage her mouth. Their privacy was disrupted by the noise of peasants' voices in the distance, and Robin worried that Marian's reputation could be harmed if someone glimpsed them embracing. He released her and stepped away.

Resuming his perusal of the stones in the ground, Robin described his mother. "The older servants and peasants in Locksley want to petition the Holy Father for her sainthood." His adoring smile was shaded by a wistful yearning. "There are several of them who routinely approach me with tales of her kindness, always helping the poor, tending to sick children, and the like. They say that her touch had miraculous healing powers."

Grimacing with sorrow as he recalled her passing, he bemoaned, "If only she could have healed herself..." His voice faded, and he fell silent for a handful of heartbeats. When he had regained control over his emotions, he recollected, "Father was so angry. I was a boy of ten summers, and I remember listening at the door, longing to go to her when she was sick, and hearing my father shout at her that it was her own fault for consorting with dirty, diseased peasants, and if she died, it would save him money, for she was too generous in giving it to undeserving people who should have been beneath her notice."

Marian gasped. "Surely, he did not mean that."

A weary sigh escaped Robin. "At the time, I assumed that he meant it. But now, as I reflect, I believe he was just frightened that he would lose her. It is one of the many things about which I will never have the opportunity to ask him."

Marian's eyes softened in understanding, and her heart felt grief for his regrets. She did not remember her own mother who had died in childbirth when she was very young.

Leaving such woeful talk of his mother, Robin remarked, "Father is not here, of course. He is buried in the town of Montlhéry, which is near Paris. When the skirmishes between King Henry and King Philippe end, we will go to France and visit his grave."

"It was such a shock when we received word of his murder," exclaimed Marian.

A thoughtful Robin mused, "Father was always so tight-fisted with his money…I have often wondered whether the thieves would have spared his life, if only he had spared some coins. I suspect that they were just poor, desperate, and starving—not intending to kill an English noble, but seeking to feed themselves and their families."

"I do not know of such things. I have never traveled further than the fortress of Nottingham," Marian confessed. She dithered, not wanting to cause Robin distress, yet anxious to tell him what she knew. "Father said that Lord Duncan had powerful enemies in France, and I know that he tried to dissuade him from going to Paris. I once heard my father speculate that Lord Duncan's death might be connected to the death of Prince Geoffrey, Duke of Brittany and son of King Henry."

Robin's brow knitted in bewilderment. "That is rather fanciful. It is true that Geoffrey died three days before my father at the same tournament in Paris. But Geoffrey perished when he was trampled after falling from his horse. I was told that the strap on his saddle had frayed and snapped. My father was killed by thieves who were trying to rob him."

An exasperated Marian acknowledged, "My father, I love him, but…" She searched for the right words. "He sees danger and intrigue everywhere. When he learned of your father's death, he collapsed! At first, I believed it was heartfelt bereavement for a beloved friend, but then…"

"What happened?" Robin's curiosity was roused by her obvious unease.

In a hushed voice, she recalled, "When he recovered, he ordered the captain of his guard to lock me in my chamber at Lenton Manor. For a sennight, I was closely guarded by half a dozen armed men. Later, one of the servants told me that Father had locked himself in the chapel, with soldiers at the door, while I was trapped in the manor."

"That is odd," he admitted.

Eager to share her disconcerting experiences with him, she divulged, "A year ago, on the first anniversary of Lord Duncan's passing, armed men were again stationed outside both my chamber and the chapel. Today, I begged Father to allow me to come here instead of enduring another imprisonment. He reluctantly consented as long as twice the usual number of soldiers escorted me. Therefore, most of the Lenton men-at-arms are here at Locksley today. I'm sorry to burden your cook with the necessity of feeding so many extra men."

"It is nothing," dismissed Robin with a wave of his hand. "If they are protecting you, then I am happy to provide them with as much food as they can eat."

Marian smiled gratefully, and then added, "As I left, I saw Father entering the chapel, and there were two sentries at the door. He will probably still be there when I return."

"Your father is very pious," Robin observed.

"True," agreed Marian, "but he seems to have devised his own Holy Days. In addition to today, there is the 25th of October." She heaved a sigh. "Yet another day when I often find myself under guard."

Robin could not suppress a short chuckle. "The 25th of October? Which saint owns that day?"

"Only Saint Crispin, the patron saint of tanners. So, it makes no sense for my father to spend two days in a guarded chapel, on his knees weeping and frantically praying for salvation and forgiveness. I heard him mention the names 'Stephen' and 'William,' but I've never heard of a Saint William, and Saint Stephen's day is December 26th. My father would not make such a mistake."

His eyes narrowed suspiciously. "And you know this because...?"

Marian sheepishly responded, "The chapel's main doors might be secured, but there is a gap in the rear wall where a relatively small person can squeeze into the vestry. That is, once this small person has climbed out her window and shimmied down a nearby tree."

Robin grinned indulgently. "A small person such as yourself, perchance?"

Marian, neither confirming nor denying his assertion, beamed at him. At that moment, the sun broke through the lazily drifting clouds and lit her pale blonde hair in a glorious halo.

Robin paused and humbly counted his many blessings. He was a man of position and wealth. He had received an excellent education and had been trained by the most talented military men of the Angevin Empire. But it was the love of this radiant woman which he treasured above all else; a woman whose beautiful appearance was surpassed only by her keen mind and her gracious, affectionate temperament.

Glancing at the overcast sky, he saw that the clouds were dispersing; the rain that had seemed so certain earlier was no longer a threat. "My lady, let us depart this place of mourning and lost opportunities. I was planning to ride into Sherwood for some archery practice. Would you care to join me? Much is at Locksley Manor, and he could act as chaperone."

Marian tentatively countered, "Robin, I would like to accompany you, but…"

A disappointed Robin prodded, "But what?"

A shy grin tugged at her mouth. "Can we go alone…just the two of us? We will not be gone long, and no one will ever know."

His heart skipped a beat, and he smiled roguishly. "That is true. We will return before anyone realizes we have left." With those words, they abandoned the two forlorn stones.

❧

Marian was laughing so hard that she was gasping for breath. She admonished, "You cannot put a hole in that cloud with an arrow."

"Why do you have so little faith in my abilities?" queried Robin with mock offense. "You are not even giving me a chance. Very well. Pick a leaf, any leaf, and I will pierce the center in one try."

Marian wiped a stray tear that had leaked from her eye during her unrestrained mirth. "How do you expect me to choose one leaf? The tree is thick with them. It does not matter which leaf I select; you will always claim that you pierced the correct one."

She beheld him as he stood there, bow in hand, his pale blue eyes sparkling with mischief, his boyishly handsome face sporting an impish smile, and his wheat-colored hair slightly ruffled owing to their spirited ride from the Locksley stables to their favorite meadow. Marian liked to imagine that it was an enchanted corner of the forest—a refuge dominated by a massive oak, one of the largest trees in this part of the greenwood.

"Well?" he demanded. "What shall I aim for next? I need a challenge, and you will not allow me to poke holes in the clouds, for fear that it will cause them to rain–"

"That is not what I said!"

Robin persisted, "And you refuse to choose a leaf, although there appears to be an abundance of leaves from which you could make a selection. I have already slain a brace of coneys and a pheasant. Elvina and the cook will be quite pleased with me."

Marian huffed in mock exasperation. "Elvina and the cook are *always* pleased with you." A sly twinkle brightened her eyes. "What about the pheasant you missed?"

"Missed!" he thundered. "No, no, I did not miss that pheasant. I never miss. Someone deliberately distracted me."

"It was accidental," she insisted with a grin.

Robin argued, "Sneaking up behind me and shouting, 'Do not miss,' just as I released the arrow was not accidental."

Their laughter faded as he took her hands into his. Marian gazed deeply into his eyes, attempting to learn every shift in the emotions that he guarded so well.

She believed that he revealed more of himself to her than

anyone else, but he was still often a puzzle. At times, he was quiet and contemplative, obviously focusing his mind on some problem or issue, yet denying that he was thinking about anything important. On some occasions, she had seen him tense with anger, only to disguise his feelings by making a jest or laughing, even though he was clearly not amused. Marian knew that when he was truly battling his emotions, he would disappear into the embrace of Sherwood Forest, for Robin was a man who found comfort in the untamed beauty of nature.

Once, in a surprisingly candid conversation, Robin had described to her what the forest meant to him. He spoke of how the forest made him feel alive, and how each of his senses experienced the greenwood: the fragrances of pine and wild blossoms, the sounds of a rushing river at his feet and the rustling of leaves overhead, the taste of freshly gathered berries, the feel of a gentle rain against his face, and the vistas that could only be viewed from tree limbs high above the forest floor. Robin had told her that the forest was both vast, as it stretched to the horizon, and intimate, as the sheltering trees sometimes seemed to be crowding around him.

Marian had frequently pondered his words, and she longed to hear him speak openly about himself again. Unfortunately, whenever she asked him about his feelings or his thoughts, he deflected her questions with either a joke or a change of topic.

As they stared intently into each other's eyes, Marian detected a shift in his emotions. No longer playful, his eyes conveyed a passion that caused her to feel anxious and aching. Cupping her face, Robin kissed her softly and hugged her close. Marian rested her cheek upon the front of his shoulder and shut her eyes, content to be enveloped in the strength and warmth of his arms.

Unexpectedly, a foreboding settled over her. In many ways, she had been blessed with good fortune and happiness all her life. She didn't remember the loss of her mother, so her greatest sorrow had been that lonely time when Robin was far away, training in Poitou.

She had missed him terribly during those seven long years. Maybe that is why she felt a kinship with Penelope when she read the story of Odysseus.

Soon it would be Michaelmas, and they would finally wed. Yet…she could not shake this feeling of disquiet that made her heart tremble like a baby bird fallen from its nest and lying helpless on the ground. Such small creatures were doomed, for they had no hope against the predators lurking in the shadows, stalking the weak and the vulnerable. Her morbid thoughts caused Marian to instinctively recoil, ending their tender moment.

"We must return to Locksley; it grows late." Robin's voice was rough as he released her.

Marian nodded wordlessly and walked to her horse. She watched as he collected the game he had slain and the arrows that he had been using for target practice. Before long, they were grudgingly making their way back to the Locksley stables.

As they neared Locksley, they rode past the church and its desolate graveyard. Robin stopped his horse and stared in the direction of the two stones that commemorated the lives of his parents. Marian also halted her horse and regarded him curiously.

Once more, regret washed over Robin. *If only…* He sighed deeply. If only his father had been willing to answer his questions or had been willing to simply *talk* to Robin. But Duncan Fitzooth, the proud and ruthless Earl of Huntingdon, had been an aloof and enigmatic man. And now…he would forever remain an unsolved puzzle.

Robin turned his horse and spurred it away from the cemetery, determined to leave the past behind and focus on his future with Marian. He knew that history was unalterable, and he believed that regrets served no purpose save to torment the mind with what could have been. But very soon he would learn that the past was not lifeless bones concealed within the embrace of the earth. Instead, history was a predator lurking in the shadows and preparing to strike the young Earl of Huntingdon in retribution for the sins of his father.

22 August 1188, Lenton Chapel, Nottinghamshire

Alfred lay prostrate before the altar of the chapel adjacent to his home. The damp chilliness of the stone floor had seeped into his bones, and his body ached from both the cold and the fact that he had not shifted his position in some time. It was a penance for his many sins.

On this day, the anniversary of Duncan's murder, he was consumed by memories of the last time he saw his lifelong friend and liege lord. He had begged Duncan to stay in England, warning him that the French court was the domain of the House of Blois-Champagne. Alfred was convinced that such a powerful and influential family would still resent the loss of the English throne after the death of King Stephen. They would be acutely aware of Duncan's role in securing the throne for Henry Plantagenet.

Duncan had irritably responded that he would be traveling under the protection of King Henry.

With trepidation, Alfred then reminded Duncan of the blood curse that hung over their heads. Duncan had just laughed in his face and teased him about his superstitions.

Nothing was more important to Duncan than pleasing King Henry, who had personally asked him to travel to Paris, where his middle son, Geoffrey, was competing in a tournament. Henry, ever suspicious of the motives of his remaining three sons, was wary of the deepening friendship between Geoffrey and King Philippe. He hoped that Duncan could monitor Geoffrey and keep him out of trouble. Instead, both Geoffrey and Duncan had met violent deaths in Paris.

Sighing in resignation, Alfred conceded that his long friendship with Duncan was built upon his own aversion to conflict and discord. Perhaps that was the reason why Duncan valued their friendship: Alfred never confronted Duncan about his cruelty to others, his disdain for the common people, or his disregard of God's commandments. From his betrayal of King Stephen to his frequent and flagrant betrayals of his wedding vows, Duncan had been a fearless pursuer of pleasure and his own self-interest. And through it all, Alfred had quietly observed—alarmed and chagrined, but too much of a coward to challenge his liege lord.

Alfred had to admit that his reluctance to stand up for what was right was cowardice, and it made him complicit in Duncan's sins.

He was also haunted by the aftermath of King Stephen's passing. His conscience was tormented by his eager acceptance of valuable lands confiscated from nobles who had been executed because their names were on Stephen's list. These lands had enriched the Barony of Lenton with revenues that stank of death and deceit. Alfred had been so burdened by guilt that he eventually used his profits to build this beautiful sanctuary and to purchase the sacred relics which were hidden under its altar.

Whenever he recalled the death of King Stephen his thoughts would inevitably turn to King Henry's siege of Toulouse, now nearly thirty years ago. He had been with Duncan and Hugh of Gisborne, camped outside the gates of the city, when they had unexpectedly encountered William of Blois.

Duncan had mercilessly mocked William, and Alfred and Hugh had had to separate the two men before they came to blows. Following that incident, Duncan kept the former prince under surveillance, concerned that he still had designs on the throne.

A few days later, Duncan and Alfred had surreptitiously witnessed William and Hugh plotting to poison Henry in a bid for William to claim the throne. Duncan had immediately warned the king and then killed Hugh in a duel.

But it was the virulent plague that struck the camp after the attempt on Henry's life that Alfred found particularly disturbing.

The symptoms of the plague had matched William's description of the effects of the poison he had given Hugh. When it was reported that William had also succumbed to the sickness, Henry sent Duncan and Alfred to search William's tent in hopes of recovering the talisman of the Conqueror, which the king believed was still in William's possession.

They were unable to find the artifact, but Duncan discovered an empty container with suspicious residue, and he concluded that William had poisoned the camp and committed suicide to avoid Henry's wrath for the regicide attempt.

A loud cry outside the doors interrupted Alfred's solitude, and he slowly and stiffly struggled to his feet. With bleak resignation, he observed his destiny stroll into the small chapel in the form of Alaric de Montabard, Baron de Argentan.

"You were warned, Lord Lenton, that vengeance would come, even if it was from beyond the grave."

Alfred despairingly beheld Argentan and disclosed, "I told Duncan that William of Blois had influential connections, and here is the proof."

Argentan chuckled maliciously, savoring the moment. "Huntingdon's arrogance was his downfall. I will always cherish the devastated look on his face when he realized that the curse would claim his life."

"So, I was right, it was the curse…in Paris when Duncan was killed," ventured a disheartened Alfred.

"Of course."

"And today, you have come for me." Alfred shuddered with dread. "Is there nothing…?"

An apparently amused Argentan shook his head and unsheathed his dagger. "Your fate was sealed many years ago. There is no escaping it. You are destined to die anyway. All men die. Their rotting corpses become dust. The dust spreads across the earth. Some dust settles in the sun, where all can see it, but there is also dust in the shadows, and it goes unnoticed by those who walk in the light."

Alfred grimaced. "I understand. The curse is a legacy of the shadows, and that explains how a dead man can take vengeance against those who still live. I am ready to die, but," he sank to one knee and beseeched, "I beg you, please spare my daughter! Do not let the curse touch her. She is not responsible for my sins. Please... I beg you."

The smirk on Argentan's face caused Alfred's heart to drop heavily and his skin to prickle with fear. There was no hope.

"Even the Lord, our God," sneered Argentan, "has decreed that the sins of the fathers shall be visited upon their *sons and daughters*. Huntingdon also begged for mercy for his son. I will tell you the same thing I told him: I promise that your daughter will suffer loss, betrayal, and heartbreak before the time comes when I must take her life as well."

"NO!" Emboldened by a deep-seated compulsion to protect his beloved child, a fierce defiance fueled Alfred as he leapt to his feet and tried to seize Argentan's weapon. Argentan tottered backwards from the unanticipated assault, but he swiftly recovered and stabbed Alfred in the heart. Alfred gasped in pain, and the world around him receded into a murky haze as he stared into the diabolical eyes of his murderer.

Argentan pulled his dagger from the dying man's chest and gleefully proclaimed, "You are the last of the original traitors. Soon the children of treachery will follow their fathers, for I will take from them the long life, happiness, and prosperity that were stolen from the true King of England."

Coughing blood and gurgling his final breaths, Alfred slumped to the floor.

"Welcome to the shadows, Alfred Fitzwalter, Baron of Lenton." Eyes glittering with both satisfaction and disdain, Argentan calmly leaned over and used Alfred's expensive cloak to wipe the blood from his blade. He then sheathed it and loudly summoned Gisborne, who was patiently waiting outside the chapel, along with the bodies of Alfred's guards. "Gisborne, take Huntingdon's dagger and plunge it into Lord Lenton at the same location where I stabbed him."

"Yes, my lord," Guy obediently took the elaborate silver dagger he had employed to dispatch the sentries and thrust it into Alfred.

"Excellent," enthused Argentan. "Are you confident that you were not seen?"

Guy scoffed, "I was able to steal the dagger from Locksley Manor while the servants were eating their midday meal. What kind of man leaves his sword and dagger in his bedchamber all day?"

Argentan rolled his eyes in disgust. "A pampered son of the nobility who probably passes the time writing poetry. Perhaps he spent the day composing love songs to some viperous woman. Huntingdon's son studied at the court in Poitiers." The two men snickered at the notion of such a pathetic excuse for a man.

Sobering, Argentan ordered Gisborne to implement the next part of the plan. "Go and arrest Huntingdon for the murder of Lord Lenton. I will arrange to have Lenton's body delivered to the castle as evidence." He paused. "And Gisborne, bring him to Nottingham *alive*. You do not have permission to kill him, yet."

Scowling, Guy entreated, "If you will not allow me to kill him, will you permit me to damage him slightly?"

Argentan indulgently consented, "Certainly, but no permanent damage. Hurt him if that would please you."

"Thank you, my lord." Gisborne promptly departed to assemble his men for the ride to Locksley. He was impatiently anticipating his first meeting with the son of the man who had murdered his father and destroyed his mother's happiness. He just wished that he could have personally slain Duncan Fitzooth, but his master had claimed that privilege. At least Guy might attain some measure of vengeance by taking the life of Duncan's son. A lethal rage bloomed in his heart, and he spurred his horse faster. His mind was filled with fantasies of torturing Robert Fitzooth, whom he pictured as a short, heavy-set, effeminate boy. Maybe he would beat Fitzooth in the same manner as Montlhéry had beaten his mother. That seemed oddly appropriate to Guy.

His dark daydreams were disrupted as a sizeable contingent of mounted men-at-arms approached them from the opposite direction. Gisborne slowed his soldiers and moved them off the road, facilitating the passage of the other men. Encircled by her guards, an elegant, lovely young woman with pale blonde hair rode past them, and Guy was instantly captivated by her noble bearing and uncommon beauty. As soon as the road cleared, he resumed his journey to Locksley.

22 August 1188, Locksley Manor, Nottinghamshire

Robin laughed boisterously as he sat at the table in Locksley Manor. He had just returned from his outing with Marian, and he was happily anticipating the fine meal that had been prepared during his absence.

His best friend from childhood, the son of Locksley's miller, was sitting with him. Many years ago, a devastating fire at the mill had left Much an orphan. Robin's mother, Lady Edith, had owned the mill, and she felt responsible for the seven year old boy whose entire family had perished on that dreadful day. She resolved to take Much into her home as a companion for Robin, who was five years old at the time.

After many miscarriages and a number of stillborn births, Edith had accepted that Robin would most likely remain an only child, and although Much and Robin would never be equals, they could be playmates. Thus, a life-long friendship was born.

On this somber anniversary, everyone was focused on lifting Robin's spirits. Leofric and Elvina, the two elderly servants who managed the Locksley estate, had started telling tales from his youth. Unfortunately, they had excellent memories.

"No! No!" Robin loudly protested as he strove to stifle his laughter. "I swear, I did not eat that pie. The dog ate it."

"Now, Lord Robin," Elvina gently chided him, "we all know it was your favorite. And how could the dog reach the window sill?"

"Well, a bird accidentally knocked it off the window sill, and then the dog ate it," Robin carefully explained.

Leofric's wrinkled face creased in a perceptive grin. "Was this a blue-eyed, blonde bird?"

Robin's eyes sparkled mischievously.

Odella, a Locksley girl who regularly helped Elvina in the kitchen, had just set a platter of food on the table when she heard Leofric and frowned in confusion. Like many of the people of Locksley, she was at ease in the presence of Lord Huntingdon and did not hesitate to join the conversation. "What kind of bird is that? I ain't never seen such a bird."

Everyone around the table roared with laughter.

Elvina, who was fond of Odella, told her the story of how a blonde bird came to Locksley. "Lady Edith," she paused as everyone reverently crossed themselves, "she found this bird in the garden, and it was so friendly that it would eat from her hand. She decided that it would be her pet, and she would take care of it."

Leofric reminisced, "Do you remember the cage I built for it? No bird ever had such a fancy cage, I reckon."

"And this bird had blonde feathers?" Odella was still befuddled.

Elvina continued her story. "No, that blonde bird made his appearance a few months later. But this other bird, after Lady Edith put it in its cage, it stopped chirping and eating, and I told her, 'You're killing that bird. Birds need to be free, my lady.' So, Lady Edith let the bird go, and he was singing when he left that cage and flew south for the winter."

Elvina walked to where Robin was sitting, her eyes shining with barely suppressed emotion. She put her hand on his shoulder and regarded him devotedly. "Not long after that, Lord Robin was born, and Lady Edith decreed that his name would be 'Robert,' but everyone must call him 'Robin.' Lady Edith said that she wanted her son to be like that little bird who courageously abandoned the safety of a cage to find his future."

As tears began rolling down Elvina cheeks, Robin stood and comforted her with a hug. Without warning, the sound of horses interrupted their poignant moment. Much and Leofric jumped to their feet as Robin hurried to the door. He was convinced that Marian had returned with her small army of guards, and he was concerned that something alarming might have happened. The rhythmic pounding at the door startled everyone, as Marian would not have bothered to knock.

Robin cautiously opened the door and was driven back into the manor's great hall as a tall knight shoved hard against the other side. Bristling at the man's aggressive stance, Robin challenged him. "Who are you?"

The knight did not seem to hear him as he barked, "By order of the sheriff, I demand to see Robert Fitzooth, Earl of Huntingdon."

His eyes narrowing in indignation, Robin coolly introduced himself, "I am the Earl of Huntingdon, and I insist that you show me proper respect in my home."

The knight spun around, theatrically drew his sword, and pointed it at Robin.

Troubled by this surprising turn of events, Robin authoritatively enjoined, "Sheathe your weapon *now*, or I will forcibly remove you from my home."

"I do not obey you," sneered the man in a strong French accent. "I am Sir Guy FitzCurzon de Gisborne, captain of the guard for Alaric de Montabard, Baron de Argentan."

"Argentan?" Robin was increasingly perplexed. "What business does the captain of a Norman baron have with me? I do not answer to Norman barons."

Gisborne smirked nastily. "When that baron is the Sheriff

of Nottingham, and you have committed murder, then you *will* answer to a Norman baron, and you will beg for his mercy."

Much and the people who lined the hall gasped and worriedly murmured amongst themselves.

A niggling memory plagued Robin, and he recalled, "Gisborne? There used to be a Gisborne barony in Huntingdonshire. Do you know of Hugh..." At that moment, the names came flooding back to him. "You...you are Hugh FitzCurzon's son?"

Gisborne did not respond, but the emotion flashing in his pale blue eyes confirmed Robin's suspicions.

Abruptly, something Guy had said registered in Robin's consciousness. "Murder? Wait, that is absurd."

"The proof is incontrovertible. You will surrender at once," Gisborne announced.

The hall quieted as a stunned Robin was momentarily speechless. Recovering from the shock, he irately asserted, "Impossible. I did not murder anyone. What is your proof? And who has been murdered? Does your master know that you are here, harassing the Earl of Huntingdon?"

With great satisfaction, Guy declared, "Your dagger was buried in the man's chest. Two additional men were found nearby, also dead from dagger wounds."

At this news, Robin felt relief. He could easily refute these spurious allegations. "My dagger is here. I will go retrieve it. And then you will apologize and leave." He took a step away, only to feel the sharp point of Gisborne's sword poke him in the back.

"No, Huntingdon," Guy growled between clenched teeth. "You are not leaving my sight. Send a servant."

Robin's blood boiled in anger, but he worked to stay calm as he commanded, "Much, it is in its sheath on the table next to the bed."

Much promptly ran to the stairs and mounted them two at a time. He then disappeared down the passageway at the top.

Robin glowered at the knight, savoring the apology he would

soon receive. The moments stretched on, and an uncomfortable silence reigned as he impatiently flicked his gaze to the stairs.

The periphery of the manor's great hall had filled with people. Soldiers stood behind Gisborne inside the front door, while servants and villagers congregated in the area nearest the kitchen after entering through the manor's back door.

Finally! Robin could see Much sluggishly descending the stairs. He was holding the dagger in its sheath with a confused expression on his ashen face. Much's curly red hair, which was always a bit wild, was practically standing on end, as if the man had been anxiously tugging on it.

Robin summoned his friend, "Bring it here, so that this Norman dog can apologize, and we can continue our meal. The food grows cold."

Much's mouth was hanging open, and he seemed both dazed and distraught. He reluctantly offered the sheath to Robin, who snatched it and immediately realized that it was empty. His dagger was gone.

Once more, Gisborne's lips twisted into a spiteful mockery of a smile. "I look forward to receiving your apology as I beat a confession out of you."

With this ominous threat, the hall exploded into chaos. The people of Locksley were shouting that Robin was innocent, and the soldiers surrounded Robin and Guy, pointing their swords at the unarmed peasants and household servants.

Two men grasped Robin by his arms. Initially frozen in shock, Robin regained his senses, dropped the empty sheath, and fought against his captors. An unexpected movement caught his eye, and Robin watched as something flew through the air and struck Guy of Gisborne on the side of his head. It plummeted to the floor, and Robin realized it was a moldy cabbage—undoubtedly taken from the garbage pile located behind the manor.

"Son of a traitor and a French whore!" someone bellowed.

Robin recognized the voice of Cuthbert, an older servant who had lived at Huntingdon Castle years ago and would have known the FitzCurzon family of Gisborne.

Guy, his sword still drawn, pivoted towards the villagers and servants who had flocked into the great hall of Locksley Manor, and a savage glint lit his eyes.

Robin feared for the safety of his people, and he attempted to sidetrack the knight. "Gisborne, take me to the sheriff," he urgently insisted. "I surrender but reserve the right to prove my innocence."

Gisborne ignored Robin and moved swiftly into the crowd as they tripped over themselves in an effort to retreat. Suddenly, Guy grabbed a man and plucked him from the throng. It was Cuthbert.

"Wait—" began Robin, but he was too late, and he witnessed Gisborne impale the old man. The people shrieked in terror and rushed to escape through the kitchen door.

Guy withdrew his sword from the man's body, and the mortally injured peasant collapsed.

"No!" yelled an appalled Robin. "You cannot come into my home and murder an unarmed man. Take me to the sheriff now. I will demand justice."

Guy disdainfully glanced at the dead body as he yanked a banner with the Huntingdon coat of arms from the wall and used it to clean his bloodstained blade. "This worthless old peasant is beneath the notice of Baron de Argentan." He then allowed the banner to flutter to the floor before he purposefully stood on it as he sheathed his sword.

Robin was not concerned about the desecration of his heraldry. Instead, he was fixated on Cuthbert, and his heart was seized with both horror and sorrow that this good man, whom he had known all his life, had been viciously slaughtered for no reason.

The men restraining Robin towed him towards the door as Much begged, "Lord Robin, what shall I do?"

"Go to Lord Lenton," Robin instructed Much as he was dragged away. "Have him assemble the other local nobles and come to the castle to defend me before the sheriff."

Gisborne doubled over in laughter. Struggling to catch his breath, he choked out, "Lord Lenton is already at the castle."

A baffled Much gaped at Gisborne's strange reaction.

Once outside the manor, one soldier bound Robin's hands, and another directed a stable boy to bring his horse. While they waited, Guy decided to entertain himself at Huntingdon's expense. He gave the earl a sharp push and guffawed as Robin, his hands tied securely behind him, stumbled and fell, face first, into the dirt.

Gisborne's sadistic glee was quickly curtailed by the outcry from the people of Locksley. Guy had never seen servants and peasants with such an attachment to their lord, and he became alarmed by the angry mob. There were fewer than a dozen soldiers, so they were significantly outnumbered by the villagers besieging them.

Outraged shouts echoed across the clearing in front of Locksley Manor.

"Someone help Lord Robin!"

"That Norman swine killed Cuthbert!"

"Lord Robin is innocent!"

Much assisted Robin to his feet as the villagers surged forward. The soldiers encircled Gisborne and Robin while brandishing their swords. Some of the people were now carrying scythes and large sticks. The situation was spiraling out of control, and Robin knew that he had to act without delay. One of the Locksley grooms brought forth a horse, and Much helped Robin mount it.

When Robin was seated on his horse, where everyone could see him, he called for their attention. "People of Locksley, do not risk a confrontation with armed soldiers; I do not want anyone else to be injured. I am going to Nottingham to resolve these unfounded accusations against me. As soon as Baron Lenton and I speak to the sheriff, I will return."

As they traveled away from Locksley and towards the fortress of Nottingham Castle, Gisborne moved his horse alongside Robin's and smugly divulged, "Baron Lenton is already with the sheriff, but he will not defend you. The last time I saw him, your dagger was planted firmly in his chest."

CHAPTER 3
A GAME OF CAT AND MOUSE

23 August 1188, Nottingham Castle

Robin slowly regained consciousness, only to be assaulted by the vilest stench he had ever experienced. He sat up on the hard planks of wood that served as his bed and groaned; his bruised body objecting to the slightest movement. His head was spinning and throbbing, and he massaged his temples in an effort to find some relief.

The previous day's ordeal had unsettled him more than he wanted to admit. Arriving in Nottingham just after sunset, Gisborne had informed Robin that it was too late in the evening to meet with the sheriff, so Robin had been dragged to the dungeons below the castle. Once there, Gisborne had beaten him, ostensibly to coerce a confession. Robin suspected that the vicious knight had been enjoying himself. Robin's resilience and strength had surprised Gisborne, who eventually tired and left.

Robin was thankful for the rigorous training he had received under the tutelage of Prince Richard, for it had greatly toughened his body and spirit. Memories of his years at the court of Poitiers inundated his mind, and he mentally journeyed far away from his foul prison cell. It had been an exciting, beautiful place for a young man to come of age. His days had been spent studying military history and tactics, while his nights had been filled with music, poetry, dancing, and courtly love. He guiltily acknowledged to himself how much he missed those exhilarating times.

Reluctantly returning to his present predicament, Robin sluggishly stood and examined his surroundings. A somewhat swollen left eye and the dim light from a sputtering torch made it difficult to inspect his dank, dirty cell. He could hear water dripping from the ceiling and the chittering and rustling of rats; apparently, they were his only companions as he waited in the bowels of Nottingham Castle. His stomach rumbled in hunger, and time stretched interminably.

At last, the rhythmic pounding of feet on stairs heralded the arrival of Gisborne and his men, and Robin silently watched as the soldiers crowded into the narrow space outside his cell, their torches illuminating the bleak stone walls. Gisborne entered, and he surveyed Robin's bruised and disheveled state with obvious pleasure.

As Robin's eyes met Guy's, thoughts of his father unexpectedly rose in his mind. Duncan Fitzooth had always said: *a man must never show fear when facing an opponent,* and Robin heartily agreed with his cold and distant father. With some effort, he mustered a devil-may-care smirk, although it felt tight against his teeth. Guy uneasily glanced away, and Robin knew that his impudence had ruffled his enemy's feathers.

Gisborne started barking orders in French. Visibly flustered, he switched to English. "Huntingdon, I will escort you to the sheriff. Turn and put your hands behind your back."

Robin grudgingly complied, and a guard reached through the bars to bind his wrists while Gisborne unlocked his cell. Deciding that the best way to resolve this outrageous situation was to appeal to the sheriff for justice, Robin said nothing and obediently walked with the men up the long, uneven stairway that ended in a hallway on the surface level of the keep.

In the past, Robin had rarely visited Nottingham; he owned many properties and typically divided his time between Locksley and Huntingdon, his two favorite estates. Nevertheless, he easily recognized the layout of Nottingham's fortress, as it was reminiscent of his family's castle in Huntingdon. Both were girdled by an imposing wall and a deep ditch, but Nottingham's moat had been allowed to drain during the preceding years of peace and prosperity. It was currently little more than a smelly, muddy ring of sludge encircling the walls. The fortress was perched upon a cliff which overlooked the river on one side and the town of Nottingham on another, and it could only be accessed via a causeway and drawbridge.

During his reign, King Henry had done much to improve Nottingham Castle; it now boasted a stone keep with a design comparable to Huntingdon Castle's keep. Turning left at a corridor, they approached the spiral stairway that led to the highest and most unassailable tower of the castle.

Robin contemplated the gloomy shadows that shrouded the upper limits of the staircase, and a foreboding slowed his ascent. With his attention diverted and his hands behind his back, he tripped clumsily on the steep stairs.

Gisborne, who was leading the group, looked back and snickered, "The Earl of Huntingdon is quaking in terror and staggering like a drunken fool. I just hope he does not wet himself." The other men tittered in amusement.

Robin clenched his fists as he strained against the bindings on his wrists. He desperately wanted to punch Gisborne. The cruel, detestable knight exemplified all the traits that Robin despised in a man: cynicism, dishonesty, and a callous disregard for others.

There was an antechamber at the summit of the stairs with a pair of impressive, heavy doors. Gisborne haughtily commanded,

"Robert Fitzooth, prepare to meet Sheriff de Argentan. You will show him proper respect."

Robin snorted in his face and derisively countered, "What would *you* know about proper respect? And why are you hiding behind half a dozen armed men, even though my hands are bound? You were very brave yesterday when you impaled an old, unarmed peasant. Your men must be so honored to serve under you."

With both hands, Gisborne grabbed the front of Robin's tunic and backed him up until Robin was teetering on the top step of the winding stairway, his toes barely finding purchase on the edge of the uppermost stair. His heart was thumping frantically in his chest, but Robin again scoffed at Gisborne, grinning at the loathsome man and disdainfully hissing, "Congratulations on defeating another unarmed man. Is this how you attained your knighthood? Throwing a bound man down a flight of stairs? You are an embarrassment to the proud heritage of Normandy."

Instantly, Robin regretted his taunts; he was in an incredibly precarious position, and enraging the man whose grip on Robin's tunic was the only thing saving him from a fatal plunge, was unwise. However, in a confusing turn of events, his adversary's fury actually abated at this last insult. Gisborne pulled Robin from the threshold of the stairs and shoved him roughly in the direction of the doors. Robin had anticipated another cowardly push, and although he stumbled awkwardly, he managed to stay on his feet.

Gisborne narrowed his eyes and sneered, "I would welcome the opportunity to fight you, and I fear no one, especially some pampered and indulged *boy*."

Robin recovered his balance and strode towards the doors, ignoring the other man's blustering and posturing. Only the sheriff could help him; nothing was more important than resolving these ridiculous accusations so that he could leave and offer comfort to Marian in her bereavement. He was also going to obtain justice for Cuthbert. This Norman dog needed to be punished for what he had done at Locksley Manor. The irony of the situation did not escape Robin: he was accused of murdering an old, unarmed man by a man who had committed the same crime in front of him and many other witnesses.

Robin and Gisborne were ushered into the sheriff's private quarters, and Robin took note of the number of men-at-arms milling around. Chuckling to himself, he wondered if this heavily guarded Norman sheriff chose to live in the tallest tower of the castle because he feared the intrepid English people whom he would be governing.

The chamber was lit by large windows, and the rays of the morning sun illuminated its rich interior. It would have normally served as a solar for the lord's family, but the sheriff was using the space to conduct his business; it certainly afforded more privacy than the great hall. The room was dominated by a massive desk covered with scrolls and piles of parchments. Behind the desk sat a middle-aged man meticulously recording entries in a book of accounts. His expertly crafted chair had been painted scarlet red, and its impressive size was more suitable for a royal throne than a royal official.

Robin stood beside Gisborne as the sheriff concentrated on his ledger. Scrutinizing the maps and parchments which were haphazardly spread across the desk, Robin saw several documents with elaborate seals. Unfortunately, he could not identify them due to the slight swelling of his bruised left eye. He glanced at Gisborne, who was patiently staring straight ahead, smirking contemptuously.

Sighing noisily at the delay, Robin observed the older man hunched over his paperwork, and he was reminded of his own sheriff in Huntingdonshire. He was also middle-aged, similar to this new Sheriff of Nottingham. As an earl, Robin was well versed in the duties of a sheriff. A sheriff received the king's writs, carried out orders from the king, maintained the gaol, and accounted for his finances. He was essentially a type of steward for the king. Of course, a sheriff could detain you, imprison you, and send you to London for trial, but he was not a judge and didn't have the power to put a man, especially an earl, on trial for a serious offense such as murder.

Robin was confident that he could settle this matter, and that Sheriff de Argentan would be reasonable. He needed to go to Marian as soon as possible; he was worried about how she was coping with the death of her father. He grimaced as he recalled the killing of Cuthbert; he would insist that the sheriff arrest his captain for this deplorable crime.

After a lengthy wait, Baron de Argentan set down his writing instrument and wearily rubbed his face. Raising his eyes to peer beyond his sea of parchment and into the faces of Robin and Guy, the sheriff startled, as if he had not realized that they were there.

Robin nearly rolled his eyes in exasperation. He had little in common with stewards and masters of accounts; men whose world centered on bits of paper and the clicking of their abacus. He inwardly shuddered at the thought of such a miserable existence sequestered within four walls, with ink-stained fingers, bleary eyes, and a stooped back.

The sheriff stood, and Gisborne deferentially dropped to one knee and then rose again. Robin was pleased to see that the mongrel next to him had a master; perhaps Gisborne's master could gain better control over his dog.

"Gisborne, who is this?" Argentan queried in French. He was average height, impeccably groomed, and dressed in black, austere clothing.

Gisborne, also speaking in French, replied, "My lord, this is the Earl of Huntingdon."

Robin knew the language well, and he wondered why King Henry had sent Normans into the heart of England for this crucial post. The people of Nottingham were predominately English; they would resent submitting to a foreign sheriff and knights like

Gisborne. Robin was annoyed that the king had made such a poor choice.

"The Earl of Huntingdon?" the sheriff exclaimed as he surveyed Robin from head to foot. "Why have you bound him? This is not how we treat an earl. Untie him immediately."

Robin breathed a sigh of relief; this Norman baron was a sensible man. He could feel Gisborne loosening the rope around his wrists as the Sheriff of Nottingham glided towards him, his dark eyes communicating concern for Robin's welfare as he briefly sank to one knee.

"Lord Huntingdon, what has happened to you?" the sheriff inquired fretfully. "Do you speak French?"

Robin responded in kind, "I am fluent in French, my lord; I lived in Poitiers at the court of Prince Richard for seven years. It is where I received my military training. I was knighted by Prince Richard himself," he added proudly, his expression shaded by unmistakable nostalgia. He then asserted, "However, if you are to be the Sheriff of Nottingham, you will need to speak English. Do you speak English, Lord de Argentan?"

Smiling faintly, the sheriff switched to heavily accented, yet flawless, English. "Allow me to introduce myself. I am Sir Alaric de Montabard, Baron de Argentan. I have been appointed Sheriff of Nottingham."

Robin bowed courteously in recognition of the man's rank. "I am pleased to make your acquaintance, although I am not pleased by the circumstances under which we are meeting."

"I humbly apologize, Lord Huntingdon." The sheriff assessed Robin carefully. "Have you been injured?"

Robin cast a withering scowl at Guy; then his gaze slid to Argentan. "My lord, I wish to make a formal complaint against this man, Guy of Gisborne. He viciously slaughtered an unarmed man in my home, and then he arrested me on absurd, false allegations.

When I was brought here last night, I was beaten in an attempt to force me to confess to a crime I did not commit."

Argentan was noticeably distressed by this news, and he frowned at Gisborne.

Robin tried not to grin in anticipation of the scoundrel's impending imprisonment in the dungeons. Maybe even the same cell. He sternly enjoined, "I demand justice for Cuthbert and amends for my inconvenience."

"Certainly, Lord Huntingdon," cried Argentan, and his glare veered to his captain as he reprimanded, "This is inexcusable, Gisborne. This man has clearly been ill-treated. He is an earl. He was knighted by Prince Richard himself. And what is this nonsense about a murder? This is the Earl of Huntingdon. He is not a killer."

Robin felt vindicated, and his demeanor brightened. He had been correct in his assumptions. Gisborne was nothing more than a dog who had escaped his leash, and now he would be punished. Nevertheless, Robin felt dismayed at the impassive reaction of the knight, particularly in light of the serious charges which had been leveled against him, and the severe rebuke he was receiving from his master.

The sheriff, his voice layered with skepticism and indignation, continued to admonish his captain. "Gisborne, I send you to find the coward who murdered poor Lord Lenton and his guards, and you bring me an *earl*? It is not possible. What is your proof?"

Gisborne answered in a rather flat monotone, and it struck Robin that his words sounded rehearsed. "My lord, I was also shocked by the earl's actions, but I was presented with irrefutable proof of his guilt."

"It is a lie," Robin proclaimed confidently. "I did not murder the Baron of Lenton. He was one of my most trusted vassals and the father of my betrothed. We were always on the friendliest of terms."

The sheriff chided, "Gisborne, you heard what the earl said. He is innocent. You know better than to harass nobles like Sir Robert

Fitzooth, the Earl of Huntingdon. A man knighted by Prince Richard himself."

Robin considered that the sheriff might be mocking him but promptly rejected the notion. "Of course, I am innocent," he earnestly avowed.

"My lord, what about the evidence?" Gisborne asked without acknowledging Robin.

Argentan waved his hand in a dismissive gesture. "I am sure the earl can explain everything. Tell us about this allegedly 'irrefutable' evidence."

Gisborne motioned to one of the soldiers who approached and passed him a small bundle of cloth before returning to his position at the door. Unwrapping the object, Gisborne showed it to Robin and the sheriff, and Robin was aghast to see his own dagger, a gift from Prince Richard on the occasion of his knighthood, cradled in rags and caked with dried blood.

"My lord, this dagger was recovered from the chest of Lord Lenton as he lay lifeless on the floor of his chapel," Guy triumphantly reported to the sheriff. "Upon close examination, I discovered that the blade fit perfectly into the wounds of the two dead sentries who had been standing guard at the chapel doors. All three men were murdered by Huntingdon using this weapon."

Robin was increasingly exasperated by this charade. "That does not prove anything." he defended himself. "Someone could have stolen my dagger and used it in this crime. And I had no reason to kill Lord Lenton."

Argentan smiled sympathetically. "My lord, be at ease. I am certain this can be explained." The sheriff paused. "Is this your dagger?"

"Yes, it was a gift from Prince Richard." Robin pointed to the ornate hilt. "You can see his heraldry there, adjacent to the seal of the Huntingdons. The prince gave it to me after the ceremony—"

The sheriff interrupted, "Was this the ceremony where Prince Richard knighted you himself? This is indeed a special dagger."

Robin felt a prickle of unease but chose to ignore it. "That is true, my lord. I treasure this dagger as a token of my friendship with Prince Richard."

"Of course, my esteemed Earl of Huntingdon." Argentan let out a strange laugh, a piercing and vinegary sound; then his expression became grim as he continued, "But instead of selling the dagger, the thief attacked an old, unarmed nobleman in a church." He released a frustrated sigh. "It is so difficult for a rational man, such as myself, to understand the mind of a criminal."

"So, you believe me? Am I free to go?" Robin impatiently asked.

"Naturally, I believe you. You are an earl," Argentan affirmed in exhilarated tones.

Again, something about the conversation nagged at Robin. He decided to think about it later—he had to go to Marian. She must be bereft at the loss of her beloved father, and she needed him. As Robin hurried towards the door, the sheriff called to him before he could exit.

"Lord Huntingdon, forgive me, but I have one more question." The sheriff's voice was grave with concern. "You are an educated man; what do you make of this situation?"

Robin hesitated and looked back at the sheriff, raising a puzzled brow. "What do you mean, Lord de Argentan?"

"Well, perhaps you could help me solve this mystery. Clearly, my captain is not smart enough to unravel this. He has obviously gotten it all wrong. Arresting an earl; how very incompetent."

Gisborne visibly bristled at the insult but did not protest.

Robin observed an enigmatic gleam in the sheriff's eyes, and he fought his mounting apprehension, preferring to focus on Alfred's tragic death and welcoming the opportunity to provide assistance. Robin retraced his steps to the cluttered desk. "Lord de Argentan, I would be pleased to help you find the real culprit. Lord Lenton was a gracious, good man. His murderer must be captured and punished. Anyone who would kill such a pious man deserves to be executed in Nottingham square in front of the whole shire."

The sheriff enthused, "That's an excellent idea." Stroking his chin thoughtfully, Argentan proposed, "We must think. How could your dagger end up in Lord Lenton's chest?"

Robin carefully explained, "It is usually kept in its sheath on a table next to my bed. The village of Locksley is quiet and peaceful, and I typically don't carry it when I am at home there."

Argentan prodded, "And who has access to your bedchamber?"

"Only the Locksley servants, myself, and my friend, Much," Robin clarified.

The sheriff excitedly ordered his captain, "Gisborne, go to Locksley at once and arrest all the servants and especially this Much creature. Bring them here, and obtain a confession."

"Wait!" Robin shouted. "Locksley was part of my mother's dowry, and I've known these servants all my life. They are not thieves. As for Much, I will personally vouch for him—a more loyal, honest man would be hard to find."

"I see." Argentan's face fell.

"A stranger," Robin offered. "I suppose a stranger might have entered the manor and stolen the dagger."

The sheriff seemed bewildered as he regarded Robin. "But why would this stranger then travel all the way to Lord Lenton's estate and kill him?"

Robin averted his eyes, unable to withstand the intensity of Argentan's ever-penetrating and unpleasant scrutiny. The sheriff's dark eyes were oddly unnerving, and he instinctively wished to recoil from him. Robin forced himself to meet the other man's stare and admitted, "I don't know, Lord de Argentan."

The sheriff's attention shifted to Gisborne, and he briskly inquired, "Was anything stolen from the chapel?"

Guy barely repressed a smile. "No, my lord."

A baffled Robin mused aloud, "It's almost as if someone wants you to think that I killed Lord Lenton."

"Do you have many enemies, my lord?" The sheriff was evidently intrigued by the idea.

"I don't have enemies," Robin firmly asserted. "And neither did Lord Lenton; he was greatly admired by everyone who knew him. Therefore, I am determined to find his killer."

"Lord Huntingdon, I agree. This despicable killer must be caught." Argentan instructed his captain, "Gisborne, I insist that you catch this fiend. I will not tolerate failure."

Gisborne replied, "Lord de Argentan, would you like to interview the witness?"

"Witness?" Robin exclaimed incredulously. "We have wasted all this time talking about the *dagger*, and you have a *witness*? This degree of incompetence is intolerable. We must question this witness immediately." He then narrowed his eyes at Gisborne, whom he had already grown to loathe with every fiber of his being. "And then I demand to know how you plan to punish this man who murdered an unarmed villager in my manor. Not to mention arresting me and attempting to beat a confession out of me."

"Quite right," the sheriff concurred. He then somberly commanded, "Gisborne, produce this witness at once."

Robin noticed that Gisborne still did not appear to be troubled by his imminent arrest, but maybe he was the type of man who could mask his emotions. He watched the tall knight saunter to the door, open it, and summon someone; then Gisborne calmly returned to stand beside Robin.

A slender young man with unusually pale skin and white-blonde hair entered the chamber. He was also dressed as a knight, wearing a surcoat and a French, black-hilted sword. As their gazes locked, Robin found the man's dead eyes disturbing. There was no flicker of personality and no warmth there—only a glint of danger in grey eyes that revealed nothing of his thoughts. The man seemed to be totally devoid of both color and emotion.

Argentan presented the knight to Robin. "This is Sir Tancred de Payen; he is second only to Gisborne in his rank, and he will help us get to the bottom of this mystery."

Payen ceremoniously dropped to one knee in front of the sheriff and rose again.

"Tancred, this is the Earl of Huntingdon, the illustrious, brilliant Robert Fitzooth," Argentan announced with an exaggerated air of deference that clearly bordered on mockery. "He was knighted by Prince Richard himself."

Robin looked sharply at the sheriff while Payen once more genuflected to give the earl proper obeisance. Robin's sense of disquiet was steadily building as he waited for the knight to begin his statement.

"*Mon seigneur shérif–*" Payen began in French.

"English, please," the sheriff requested. "The earl was kind enough to remind me of the importance of speaking English here, in the wilds of Nottinghamshire."

The sheriff flashed an insincere smile at Robin, who winced slightly as his suspicions that the sheriff was ridiculing him were gradually being confirmed.

The knight switched to heavily accented English. "My lord, I went to Lenton and searched for the baron, intending to deliver your invitation to the castle."

Argentan disclosed, "I had planned to meet with all the local nobles, in order to introduce myself. I would have sent you an invitation as well, but I assumed you were at Huntingdon."

Payen politely resumed his testimony. "At the baron's home, I was told that I could locate him in the chapel. Upon my arrival, I saw this man–" He pointed at Robin.

Robin gasped in disbelief. "What?"

"I saw this man leaving the chapel," Payen repeated nonchalantly without glancing at Robin. "I don't think that he noticed me. He jumped on a horse and rode away. In front of the chapel, I found two dead guards. I heard moaning and hastened into the sanctuary, where I discovered an older man on the floor with a dagger in his chest." His voice rose an octave, the first hint of any emotion from the colorless knight. "I knelt next to him and asked him, 'who did this?' His reply was 'Robert Fitzooth stabbed me.'"

The audacity of the lies and the composure with which they were uttered stunned the young earl into silence. His fleeting mental fog was dispelled by a burst of bright fury that assailed his mind like a lightning strike in a tempest. Finding his voice, an enraged Robin yelled, "No! He is lying. That did not happen."

Two soldiers seized Robin by his arms and firmly restrained him, and he struggled against their tight hold, his heart hammering a frenzied rhythm.

Gisborne showed Payen the dagger. "Do you recognize this weapon, Tancred?"

"*Oui*, that is the dagger that I found in Baron Lenton's chest," Payen impassively affirmed.

Robin vehemently roared, "That is a lie! I did not do this. Alfred was my friend. I am marrying his daughter. He was like a second father to me."

Argentan's piercing stare assessed Robin with a sharpness that rivaled a blade's edge. "My lord, what am I to think? It is your dagger, the victim is a man known to you, and I have a witness who saw you leave the scene of the crime. Can you prove that you were somewhere else at the time of this murder? I believe that it occurred after midday."

Robin calmed and endeavored to remember his movements from the previous day. "Well, I was in the cemetery, and then I rode into Sherwood–"

"Alone?" Argentan inquired.

Robin momentarily froze. He had been with Marian. It had been just an innocent ride along the forest trails followed by some archery practice, but it would reflect badly on her character if he divulged the truth. They were not supposed to go off together without a chaperone. Robin's code of honor and his love for Marian prevented him from besmirching her reputation.

"Yes, I was alone," Robin lied.

The sheriff declared with feigned sorrow, "How unfortunate. What a pity for our beloved Earl of Huntingdon."

Robin's gaze darted between Payen, Gisborne, and the sheriff. He desperately wanted to grab the pale knight and force the truth out of him, but his only prudent recourse was to convince Argentan, so he persisted, "I don't know this man. For some reason he is lying."

Argentan frowned. "I have known Tancred since he was a boy. His father was a talented apothecary who desired a better future for his son." He queried Payen, "Tancred, will you take an oath that this is the truth?"

Payen respectfully consented. "Certainly, my lord."

As Robin frantically tried to understand what was happening, he suddenly realized something and urgently questioned, "What was it that Lord Lenton told you? What did he say?"

Payen blinked a few times, and then he dispassionately repeated his testimony. "Baron Lenton said, 'Robert Fitzooth stabbed me.'"

"That is impossible!" Robin shouted, his control slipping away. "There is the proof. Never in my life has anyone who knew me called me Robert. Everyone knows that I am called Robin."

Payen coolly reiterated, "That is what he said, 'Robin Fitzooth stabbed me.'"

"No!" Robin screamed in an appalled voice, but no one seemed to be listening to his protestations. "Lord de Argentan, did you hear that? He changed the words. First, he tells us that Alfred called me Robert and now he claims that he called me Robin. Does this not prove that he is lying?"

Argentan observed Robin curiously. "I distinctly heard Payen say 'Robin.'" His gaze slid to Guy. "What did you hear, Gisborne?"

Gisborne's lips twisted into a wolfish smile. "My lord, I also heard Payen say 'Robin.'"

And that was the moment when Robin realized that he had been the unwitting mouse lured to his demise by a ruthless feline who took great pleasure in slowly tormenting his prey. Glowering at Argentan, he simply asked, "Why?"

The sheriff's voice cracked as he fought the impulse to laugh at Robin. "My lord, do you still deny your guilt? Are you trying to deceive me, the king's lawful representative in Nottinghamshire?" He placed his hand over his heart in mock distress, and Robin glimpsed a bulky signet ring with gold shapes on a field of red. It looked familiar, but before he could identify it, Argentan lowered his hand and taunted Robin, "Such a young and handsome face, yet it is the mask of a cruel, cold-blooded killer. You have brought infamy to the Fitzooth family."

Robin straightened to his full height, despite the fact that two guards were restraining him. He was consumed by rage and panic, and the opposing sentiments were vying for supremacy in his heart. With extraordinary effort, he reined in his emotions. "I demand that you deliver me to London for trial. There are people at court who will vouch for me. I will appeal to King Henry, and he will put a stop to this injustice." He paused to catch his breath. "I will also dispatch a message to Prince Richard. He will defend me as well. This nefarious scheme that you have devised to blame me for Lord Lenton's murder will not succeed."

Still battling to maintain a neutral façade, Argentan retorted sarcastically, "I had almost forgotten that you were knighted by Prince Richard himself. Alas! I fear Prince Richard will be quite disheartened when he receives news of your wickedness. The Lionheart has allowed a jackal into his lair."

Gisborne, Payen, and Argentan all burst into laughter, which unnerved and perplexed Robin; he could not fathom why they were so amused by his association with Prince Richard.

Robin reminded Argentan of the law. "I know that you have the power to arrest me, but for a serious offense, you are obligated to send me to London for trial."

"Wrong," Argentan countered. He snatched a parchment from his table and started reading it aloud. "In these uncertain times, when the king and many of his courtiers are in Normandy, it is difficult for the remaining officials in London to cope with the flow of prisoners from remote shires such as Nottingham. Therefore, Prince John—"

Robin interjected, "Prince John? He has no authority in these matters."

The sheriff cleared his throat and resumed, "Therefore, Prince John has decreed that sheriffs in shires which are farther than three day's travel from London shall be empowered to conduct trials and dispense justice."

"No, that cannot be correct," Robin disputed.

"On the contrary, my lord, it is plainly stated in this proclamation." Argentan rolled the parchment and tapped it against his chin. For a few moments, he appeared to be deep in thought. "Well, Gisborne was right: the evidence is irrefutable. I have no choice but to find you guilty—"

Robin brusquely cut him off. "This is not a proper trial."

"Lord Huntingdon, I find you guilty of murder," the sheriff ruled. "Now, for your punishment, I believe I must defer to you. After all, you are an *earl*. I am merely a baron."

Gisborne and Payen snickered maliciously as the sheriff gleefully quoted Robin, "Anyone who would kill such a pious man deserves to be executed in Nottingham square in front of the whole shire."

"No, you cannot—" Robin gasped.

"I can do whatever I want in *my* shire," the sheriff snapped. "Gisborne, how soon can we hang this evil killer of a defenseless old man?"

"My lord, I can arrange to have a gallows built tomorrow, and then we can proceed with the execution." Gisborne grinned brutishly, his eyes gleaming with anticipation.

Argentan enthusiastically approved. "Very good. In two days, Robert, I mean *Robin,* as-everyone-calls-him, Fitzooth, Earl of Huntingdon, will hang for the crime of murder. Tomorrow, I want this posted and announced throughout Nottinghamshire."

Robin stared at the sheriff and saw the truth. For whatever reason, this vile man was happily sending him to the gallows, disregarding all standards of justice and the rule of law. As their eyes locked, Robin recalled his earlier uneasiness. There was a malevolence within Argentan that Robin had instinctively sensed, yet he had ignored his feelings of disquiet. It was a mistake that was going to cost him his life.

Before the soldiers escorted him from the chamber, the sheriff smugly proclaimed, "For too long, Huntingdon, you have enjoyed the blessings and warmth of the sun. It is time for you to dwell in the shadows where you will finally see everything that the sun has hidden from you." With those cryptic words, Argentan returned to his throne.

CHAPTER 4
MAID MARIAN

n eerie stillness had descended upon the village of Lenton. Everyone was numb with grief at the loss of Alfred. No one could recollect the last time there had been a murder in the small barony, and to have their beloved lord cruelly slain in his own chapel was unthinkable. Whispers about foreigners in the area and rumors of a witch living in the nearby forest had excited the imagination of the people. When news of Robin's arrest reached Lenton, the absurdity of the notion that Lord Huntingdon had murdered Lord Lenton only fueled these wild speculations.

Marian was seated on a bench in the flower garden adjacent to her family's ancestral home. Her father had lovingly tended this patch of ground for as long as Marian could remember. It had originally been planted by her mother, and Marian had once asked him why he personally cultivated it when they had servants who could do the work. She would never forget his soft and wistful expression as he described how spending time in his wife's garden made him feel closer to her. Marian's only comfort in her bereavement was the thought that her parents were finally reunited. She closed her eyes and imagined them sitting together on a bench in one of the resplendent gardens of heaven, her father tenderly embracing her mother.

Marian sighed deeply and reluctantly opened her eyes. She had hoped to find solace in the beauty of her parents' garden. Instead, she felt as if her heart were grain under a millstone.

Perhaps it was all a mistake; the body had been transported to Nottingham prior to her arrival, so maybe the murdered man was really someone else and not her gentle, doting father. But then she vividly recalled pushing her way into the chapel through a crowd of well-meaning servants and glimpsing the pool of blood on the floor near the altar—exactly in the spot where he often spent hours in prayer.

A single tear slid down her cheek, and Marian fought to stem the flood of tears that threatened to follow it by focusing on the other emotion which plagued her: indignant outrage. According to Much, her brave and honorable Robin had been accused of her father's murder. It was beyond her comprehension how anyone could believe such a ridiculous allegation. A steely determination sustained her as she resolved to secure his release. For the first time in their lives, Robin needed her help, and she would not disappoint him.

"My lady?"

Marian anxiously leapt to her feet as Much came into the garden. The short, barrel-chested peasant with his curly red hair was normally friendly and cheerful, but on this sorrowful day, he was uncharacteristically grim. He was carrying a basket from the kitchen which was packed with tasty treats.

Her spirits lifted as she anticipated Robin's happiness at receiving such a surprise after his dreadful stay in the dungeons. She eagerly inspected the basket's contents, and when she found an apple on top of the other food, she cocked a curious brow at him.

Much blushed and sheepishly explained, "It's from a tree next to Locksley Manor. He's partial to the apples from that tree."

"Thank you, Much. I know Robin will be pleased to have it." Smiling kindly, Marian handed the basket back to him as they departed to begin their journey to Nottingham.

✥

A small contingent of men-at-arms from Lenton accompanied Marian and Much as they traveled in melancholy silence towards Nottingham. It was midday when they arrived at the formidable castle, and Marian shuddered to think of her Robin caged in such a place. Robin was a vigorous man who relished his independence and abhorred any type of confinement.

Upon entering the bailey through the gatehouse, Marian and Much went directly to the keep where she demanded to be escorted to Robin at once. A guard offered to take the basket, but she was not so naïve as to give it to anyone except Robin. The man temporarily left them to confer with his superior, and when he returned, he informed them that they could not visit the prisoner without the sheriff's permission.

Marian started to argue, but she promptly realized that this was for the best; as soon as she advised the sheriff that Robin did not murder her father, he would be freed, and then they could leave the castle together.

The man shepherded Marian and Much through a maze of corridors that led to a winding stairway. At the summit, they were ushered into a spacious chamber, where a middle-aged man sat on the far side of a desk covered by papers and scrolls. Two men stood on opposite ends of the desk. One was tall with angular features and reddish-brown hair, and the other was thin and exceedingly pale, with white hair despite his obvious youth.

The older man looked up. "Yes? Who are you?" he asked in thickly accented English.

Marian politely curtsied. "I am Lady Marian Fitzwalter of Lenton. I'm requesting the return of my father's body for burial, and

I wish to resolve this misunderstanding concerning my betrothed, the Earl of Huntingdon. I insist that he be set free immediately."

The man rose and approached her. Bowing respectfully, he somberly extended his condolences. "My lady, you have my sincere sympathy. I am Alaric de Montabard, Baron de Argentan and Sheriff of Nottingham. I was not privileged to make Baron Lenton's acquaintance in this life, and that saddens me profoundly."

Marian relaxed somewhat at his cordial greeting. He seemed to be reasonable, and hope stirred in her heart that this preposterous situation could be speedily settled. "My lord, you must help me sort out this terrible mistake," she appealed to him earnestly.

"Mistake?" The sheriff's eyebrows shot up in astonishment. "My lady, I have only recently arrived here in this beautiful green land, and as sheriff, I promise to work diligently to avoid any mistakes. Tell me what has happened, and I will assist you in any way that I can."

She felt relief sweep over her. "Lord Huntingdon has been arrested and imprisoned here in the castle. You must release him. This is a mistake; he would never hurt my father."

"I see." Argentan crossed his arms and rubbed his chin, as if he were pondering her words carefully. "Regrettably, I cannot release him; Lord Huntingdon's dagger was the murder weapon."

"It was stolen," interjected Much.

Argentan's eyes narrowed. "Who is this peasant? Why is he here in my castle?"

Marian was stunned. The sheriff had been courteous and sympathetic, but now he was glaring at Much like a hawk ready to swoop down and snatch its prey. She was embarrassed to realize that she had not introduced her companion. "My lord, this is Much. He is Lord Huntingdon's friend. He knows that the dagger was stolen."

Argentan ruthlessly scrutinized Much as he queried, "Is that true? How do you know that it was stolen? Did *you* steal it? Perhaps you sold it to another thief who used it in this despicable crime."

Much's eyes nervously darted between Argentan and Marian as he denied any involvement.

"Was the murder of Baron Lenton a conspiracy? Would you like to join your *friend* in the dungeons?" proposed the sheriff.

Marian hastily interceded. "Much has done nothing wrong. We have come to secure Robin's freedom. He didn't kill my father. Robin's dagger was missing from Locksley Manor."

Argentan smirked slyly. "Forgive my lack of delicacy, my lady, but the dagger was not missing at all. It was in your father's chest."

Marian gasped in shock. "But that does not mean that Robin was responsible. He loved my father."

The sheriff disclosed, "After an extensive investigation, I have established that Lord Huntingdon rode from Locksley to Lenton, using forest paths instead of the main road. A witness observed him leaving Lenton chapel just prior to the discovery of your father's body."

"No, no, no," Marian emphatically countered, wagging her head in denial; she was determined to correct these fallacies. "That is not what happened. Whoever told you that story is mistaken; I was with Robin yesterday. We went for a horseback ride, and I watched him practice with his bow. We were nowhere near Lenton."

"Alone?" prodded Argentan.

Marian wavered, worried about becoming the target of malicious gossip; however, nothing was more important than exonerating Robin. "Yes, we were alone," she confessed in a small voice.

"Hmmm." Argentan's dark eyes studied her. "Do you have any brothers, Lady Marian?"

She blinked at the unanticipated question. "No, I am the only surviving child in my family."

"This is an unfortunate state of affairs. You have no brothers. Your father, God-rest-his-soul, is gone. Who will take charge of you?" The sheriff appeared to be quite concerned.

She was momentarily dumbfounded, but when she perceived

the derisive glint in his eyes, she bristled. "I don't need anyone to take care of me. I am not a child."

Argentan pursed his lips and shook his finger at her, as if she were an insolent little girl. "Lady Marian, you are a woman of poor judgment, traipsing through the woods alone with a man. Apparently, you *do* need someone to take charge of you. You have definitely exhibited a lack of prudence."

"But...but," Marian stammered in surprise.

The sheriff's disapproving verbal assault was measured, calm, and utterly devastating in its logic. "If you were alone in the woods with Huntingdon, then you did not display proper decorum for a lady of your age and rank. If you were *not* in the woods with him, then you are demonstrating a lack of integrity by lying to an officer of the king."

"What...?" Taken aback, Marian labored to refute his accusations.

There was a wry chuckle from Argentan. "You really leave me no choice, my lady. I am declaring you my ward. You have no male relatives, and it is obvious that you require rigorous supervision, so I will assume that role. I am a strict man, and I will not tolerate disobedience."

All the color drained from Marian's face, and her heart was thumping with growing alarm and resentment. Desperately trying to understand what was happening, she assessed the two men standing behind Argentan. The blonde man was cold and calculative; his stare chilled her to the bone. The tall man's gaze was burning with a fervency that left her feeling self-conscious and vulnerable. She instinctively recognized that she could not trust either of them.

Breaking free of her mental fog, Marian strenuously objected, "Robin will not consent to this. Our wedding is next month, at Michaelmas."

Argentan scoffed, "It will be difficult for Huntingdon to marry you. He has been sentenced to hang for your father's murder."

Marian's panicked voice rose an octave as she shrieked, "You can't do that! He is innocent. I told you that I was with him all afternoon. I don't care what you think of me, but I have just proven that Robin is innocent. You must release him!"

"Yet, when I interrogated him during his trial, he testified that he was alone." The sheriff shook his head as he feigned deep disappointment. "Clearly, you are a woman whose word is not trustworthy. If you are willing to go into the woods for an indecent rendezvous with your lover, then you are certainly capable of lying to save him."

Marian gasped again, humiliated and scandalized by his denunciations. She was losing her temper, and although she knew it would only make everything worse, she couldn't stop herself. "How dare you call me a liar and a wanton," she fumed. "Robin is my betrothed. He is an honorable man who respects me."

Argentan made a slow perusal down her body, pausing to ogle her breasts and hips before refocusing on her face. Marian blushed furiously, mortified by his frank appraisal. He moved until he was uncomfortably close, and then he scolded her in a quiet, menacing voice, "Are you so pure that you consider yourself unconstrained by the rules we sinners have to follow? I know your type: the self-righteous, innocent maiden." He barked a short, humorless laugh. "That is what I will call you: 'Maid Marian.'"

Then the sheriff softly brushed his knuckles along her cheek, and she visibly cringed. His voice became soothing, almost tender, as he asserted, "Appearances are deceiving, and like any viper, you lull your victims into a dreamlike state before you strike; your venom offers a sweet death, but it is death all the same." He abruptly stepped away from Marian, who swayed on her feet as if his words had been physical blows.

Payen giggled obnoxiously as he regarded her with repugnance and contempt.

In contrast, Guy was spellbound by a fantasy of Marian

expressing the same devotion for him as she had for Huntingdon. Knowing that her heartfelt pleas were actually for his enemy fueled his hate with the smoldering fire of envy. Guy desperately wanted this flaxen haired English beauty, and the seed of an obsessive desire was sown. It flourished in the barren landscape of his soul and blossomed into a single thought: he would take her from Huntingdon, and Lady Marian would belong to him.

"Gisborne!" the sheriff summoned his captain. After a lengthy pause, he looked back at Guy who was gazing intently at the young lady, evidently lost in a haze of lust and longing. Argentan rolled his eyes in disgust; Gisborne's weakness for women was tiresome and inconvenient. Suddenly, a spark of inspiration brightened the devious eyes of the sheriff.

He commanded, "Payen, escort my new ward to the guest quarters and arrange for sentries to be stationed at her door. I want everyone to know that I will be vigilant in my protection of Maid Marian."

Marian and Much shared uneasy glances, speechless and shocked by this bewildering turn of events.

"Guards!" yelled the sheriff. "Remove this dirty peasant from my castle."

Two soldiers grabbed Much, causing him to drop the basket they had brought for Robin.

As Marian bent to retrieve it, Payen firmly grasped her arm and pulled her to the door. Marian flinched as the colorless knight touched her; his hands were icy and bony with nails that were much too long, like the claws of a predatory bird. A memory of watching such birds feasting on the flesh of a dead deer made her skin crawl with dread. She stared into his impassive grey eyes and felt a kinship with the small, defenseless animals of the forest as he dragged her away.

As soon as he was alone with Guy, Argentan demanded, "Clean Huntingdon's dagger, and bring it to me."

Guy quickly obeyed while the sheriff extracted his old dagger from the sheath secured to his belt and laid it on his desk.

The sheriff took Robin's dagger and carefully studied the intricate designs on the hilt. "I will forever treasure this little memento of our victory over the last member of the Fitzooth family," he proclaimed with ghoulish delight. He unexpectedly raised the blade and pointed it at Guy's face.

Gisborne recoiled and warily asked, "My lord?"

"Tell me, Gisborne, would you also like a memento?" Argentan lowered the weapon, but Guy's sense of vulnerability persisted and was heightened by the exultant malevolence of his master. Guy did not answer, knowing that his wishes were irrelevant.

The sheriff viewed his captain with an air of brisk interest. "What do you think of the fair Maid Marian?" He snorted derisively, "I have no doubt that her outings with Huntingdon were innocent; she still blushes like a virgin." He stepped closer and murmured, "Just imagine tasting her honeyed lips, threading your fingers through her yellow hair, cupping her plump breasts...What ecstasy awaits the man who captures such a prize. If she belonged to *you* instead of Huntingdon..."

Gisborne shifted uncomfortably on his feet, as the sheriff's lascivious words ignited lustful thoughts and tantalized him with vivid images. He shut his eyes and endeavored to clear his mind and calm his body, while Argentan laughed at him.

At that moment, Payen returned, and Guy's awkward position became unbearable. He absolutely loathed the younger knight, whom he considered a dishonorable coward. Payen's apothecary father had been a favorite of Montlhéry, and so Payen had been elevated to lieutenant due to his talent for mixing poisons and not his fighting skills.

"My lord, please excuse me," Gisborne implored. "I must attend to my other duties."

An apple had spilled from Marian's basket, and Payen had just picked it up when Argentan insisted, "Bring that to me."

Guy observed the pale knight slither across the room and hand the apple to the sheriff, who sheathed Robin's dagger and examined the ripe fruit. Argentan then held it aloft and pontificated, "The daughters of Eve will tempt a man to his ruin." He eyed Payen. "Do you agree with me, Tancred?"

Payen fawningly affirmed, "Of course, my lord. Your wisdom has been a magnificent gift to me, and you are never wrong."

This greatly pleased the sheriff, who swung his gaze back to Guy. "Did you hear that, Gisborne? I am never wrong. So why do you continually ignore my warnings about the dangers of women?" When it became apparent that Guy was not intending to reply, the sheriff mused, "I find it curious that you and Huntingdon covet the same woman. Maybe you have more in common with your enemy than you realize."

Guy released an exasperated breath. "My lord, I have nothing in common with him. He is a pompous fool."

Yet again, Argentan's eyes gleamed with amusement. "Gisborne, what would you do to gain the hand of the exquisite Maid Marian? In two days, she will no longer be betrothed, and she needs a man to guide her along the right path."

Guy apprehensively beheld his master. From past experience, he was fully aware that remaining silent was likely the most prudent strategy.

The sheriff huffed in annoyance. "I have it within my power to give you this woman. What would you do to earn such a prize?"

Gisborne recognized that Argentan would not be satisfied until he actually spoke the words, for doubtless the sheriff already knew his answer. Sighing in resignation, he confessed, "My lord, I would do anything to have Lady Marian for myself."

The sheriff cackled with pleasure. "You are dismissed. Go fantasize about your yellow-haired daughter of Eve, a lovely viper whose sweet venom you are so eager to taste. As my dear Tancred would tell you: ultimately, it makes no difference whether a poison is fast or slow, sweet or bitter; the result is always the same."

Beaming with satisfaction, Payen basked in Argentan's affectionate approval.

Guy scowled fiercely at the shameless poisoner before genuflecting to the sheriff and leaving. As he descended the winding stairs, he could hear the raucous laughter of the two other men, and he punched the stone wall in frustrated mortification that stung his pride like a nest of irate hornets.

25 August 1188, Nottingham Castle

Robin closed his eyes and listened as another drop of water landed somewhere in the shadows beyond his cell. He was alone, and it was dark and quiet, except for the rats who roamed freely and that damned dripping. Of course, there were the sounds of his breathing and his heartbeat, but these signs of life merely underscored the fact that his life would soon end. He preferred not to think about that anymore.

Instead, he thought about the trickling water. For a time, he had counted the drops as they splashed onto the stone floor. He eventually grew tired of that, and began to speculate where the water might have originated. Was he below the kitchens? Was he near an outside wall? Was it raining?

Plunk.

Another drop. What aggravated him most about the dripping was the absence of any sort of rhythm or regularity. Sometimes the water dribbled steadily, and other times he found himself waiting for that next drop, holding his breath in anticipation, and exhaling with excessive relief when it finally came.

Plunk, Plink.

Two drops in rapid succession. Robin sighed loudly and sat up, cradling his head in his hands. Perhaps he was losing his mind, but thinking about the dripping water provided a respite from the gloomy thoughts and emotions which had tormented him since his return to the dungeons.

He had been a fool. An arrogant, conceited fool. He had naively assumed that with his clever tongue, keen mind, and lofty title, he could solve any problem and defeat any challenge. In truth, Robin had never really failed at anything before. From archery contests to jousting tournaments, from poetry competitions to wooing the prettiest courtesans and widows, Robin had always been the victor, and winning had become a way of life for him.

However, the one time when it had truly mattered, he had failed spectacularly. Why hadn't he recognized the gravity of his situation? Why hadn't he left immediately when the sheriff told him he could leave? Instead, he had allowed himself to be lured back into the clutches of the sheriff, in order to prove that *he,* Robin Fitzooth, was smarter than everyone else and could unravel the murder mystery—only to realize that he was the only person in the room who cared about the truth. Robin wondered who had actually killed Alfred, and ominous suspicions plagued him.

Plink.

Robin took a deep breath to calm himself. He had already spent an inordinate amount of time seething in various shades of anger: outraged at the injustice of it all, furious at the bastards who had stood there, lying and laughing at him, and vexed beyond measure at his own stupidity. Why had he been so oblivious to the truth until it was too late?

Plunk.

He glowered in the direction of the irritating sound and wished that he could just make it stop. Another drop, and he would lose what remained of his sanity. Rubbing his face vigorously, Robin once more sought the mercy of God, begging and negotiating for his life with fervent and sincere prayers. If God spared him, then he would never again curse or skip Mass. Prince Richard had spoken of taking the cross and going on a Crusade, and at that moment, Robin promised that he would go on the next Crusade, if God saved him from the gallows.

An abrupt clattering disturbed the funereal silence of Robin's cell as half a dozen guards appeared, their torches illuminating the narrow space and causing Robin to squint while his eyes adjusted to the light. He was thankful that Gisborne was not with them.

"It's time, my lord," one of them dutifully announced.

All too soon, his hands were bound behind his back, and he was marching with the men who were ushering him to his demise. Robin was no longer fuming, or despondent, or hopeful. He felt numb and hollow—like an ale barrel that had been drained and was empty of everything that gave it a purpose. He was not dying in some glorious battle as a hero bravely defending his king. Instead, he would die in disgrace at the end of a rope. It all seemed so illusory, so impossible—as if he were in a waking nightmare.

The small group trudged up the uneven stairs and proceeded along a murky passageway until they reached a fortified door. One man pushed it open as another shoved Robin forward, and he was briefly blinded by the dazzling midday sun. A portentous stillness hung in the air as Robin was greeted by a sea of faces. He scanned from left to right and realized that the courtyard was teeming with men.

Robin's heart constricted with grief and disappointment. Had they come to watch him die? He knew that the people respected and admired the benevolent, pious Baron of Lenton. Robin had always cherished his close relationship with his future father-in-law. Why would the people believe that Robin had slain him? Were they here to witness the spectacle of a public hanging? He could not accept the idea that the good people of Nottinghamshire would find his execution entertaining. He knew these men, and they knew him.

Robin had seen large gatherings in the past, especially during his years in Poitiers, but he had never encountered such a hushed and solemn multitude of people. It was eerie, and again he contemplated the dreamlike nature of the moment as he trailed the soldiers.

Then he saw it: a simple gallows, with two upright supports that were set into the ground, braced front and back, and topped by a crossbeam with a single noose.

"Lord Robin!" a familiar voice beckoned him.

Robin tore his gaze from the gallows and spotted Much, who was standing with Will, a youth from Locksley. He nodded at his friends and offered them a wan smile. Beside them was Osmund, Odella's father and the Locksley blacksmith. He seemed to have a long wooden handle protruding from under his tunic, which struck Robin as odd. He then glimpsed a cluster of unkempt men behind Much and Will. Their clothing was ragged and grimy, and their faces were obscured by hooded cloaks.

Gisborne was waiting for him beneath the noose, beaming triumphantly. Robin felt loathing for this stranger who evidently coveted his demise for no apparent reason; a man who could strike down a harmless peasant without remorse.

He halted next to a small, three-legged stool and surveyed the spacious balcony which was only thirty feet from the hastily built gallows. Argentan and Payen were there, both of them manifestly jubilant. However, it was the sight of a distraught, terrified Marian that caused Robin to frantically rush towards her.

The guards promptly grabbed his upper arms and dragged him back.

"Marian!" cried a despairing Robin, his heart somersaulting in the throes of excruciating grief.

She lunged towards him and shrieked, "Robin!" She was openly sobbing as she struggled against the pale knight's hold.

With an air of profound dignity colored by inconsolable anguish, Robin earnestly proclaimed, "Marian, I swear by all that's holy, I did not kill him." He had to make sure that she knew of his innocence. He could not face eternity believing that she thought he had harmed her father.

"Robin, I know you are innocent, I told–"

Payen covered Marian's mouth and jerked her away from the front of the balcony. He shook her roughly, and indignant murmurs rippled through the crowd at the disrespectful, harsh treatment of Lord Lenton's daughter.

Then the sheriff raised his hand, and the audience quieted. "I am Alaric de Montabard, Baron de Argentan," he announced loudly in his thick French accent. "Now that I am Sheriff of Nottingham, laws will be strictly enforced. Punishment will be swift and severe. Even an earl is not above the law. This man murdered Baron Lenton, an elderly, unarmed man, as he was praying in his family's chapel."

Someone yelled, "He's innocent!"

A strident voice rang out, "Free Lord Robin!"

The throng pressed forward, and amid the shouting, another man angrily bellowed, "Go back to Normandy! We don't want you here!"

Robin noticed that Gisborne's mood had transformed from gloating to apprehensive as he perceived the ugly temper of the men congregating around the gallows.

The executioner walked up to Robin clutching a black cloth—the hood that was placed over a man's head during his hanging. "My lord?" he tentatively entreated as he lifted the hood towards the prisoner.

"No," Robin emphatically responded. He then raised his voice, addressing the onlookers and hoping that they could hear him. "No hood! I refuse to wear a hood of guilt and shame, the hood of a man condemned for committing crimes. I stand here an innocent man.

I will not depart this life with my face hidden. Instead, I will meet my death with the clear conscience of a man who is being unjustly executed. I did not kill Baron Lenton!" The multitude roared with approval for Robin's defiant courage.

Once more he looked up at Marian. His heart dropped as he saw Payen holding her head and forcing her to observe his death.

Argentan impassively regarded Robin, obviously unimpressed with his final statement. "Very well," he declared. "We will send you to the devil without a hood. I will enjoy watching your face contort in pain and turn blue."

At this, a clamorous outcry erupted, and Gisborne nervously clasped his sword's hilt, although he kept it sheathed.

"People of Nottingham," again the sheriff raised his voice, and the crowd reluctantly hushed. "For the crime of murder, I sentence Robert Fitzooth, Earl of Huntingdon, to death. Burn in hell, Robin the Hoodless." Thunderous noise from the spectators echoed across the courtyard, and the half dozen soldiers who had escorted Robin out of the dungeons arranged themselves in a defensive circle around the gallows.

Robin stepped carefully onto the stool, which wobbled slightly under his weight. Gisborne slipped the noose over his head and tightened it. Smirking cruelly, Guy leaned closer to Robin and hissed into his ear. "Do not worry about Lady Marian. She belongs to me now. I will be bedding her soon, and I have no doubt that she will bear me many fine sons."

A bolt of fear and fury tore through Robin, but he could not attack the odious knight—not with the noose securely around his neck. "I swear to God, Gisborne, if you touch her, I will sell my soul to the devil and come back to haunt you; I will pursue you like a demon from hell."

Gisborne's confident, spiteful grin caused Robin to descend into absolute hopelessness, for he knew his words were an empty, meaningless threat. He beheld Marian for the last time, and his heart shattered into an infinite number of small pieces; she would soon be at the mercy of these evil men, and there was nothing he could do to save her.

Guy instructed the executioner, "The sheriff demands that you slowly remove the stool. He does not want a broken neck or an easy death for this vile butcher of a helpless old man in a church."

"Yes, my lord," the hangman meekly replied.

Robin's heart was beating so wildly that he could hear his blood rushing through his body. He closed his eyes and thought about Marian. He wanted the last image in his mind to be his beloved Marian. In the distance, beyond the roaring in his ears, he could hear shouting. Suddenly, he was falling, and he felt a sharp burning on the outside of his neck. He gasped for air, but he could not breathe, and his lungs began to painfully constrict. The whooshing in his ears grew louder.

And then the world around him receded, and he plummeted into a black abyss.

◈

A devastated Marian had ceased thrashing against the iron grasp of Payen as he gleefully compelled her to watch the destruction of her past, present, and future, leaving her bereft and utterly alone. Whenever she started to faint, the fiend slapped her, bringing her back from the haze of a swoon to the reality of a nightmare. Through watery eyes, she witnessed Robin fall and begin to twist at the end of a rope.

Like her beloved, she felt herself plunging into oblivion, but the jolt of landing on the stone floor and the din of a tumultuous outcry brought her back to full alertness. Opening her eyes, she realized that the knight had dropped her and hastened to the low wall at the front of the balcony, and a sense that something unexpected was occurring gave her the strength to regain her feet and stagger to the wall beside Payen.

The sight which greeted her was so amazing that she feared it was an illusion. The throng had surged forward and stormed the gallows. Much and another young man were gripping Robin's legs, lifting him and releasing the pressure of the noose around Robin's neck. A blade flashed in the bright sun as another man swung a scythe and severed the rope that tethered Robin to the crossbeam. The sheriff's captain was so tightly surrounded that he couldn't unsheathe his sword as the crush of men shoved him away from Robin. The six guards hastily retreated into the keep under a hail of rocks.

A livid Argentan was screeching in French, and Payen hurriedly left.

Marian watched Much carry Robin over his shoulder as he sprinted through the portcullis, followed by a swarm of men flowing from the bailey like a river of humanity. The peasants had used sticks, farming tools, and rocks to distract the soldiers during Robin's rescue.

Gisborne had managed to draw his sword, and a giant man in ragged clothes boldly approached him, laughing and taunting the knight. Marian was afraid for the man's life because his only weapon was a long wooden staff. Gisborne viciously slashed at him, but in an agile movement that belied his great size, the man blocked Guy's strike with his heavy stick. Gisborne's sword became lodged in the wood, and the big peasant wrenched it from his hands.

A stunned Gisborne stood there, open-mouthed and defenseless, as the man punched him in the face. Guy crumpled in a heap on the ground, and the peasant spat on him. At that moment, Marian glimpsed the pale knight run into the courtyard, and she silently prayed that the big man would hit him as well. However, as soon as Payen saw that Gisborne was unconscious, he pivoted and dashed back into the safety of the keep.

Marian glanced at the sheriff, whose face was purple with rage. He was screaming at the soldiers stationed along the castle wall, but they were either gaping in shock at the riot below them, or they were frowning at Argentan in confusion. Marian wanted to laugh; the sheriff was shouting in French! No wonder the men were perplexed. She understood a little of the language, and she believed he was shrieking at them to shut the gate. By the time the portcullis was finally closed, the crowd had escaped and dispersed.

Marian was convinced that Robin had survived. Those few moments of hanging would not have killed him. The sheriff's icy voice interrupted her thoughts, and she uneasily flicked her eyes to him.

Argentan was visibly struggling to contain his wrath, and he sneered, "Maid Marian, your lover is a very dangerous criminal; he is a murderer and a traitor who incites rebellion among the populace. As your guardian, I must act in your best interest. Therefore, I am dissolving your betrothal to Huntingdon."

In a broken voice, Marian cried, "You cannot do that!"

The sheriff swiftly advanced towards her, making her skin prickle in fear and revulsion, and she recoiled, bumping into the rough stone wall at her back.

The menace in his quiet voice was much more terrifying than his shrill screaming at the soldiers. "Never tell me what I can or cannot do, Maid Marian. I rule Nottingham with the authority of a king; I decide who lives and who dies with the power of an immortal god. You are alive only because it serves my purpose."

Marian's eyes widened in abject horror as Argentan reached up and wrapped his hand around her neck. She could feel each one of his fingers and the band of his heavy signet ring against the delicate skin of her throat. Her heart sped faster as she observed the emotion in his eyes shift from festering hatred to sadistic pleasure.

Argentan's voice became gentle and honeyed, as if he were soothing a frightened child. "It would be so simple to kill you now. All I have to do is squeeze." His fingers tightened, and it became harder for her to breathe. Marian seized his forearm with both hands and desperately tried to pull his hand from her throat. His dark eyes bore into hers as he reveled in a lurid fantasy of death. "And while I squeeze, your eyes will beg me to stop, they will stare at me, pleading for your life. Soon the light in your eyes will fade away as you descend into the shadows; you will belong to me for eternity while your eyes will be forever staring into the distance, full of fear and longing for the life that I have taken from you." He exhaled noisily, as though he were experiencing immense satisfaction at the thought of killing her, and she felt his hot breath puff across her face like a blast from the fiery pit of hell.

Abruptly, the sheriff released Marian, and she doubled over, coughing and trying to catch her breath. Tears were streaming down her cheeks, and she was filled with a terror that left her stomach nauseated and her mind jumbled.

Argentan calmly asked, "I'm curious, Maid Marian, what is your opinion of Gisborne?"

"Who?" she sputtered, still winded and wheezing.

"The tall, handsome knight." Argentan smirked wickedly. He was now amused, as if he had not just threatened to strangle her with his bare hands. "He has expressed an interest in bedding you." He paused, and his grin broadened. "Ah, pardon my poor English, I meant to say he has an interest in wedding you. Perhaps I will give you to him as a reward for his loyal service."

At that moment, Payen returned.

Argentan's focus never strayed from Marian's horrified face as he commanded, "Payen, escort Maid Marian to her chamber. I am done playing with her for today."

CHAPTER 5
THE EARL OF SHERWOOD FOREST

25 August 1188, Sherwood Forest, Nottinghamshire

Heaven was exactly like Sherwood Forest.

Robin's head was throbbing, but the familiar smells and sounds of the greenwood were slowly making their presence known to him, and he was delighted to discover that the afterlife was very much like his favorite place on earth. He did not have the strength to move, but he could hear the murmuring of angels along with the rustling of leaves and the chirping of birds.

"Lord Robin?" An anxious voice summoned him.

Robin stirred slightly, but his eyes remained closed as he lingered in a hazy world between sleep and wakefulness. Much had been his constant companion for many years, but Robin hardly expected his loyal friend to accompany him in death. With great effort, Robin cracked open an eye. Just as he had hoped, heaven was a beautiful forest. His vision was somewhat blurred, but he could distinguish leafy branches above him. Suddenly, a ruddy face framed by unruly red hair loomed over him, blocking his view.

He moaned; the skin on his neck felt raw, and his throat was sore. A stray thought occurred to him: why did he have to suffer like this in heaven? No sooner had that notion entered his mind when another, more lucid, thought emerged: he was alive.

"Where?" Robin managed to choke out.

"We are in Sherwood with the Little Band." Much was visibly relieved that Robin was at last awake, and he helped him to sit up.

Robin had not eaten in days, and his ordeal had left him faint and dizzy. He deeply inhaled the savory scent of something cooking, and when Much pressed a rough earthenware cup against his lips, he eagerly drank the cool, refreshing water. The pounding in his head quieted, and Robin finally opened his eyes to inspect his surroundings. He was in a tidy camp, and although he could hear the River Trent flowing nearby, this clearing was unfamiliar to him.

His initial pleasure at being in Sherwood was replaced by unease as he observed a dozen men with scruffy beards and ragged clothing standing behind Much and staring at him intently. Immediately, he remembered them from the crowd in the courtyard.

Robin apprehensively looked at Much, who calmly introduced the men. "My lord, this is John Little and his men. They live in the greenwood, and they helped rescue you from the gallows. Everyone knows that John Little can outwit sheriffs, forest officers, and nobles."

It took a moment for Robin to comprehend Much's words, and he was alarmed to realize who these men were. Hoarsely, Robin queried, "Poachers?"

This caused the men to irritably mutter and scowl at Robin and Much. The largest of the men stepped forward and disdainfully asked, "Are you going to report us to the sheriff for poaching, Robin Hoodless?"

Robin heaved a sigh and attempted a more diplomatic approach. His voice was still raspy as he respectfully answered, "Of course not. I didn't mean to insult you, and I am thankful for your assistance. Are you the leader of these men?"

The man brusquely affirmed, "I am John Little, but my men call me Little John. I don't much care for nobles like you: selfish men with soft hands who speak fancy words."

Robin was sitting on the ground, and he contemplated the tall and muscular "Little" John, whose long hair and bushy beard were streaked with grey, giving him a feral, unkempt appearance. Nevertheless, he discerned an unmistakable intelligence in the man's shrewd eyes. Again, he endeavored to thank him. "I appreciate your willingness to save me, despite the fact that I am a noble."

Little John frowned. "I didn't do it for you. I did it for Lady Edith."

"My mother?" Robin was surprised by the mention of his mother, who had been gone for twelve years.

John gruffly explained, "Lady Edith saved my son after a sickle sliced open his leg during the harvest. She cleaned and stitched his wound herself, even though she was a high born lady, and he was just a peasant boy. She saved him, and now I have saved you. My debt to your family is paid."

Robin often heard such stories about his mother. He briefly scanned the faces of the other men before asking, "Where is your son? I would like to meet him. Is he here in this camp with you?"

John abruptly tensed and tersely replied, "My son is always with me." With that cryptic statement, he walked away with his men deferentially following.

Much tapped Robin's shoulder and disclosed, "Elvina sent a special broth to rebalance your humors and this salve for your neck." He produced a small pot containing a foul smelling ointment.

Robin refused it and tried to get up. "There's no time for that. I have to go to the castle; Marian is in terrible jeopardy."

Much restrained him and contended, "I'm sorry, Lord Robin, but the sun is setting, and tonight is a new moon. It will be too dark to travel."

Robin's voice was wispy and hoarse, but he countered as

vehemently as he could, "If necessary, I will crawl on my hands and knees through the black of night. I must rescue her from those evil bastards."

"But you are still weak," argued Much. "I have sent Will to Lenton to gather news of Lady Marian. He will be back tomorrow. Besides, I don't think Little John will let you leave his camp. This is a secret location."

Robin's eyes narrowed skeptically. "A secret location that is well-known to you."

Much had the decency to blush. "It's true, Lord Robin. I've known Little John all my life. He used to live in Locksley."

"Are you friendly with his son? I'm guessing he would be our age." Robin glanced at the other men who were loitering at the far side of the camp.

Much offered Robin a bowl filled with soup. "Elvina insisted that you must drink all of it."

Although Robin was impatient to be on his way to save Marian, he conceded that some food would give him the energy he needed. The broth smelled delicious, and he greedily drank it down. Returning the empty vessel to Much, he demanded, "We will leave at once." Robin struggled to stand, but his body felt very heavy. He shook his head to dispel the fog descending upon his mind.

"Forgive me, Robin. Elvina said the broth would help you sleep. You will feel better tomorrow, and we will go to the castle then," promised an apologetic, yet resolute, Much.

Robin wanted to be angry, but he was too drowsy. Without complaining, he allowed Much to ease him back upon his make-shift bed. Closing his eyes, a sense of calm washed over him like a gentle breeze as he listened to Much's wistful recollections.

"I knew Little John's son; we were the same age. But John's son, his wife, and all his children, they died from the same plague that killed your mother. That's when John abandoned his home in Locksley and went to live in the woods."

Robin's last thoughts before slipping into a dreamless slumber were about John Little, a wild, coarse man of the forest. How could any man survive the death of his entire family? Such a man deserved more than the easy pity of a compassionate heart; he deserved respect for having the strength to continue living.

✍

When Robin awoke the next morning, he felt much stronger. His nose wrinkled at the smelly salve which Much had slathered on his neck during the night, but he also had to admit that his neck was no longer so tender and chafed.

He promptly attended to his personal needs, and when he returned, he found his bow, sword, and some of his clothes in a pile alongside a sleeping Much. He knelt on the ground and roused his friend. "Much, we must leave. Marian is in danger."

Much startled and sat up, just as a booming voice reverberated behind them.

"You're not going anywhere."

Jumping to his feet, Robin spun around and glared at Little John. He indignantly retorted, "We are leaving now."

Little John gestured to his men, and they encircled Robin and Much, confirming that they intended to detain them in the camp.

Much bravely argued, "Little John, you can't keep the Earl of Huntingdon here against his will."

John sneered, "His title means nothing in *my* forest."

"*Your* forest?" Robin cocked an inquisitive brow at the big man.

John grinned broadly and pronounced with great fanfare, "Let me introduce myself: I am John Little, the Earl of Sherwood Forest, and these are my vassals." He waved at the other men with a sweeping flourish, and they all genuflected with exaggerated formality as they snickered and chortled.

Enjoying the humor of the situation, Robin bowed to the Earl of Sherwood Forest, the usual form of greeting between men of equal rank. He curiously inquired, "If these men are your vassals, how do they serve you?"

Several of the men spoke up, and their overlapping chatter echoed loudly in the early morning stillness. Little John silenced them with a flick of his large hand and responded, "As the Earl of Sherwood Forest, it is my duty to provide timber, venison, and animal skins to the villagers. My vassals assist me in this mission. In return, the villagers supply us with whatever we need. It's a comfortable life, and everyone is happy."

Robin carefully considered his words. "I have heard vague tales of men living in the woods, but I didn't realize that the poachers were so numerous and well-organized. I can appreciate how your arrangement benefits both you and the villagers; however, I suspect that the sheriff and the local forest officers are not so tolerant of your scheme."

John shrugged. "After twelve summers of dwelling in Sherwood, I have yet to be captured or punished. The same is true for my men." He raised his voice and asserted with zealous conviction, "I do not recognize the authority of any king over this forest. The Lord, our God, gave the people this greenwood and everything within it. For four generations, the story has been passed down from father to son of how the Normans–" at this word, John leaned to the side and spat, "came here and claimed ownership of the forests. They seized the forests from us, and now we are taking them back."

The outlaws cheered and pumped their fists in the air as they enthusiastically seconded Little John's defiant speech.

Robin sympathized with the men and their plight. He was well aware of the hardships that forest law imposed upon the people. These edicts had been brought to England by William the Conqueror, a Norman, and they had been expanded and vigorously enforced under King Henry, an avid hunter eager to control all the woodlands within his domain.

"I am not interested in reporting you to the sheriff or the forest officers, but you must permit Much and me to leave. I have to return to the castle–" Robin's announcement inspired howls of laughter among the men.

Little John huffed in annoyance. "I just saved you from hanging. Do you want to die? You are an outlaw now."

Someone shouted, "There's a huge bounty on your head, Robin Hoodless."

Robin's brow creased in confusion, so Much enlightened, "The people are calling you that because of what you said at the hanging, when you refused to wear a hood."

Understanding dawned as Robin recalled his address to the crowd.

John was apparently unmoved by Robin's testimony at the gallows. "I heard you proclaim your innocence. But not one of us sinners is innocent. It's just that some men are more successful sinners than others. There's another problem though." He motioned for one of the outlaws to come forward. "Kenric, tell us what you discovered."

A somber young man approached and grimly informed, "The sheriff is punishing the people for the riot. The harvest is underway, and he's declared that half of all the grain must be surrendered to him. Everyone is afraid that there won't be enough food for the upcoming winter." Swallowing nervously, Kenric delivered some gruesome news from his reconnaissance in Nottingham. "The six soldiers who were guarding the gallows were executed for allowing Lord Huntingdon to escape and refusing to reveal the names of the villagers who were there. Lord de Argentan has hung their naked bodies from the walls of the gatehouse, so that all those entering Nottingham Castle will see what happens to men who disobey the sheriff."

Robin's heart sank. Those men had been doing their duty—merely following orders, and he held no animosity towards them. His hatred was reserved for Argentan, Gisborne, and Payen. He asked, "Did the soldiers have families? I want to provide assistance to them."

Kenric answered, "My lord, most of the men were unmarried; only one had a wife, but another was supporting his elderly parents."

Robin's anger over the slaughter of the soldiers exploded as he heatedly avowed, "I pledge to obtain justice for these families; this malevolent sheriff must be stopped. First, I will rescue Lady Marian from the castle, and then I will send dispatches to King Henry and Prince Richard–"

Once again, a chorus of heckles resounded, and Robin realized how his remarks might be received by a dozen cynical poachers who were brazenly defying the king's law of the forest.

"Robin Hoodless, you are not in command here, I am," decreed John. "However, since you are now a fellow outlaw, I am willing to accept you as one of my vassals. Are you prepared to swear an oath of fealty to me?"

Robin hesitated as he warily assessed the older man. He was being tested, and he would not, could not, fail; Marian was alone and vulnerable in the castle. He parried Little John's taunt with an audacious, yet prudent, suggestion. "Or, you could become my vassal. I will accept an oath of fealty from you and your men. I have military experience; I have fought alongside Prince Richard in Aquitaine."

Little John was also scrutinizing Robin as he scoffed, "This ain't Aquitaine; you're in England now. I'll wager that your foreign training won't do you any good here in the woods." He smirked at Robin, hoping to provoke the younger man. "If you become my vassal, I will need to train you to fight like a real man and not a Norman dog." Then John leaned to the side and spat.

Most of his men mimicked him by theatrically spitting on the ground.

Robin was growing impatient. "Instead of crowing about ourselves like roosters at dawn, let's put our boasts to the test." He coolly proposed, "I will fight your best man. If I win, then I will be the leader of this band."

With a glimmer of confident anticipation in his eyes, John bragged, "I have never lost a fight, and you're nothing but a little boy. It will hardly be a challenge for me to defeat you."

Robin promptly replied, "I accept your challenge—"

"Robin, no," protested Much, who was panicking at this unforeseen turn of events.

A determined Robin silenced Much with a peremptory gesture as he resumed, "Just to clarify: if I defeat you, then I will be the leader of these men. I will have the authority to pursue the rescue of Lady Marian."

"I won't let you send these men on a doomed mission that promises them only death," growled a fuming John.

Robin hastily reassured everyone, "My plan will not require anyone to sacrifice themselves." Unfortunately, he was not telling the whole truth, as he had not actually formulated a plan, but he reasoned that he *planned* to devise a plan where no one would die, so he wasn't really lying.

The outlaws escorted Much and Robin to a clearing on the banks of the River Trent, where John faced Robin and instructed, "We will use staffs instead of swords. The first man to yield will become the vassal of the victor." John was already holding his staff, and another man gave a similar thick wooden pole to Robin before returning to stand with the others.

"What are the rules?" asked Robin.

At that moment, Little John swung his staff against the side of Robin's knees, knocking him to the ground with a humiliating thump.

"Rules?" John laughed scornfully. "We follow outlaw rules."

A spectator excitedly yelled, "Which means there ain't no rules!"

Little John was still snickering as he chided, "Had enough?"

"No, it will take more than a sneak attack to deter me." Robin stood and grinned roguishly, even though he was mortified and thoroughly annoyed with himself for his naiveté. He raised his staff and held it with both hands in front of his chest while he tamped down his emotions and focused on what was truly important: winning this contest as a first step to rescuing Marian.

John swung hard, aiming for Robin's head and intending to render him unconscious. Robin's training and quick reflexes enabled him to avoid the blow by diving to the ground as John's staff passed harmlessly over his back. John was off balance from the momentum of his swing, and he wobbled awkwardly while Robin nimbly regained his feet and struck the big man forcefully in the stomach.

Little John grunted and was evidently unscathed, although Robin noticed that he was favoring his left leg as he shuffled to the right in preparation for his next assault. Robin braced himself for the coming onslaught; he had fully expected to topple his opponent with such a solid hit, and John's nonchalant reaction was unnerving.

John's subsequent strike was bone-jarring, but Robin successfully blocked it as he pondered his adversary's strength and apparent invincibility. Robin knew from past experience that even the sturdiest fortifications have some weakness; he would just need to find John's Achilles' heel, and find it fast.

Robin modified his grip until he was holding his pole like a spear. He poked John's left shoulder and hurriedly stepped back. Little John swung again, and Robin ducked. Then he sprang forward and jabbed his staff into John's right shoulder, essentially repeating what he had done to the left.

Little John grumbled derisively, "Are you going to just poke me with your little stick? Maybe that impresses all those foreign women at court, but I'm getting bored."

Robin chuckled despite himself. The big man was smarter and wittier than he looked. Meanwhile, the outlaws guffawed and mocked Robin, obviously enjoying the entertainment.

Robin refocused on his methodical search for John's

vulnerabilities: John had flinched when prodded in the left shoulder, but not the right. He had a barely perceptible limp, also on the left. This was predictable since injuries on the left side were the common result of two right-handed men engaging in combat. John was brawny and resilient, but his movements were slow, and Robin could easily read his intentions.

Little John goaded Robin. "Is this your fancy foreign training? You have a lot to learn about fighting."

The onlookers gleefully offered their own advice and opinions.

"Knock him down!" hollered someone.

Another bellowed, "I think he's scared of you, John."

"I've seen women fight better than Robin Hoodless," jeered a loud voice.

Robin smiled serenely; he was too well-trained to allow taunts to unsettle him. In the meantime, he hoped to find one more weakness as the two men cautiously circled each other, clasping their staffs and ready to thwart any attack. Robin lurched to the side and swung. The outlaw simply checked Robin's strike, confirming that there was nothing wrong with John's left eye.

They were still circling, but Robin was now moving faster, executing a series of short thrusts and feigned swipes. Little John did an excellent job of opposing his maneuvers, and Robin was surprised by his skills. Abruptly, he lunged to John's right, mirroring the action he had performed earlier on his left. This time, there was a delayed response, and Robin grinned in satisfaction; John's right eye did not have the acuity of his left.

Robin increased his pace, and he started pressing closer to John, driving him to back towards the river. He concentrated on hitting the left side of John's body while maintaining his stance to the outlaw's right, where John's vision did not seem as clear.

The older man was growing winded and tired, and he was sweating profusely in the humid August air. Unexpectedly, John managed to whack Robin's leg, nearly toppling him, and the other outlaws cheered.

Little John made the mistake of savoring his small victory a bit too long, even raising his arms in triumph. Robin seized the opportunity to charge John's right side, where his eyesight was weaker. He adroitly moved behind his adversary and walloped the back of John's knees with his staff, causing the big man to plummet to the ground with a heavy thud.

Without warning, John swiveled on his knees and swiped his staff towards Robin's ankles. Robin leapt on top of his foe, briefly pinning him, but he was not strong enough to keep him in place. The outlaw rocked sideways, and Robin found himself underneath Little John. But momentum took over, and suddenly the two men were rolling down the embankment until they splashed into the shoals of the River Trent, where Robin remained in the shallows while John continued tumbling into much deeper water.

Little John was floundering as the outlaws rushed to the edge of the river, some of them anxiously shouting to their leader, encouraging him to swim to safety.

In a horrified voice, someone recalled, "He can't swim!"

Another man screeched in a panic, "Can anyone swim?"

Robin unhesitatingly dove into the water and swam to John, whose frenzied thrashing was unintentionally propelling him further from dry land and out into the powerful currents of the river. As Robin reached for him, a terrified John almost smacked Robin in the head. Little John kept dropping beneath the surface, and Robin could not get a good grip on him. John's agitated movements presented a very real hazard to Robin, who had to dodge the outlaw's flailing arms and kicking feet.

Just then, something floated by, and Robin recognized John's staff. One of the other men had tossed it to him, and Robin was grateful for the man's quick thinking as he grabbed it. John was rapidly tiring, and he sank lower into the murky depths. Robin extended the staff to the drowning man, and John instinctively clutched the familiar piece of wood. With John holding onto one end of the staff, Robin steadily towed him to the shore.

As they neared the embankment, the other outlaws waded into the shoals and pulled the two men to safety. Wheezing and coughing up water, Robin and John sat beside each other, laboring to catch their breath.

"Shit!" cried Little John as he slapped the ground in exasperation.

"What?" Robin was momentarily befuddled by the other man's outburst.

"Just when I finally repaid my debt to your family, you go and save my worthless life, and now I owe you a life again. Shit!" The playful gleam in John's eyes was unmistakable, and he was clearly suppressing a grin at the young man who had rescued him from drowning.

Robin snorted in amusement, and soon everyone dissolved into waves of joyful laughter triggered by the tremendous relief that a tragedy had been averted.

When the group quieted, Robin stood and faced the men. "Let us call this contest a draw. I am not seeking leadership because I am an earl, and you are peasants. You are free men of the greenwood, and I don't care if you are poachers. I am no champion of forest law; it hurts peasant and noble alike."

Robin gathered his thoughts. "This Norman baron is not like the previous sheriff, God-rest-his-soul. Argentan is a lawless man who does not value justice and fairness. Consider the fate of those soldiers—men who did not deserve death."

Much indignantly exclaimed, "And the sheriff tried to execute Lord Robin for a murder he didn't commit."

The men murmured in agreement; no one believed that Robin was guilty.

Robin sent his friend a brief nod of thanks before confidently asserting, "I can lead you through the difficult days ahead. I will welcome Little John as my captain; he has proven his skills to me. Perhaps you are not impressed with my foreign military training, but this knowledge will help me oppose these men from Normandy. I will be acquainted with their tactics, and more importantly, I will know how to counter them."

He surveyed the men and boldly proposed, "Accept me as your leader. I have been declared an outlaw, but I will not be called Robin Hoodless. Until I can return to my life as Robin Fitzooth, I will be Robin Hood. I will wear a plain hooded cloak just like you—not an earl, not a lord, but just a man protecting the people from this malicious sheriff and fighting to restore my good name. Follow me."

Silence reigned along the banks of the River Trent, and Robin worried that they would reject him. The time had stretched uncomfortably when Little John stiffly rose to his feet. "I'm an old man, but I want to fight against this Norman sheriff. I will follow you." With John's endorsement, the others promptly pledged to support Robin as their leader.

Robin outlined his priorities. "First, we will give those soldiers a proper burial after we retrieve them from the walls of the gatehouse. We will not tolerate Sheriff de Argentan's desecration of their bodies. Then we will work to undermine the sheriff and drive him out of Nottinghamshire, but we will not kill. We are honorable Englishmen, not murderers. In our quest for justice, we will treat every man, whether he is a noble or a peasant, friend or foe, with fairness and mercy. The soldiers are not the enemy—the Norman sheriff and his knights are the enemy."

He paused, knowing that he must convince them of his next directive, or they would be doomed to fail. Emphasizing each word, he demanded, "However, we cannot kill the Normans. King Henry sent them here. We cannot become enemies of our king. Despite what you think about forest law, King Henry is a good and fair king. But if we murder his representatives here in Nottinghamshire, then we will have no hope of surviving his vengeance."

Pleased to see the men nodding in agreement, he suggested, "Instead of killing these Normans, we will make them so miserable that they will be desperate to leave England."

The outlaws cheered at this idea, and one yelled, "We'll send those dogs back to Normandy with their tails between their legs."

Robin was thankful that the men understood his reasons for avoiding bloodshed. Now, he had to persuade them to save Marian, and he knew exactly what approach to use. "We must also rescue Lady Marian, the daughter of Baron Lenton. She is a virtuous woman, who is in great danger at the castle. The tall Norman knight has vowed to take her by force. We cannot let our women be violated by the Normans."

A battle cry arose among the men; they were eager to defend the virtue of the lovely Lady Marian.

Everyone returned to camp, and Robin sat beside a warm fire, deep in thought as he considered various rescue strategies. A blade flashed in the periphery of his vision, and Robin leapt to his feet, pivoting to confront the perceived threat.

Little John was offering him a sword. "I took this from the Norman dog who put the rope around your neck."

Robin accepted it and thanked John as he divulged, "That was Guy of Gisborne. His father was a traitor who tried to murder King Henry, and he is the man who is menacing Lady Marian." As he examined the unusual weapon, he requested, "May I keep this?"

John shrugged indifferently. "Take it. Blades are for weak men who can't fight with their fists." He then left to sit with his men at another campfire.

At that moment, Will of Locksley entered the camp and joined Much and Robin.

Much queried Will, "How are things in the village?"

A solemn Will advised, "Quiet at present, but my father says it feels like the lull before the storm. I went to Lenton; Lady Marian is a prisoner in the castle, but there are no reports of any wedding. The Locksley priest says that she cannot be married against her will. Such a marriage is invalid and will not be recognized by the church."

Robin roughly dragged his hand through his hair and argued despairingly, "The men who have taken Marian captive will not care whether the marriage is valid. An invalid marriage will not stop that man from—" He broke off, images of Marian being assaulted swamping his mind and hindering his efforts to think about anything else, including a plan of rescue.

Forcing himself to redirect his thoughts away from Marian's perilous circumstances, Robin returned to his scrutiny of Gisborne's weapon. He frowned at the sword and mumbled, "Interesting."

"What is it, Lord Robin?" inquired Much.

Robin revealed, "This sword is quite distinctive."

Will leaned closer for a better view. "It looks like any other sword, except for all those marks on the blade."

Robin inspected the extravagant weapon as he described it. "This is an excellent sword, equal to the one I carry. It's unlikely that a landless knight like Gisborne would own such a weapon, although sometimes a wealthy noble will award a superior sword to his favorite squire on the occasion of his knighthood, especially if the knight will be tasked with guarding the lord."

Much felt confused. "Gisborne is Argentan's captain; he was probably his squire too. Why does the quality of this sword surprise you?"

Robin countered, "Much, do you remember the Barony of Argentan from our travels through Normandy?" At the quick shake of Much's head, he disclosed, "Well, *I* remember it. Argentan is not prosperous; it is small and insignificant. I wonder how Baron de Argentan could afford to give such an expensive weapon to his captain."

Rising, the three men strolled to a nearby spot brightened by a shaft of light, and Robin held the blade where the sun's rays could illuminate its elaborate designs. He continued to study it as Will and Much watched.

Much commented, "Those marks look like letters."

An amazed Will stared at Much. "You can read?"

Much's ruddy complexion darkened slightly in self-consciousness. "I can read a little. I was allowed to listen to Lord Robin's lessons, and his tutor kindly taught me many things."

Robin pointed to the elegant etching on the blade. "Notice these two lions—I saw something similar on Argentan's ring. Above the lions is a rising sun, and below them is a peculiar inscription."

Much squinted at the blade and grumbled in frustration. "I know my reading is not as well-practiced as yours, but I cannot decipher any of those words."

Robin smiled affectionately at his friend. "Be at ease, Much. It is not English; it is written in Latin. I've seen this style of inscribed sword in the past, but typically they are engraved with prayers, such as 'In the Name of the Father.'"

"Do you know what it says?" asked Will.

Robin replied, "I can translate it, even though the letters are crowded together. It says, 'From Shadows to Glory: I am Immortal, and My Kingdom Awaits.'" He harrumphed grimly, flustered by the unexpected phrase. He lowered the sword from the patch of sunlight as he became lost in his thoughts.

Robin blew out an exasperated breath. "Argentan mentioned shadows, but he was speaking in riddles. I must think on this more. For now, I will keep this sword; I want Gisborne to know that I have it."

Following Much and Will back to the campfire, Robin plotted Marian's rescue.

26 August 1188, Nottingham Castle

Gisborne smirked at the three young women who were flirting with him. Argentan was holding a feast to celebrate his arrival in Nottinghamshire, and they were the daughters of several local barons. They were pretty, and their eyes shone with admiration for the tall, handsome, and mysterious knight. The aura of danger surrounding Guy often attracted women like moths to a flame.

"Can you talk French to us?" one of the girls breathlessly entreated.

Startled by her request, Guy slanted his eyes in her direction. "Why? Do you know the language?"

She giggled. "No, of course not, but it sounds so beautiful when I hear you talk like that to the sheriff." The girls tittered with excitement.

Guy, not caring if he insulted them, rolled his eyes. He scanned the great hall, evaluating the other available women. He was in no mood to deal with innocent maidens, particularly the daughters of nobles who might squawk and complain if Guy took one of them to his bed without any intention of marriage. He needed someone without expectations who could distract him from his preoccupation with Lady Marian. That was when he spotted her: a blonde who was old enough to know her way around a man's bed. Without another word to the simpering girls fawning over him, Guy stalked towards his prey.

He would wed Lady Marian as soon as Argentan granted him permission. In the meantime, he would entertain himself with blondes who vaguely resembled his future bride. Gisborne was halfway across the great hall when Payen stepped into his path.

"What do you want, Payen?" Guy snarled. As usual, whenever the men spoke to each other or to Argentan, they reverted to French.

"What is it that *you* want, Gisborne?" the younger man's grey eyes were amused.

"At this moment, I plan to have that woman over there." Guy tilted his chin towards the lady who was now smiling seductively at him.

Payen scolded him, "Argentan is right: women are treacherous vipers. You should heed his warnings."

Guy snorted derisively and launched a scathing attack. "Have *you* ever bedded a woman? Shall I help you locate a blind whore who is willing to make you a man? It is not my fault that women are so eager to warm my bed, while they find you repugnant."

Payen's eyes narrowed in resentment, and he retaliated. "Gisborne, where is your sword? That is not your customary weapon."

Guy grabbed the front of Payen's tunic and yanked him closer as he growled menacingly, "I will reclaim it shortly. Do not say anything about the sword to the sheriff, or I will beat you senseless and tell him that you were injured while running away from some village children."

Unimpressed by Gisborne's bullying, Payen gleefully taunted, "I cannot believe that you lost the sword that Montlhéry gave you when you attained knighthood. When I mentioned it to the sheriff earlier, he was very disappointed in you."

Guy's face briefly paled before it reddened in fury, and he lifted the smaller man off his feet and hurled him into a nearby wall, much to the chagrin of shocked bystanders. As a shaken Payen stood, Guy irately marched towards the blonde waiting at the far side of the hall. He just hoped that she was prepared to submit to a vigorous bedding.

CHAPTER 6
THE UNWANTED SUITOR

27 August 1188, Nottingham Castle

A thunderous pounding at her door caused Marian to startle and jump to her feet.

It was the third day of her imprisonment, and Marian had been listlessly watching the clouds drift across the cerulean canvas outside her window. She was exhausted from the intense emotions tormenting her: worry about Robin's safety, terror over Argentan's threats to kill her, and panic that she might be forced to marry a stranger. When she slept, she was haunted by nightmares of Robin hanging from the gallows, his face blue, and his handsome features twisted in a grotesque mask of pain.

These fearful emotions were foreign to her. Throughout her life, she had been treated much like the precious relics which her father had hidden in the altar of his chapel: she had been sheltered, guarded, and venerated. The adoration and respect which she had received from her father, Robin, and everyone else around her, had been crucial to her development into a self-confident and accomplished woman.

But did she have the strength to confront the powers now arrayed against her? Never before had she felt such vulnerability and uncertainty in her life, and she loathed these timid, trembling emotions with the same vehemence with which she abhorred the sheriff and his knights. After all, it was their fault that she was experiencing waves of terror and panic.

The sound at the door resurrected all her anxieties, and she resolved to conquer these fears plaguing her. Irritated that her hands were shaking, she huffed in exasperation as she walked to the door and asked, "Who's there?"

The muffled voice only heightened her sense of alarm. "My lady, it is Sir Guy of Gisborne. Open the door."

She did not want this horrible man anywhere near her. "Sir Guy, I cannot allow you to enter my chamber...Uh, the sheriff would not approve of me being alone with a man." Marian prayed that he would leave, but to her dismay, the door began moving. She scurried backwards as it swung open, and the tall, imposing knight barged into her chamber.

"My lady, it pleases me that you are taking Sheriff de Argentan's admonishments to heart, but he will not object to me visiting you. Besides, I am not alone, and there are guards in the corridor."

Marian spotted a young woman with dark blonde hair trailing Gisborne. The girl's eyes were wide with fright, and they seemed to beseech Marian with some unvoiced entreaty. It was then that Marian recognized her as one of the Locksley servants.

Gisborne grinned as he proudly disclosed, "I dispatched a message to Lenton that your possessions must be delivered to the castle. They have sent your maid with a few of your belongings, and she tells me that the rest will follow soon." He paused as he noticed Marian's tentative expression. "Aren't you pleased that I am taking such good care of you? Is this girl your maid?"

Marian broke out of her nervous trance and alleged, "Of course, I am delighted to see my maid from Lenton." She impulsively moved forward and hugged the servant, briefly shielding the girl's face from Guy's view.

The girl whispered into Marian's ear, "Odella."

Marian stepped back and smiled amiably. "Odella, I am so glad that you are here. Put that bundle on the bed."

When Odella had complied, Gisborne barked at her to leave at once.

Odella hesitated, and Marian assured her, "It's all right, but don't go far. I will need your help after I speak with Sir Guy."

As soon as the girl had left, Marian's focus reluctantly veered to Gisborne, and she instinctively recoiled from his hungry leer.

He boldly approached and took hold of her hands. Marian gasped in shock and looked down at his hands; they were well-groomed with long, graceful fingers. Nevertheless, all Marian could see were the hands that had placed a noose around Robin's neck. Her skin crawled in revulsion at Gisborne's touch, and she tugged her hands from his grasp.

His brow creased in puzzlement at the unanticipated rebuff, but he quickly recovered and revealed, "My lady, I have come to declare my passionate devotion to you. Sheriff de Argentan has annulled your betrothal to Huntingdon. He is an outlaw with a bounty on his head–"

"He's alive?" exclaimed Marian, hope surging in her heart.

Gisborne's eyes narrowed in annoyance as he observed the joy and warmth that illuminated Marian's face at the mention of Robin. He sternly advised, "He will be captured and executed forthwith, my lady. He is a dangerous criminal who coldly murdered your father–"

"That's a lie!" Marian defiantly interrupted him.

Guy moved so swiftly that Marian was unprepared to find herself trapped by his iron grip as he grabbed her shoulders and shook her, his face contorted in dark fury. She squeaked in distress, and he resentfully raised his voice. "Stop defending him! You are no longer betrothed to Huntingdon. Argentan has given you to me."

Marian's heart was thrumming like a frightened bird's, and

she pulled away from him, imploring, "Please, let go, you're hurting me."

He promptly released her, pleading with a remorseful gaze and a soothing voice, "My lady, forgive me; my love for you overpowered me. You must forget Huntingdon; he has abandoned you, but I will never forsake you because I love you more than that criminal. You will know great contentment as my wife."

"Wife?" Marian hoarsely whispered, appalled by the prospect. She found his repeated assertions of love and devotion quite disturbing. He was a stranger!

"We will be married in a few days," he eagerly explained.

"No!" Marian shouted. The reappearance of Guy's wrathful glare compelled her to moderate her tone. "I am in mourning." It was the first excuse that entered her mind.

"Your father would want you to be wed without delay. You are at risk from unscrupulous men who will aspire to become Baron of Lenton by right of wife," Guy evenly countered, although his eyes were still flashing with anger at her rebuke.

Marian bit her tongue at the obvious retort to his supposed concern about 'unscrupulous men.' Searching her mind, Marian found the perfect reason to postpone their wedding, assuming she could convince him. She argued, "But no marriage can take place until it has been announced by the priest for three consecutive Sundays."

"What?" Gisborne was clearly surprised by her claim, and Marian prayed that he would believe her. These proclamations were not strictly required, but the church had begun encouraging them for unions of prominent noble lineages. Her betrothal to Robin had been formally publicized numerous times throughout the summer at various family estates.

"It's true," she insisted. "If it's not announced properly, it will not be valid in the eyes of the church. I will not enter into an invalid marriage."

A frustrated Guy sighed heavily. "Very well, I will speak to the priest and demand that he make the first announcement this Sunday. We will wed in three weeks."

His face brightened. "While we are waiting, we shall become better acquainted. Whenever I am not attending to my duties for the sheriff, I will spend time with you." He smirked as his eyes skimmed suggestively over her form, evidently confident that she would welcome his company.

Marian concealed her mortification as she forced a smile. "I do not want to marry a stranger," she confessed, hoping that her vague statement would placate him, and that he would not comprehend the true meaning of her words.

Suddenly, they heard a loud shriek from the corridor. Marian followed Guy as he rushed to the door and flung it open. In the hallway, Payen was embracing Odella as she struggled against his unwanted advances. She brought her knee up sharply into the man's groin, and he instantly let go of her and doubled over in pain.

Odella darted into the chamber and cowered behind Marian, while Gisborne howled with laughter. Payen, his eyes blazing with hatred, pursued Odella, but Gisborne detained the younger man by roughly seizing his arm, and they spoke to each other in French before the pale knight spun on his heels and irately stomped away.

Gisborne queried, "My lady, do you speak French?"

Marian understood a little of the language, but it had been several years since she had practiced it with her tutor. She lied, "No, Sir Guy, I do not."

Frowning in disappointment, he offered, "I will teach it to you; it is the most beautiful of all languages."

He then translated, "I commanded Payen to leave your maid alone; he will not molest her again." Rising to his full height, he pompously declared, "Sheriff de Argentan needs me; he has given me many important responsibilities. I will return to visit you later."

As soon as the door closed, the two women nearly collapsed in relief.

"Lady Marian, are you all right?" cried Odella. "Lord Robin—"

"Shhh!" Marian prudently hushed the girl as she clutched her hand and towed her as far from the door as possible.

Odella quieted her voice. "Lord Robin sent me to find out if you are safe and the location of your chamber."

"Is Robin safe? Was he injured from the hanging?" Marian worriedly asked.

Odella smiled at her kindly. "My lady, he is hale and hearty. But that tall Norman told Lord Robin at the hanging that he was going to marry you. Lord Robin is coming to rescue you, but he would like to wait until the next full moon, and that's twelve days from now. Will you be safe until then?"

Marian's initial reaction was to insist that Robin come immediately to save her, but as she reflected, she concluded that she must be patient. Robin was clever and competent, and she ought to have faith in his strategy. Moreover, she had told the sheriff that she wasn't a child, and now it was time to prove it.

She courageously proclaimed, "I will be safe here. Sir Guy has agreed to wait three Sundays before marrying me, and the full moon will arrive in less than a fortnight. In the meantime, I can manage Sir Guy. Do you know what Robin is planning?"

Odella shook her head. "I'm sorry, my lady; I don't know the plan. But considering what Lord Robin did last night, it would probably be best for him to wait a while before returning to the castle."

"Last night?" echoed Marian in confusion. "Are you saying that Robin was here last night?"

"No, he wasn't here inside the keep. Lord Robin and some other men cut down the bodies of the executed soldiers from the walls of the gatehouse in order to give them a proper burial."

Odella unexpectedly snickered. "But Lord Robin left a message for the Normans, and that's the real reason why they are in a snit today. I saw it myself this morning: a badger and two squirrels were hanging from the gallows, and one of the squirrels was painted white. I didn't understand why until I saw that knight who grabbed me." Odella lowered her eyes in shame; she was visibly unnerved by Payen's assault.

"Did he hurt you?"

"I'm not hurt. He got the worst of it, I think." Odella chuckled, although it was a grim sound.

"Odella, you must return to Locksley. I will be all right, but I fear for your safety. That man with the pallid skin makes my blood run cold. I know that Sir Guy will protect me, but I do not trust him to protect you."

Odella dithered over what to do, and Marian recognized that the girl wanted nothing more than to go home. She reassured her, "Tell Robin that I am safe, and that I will be awaiting him when the moon is full. I will inform Sir Guy that you had to leave to tend a sick family member. That way, you will not be blamed for aiding my escape, because you will not be here."

After relaying the rest of Robin's instructions, Odella cautiously departed the castle, peeking over her shoulder at every turn.

As the sun descended into the lush forest west of the castle, Marian lingered at her window and called softly to Robin, even though she knew that he was far away and could not hear her.

"Oh, Robin! My brave and dear Odysseus,
I am your beloved, faithful Penelope.
Two hearts joined by love's brightness,
Cannot be dimmed by the shadows o'er me.
The unwanted suitor, I will deceive,
As I weave a shroud of clever lies.
Penelope will remain true and believe,
Her Odysseus will appear with the full moon's rise."

1 September 1188, Nottingham Castle

Marian nervously twirled a strand of hair around her finger as she peered out her window. The sun was setting, and it was the time of day when Sir Guy typically visited, eager to woo her, bringing gifts and poetry, and regaling her with tales of his importance and valor.

She touched the expensive brooch pinned to the front of her scarlet bliaut, just to be certain that she was wearing the ornate gift from Gisborne. He had been annoyed when she had forgotten to put it on the previous day, and Marian was laboring tirelessly to achieve a balance between friendly warmth and demure reserve in her relationship with the knight.

Robin's planned rescue was still a sennight away, and every evening she studied the waxing moon, rejoicing as it became brighter and fuller with each passing night.

She contemplated the cryptic message Odella had delivered from Robin: *Wear red, especially as it nears the time of the full moon.* Apparently, Robin had sent every piece of red clothing that she owned in the bundle brought by Odella. Marian preferred to wear green or blue, and she knew that Robin loved to see her in green; he had once admitted as much. So, why did he want her to wear red at the castle? She had pondered this at first, but then she resolved to simply obey his directives, trusting that he would explain everything later.

Marian closed her eyes and imagined that she was with Robin in their special meadow and enveloped in his arms. In this fantasy, her father was still alive, and she would awaken to discover that the events of the last fortnight were merely a nightmare.

Reality rudely interrupted her daydreams as a brisk pounding on her door heralded Guy's arrival. Marian strolled leisurely to the door; she was in no particular hurry to spend time with the odious man. At least he had not touched her again, and she was thankful for that small mercy.

"My lady," Gisborne beamed with obvious delight as he entered her chamber and sat in his usual chair by the hearth. "You are wearing my gift. This pleases me very much. I noticed your love of the color red, and so I selected this brooch for its red stones."

Marian smiled weakly as she shut her door before sitting in the chair next to Guy's. "It is lovely; thank you." She wondered how many times she would have to thank him and fawn over his gift.

Guy alleged, "If Huntingdon had really loved you, he would have given you expensive gifts. Did he ever give you a brooch with red stones? Did he ever compose poems for you?"

A wave of irritation surged through Marian. During Guy's visits, there was always a point when the conversation turned to Robin, and she quickly learned that defending Robin, or speaking favorably of him, irked Gisborne. He had not grabbed her again, but his volatile temperament was worrisome. She professed, "You are right; Robin never gave me a brooch with red stones or wrote poems for me." In truth, Robin knew her well enough that he would have given her a brooch that better fit her tastes. As for poetry, Robin had once composed a poem for her, but it was so precious, so dear to her heart, that Marian could not bear the thought of divulging its existence to this loathsome man.

Gisborne retrieved a piece of parchment from under his tunic, and Marian braced herself. His verses were well-constructed, but they lacked genuine emotion as they were usually either extravagant descriptions of her perfection or odes to his prowess with a sword. He proudly handed it to her, oblivious to the fact that Marian's brittle smile did not reach her eyes.

She silently read:

My heart is your vassal;
Your heart is my lord;
My arms are your shield;
Your arms are my shelter;
My legs are your servants;

Your legs are my gatehouse;
My sword is your champion;
Your body is my castle.
My lady, your champion awaits;
Open the gatehouse, and surrender the castle.

It took a moment for Marian to decipher the meaning of the poem, but then she gasped in embarrassment and blushed furiously at the brazen sexual references. Her heart raced, and her stomach fluttered in trepidation, for this was very different from his other poetry.

Without warning, he dropped to his knees in front of her and clasped her hands. "Marian," he exclaimed, his eyes shining with a lascivious glint, "my heart cannot abide this continued distance between us. We will be wed soon enough; let us become one now. You will find great pleasure in my arms; I am a man who knows how to please women."

"No!" whispered an aghast Marian.

Before she could utter another word, Guy wrapped his large hand around the back of her neck, dragging her face to his and pressing his lips firmly to hers. He stood and pulled her out of her chair, trapping her within the circle of his arms. Initially frozen in shock, Marian rapidly regained her senses and pushed against him.

Guy just tightened his grip on her, and when Marian tried to speak, to beg him to stop, he deepened the kiss. Marian was truly horrified; this was nothing like the kisses that she had shared with Robin: kisses that filled her with warmth and often caused her to ache with yearning. Guy's kiss was an intrusion into her very soul, and a profane attack on her love for Robin.

Desperate, Marian bit his tongue and shoved him with all her strength. Guy yelped in pain and relinquished his hold on her. As soon as she was free, Marian seized the fire poker and shakily held it in front of her as she backed away from him. The fury that flared in his pale blue eyes morphed into confusion, and Marian realized that he had assumed that she would welcome his embrace.

He roared, "*Merde!* Why would you do such a thing to me, Marian?"

Marian's mind sorted through the various answers that she would like to offer, such as *you disgust me* and *I loathe you*, but she knew that diplomacy was her only option. She beseeched, "Sir Guy, forgive me for hurting you, but I will not allow such liberties from a man who is not my husband. Such behavior is a sin against God. How could you treat me so disrespectfully?" She then burst into tears, terrified that her unwanted suitor would persist in his lecherous advances.

Guy believed that her distress was due to her pure heart and dedication to church teaching. He regretfully entreated, "My lady, I apologize. You are the most perfect, virtuous, and noble woman I have ever known, and I will honor your wishes. We will wait until we are wed." He struggled to settle himself. "I confess that my passion for you is overwhelming. I have never desired a woman with such fervor. Please, sit down; I have important news."

Marian unsteadily returned to the chairs by the hearth, and Guy warily took the fire poker from her. They sat in silence for a short time, as Marian wiped the tears from her face and attempted to calm herself.

Breaking the tense hush, she demanded, "Tell me your news; then I wish to be alone."

"Of course, my lady," Guy politely assented. Then he became animated as he revealed, "I have been granted the Locksley estate. I am now Lord of Locksley. I will be bringing my own wealth to our union and not solely relying on your inheritance. You will see that I am worthy of becoming Baron of Lenton by right of wife."

Marian was speechless for a few heartbeats. When she imagined this awful man becoming Baron of Lenton and stealing Robin's beloved Locksley, her temper ratcheted up a notch.

Guy perceived the flame in Marian's eyes and the rigid set of her jaw, so he endeavored to put her at ease. "My lady, I am not marrying you to gain control over your family's barony. My father was a baron whose title and lands were stolen from him. Sheriff de Argentan has assured me that I will be restored to my father's barony, and more, when–" He abruptly broke off.

A frown creased her brow. "When, what?" she prodded.

"When I have proven myself worthy of the Gisborne barony," he finished after a brief pause. "Until then, I will demonstrate that I am a capable administrator for both Locksley and Lenton." He sighed and grudgingly conceded, "My lady, it grows late, and I must bid you a good night." He arose and promptly left.

The instant the door closed, Marian started feverishly rubbing her mouth with her sleeve, seeking to remove his taste from her lips.

She glanced down and saw the parchment with Guy's vulgar poem on the floor where it had fallen from her lap. She bent to pick it up, intending to burn it, when she realized that she was looking at the flipside, and it had writing in a different hand. She had noted that all Guy's poems were written on parchment with jagged edges. Considering how costly parchment was, it was not surprising that he had probably torn the fragments from other, larger documents.

Marian lit several candles as she prepared to examine the back of Guy's poem. It had definitely been torn from an official manuscript of some kind. Inspiration struck her, and she strode to another small table where she was keeping his other poetry. She would have preferred to burn them, but she was afraid that he would notice that they were gone, so she kept them where they could be easily observed during his visits. She cleared the table where she ate, spread out all five poems, and hastily flipped them over.

A tingle of excitement coursed through her as she realized that four of them had writing on the back. She moved them around and discovered that two seemed to be torn from the same document. Squinting at the words, Marian grumbled in frustration. French! If only she had paid more attention to her tutor. She knew a little of the spoken language, but she had never thought it would be necessary to learn to *read* French.

At one corner was: *Paris.* She recognized that. She scanned the scraps with the utmost concentration, and she suddenly spotted the name *John.* She soon identified two more names: *Philippe* and *Henri.* Marian grinned in triumph, convinced that these fragments were talking about the kings of France and England.

At that moment, the servant bringing the evening meal knocked, and Marian gathered the mysterious papers and set them aside. She would show them to Robin later.

8 September 1188, Nottingham Castle

Guy was following at just the right distance to fully enjoy the view of Marian's hips gently swaying as she slowly climbed the spiral stairs of the sheriff's tower. Marian's bright scarlet bliaut enhanced her visibility in the dimly lit stairway. He was pleased that she was again wearing the expensive brooch he had bought for her. He contemplated Marian's devotion to the color red with fond amusement.

In another sennight, Marian would finally belong to him. After twelve days of gifts, poems, and companionable conversation, he was confident that he had won her heart. No other woman had ever led him on such an ardent pursuit, and now Guy better understood the troubadour songs describing virtuous rejection and unsatisfied passions. He knew that the upcoming consummation of their love would surpass all his fantasies.

He was especially gratified that Marian no longer cared about Huntingdon. She had ceased asking about him and had admitted that Huntingdon had never given her such fine gifts or bothered to write poetry for her.

Guy grimaced in annoyance; he had hoped to give her another verse, but the sheriff had been in his tower all day, making it impossible for him to steal a scrap of parchment from Argentan's messy desk.

As Guy escorted her towards the sheriff's tower room, Marian stumbled. He politely steadied her, and he noticed that she was ashen and trembling. "Lady Marian, what troubles you?"

"Sir Guy, why did the sheriff summon me?" Marian's voice was shaking with dread.

Guy was also uncertain about the upcoming meeting, but he strove to soothe her nerves. "My lady, it has been almost a fortnight since he last saw you. He merely wants to ensure that you are comfortable and in good health."

The guards opened the doors for Guy and Marian, and they entered the sheriff's lair. Payen and a merchant were already in the chamber, which was weakly illuminated by the fading light of a setting sun. Since Argentan was still conducting business, Guy steered Marian to one side.

The merchant fretfully wrung his hands as he tried to explain, his voice quivering with fear. "My lord, it is not my fault. Forest bandits ambushed me along the road to Nottingham and stole half of the red cloth that I was transporting to you."

"Forest bandits?" Argentan echoed. "You expect me to believe that they stole my red cloth? That is absurd. Why would they steal *red* cloth? Will they be hanging red banners from the trees?"

"My lord, I'm sorry, but I don't know why they took it. However, I still have half of your order, and I can obtain more fabric for you, but red dye is expensive. Perhaps if you could pay me for the material I delivered today–" The merchant lapsed into silence at the sight of Argentan's stony glower.

"You will supply more cloth as soon as possible," the sheriff growled between gritted teeth.

"My lord, give me a fortnight, but in the meantime, there is enough to make a tablecloth for the high table and several banners. I have arranged for the finest seamstresses to sew a rising sun at the top of the banners which will hang behind the high table. When I deliver the rest, there will be sufficient material to cover the walls of the great hall with red fabric."

The sheriff was quite aggravated by the delay, and doubting the man's competence, he inquired, "The cloth, it is red like blood, no?"

The merchant gulped. "Yes, blood red, as you requested. The great hall will be swathed in crimson, and you will be pleased to know that I procured red paint for the chairs used at the high table. Everything will be red; I will not disappoint you again."

Argentan narrowed his eyes. "Are you aware of what happens to men who disappoint me? Hanging naked from the walls of the gatehouse will be the least of your worries if I do not receive my red cloth in a fortnight."

Guy leaned over and whispered affectionately into Marian's ear, "The sheriff shares your love of red."

Marian uneasily watched the frightened merchant dash to the door as he fled his audience with the sheriff.

"Ah," cried Argentan as he swung his scrutiny to Guy and Marian. "My dear Maid Marian, it has been too long since I have enjoyed your company. Come closer."

Guy took Marian's arm and guided her to where Argentan was standing next to his cluttered desk. Marian timidly bobbled a curtsey.

Payen cast a contemptuous scowl at Marian and wrinkled his nose in distaste, while Guy leveled a warning glare at the pale knight.

The sheriff blatantly inspected Marian's form, and he chuckled at her discomfiture. "I suppose I can no longer call you 'Maid' Marian. Please accept my apology for missing your wedding. Are you *satisfied* with your husband?"

Payen and Argentan snickered obnoxiously.

Guy's heart sped with alarm; he did not realize that the sheriff assumed that they were already married. He should have coached

Marian to simply agree with whatever Argentan said—that was always the best strategy when dealing with him. He glanced at Marian whose eyes were alternating between him and the sheriff, her confusion and distress unmistakable. *Merde!* There was going to be hell to pay. Guy braced himself as the sheriff's cruel eyes returned to him.

"Gisborne? I ordered you to wed this girl. Have you obeyed me?" Argentan hissed.

Guy nervously blinked and cleared his throat. "My lord, the marriage will not be valid unless it has been announced by the priest for three consecutive Sundays."

Irritation flared in the sheriff's eyes. "And where did you hear that?"

Without thinking, Guy looked at Marian, and Argentan had his answer.

"Do I understand you correctly? You trusted the word of this woman regarding what constitutes a valid marriage? You are pathetic, Gisborne."

The sheriff's scathing condemnation caused Guy to shift anxiously on his feet.

Argentan resumed, his words thick with derision. "There is no such requirement unless the bride and groom's families might share blood ties. You're not Baron Lenton's long lost son, are you?" he scoffed. "No? I will tell you what you are: you are a weak fool, and this viper is manipulating you."

Guy observed Marian, and her panicked expression confirmed that the sheriff was speaking the truth. His ire and mortification intensified until his face was as crimson as Argentan's new cloth.

The sheriff salted Guy's wounds. "As long as she remains untouched, Huntingdon can reclaim her. Once you have taken her maidenhead, he will no longer want her. I am telling you to bed her *now*, or I will give her to someone else."

Argentan flicked his gaze to his apothecary. "Tancred, would you like to take the lovely Maid Marian to your bed?"

Grinning triumphantly, Payen replied, "My lord, I will happily bed her immediately, if it is your wish."

Without another word, a furious Guy seized Marian and slung her over his shoulder, exiting the sheriff's tower room and hurriedly making his way to Marian's quarters while she flailed against him, pelting his back with her fists and repeatedly screaming, "No!" and "Help!"

Bursting into her bedchamber, he kicked the door shut behind him. He carried Marian to her bed and tossed her on it. When she tried to roll away, he dropped heavily on top of her, pinning her beneath him. His lips crashed into hers, but he was not willing to risk another sharp bite on his tongue, so he kissed a trail down the side of her neck as he cupped her breast with one hand.

Marian begged, "Guy, I wasn't lying. Please, don't do this." She was crying and squirming under him, and she shrieked hysterically, "Stop, you're hurting me!"

At that moment, Guy stilled and exhaled so forcefully that all his rage, humiliation, and frustration seemed to be escaping his body in one long, tortured breath. He closed his eyes and laid his head on her shoulder.

"Please, Guy, I told you the truth. Such announcements are expected." She dissolved into more sobs.

Guy lifted his head and beheld her terrified, tear-stained face. He tenderly stroked her cheek, only to see her cringe at his touch. His heart tightened, and his wrath transformed into guilt and regret. He loved this woman; he did not want to destroy her affection for him.

"Marian," he whispered. "I'm sorry. I love you, and I don't want you to be afraid of me."

Marian remained silent, her eyes tightly shut.

Guy sighed despondently. If he took her by force, he would

be no better than Montlhéry—a brutal, heartless demon who had often beaten his dear mother. And now that Guy was a grown man, he knew exactly what Montlhéry had been doing to his weeping mother after dragging her into the bedchamber by her long, dark hair. He would never forget her muffled cries: *Please stop! You're hurting me!* Echoes of Marian's desperate pleas. As a young boy, he had cowered under a table with his hands covering his ears, as he struggled to ignore his mother's screams and shrieks. When he became a man, he had vowed to never beat or rape a woman, yet here he was, assaulting this exquisite, innocent creature.

Guy promptly moved off of Marian and stood by the bed. He reached for her, and she turned her back to him, hugging her knees to her chest. Again, he was filled with remorse. "Marian," he murmured, but she did not respond. He picked her up, easily defeating her weak attempts to elude him. Carrying her to the chairs by the hearth, he sat her in one and knelt in front of her.

Guy eyed her apprehensively. "Marian, I am a passionate man, and sometimes my emotions overpower me. I was angry when I thought you had deceived me, but if you tell me that your words were true, then I believe you. I will advise the sheriff that I took your innocence, but I promise that I will never take you by force. When we join together, it will be an occasion of joy and love. I never again want to see fear in your beautiful eyes when you look at me. Do you believe me?"

He closely studied her as she reluctantly opened her eyes. Staring fixedly at her lap, she jerked her head in what he interpreted as a nod.

Guy felt relief sweep over him, and he silently thanked God that he had not extinguished her regard for him. "Marian," he savored the sound of her name, caressing each syllable. When she at last focused on him, her expression tense and guarded, he endeavored to further reassure her. "I swear, everything will be all right, and I will wait until we are wed."

She still did not speak, so Guy quietly stood and left.

❦

When she heard the click of her door latch, Marian sank to her knees in front of her chair and buried her face in her hands. Uncontrolled sobs shook her body, and she unconsciously rocked back and forth, instinctively seeking the comfort that a child finds in the arms of a parent. Except that she was all alone; she was so very alone.

In her mind, harsh words and laughter echoed, taunting her with her own hubris:

I will be safe here. I can manage Sir Guy.

The mocking sound of her own voice was joined by the deep, scornful words of the sheriff: *Once you have taken her maidenhead, Huntingdon will no longer want her.*

And finally, the ultimate mental violation: Guy's declarations of love repeating over and over—words which Robin had never spoken to her. Did Robin love her? Would he come for her? Maybe he had changed his mind!

Marian began crying harder and rocking back and forth faster and faster, until a warm hand on her shoulder sent a shock of terror through her body, and she ceased thinking about anything at all, as she frantically crawled away from the unexpected and unwelcome touch.

CHAPTER 7
A GAME OF HIDE AND SEEK

8 September 1188, Nottingham Castle

Robin was feeling confident about his rescue plan as he jauntily tapped on Marian's door.

Little John was dragging two unconscious and bound guards into an adjacent empty chamber while Will collected their surcoats and helmets. The men's uniforms would be used as disguises during their escape from the castle.

There was no response, and Robin's brow creased in concern. He knocked more forcefully and heard a muted noise. It did not sound like an invitation to enter, but surely, Marian had not forgotten that he would arrive on this night. Apprehensively peeking into the chamber, Robin saw Marian weeping hysterically on the floor next to the hearth, and he was seized with panic as he sprinted towards her.

Little John and Will trailed him, closing the door and vigilantly remaining near it.

Robin touched Marian's shoulder and called to her softly. Instead of a warm welcome, she cried out in terror, crawling away from him as he reached for her.

When he managed to take hold of her arm, Marian looked up

at him; her hair and clothes were disheveled, and her eyes were wide with fear. For the space of two heartbeats, it seemed as though she did not recognize him, but then she whispered, "Robin?" At his nod, she reached for him, and he helped her climb to her feet.

"Marian, what troubles you? Have you been injured?"

She frantically embraced him and buried her face into his chest as she mumbled, "No, he stopped before–" Her words faded into a stifled sob.

Robin was understandably disturbed by this fragment of a sentence, and he drew back to scrutinize her as he demanded answers. "Who stopped? Before what? Did someone touch you? I will–"

Marian dissolved into tears, and Robin felt remorse for his harsh tone. He gathered her into his arms and gentled his voice as he comforted her. "Marian, I am here now, and I will not let anyone hurt you. Tell me what happened."

In a hushed murmur that he could scarcely hear, she asserted, "Nothing happened, but I'm not safe here; I want to leave immediately. Do you believe me?"

Again, Robin leaned away slightly so that he could peer into her worried eyes. "Marian, of course I believe you." Anxious to put her at ease, he grinned breezily and joked, "And why else would I be here, except to rescue you? Do you think the sheriff has invited me to join him for a feast?"

Little John and Will chuckled at his jest, and the unexpected sound of strangers startled Marian.

Robin introduced his companions. "Marian, this is John Little and Will of Locksley."

To his profound relief, Marian relaxed and smiled. "I remember both of you!" she exclaimed. Pointing at Will, she recalled, "You helped Much hold Robin's legs at the gallows." Shifting her attention to Little John, she became even more animated. "And you! You defeated Sir Guy and hit him in the face."

Little John and Will briefly dropped to one knee to show their respect for Lady Marian.

John admitted, "My lady, I will gladly punch any Norman who tries to molest you." He barked a laugh, "Ha! I will defend you from the Normans even if they merely look at you in a way I don't like."

Robin snorted in amusement. "John is eager to conquer the Normans who have invaded Nottinghamshire." He clasped Marian's hands and gazed tenderly at her tear-stained face. "Let me explain the plan. First—"

Three loud knocks boomed, and Marian gasped, "Oh, no, it is Sir Guy."

The thick wood muffled Guy's deep voice as he implored, "My lady, I wish to apologize; I cannot sleep unless I hear your words of forgiveness."

As the door swung open, Little John and Will found themselves behind it. Robin shook his head at John, signaling that they should stay hidden, if possible, while he stood between Marian and Gisborne as the tall knight sauntered into the chamber.

Guy froze in astonishment at the sight of Robin before recovering and promptly drawing his sword. He roared, "Move away from Lady Marian! She belongs to me."

Robin scoffed, "You do not own Lady Marian." With a dramatic flourish, he also unsheathed his sword.

Guy gaped in disbelief as he recognized the unique sword that had been a gift from Count de Montlhéry. "That is *my* sword," hissed Gisborne.

Feigning bewilderment, Robin replied, "But, it is in *my* scabbard. And consider the inscription: 'I am immortal.' This obviously refers to me, since I am the one who survived a hanging. Therefore, this sword is mine and not yours."

"You are a thief and a liar," Guy irately contended. "You *know* it is my sword, and now I will take it away from you."

There was an impish gleam in Robin's eyes. "I have seen you

bravely murder an old, unarmed peasant, and I am quaking with dread. You once proclaimed your willingness to fight a pampered and indulged boy like me. Well? Here I am."

Never taking his eyes from Huntingdon's, Guy bade Marian, "My lady, please stand back. I do not want you to be harmed as I trounce this criminal and retrieve my stolen sword. I pledge to protect you from him."

Marian made a strangled sound, and she was trembling with fear as she faced the man who had nearly assaulted her. In her mind, he had become the personification of the terror and vulnerability which she had experienced since her imprisonment in the castle. And now, this same horrible monster was threatening to kill the only man she could ever love.

Robin softly murmured to her, "Go, Marian. I will be all right."

As soon as Marian had fled to the periphery of the chamber, Guy charged recklessly at Robin, who easily checked his blow. Adhering to his usual strategy, Robin took a restrained approach while evaluating and testing his opponent. Gisborne again slashed wildly with his sword, which Robin adroitly sidestepped, causing the other man to stumble.

Gisborne had a natural advantage; he was one of the tallest men Robin had ever met, and his height rivaled that of Prince Richard. Such great height afforded both a longer reach and stride.

Will and John lingered in the shadows while a poised Robin calmly deflected Guy's strikes. Thrust and parry and repeat, with none of Guy's maneuvers successfully penetrating Robin's defenses. The only sound beyond the clanging of steel was the occasional witty retort from a gleeful Robin, and the ensuing snarling response from Guy.

Robin's skills clearly surpassed Gisborne's. Moreover, his adversary was an emotional combatant, which was a hindrance in a contest requiring strategic thinking. Robin decided to taunt

Gisborne in hopes of goading him into an impulsive action. He scornfully decreed, "I have never seen a knight so lacking in grace."

"Fight me, you coward," urged Gisborne, as the two men began circling, each waiting for the other to make the next move.

Robin disdainfully heckled him. "Watching you blunder about and embarrass yourself is so diverting. I'm not sure I want to defeat you quickly."

At this, John and Will snickered, and Gisborne spun around, alarmed to discover that there were two additional men in the room. Facing Robin again, Guy accused, "You are not man enough to fight me alone; you have brought these men to rush me from behind."

"Nonsense," dismissed Robin. Still focusing on Gisborne, he admonished his men, "John, do not interfere; this fight is between me and this poorly trained buffoon."

John laughed heartily. "As you wish, Lord Robin. We are just here to enjoy the entertainment."

An incensed Gisborne furiously sprang forward, and Robin smiled to himself in satisfaction. The knight had lost all control over his emotions, thus ensuring that Robin would triumph. Robin now countered Guy's attacks more vigorously, which momentarily stunned the sheriff's captain. The next time that Gisborne lunged at him, Robin blocked his strike and then deftly rotated his wrist in a tight circle, wrenching Guy's sword from his hand and sending it clattering across the floor.

The color drained from Guy's face as he slowly raised his hands in surrender. He glanced worriedly at Marian, who was visibly frightened and silently witnessing the duel.

Robin aimed his sword at Guy's chest and glared into the other man's pale blue eyes. "I have a message for your master: the men of Nottinghamshire will not meekly accept his lawless ways. I will not allow the sheriff free rein to abuse his post."

"Are you leading a rebellion against an agent of your king?" Guy's allegation was unmistakable.

"I know King Henry, and he knows me. My father was one of his most trusted vassals. Henry is a wise and honorable king, and he would never endorse Argentan's conduct. This is not an insurrection; it is a defense of what is right."

Narrowing his eyes, Guy sneered, "Your father was Henry's pet hound."

Robin shrugged indifferently. "I don't care what you think about my father." Then he paused and fervently announced, "Until the king restores my title and reputation, I have taken the name Robin Hood, and I will work tirelessly to oppose Argentan's tyranny and protect the people."

"Are you threatening Baron de Argentan? You have acknowledged him as an agent of your king." Once more, Gisborne endeavored to lure Robin into a treasonous statement.

"I will not kill an agent of my king, but I will notify the king of what Argentan has done, and you and your master will be expelled from Nottingham," insisted Robin.

"Your king is far away from England. You will fail," Guy evenly remarked.

Gisborne's repeated disavowal of Henry was quite odd, and a perplexed Robin asserted, "Henry is your king too, and as Duke of Normandy, he is Argentan's liege lord."

Guy pursed his lips as if he were formulating a reply, but he said nothing.

Robin smirked as he suggested, "Little John, I think Gisborne needs to rest in order to recover from his humiliating defeat at the hands of a pampered and indulged boy."

Guy nervously stepped back as John immediately advanced and punched him. For a second time, Gisborne collapsed into an unconscious heap at the feet of the big peasant, and John spat on him.

Marian dashed to Robin, hugging him tightly, and he reveled in her eager embrace. Reluctantly, he released her. "Marian, we must hurry. Gisborne has delayed us." Robin motioned to Will, and the younger man handed him a leather bag. Giving it to Marian, Robin instructed her, "Marian, wear these clothes, and give me your bliaut. Will you be disappointed if I ruin it?"

"I never want to see this bliaut again," huffed Marian.

Robin nodded. "Very good. Please hurry."

Marian yanked off Guy's ostentatious brooch and threw it at him before retreating behind her privacy screen. The bag contained dark-colored male clothing, which hung loosely on her slender form. She gave Robin the hated red bliaut and watched with fascination as he sliced open the side seams and pulled it over Will's head, securing it with a rope around his waist. The poor boy looked ridiculous, and Marian smiled as she fought the urge to laugh.

However, John made no attempt to stifle his amusement. "Well, ain't you a sight. You and your fancy, orange clothes."

Will blushed until he was nearly as red as Marian's bliaut. Without thinking, he argued, "This ain't orange. Are you blind, old man? This is scarlet."

Little John just laughed harder, and Robin and Marian also chuckled, in spite of their best efforts to maintain their composure.

Still chortling, John proclaimed, "You ain't even a member of my gang, and you have already chosen your outlaw name. Come on, Will Scarlet, let's go."

"Wait," demanded Robin. "Where's the scarf? Will must cover his head."

"Do you mean this?" asked Marian, as she reached into the bag and retrieved a large square of red fabric which she had found with the other clothes.

Sighing in resignation, Will sullenly snatched the cloth. He folded it in half, creating a triangle that he wrapped around his head and tied beneath his chin.

Robin then repeated his plan one last time to John. "Remember, I want people to see Will, but from a distance. Go to the great hall and run by the entrance. From there, proceed to the kitchens, and make sure that some of the servants glimpse the two of you. Exit the keep through the bakery, then run north across the bailey and allow the soldiers on the curtain wall to observe you. The full moon is our friend tonight. When you see a stack of barrels, duck behind them and change into the guard uniforms. We will wait for you at the church." Robin then confiscated Guy's sword and dagger and gave them to John.

As they strode towards the door, Marian detoured to a small table. She hastily collected Guy's poems and a few of her personal items and stuffed them into the bag Robin had brought.

"What are those papers?" inquired a curious Robin as he took the bag from her and tied it to his belt.

"It is something I will show you later," Marian cryptically replied.

⚬

Robin was stealthily moving through a section of the castle used for storing armaments and tools when Marian tugged on his sleeve.

"Robin," she impatiently whispered. "Where are we going? How will we escape the castle?"

Since they were alone and had not spotted anyone else recently, he paused and answered in a hushed voice, "We are going to the postern gate. John and I have bound and gagged the guards there, but the four of us must exit prior to the beginning of the next watch, when it will be discovered that the gate has been breached."

Marian frowned in confusion. "What is a postern gate?"

Robin realized that she would not have knowledge of such things, and he briefly explained, "It is a small passageway that is hidden in the castle's wall. If the castle was under siege, then soldiers could secretly exit through this gate to attack the besieging force."

Marian's forehead creased in concentration while Robin resumed a swift pace. They were almost there. Again, she tugged on his sleeve. "How did you learn about this 'secret' gate?"

"Huntingdon castle also has a postern gate. I just had to spend several nights exploring the castle wall until I located it."

Robin abruptly halted and scrutinized her as he assessed her reaction to his next words. "Marian, once we have passed through the postern gate, we cannot speak, even to whisper. Our voices will carry in the still night air, and there will be men above us, patrolling on top of the curtain wall. It will be a challenging journey as we descend a steep slope in order to traverse the castle ditch. The moat is significantly depleted, and I have fashioned a temporary bridge using a plank of wood, but it's going to be muddy and smelly."

Robin apprehensively questioned, "Can you do this? I cannot carry you; I must be ready to fight in case we are discovered." He noticed Marian tense with dread, but then a fire of fierce resolve ignited in her beautiful green eyes, and he was utterly captivated.

"I can do this," she insisted. "I am ready to do anything to get away from the sheriff and Sir Guy. And I won't need to be carried. I'm not scared of mud or unpleasant odors."

Robin chuckled at her grim tenacity, only to instantly regret it as she scowled at him with unmistakable irritation. He soothed her wounded pride. "Marian, I'm confident that you can do this. I would not have devised this plan, if I doubted your ability to prevail over such obstacles."

This mollified her somewhat, and Robin silently chastised himself; he was lying to her, of course. He had agonized over this part of the plan for days, worriedly envisioning his lovely and genteel Marian sliding down the filthy embankment of the castle ditch and walking across a wobbly plank with fetid water flowing underneath it. He just prayed that she would live up to her brave words.

When they arrived at the postern gate, the two soldiers assigned to guard it wriggled against their bindings and tried to shout a warning. However, their cries were merely muffled grunts behind their gags.

Robin advised, "We will have to crawl out on our hands and

knees. I will go first to ensure that there are no dangers on the other side. Remember, no talking or whispering. We will emerge on a narrow berm on top of the cliffs. Stay close to the castle wall and follow me. The moonlight will help us navigate."

Marian nodded, and despite the anxiety shining in her eyes, the set of her jaw revealed her determination to surmount any difficulty. Robin suppressed a smile; it was the first time he had ever seen such resiliency in his betrothed, and he liked it very much.

⚬

The bright harvest moon shimmered overhead, and the landscape below was cast in a soft, dreamy light. Robin and Marian carefully crept along the curtain wall as they hurriedly made their way to the great castle ditch and the foul, stagnant water oozing along its soggy bed. In late summer, the moat typically shrank to its lowest level, and since Nottingham had been peaceful in the years following Henry's ascension to the throne, previous sheriffs had not bothered to keep it filled. Robin predicted that his audacious plan to rescue Marian would result in a heightened emphasis on the castle's security, but for now, all that mattered was Marian's safety.

Soon they were at the edge of a steep slope, and Robin studied Marian with concern, endeavoring to gauge her reaction. He watched her eyes widen in alarm, and he suspected that the blood had probably drained from her face, although in the silvery glow of the moonlight, her features already seemed rather pale. He reached for her, intending to take her hand and perhaps even carry her, when she surprised him by jerking her hand away and stubbornly beginning her descent into the shadows of the gulch without his assistance.

Alternately stepping and sliding, the two fugitives cringed whenever the ground beneath their feet crumbled and sent a spray of small stones rolling ahead of them. Within the depths of the castle ditch, the soft light of the moon was weak and distant, but the plank of wood that Robin had detached from a nearby building was plainly visible. Robin firmly took Marian's hand and guided her to the makeshift bridge. Before she could object, he lifted her and nimbly crossed to the other side, where the upward slope of the ditch was more gradual. He set her back on her feet, and they continued their flight as they scurried past the row of brew houses flanking the castle wall.

Robin and Marian crossed a fallow field and then entered a cemetery adjoining a large church. She tapped his shoulder, beseeching him with her eyes for permission to speak.

Overflowing with relief and joy, Robin enveloped her in his arms and praised her. "Marian, you did well. I never knew that you were so intrepid. We have fled the castle, but we have to keep moving."

"You said we were going to the church." Marian pointed at the imposing structure of St. Nicholas' Church.

"No, this church is in Nottingham's Norman Borough. We are going to St. Mary's Church in the Anglian section of town." Robin beamed affectionately. "Besides, it is only fitting on your special day."

Marian arched a brow, and he realized that she did not know the date.

"Marian, it is September 8th."

"Oh!" she exclaimed in surprise. "I have been so focused on the waxing moon that I didn't count the days. It is the Nativity of the Virgin."

"And the eighteenth anniversary of your nativity as well," Robin cheerfully announced. "I'm sorry that I do not have a gift—"

Marian rolled her eyes. "Please, no gifts. I have received enough gifts lately." She laughed at his puzzled expression. "Being with you is the best gift, Robin."

Unexpectedly, someone interrupted their exultant moment. "Hey! Would you two be quiet over there? You're going to wake the dead."

Robin pivoted, smoothly drawing his sword and standing between Marian and a voice emanating from the shadows scattered amongst the grave markers.

A young man appeared, rubbing his face and yawning. When he caught sight of Robin's sword, he stopped and raised his hands in surrender. "I don't have any money. Do you think I'd be sleeping in a graveyard, if I had money for a bed at the inn?"

Robin declared, "I'm not here to rob you. Come closer, so that I can see you, and keep your hands up." The man obediently strolled into a circle of moonlight, and Robin queried, "Who are you? And what are you doing here?"

"My name's Allan-a-dale. I'm sleeping, or I'm trying to sleep. Ain't that obvious?"

Robin inspected the open, unguarded countenance of the man. "If you do not have a place to sleep, then I can only assume that you are a stranger here. Why are you in Nottingham?"

"I came for the festival of the Virgin's Nativity, hoping to earn some coins. I'm a traveling minstrel, and I usually make good money here in Nottingham, but today my luck was bad." Allan lowered his hands but maintained a relaxed, non-threatening stance.

Robin sheathed his sword. "Allan-a-dale, I am Robin Hood, and I'm on a mission."

"Robin Hood!" cried an exhilarated Allan, too loudly for Robin's comfort.

"Shhh!" Robin urgently hushed him. Grinning, he cautioned, "You're going to wake the dead."

Allan strove to be more restrained as he happily divulged, "I've heard about you. The men in the tavern were talking about your hanging. I wrote a ballad about you. Do you want to hear it?"

Marian, who had been uncharacteristically silent, spoke up. "I would like to hear it."

"My lady, I would be honored to sing it for you." Allan briefly dropped to one knee.

Robin did not want to reveal Marian's identity to this stranger, so he purposefully did not introduce her. "Allan, we will listen to it another time. We must be on our way."

"I will join you. Afterwards, I will compose a new song about our adventure." Allan was so enthused about the idea that he promptly gathered his few possessions and his lute.

Robin attempted to dissuade him. "Allan, this is a dangerous undertaking. You should remain here."

Unfortunately, this made Allan even more determined as he asserted, "People love to hear ballads where the hero conquers some great peril. If I'm with you, I'll be able to describe every detail. Where are we going?"

As Robin sought to politely separate from the minstrel, Marian stepped forward and complicated the situation. "Allan-a-dale, I believe that Lord Huntingdon has forgotten his manners. I am Lady Marian of Lenton. We are going to St. Mary's church. Please, come with us. Later, I want to hear the song you've written about Robin Hood."

An exasperated Robin cursed under his breath. Thanks to Marian, Allan now knew too much, and Robin would have to keep an eye on him until they were ready to leave Nottingham. He grudgingly led Allan and Marian from the cemetery and towards Castle Gate Road, which would eventually take them to the Anglian Burgh and St. Mary's Church.

As they traveled along the roadway, a clamorous outcry from the castle alerted Robin that the bound guards at the postern gate had been discovered. He only hoped that John and Will had escaped in time and were on their way to St. Mary's.

The rhythmic rumbling of swiftly marching feet behind them caused Robin to hastily pull Marian and Allan into the dark alcove of the nearest building. Robin jiggled the door's latch, but it was barred from the inside. There was nowhere else to go, as all the structures along Castle Gate Road were crowded tightly together, and the torches of the approaching soldiers would soon illuminate their hiding place.

Robin retrieved the bow slung across his back and grabbed several arrows from the quiver at his belt. His heart sank with despair; he was vastly outnumbered, and Allan did not seem to have any weapons beyond a small dagger sheathed at his belt.

Allan whispered, "I know what to do." He suddenly sprinted towards the soldiers.

Fury coursed through Robin as he realized that the impoverished minstrel was planning to betray him and collect a bounty.

"Halt!" yelled the lead soldier. "Who goes there?" The men quickly surrounded Allan.

Showing them his lute, Allan calmly replied, "I'm here to entertain at the feast for the Nativity of the Virgin."

One of the men disclosed, "We're searching for a man who abducted a woman from the castle. She's a ward of the sheriff, and he wants her returned to him. Did you see anyone else out here on the road?"

"You say you're looking for a man and a lady?" Allan eagerly inquired.

A second soldier hollered, "The lady's wearing red!"

Still another man interjected, "And the man's in a hooded cloak."

"Yes, I saw them," Allan triumphantly confirmed. "Is there a reward for finding this lady?"

A frightened Marian gasped softly, and Robin pushed her behind him as he nocked an arrow and prepared to defend her, probably to the death. He would disable as many men as possible with his bow and battle the rest with his sword. But his first arrow was reserved for the heart of Allan-a-dale.

"Yeah, there's a reward." The commander squinted at Allan suspiciously. "Where did you see them?"

Allan confessed, "I was near St. Nicholas' Church, and I saw a man in a hood and a beautiful lady dressed in red. They ran past me, and they were headed north."

The soldiers began murmuring excitedly as their leader grabbed Allan by his tunic and shook him roughly. "You sure about this? You ain't lying?"

"I swear that I saw them," insisted Allan. "They were traveling in the direction of the market and St. Peter's Church. Can I have my reward?"

The soldier shoved Allan to the ground as he sneered, "Your reward is that you get to live." He then ordered his men to reverse course and go north, towards the other side of town.

As soon as the soldiers were out of sight, Robin and Marian emerged from their hiding place, while the minstrel was brushing the dirt from his clothes.

Grinning broadly, Allan exhorted, "Well, Lord Robin Hood, we should continue our quest. I already have two stanzas composed in my head."

"Allan, thank you," declared an incredibly relieved Robin. "Next time, you must tell me what you are planning."

"Next time?" Allan echoed. "You want me in your band of men? You won't regret this. I will chronicle all your adventures and write many songs about your brave deeds and heroic victories."

"Oh, yes!" Marian exuberantly agreed. "You must join us and write songs about Robin."

Robin heaved a sigh. He had doubts about Allan's usefulness as an outlaw, and a niggling alarm also sounded in the back of his mind at Marian's casual inclusion of herself in his band. He would have to sort it out later; they needed to get to St. Mary's as soon as possible.

❧

Guy's anger was escalating like a wildfire in a parched forest. His pursuit of Marian and Robin had reached a dead end at the northern most section of the castle's inner bailey. Just then, a soldier appeared and breathlessly informed Guy that the men guarding the postern gate had been attacked. Guy immediately realized that Robin, Marian, and the two outlaws had already fled the castle.

With a roar of frustrated rage, he toppled a nearby stack of barrels, and his men cowered apprehensively. Guy ferociously cursed as he tried to comprehend why so many people had claimed to have seen Marian in the great hall, the kitchens, and the bailey, when the postern gate was in the opposite direction. He called for his horse and commanded all available men to assist in the hunt for the fugitives. At least Marian, in her vibrant red bliaut, would be conspicuous and easily found.

Much to his chagrin, Payen accompanied him as they rode through the portcullis and into the town of Nottingham proper. They had not gone far when a group of soldiers intercepted them with news that Marian and Robin had been spotted running towards the market. Guy and Payen spurred their horses into a trot; their men followed on foot.

Rounding a corner, they surged into the marketplace. Since it was a feast day, the taverns were still crowded, and the square was gaily lit with numerous torches, despite the late hour. Men were celebrating in the street, drinking and carousing.

Gisborne and Payen brought their horses to an abrupt halt and gawked in befuddlement at the bizarre sight that greeted them: every man in the square was wearing a bright red cape.

They dismounted and stalked towards the revelers. Seizing the closest man, Guy growled, "What is the meaning of this? What are you wearing?"

The man, who was obviously drunk, beamed with joy. "God bless Robin Hood!" he shouted boisterously. "He gave me this cloak, and it's the nicest one I ever owned."

Another man staggered over to them and added, "And he gave us barrels of ale to celebrate the Nativity of the Virgin. God bless Robin Hood!"

Stunned speechless, Guy released the inebriated man and watched as the two staggered away.

Standing next to Gisborne, Payen commented, "Now we know what happened to the sheriff's missing red cloth."

✑

Marian was uncomfortable to be walking into the sanctuary of St. Mary's in her bare feet. But since her shoes, as well as Robin's, had been caked with the foul mud of the castle ditch, they had left them outside, at the back door of the church. They were anxiously awaiting the arrival of John and Will, and Robin had announced that they could only linger a short time.

Allan and the priest were affably conversing about music, when Marian pulled Robin aside. "Robin, we are here. The priest is here. Allan can be a witness."

Robin was distracted by his concern for Little John and Will, so he looked at her in confusion. "A witness to what?"

Marian impatiently proposed, "We can marry now—tonight. I don't want to wait until Michaelmas."

Robin's initial bewilderment morphed into something akin to horror. He was rarely at a loss for words, and if the situation had not been so dire, Marian might have found it humorous. Instead, she became indignant at his hesitation and lack of enthusiasm for her splendid idea.

"Marian, no," Robin sputtered after a moment's pause.

Marian's heart started pounding, and she frantically queried him. "Have you changed your mind? Do you still want me as your wife?" Her rapid questions dissolved into sobs. "Please, do not abandon me!"

Robin tenderly asked her, "Marian, why would you think that? I will never forsake you. You are the only woman I want as my wife."

Annoyed with herself for crying, Marian struggled to control her emotions as she dried her damp cheeks with her sleeve. "The sheriff says that I am his ward, and that he has ended our betrothal.

If you had not come tonight, he would have forced me to wed Sir Guy. If we marry now, then no one will ever be able to separate us again."

Robin argued, "Argentan is speaking nonsense. First of all, as an orphaned daughter of the nobility, you are King Henry's ward. Secondly, Argentan cannot end our betrothal. There is a formal document, and it would be among your father's papers. Any marriage between you and Gisborne would have been illegal because of this contract. I will go to Lenton and retrieve this agreement so that I can safeguard it." He then disclosed, "Furthermore, you cannot be forced to marry against your will; that alone would have rendered the marriage invalid."

Marian's relief was palpable. She explained, "My father's important papers are hidden in the altar of our family's chapel. The sheriff will never find them."

"Very good; we will leave them there," decreed Robin.

He put his hands on her shoulders and peered steadily into her eyes. "But there is no need for us to wed in the dark of night in our bare feet. We will stand at the altar of God in the light of day; that is what your father would have wanted for us, and it is how the Lord expects His children to show reverence for the holy sacrament of matrimony. Then we will have a grand feast, and everyone will be there to celebrate with us."

"I don't want to wait. I don't care about feasts or celebrations. I just want to be married. I want your name and your protection from the sheriff and Sir Guy." Tears sprang into her eyes, but Marian refused to let them fall.

He implored, "Marian, please, give me my pride. I'm an outlaw, and I cannot take a wife right now. You know that King Henry will support me. Prince Richard will also defend me. I will not fail, and Argentan will not win. I'm asking you to wait until I have been absolved of your father's murder, and I have been restored to my title and lands. Then I will make you my wife and my countess."

Marian's anger abated at Robin's earnest pleas. She was about to consent to his request, when Robin summoned the priest. "Father, we wish to make a solemn declaration before God with you and Allan as our witnesses."

Without another word, Robin ushered Marian to the altar of St. Mary's church, where he encouraged her to kneel next to him while Allan stood nearby.

Robin cradled Marian's hands, and they regarded each other intently. "Marian Fitzwalter, I promise that I will marry you once my troubles are resolved." He then reached up and tugged on a cord that was around his neck, breaking it and revealing the silver ring that he had worn over his heart for twelve years.

He continued, "I had planned to give you this ring on our wedding day; it was my mother's. Instead, I will give it to you now, as a pledge that you will be my wife as soon as I am exonerated." Robin slid it on her finger.

Marian's heart leapt with joy as she beheld the ring; its simplicity and elegance were exactly to her taste. Refocusing on Robin, she affirmed, "Robin Fitzooth, I promise to marry you. Only you. You are the only man I will have as my husband."

The jubilant priest proclaimed, "These vows bind the two of you together. The Lord will undoubtedly bless your future union." He then recited several prayers.

They had scarcely regained their feet when Little John and Will finally arrived. Robin introduced Allan to them and instructed John to take the minstrel to the outlaw camp.

"Where are we going?" Marian was surprised that the group was dividing up.

Robin explained, "Marian, if we all take the same route, it creates a recognizable trail. Will is returning to Locksley, while John will escort Allan to his camp. We will be on horseback as we follow yet another pathway into the woods."

Marian contemplated this, and she was excited to realize that she understood perfectly what Robin meant. This was a completely new way of thinking for her, and she was both intrigued and energized by the thought that her life was moving towards an unforeseen and adventurous future. As she and Robin rode along a moonlit forest path, Marian decided that she must learn more about such tactics and strategies. She silently swore that never again would she be at the mercy of men like Argentan and Gisborne.

CHAPTER 8
SURRENDER

8 September 1188, Hunting Lodge owned by the Fitzooth family,
Sherwood Forest

Marian opened the window's shutter and peered out into the shadows surrounding the lodge. Above her, the full moon hung over the crowns of the trees like a giant pearl nestled in the velvet folds of the night sky. A soft breeze caused the highest branches to sway languidly, and moonlight danced merrily across shimmering leaves.

A profound sense of tranquility descended upon Marian. Maybe it was the quiet stillness of the woods outside the lodge. Perhaps it was her utter relief to be liberated from her captivity in the castle. Most likely, it was the joy of being reunited with her Robin. Marian caressed the silver ring that now adorned the third finger of her left hand—the finger with a direct connection to her heart.

She took a deep breath and inhaled the unique fragrances of the forest. Ever since the sudden passing of her father and her imprisonment in the castle, she had been burdened by despair and dread, but finally, she could relax and breathe; she was with Robin, and she was safe. Whatever else the future might hold, Robin would be at her side.

She was alone while Robin tended to the horse, so Marian shifted her scrutiny from the window to thoroughly inspect his family's rustic hunting lodge hidden within the greenwood. It was a cluttered space containing nearly every item she owned. Robin had arranged for her belongings to be delivered here from Lenton, and the result was a colorful, chaotic mess that warmed her heart. The green and gold brocade draperies from her bedchamber were suspended from an aging canopy frame that was straining to support the heavy fabric. Two large chests were overflowing with her clothing, and a privacy screen that had once belonged to her mother stood guard at the far corner.

Robin's personal possessions were crowded into the opposite corner of the lodge. There was a trunk of clothing, a pile of pelts, and a trestle table laden with rolled parchments and books, some bearing the seal of his earldom. Apparently, Robin had salvaged these things from Locksley Manor after he had been outlawed. The two walls beyond the table were covered with all manner of weaponry: swords, spears, axes, daggers, and several styles of bow, including a crossbow. On the floor, below the bows, arrows were stacked next to a few crossbow bolts.

As pleased as Marian was to have her things from Lenton, it was this impressive collection of armaments that truly fascinated her. She was diligently studying the weapons when the creaking of the door alerted her to Robin's arrival.

Robin carried a bundle of wood to the hearth where he crouched and stoked the fire by adding kindling and a small log. Marian observed the lines of his handsome profile and pondered how his square jaw and high cheekbones gave him a rugged, yet boyish, appearance. Her heart quickened with the realization that it was the first time they had ever been together in a bedchamber.

When he rose and faced her, Marian spontaneously rushed to him, smiling festively and excited to be able to move so effortlessly in her male clothing. Robin chuckled and opened his arms to her,

Chapter 8

cheerfully bracing himself for her enthusiastic onslaught as she fell into his arms.

They laughed breezily as a sense of elation and freedom overmastered them. He picked her up and spun around before restoring her to her feet and planting a brief kiss on her lips, which led to a series of carefree pecks on her nose and cheeks, coaxing a rich torrent of giggles from her.

Marian touched his cheek. "It is so good to be with you at last."

Robin captured her hand and brushed his lips against her palm before smugly announcing, "Obviously, you missed me a lot."

She extracted her hand from his and teasingly waggled a finger at his grinning face. "Haven't you missed me?"

He warmly conceded, "More than you can know."

"Robin," she drawled, savoring the word. "My Robin…"

"Marian," he murmured. Cupping her face with his hands, he kissed her with a reverent tenderness. "My Marian…"

Staring intently into Robin's pale blue eyes, Marian was perfectly content, as if she and Robin were standing within the gilded gates of paradise. Whenever he smiled at her, she experienced divine lightness, immeasurable joy, and another sensation, sweet and burning her from the inside out, which her young and innocent heart identified as desire for him. She again raised her hand to his face and traced its contours. An overwhelming feeling of love inundated her like a spring flood, flowing from the tips of her fingers and spreading until something clenched deep within her. It was an exhilarating stirring that she felt only when Robin kissed her ardently or enfolded her in his arms.

A fierce urgency consumed her: she *must* confess her love for him. In the past, she had been too shy to tell him that she loved him, but that was before she had witnessed his hanging. In that horrifying moment, prior to his rescue by the peasants, Marian was devastated to realize that he would die and never know that she loved him. Suddenly, her maidenly hesitations and worries seemed childish and foolish.

She dreamed of hearing Robin declare his love as well. Even though she had been patient in the past, Marian needed to know whether he really loved her. Maybe it was the agony of having to suffer through Guy's repeated, empty pronouncements of his obsessive devotion. Each time that Guy had professed his undying love, Marian could not stop thinking about how she longed to hear sincere assurances of love from Robin.

Marian, looking absolutely enamored, gazed into his eyes and bared her soul. "Robin, I love you so much." Once she had begun, her words poured out in a giddy burst of heartfelt admissions. "I loved you from the moment when I first saw you at Huntingdon Castle after your return from Aquitaine. I love you more than life itself, and I cannot imagine my life without you. I love you more than Penelope loved Odysseus!"

Robin's surprise at her words blossomed into magnificent delight. He impulsively pulled her into a close embrace as he worked to restrain the strong emotions which engulfed him. It dawned on him just how much he had needed to hear words of love from her. When Marian had accepted his marriage proposal, he had been encouraged by the joy and affection that had shone in her beguiling green eyes. And now, he had finally received an unequivocal affirmation of her devotion. It was a divine gift that he would forever cherish.

He closed his eyes and buried his face into her silky flaxen hair as he hugged her tightly and reflected on how different she was from any other woman he had ever known.

Women had eagerly flocked to the handsome, athletic, and charming heir to the Huntingdon Earldom. His spirited, mischievous demeanor, his enthusiastic bravado, and his versatile, intelligent mind had made him the center of attention among both women and men. His close friendship with Prince Richard, who became heir to the throne after his older brother's unexpected death, only enhanced Robin's desirability among the women at court. He was also lauded for his renowned marksmanship and many tournament victories in Aquitaine, Poitou, England, and Normandy.

Robin had exulted in the adulation. He had not been chaste during his years on the continent, although he had not been detestably lecherous either. Court was teeming with willing women, and he had not resisted their determined entreaties. He had indulged in a number of affairs while living at the royal courts in Aquitaine and Poitou, but he hadn't developed an attachment to any of the courtesans or widows whom he had bedded. Unlike some of the other men at court, Robin never sinned by initiating virgins into the pleasures of physical love because his honor prevented him from such despicable behavior.

Besides, deflowering the daughter of a noble was tantamount to an offer of marriage, and Robin had always known that his father intended for him to wed the daughter of Baron Lenton. During his years at court, Robin often thought about the young girl whom he had left behind in Nottinghamshire. In his youth, little Marian had frequently tagged along after him, both annoying him and warming his heart with her childish adoration.

Robin would contemplate the Poitevin sunset and fondly recall the times when he took young Marian to his favorite meadow. She would cling to his back as he climbed the thick branches of a great oak, and they would watch the dying sun's rays paint the sky in brilliant hues. The little girl's innocent and rapturous delight at viewing these sunsets, and her worshipful admiration, had made Robin feel like a hero who could slay dragons and conquer the world.

Upon his return home, Robin had been astonished by the changes in his little friend. Marian had grown into a beautiful woman, and his feelings for her were nothing like what he had experienced with other women. Her smile sent his heart racing and humming sweet romantic songs. Marian was everything Robin coveted in a wife: she was supportive, compassionate, and quickwitted; there was no denying that she was the queen of his heart.

His love for Marian was in his blood, in his bones, and in every part of his being, and he needed her as much as a man needs air to breathe.

Robin relaxed his firm hold on Marian so that he could once more bask in her loving gaze, but he was alarmed to see that her eyes were filled with guarded trepidation. Searching his mind to try and understand why she might be so apprehensive, he suddenly realized that he had never told her that he loved her.

Robin stared meaningfully into her eyes and proclaimed, "Marian, when I proposed to you, I had already fallen in love with you." His arms tightened around her. "I love you wholly and unconditionally."

To his great joy, embers of happiness rekindled the light in her enchanting eyes. Their lips met in an eloquent kiss that blessed the union of their hearts, defining the deeper sense of their relationship—an amalgamation of love, trust, and friendship.

"My love for you strengthens with each passing day, and nothing will change that," he averred.

"I love you, too," repeated a jubilant Marian, her eyes flicking to his lips.

Robin was still holding her close as a surge of desire swept through him. His resolve was weakening; he wanted her with a fervency which he had never before experienced. He kissed Marian achingly, and she readily deepened the kiss as she leaned into him, her body pressed against his, her hands entangled in his tousled hair. There was no doubt in Robin's mind that she wished to become one with him in every way.

Abruptly, Robin extricated himself from their embrace and strolled to the window. He was breathing heavily and attempting to regain control over his lust-fogged mind and all-too-eager body. Needing a distraction, he glanced out the window and glimpsed the trees swaying in a gentle breeze as the moon cast a silvery sheen on the clearing around the lodge.

He returned his gaze to Marian who was standing in the middle of the chamber, her expression lost. As their eyes met, she bestowed upon him an empyreal smile that was more intoxicating than the prized wines from vineyards of Poitou.

"Robin?" She walked to him, a quizzical brow raised.

Robin pondered his comparison of Marian to wine. His state of yearning for her was reminiscent of a drunken swoon, and he was struggling to think coherently. After a moment's hesitation, he announced earnestly, "Marian, I am so pleased that you are safe, and that we are reunited, but it has been a long day, and I must let you sleep. I will be nearby, so if you have need of me, go to the window, and summon me."

Marian's eyes narrowed in aggravation. She then boldly asserted, "I have a need for you now; there is no reason for you to leave."

Robin studied her attentively. Her luminous eyes were darkened with passion, and he could read her lascivious thoughts very well. "Marian, we should not do this until we are wed."

"We love each other," she persisted in a steady, self-assured voice. Unquestionably, she was set on a particular course of action. Drawing near to him, she put her left hand on his chest over his heart, and his mother's ring gleamed in the glow of the fire as she recollected, "And when we were in the church, we exchanged solemn vows to marry in the immediate future."

"It is not the same as an official wedding with a priest's blessing," Robin contended. His words were sensible, but his thoughts were focused on how delightful it would be to taste the sweetness of her mouth while he removed the boyish disguise from her voluptuous form.

His mind continued its journey down a road paved with justifications and excuses. They were officially betrothed; they had affirmed their mutual devotion, and now she was offering herself to him. Surely, he would be cleared of these false charges before the feast of All Saints on the first of November. Hence, they would wed very soon. Besides, Robin hadn't been with a woman in over two years because he had been happily and unwaveringly faithful to Marian. He was profoundly tempted by her, and he could easily imagine the intensely sensual pleasure of claiming her as his own. At the same time, his conscience was vigorously objecting and reminding him that waiting was the right thing to do.

"We are as good as married," declared Marian. "You proposed to me, and I accepted. My father loved you like a son and whole-heartedly approved of our wedding plans." She paused for a moment, and then affectionately decreed, "My dearest Robin, we are betrothed, and we have pledged to marry soon. Nothing else matters."

Robin had sufficiently recovered his composure, and a smug and insolent grin manifested on his face. It was an expression that infuriated his enemies with its playful self-confidence and bewitched women with its charming impudence.

He alleged, "Of course, Baron Lenton wanted the most impressive man in England—I mean in the entire world—for his beloved daughter." His grin widened, and he cocked his head. "Your father knew that my brilliance overshadowed all other possible suitors: young, eager boys who must have wept bitterly when they realized that you had chosen me. We are fortunate that we did not drown in the sea of tears created by your rejected suitors."

"The exhilaration of our bold escape has made you too sharp-witted, Robin," commented Marian with disapproval. "Usually, I enjoy your jests, but this is not the time."

He broke into a buoyant chortle, ignoring her admonishment. "You will be pleased to know that I can swim, in case we have to cross an ocean of tears. In addition to my skills with a sword and the bow, I am a master of amusing dialogue," he replied daringly. "Because I am an outlaw, my bravery, along with my sharp blade and sharp wit are the only treasures I can offer you."

"Robin, be serious," chided Marian.

Desperate to sidetrack her from thoughts of the marriage bed, Robin's eyes twinkled knavishly as he wrapped a long strand of her pale yellow hair around his finger and gently pulled, mimicking a nervous gesture which he had often seen Marian perform. She squawked and huffed in annoyance. Nevertheless, she couldn't help but smile at him fondly, for his mischievous nature was one of the many things she cherished about him.

Robin resumed his lighthearted banter. "Why should I be serious? Humor keeps your body's humors balanced and healthy. I cannot go a day without laughing. Life in the woods is not easy, and good humor keeps my men and me in good spirits."

Marian unraveled his gambit: he had them embroiled in a witty sparring match to maneuver away from the topic of their physical joining before marriage. Playing along, she seductively suggested, "Robin, there are many ways to balance humors, and I believe arguing with me is not one of them. My father always insisted that we were well-suited for each other because our dispositions are complementary. Therefore, our union will result in perfectly balanced humors."

Robin beamed at her, adoring her keenness, for she had deciphered his game. "Lady Marian, your father was a wise man; he once advised me that keeping your wife in a good humor is the secret to marital bliss. However, I must remind you that I have just courageously saved you from the lion's den and delivered you to this enchanted castle in the forest. I am a hero, not a healer."

"You are my hero!" Marian exclaimed, her eyes sparkling with a touch of mischief.

He took her hands in his and entwined their fingers. "When I was younger, I yearned to be a hero without really understanding what that meant. But now, I find that people are looking to me for leadership during these uncertain times, with King Henry far away, and Argentan ruling the shire as if he were the King of Nottingham and not merely sheriff." His smile faded a bit, becoming wistful.

"If I am your hero, then I am content, for only your opinion truly matters to me. But I'm in a situation that worries me. I might need your assistance."

This slightly alarmed Marian. "Of course, Robin, I would do anything for you." As soon as the words left her mouth, she recognized the impish glimmer in his eyes.

Endeavoring to sound sincere, he disclosed, "It seems that every good person in Nottinghamshire loves me and calls me their hero. I'm concerned that the adulation of the people will cause me to commit the sin of pride. And since pride goeth before a fall, I am asking you to humble me before I stumble."

She rolled her eyes at his immodesty. "Lord Huntingdon, you are already so proud that I fear a fall is inevitable. I think the real question is whether you will fall on your face or…in the opposite direction."

He threw his head back and guffawed. "Lady Huntingdon, I surrender. Chastise me for my pride now, and let us be done with it. Perhaps a slap to my face for my conceit will set me on the path to righteousness." Grinning in anticipation, he released her hands and spread his arms wide.

"I am very tempted to punish you in such a manner, Robin."

"Before you enact my punishment, I must warn you: my smile will disappear, and you will miss it sorely." supplied Robin in a voice laced with notes of merry laughter.

"Close your eyes, and prepare to receive your comeuppance," Marian cried.

Robin gamely shut his eyes and stood still, his arms outstretched, as if he were inviting her into his embrace.

Marian shook her head in wonder as she beheld the charming, clever, irresistible man who owned her heart. A rush of blood clamored in her ears, and lustful demons clawed underneath her skin. She approached and raised up on her tiptoes, plunging her fingers into his hair and kissing him on the lips.

At first, a startled Robin winced as she tugged his hair; but her passion fanned his desire, and he promptly wrapped his arms around her waist, hugging her even closer. She gave him entrance to the silken depths of her mouth, and her feverish ardor equaled his own. He abandoned her lips and kissed her throat, his teeth lightly nibbling at the sensitive flesh.

Suddenly, Robin pulled back and assessed the all-absorbing hunger in her eyes. "Marian, do you really understand the implications of what we are going to do?"

"Yes, I do, Robin," avouched Marian. "I have learned just how tentative and fragile life can be." She blanched as she recalled the terror of his hanging. "We can never be sure how many sunrises and sunsets God will give us. In the castle..." Her voice trailed off as she searched for the words that would persuade him to take her as his wife *tonight*. She did not want to ever admit to him that she had nearly lost her innocence to another man; she was determined to take this opportunity and ensure that Robin, and *only* Robin, would be the man to teach her about physical love. She resolutely set her shoulders and asserted, "In the castle, I had time to think about how close you came to dying—I almost lost you forever. Nothing is more important than to seize this opportunity. I cannot live a life of regret."

Robin regarded her curiously; he did not completely comprehend the shifting emotions on her face, but he distinctly remembered those final moments at the gallows, when he had believed that his future with Marian had been irretrievably stolen from him. He embraced her again and spoke in a husky voice, "Marian, my desire for you is robbing me of my wits. I love and respect you, but I am only a man, and I can no longer resist you. Are you willingly giving yourself to me?"

Marian met his eyes as she emphasized, "I need you, and I want to belong to you. Only you."

"I promise, as soon as King Henry clears my name, and I am

reinstated as the Earl of Huntingdon, then I will immediately marry you."

Abruptly, Marian sighed and stepped away from the shelter of his arms, briefly staring at the flames dancing within the hearth. "Robin, there is something that I must tell you." When she veered her gaze to him, her eyes were full of tenderness. "I don't love the Earl of Huntingdon. I don't love the Lord of Locksley. I don't love a rich nobleman or a hunted outlaw with a bounty on his head. I love you and only you, my Robin."

"Marian," Robin murmured, drawing her back into his arms. "God blessed me with a heavenly gift—you and your affection. I swear that I will always take care of you and devote my life to you. I will protect you from all threats; I will love you more than Odysseus loved Penelope." He paused to gather his thoughts before continuing, "When King Henry returns and rights the wrongs endured by me and the people of Nottinghamshire, we will be so happy together. I will be your safe retreat and your fortified place whenever you are besieged by the troubles of life."

Marian was surprised by his poetic frankness, for Robin wasn't a man who wore his heart on his sleeve. His words stirred the innermost recesses of her heart, and the joyful life that she had once anticipated seemed to beckon to her like a branch whose ripe fruit was so close that her fingertips could brush against it. She only needed to lean a little further into the chasm, and she would be able to firmly grasp the idyllic future dangling from that nearby branch.

She flung her arms around his neck. "I treasure your love, Robin. I will always be with you: through good times, bad times, triumphs, and defeats. And if I cannot be with you, I will be your Penelope, patiently and faithfully awaiting your homecoming."

"I would gladly give my life for you," he vehemently proclaimed with both pathos and a genuine resolve. "I would die a thousand deaths, if my suffering gave you another day of life."

Shuddering in dread at his gallant words, she buried her face into the front of his shoulder, fighting to dismiss nightmarish visions of Robin twisting slowly at the end of a rope, his head at an unnatural angle, his skin ashen, his lips blue, and his clouded eyes eternally fixed on a distant horizon.

The thought of Robin dying—of losing him forever—horrified Marian beyond reason. She could not live without Robin; her life would become a pointless exercise in breathing as she awaited her own demise. She raised her eyes to his. "Please, don't say such things, Robin," she implored, her heart shrouded in an imaginary grief. "If you had died, I would have begged God to grant me a swift death to be reunited with you." A fat tear trickled down her cheek.

"I am sorry, Marian. I didn't mean to upset you. Forgive me," Robin earnestly entreated. "I am not going to die, and neither are you."

"Never say this again, Robin. I do not want you to die for me." Her voice quivered with anguish.

"Marian, don't worry; we will marry soon, and we'll have many wonderful years ahead. We will raise a family and grow old together." He pulled her close and tried to comfort her as he caught sight of the wall where his weapons were hung. The fire's flickering flames were reflected in the polished steel, giving the blades the appearance of being ablaze without being consumed.

Unwelcome recollections of promises hastily given suddenly crowded his mind. He had pledged to accompany Prince Richard on a Crusade to liberate Jerusalem from the infidels. The prince's most sacred dream was to re-conquer the Holy Land for Christendom. Robin had zealously supported his liege, but that was before his return to England and his betrothal to Marian.

With mounting trepidation, Robin remembered his desperate bargain with God during his stay in the dungeons. Robin had vowed to take the cross and join the next Crusade, if God saved him from the gallows, and the Lord had answered Robin's prayers. There was no escaping such oaths.

Even the voice of his stern father invaded his musings. *A loyal, honorable vassal follows his liege lord to war.* Words which were inarguably true.

And then a guilty realization struck Robin: he craved adventure, glory, and fame. In all honesty, he was excited by the idea of going on a Crusade. His enthusiasm for war was unsettling, and remorse fell upon him. He should be thinking only of Marian. Prince Richard was not yet King of England, and King Henry was a healthy and vigorous man. Robin resolved to focus on reclaiming his title and property in order to wed Marian.

Marian must have sensed his unease, because she looked up at him. Robin contemplated her despondent face, and regret pierced him. He wished to assuage the pain that he had inflicted by his impassioned speech about dying for her sake. Of course, he wasn't going to die—not when he was so young, and when he had so many reasons to live.

Marian was already engulfed in his arms, but he tightened their embrace and kissed away her tears. They were pressed so close to one another that it drove their carnal yearnings, and their amorous fires were rapidly rekindled.

He solemnly whispered, "I promise; I will not die."

The tempest of Marian's emotions abated as she affirmed, "I have faith in you, but fortune is a mutable and whimsical creature. You must promise to be careful and not do anything reckless or dangerous."

Robin suppressed an inappropriate urge to chuckle. "I'm always careful. Everything will be all right," he declared as he avoided making promises he could not keep.

They fell quiet and gazed into each other's eyes. The fire was slowly dying, and the moon was now descending towards the far horizon. Without another word, Robin reached for Marian and kissed her with the possessive intensity and wild desperation of a lover who had long been absent from his beloved.

Marian felt as if she were flying through the air only to realize that Robin had swept her off her feet and was carrying her to the bed. He set her on the feather-filled mattress and promptly joined her, covering her body with his own. Marian instinctively tensed, and disgusting memories of Guy's body pressing down on top of hers tormented her mind. Cringing in fear, she silently cursed Gisborne's intrusion into this special moment with Robin, and she smoldered with hatred for the loathsome knight. When Robin unintentionally mimicked Guy's fondling of her breast, Marian flinched and choked out a distressed whimper.

Robin immediately rolled off of her, and in the dim light, she could see his brow creased in confusion. "Marian, did I hurt you? You are shivering; are you cold?"

Lying to him, Marian anxiously blurted, "Yes, I'm cold."

Robin quickly got off the bed, and as he stoked the fire, Marian dragged several deep breaths as she worked to calm herself. She would not allow Guy's assault to cast a shadow over the consummation of her love for Robin, and she frowned in concentration as she focused her mind.

"That is quite a fierce expression on your face, Marian. Is it safe for me to rejoin you?" Robin was standing next to the bed, warily observing her. He was jesting, but his tone revealed that he was alarmed by her response to his touch.

Marian forced a smile, and she was grateful that the low light in the lodge hid the extent of her discomfiture. "I'm sorry, Robin. Please, don't be concerned. It's just that…" She sought an excuse which would explain her reaction without divulging that Guy had lain on top of her.

She nervously asked, "I was wondering, will I conceive a child?" A blush darkened her cheeks. Although Marian hoped to give him many children, their circumstances were uncertain: they weren't married, Robin was an outlaw, and they were hiding in the forest.

Robin nodded in understanding; he knew that the fear of child bearing was common among women. He laid down next to her. "You will not conceive the first time," he told her confidently, quoting what he had heard from other men at court—a few of them dishonorable scoundrels who preferred virgins for that very reason. "Be at ease, my love. I will be careful and gentle. Do you trust me?"

"I do."

Once again, his mouth covered hers, and the real world ceased to exist as Robin and Marian dwelt in an enchanted meadow of perfect happiness.

CHAPTER 9
TROUBLING TIMES

Late October 1188, Sherwood Forest, Nottinghamshire

Robin's muscles were becoming stiff from crouching behind the thick brush that lined the road which extended south from Nottingham towards Leicester and London. He cupped his hands and gently blew into them before rubbing them together in an effort to warm himself. The crisp air and short days of autumn were a constant reminder that winter would soon arrive, and he was no closer to resolving the difficult position in which he found himself.

He was hiding with six of his men on one side of the road. Robin made eye contact with Little John, who was stationed on the other side with the remaining outlaws. They exchanged a brief nod, and Robin decided to risk disturbing the morning stillness as he silently summoned Kenric.

Kenric moved until he was squatting between Robin and Much. Robin was very impressed with the young outlaw; he had a remarkable talent for lurking unnoticed in the shadows while hearing and seeing everything around him. Kenric also had trustworthy friends among the castle servants. His spying had revealed that Argentan periodically received a box of silver from an unknown source, and it was customarily transported over this road. Unfortunately, Kenric had been unable to determine the frequency of these deliveries.

Robin whispered to him, "You are certain that someone is coming today?"

Kenric confirmed, "Yes, but I do not know if they are bringing the silver."

The soft whistle of a bird call drew Robin's attention back to John, who lifted his chin and cocked his head to the side, indicating that someone was approaching. At first, all Robin could hear was the thumping of his own heart and a light rustling from the branches above him. He started to wonder whether he had misread Little John's meaning, but then he heard the rhythmic beat of horses' hooves. Once again, Robin was amazed by John's uncanny ability to perceive what was happening in the forest around them.

Soon, three knights crested the hill at a stately pace; behind them, a richly dressed, rotund young man sat astride a magnificent destrier. He was followed by a wagon loaded with trunks, and three additional knights brought up the rear. The horses of the leading men began to snort and sidestep; the intelligent beasts had sensed the presence of the outlaws. This caused the knights to apprehensively survey the tree line on either side of the road.

When the procession was within Robin's trap, he signaled to his men, and before the knights could draw their swords, a dozen outlaws suddenly appeared, bows at the ready with arrows nocked and aimed at the men. The knights and wagon driver halted and raised their hands in submission. Several of the outlaws lowered their bows and promptly grabbed the horses' reins.

The noble shrilled, "Fight them! I pay you to defend me, not to surrender."

The oldest of the knights sighed loudly and wearily responded, "My lord, we are outnumbered."

Robin strode onto the road and commended the man who was evidently the noble's captain. "A wise man knows when to fight and when to surrender," he announced, as he watched Allan and Will move from man to man, seizing their swords and daggers. After the men were disarmed, they were ordered to dismount and kneel with their hands resting on top of their heads.

Robin approached the noble who was now nervously standing next to his wagon. He was dressed in expensive, fashionable clothing that strained to cover his corpulent figure. Pale with dark eyes and brown hair that was stylishly cut, he was obviously a man who belonged at court, not the wilds of Nottinghamshire, and Robin's curiosity was roused. As he beheld the man's face, a shock of recognition coursed through him.

"Eustace Clisson, the Earl of Bedford," Robin exclaimed in surprise. He politely bowed to greet this man whom he had not seen since they were boys training in Poitou.

A confused Bedford scowled. "Huntingdon? Why are you hindering me like this?"

Robin answered amiably, "I was expecting...well, someone else, not you. We mean you no harm, and I will release you and your men soon. But first, I would like to speak to you privately. Come with me." Robin steered Eustace a short distance away as he directed John to take charge of the others.

Bedford lumbered along, and Robin endeavored to recall everything he knew about this man. Clisson's father had died when he was just a babe, so Eustace was already the Earl of Bedford when he arrived in Poitou. Regrettably, Eustace had been a large, clumsy boy who had not been able to master the bow or the sword, although he had been a skilled backgammon player, even defeating Robin in one of the tournaments. Eustace had left without completing his training; he had suffered a minor injury during jousting practice, and his mother had demanded that he return to Bedford because she could no longer allow her only child to risk his life with such dangerous pursuits.

"What brings you to Nottingham? You are very far from Bedford and London," observed Robin.

Eustace shrugged his shoulders nonchalantly. "I have an estate near Duffield. I am traveling there. When Baron de Argentan learned that I would be passing through this area, he invited me to visit him in Nottingham."

The casual mention of his hated adversary worried Robin. "How do you know Argentan?"

"Baron de Argentan was in London last month for a meeting with the prince. As one of Prince John's closest friends and advisors, I was also in attendance," Bedford haughtily proclaimed.

Robin cautiously probed, "What was your opinion of Baron de Argentan?"

Again, Eustace shrugged. "I did not form any particular opinion of him, but I am grateful for his offer of hospitality as I travel north."

This seemed reasonable, so Robin turned his attention to more important matters. "Have you received any news from Normandy? Do you know if King Henry plans to return soon?"

Eustace drew himself up to his full height, pleased to have knowledge which Robin lacked. "On the 7th of October, King Henry was in Châtillon-sur-Inde, near the border of Touraine and Berry, negotiating peace with King Philippe."

Robin pressed for more details. "Another peace conference? The last report that I read touted that they had met at Gisors and made peace there."

"That was in August," Bedford confirmed. "After that, King Henry marched to Mantes, but then a new conflict developed. These are troubled times."

"Yes, indeed; these are troubling times," concurred Robin.

Robin leaned closer to the other man. "I have been trying to contact King Henry and Prince Richard through the usual channels, but I have not received any reply. If they are in Châtillon-sur-Inde,

I should have heard something by now. Is Prince Richard with the king?"

Bedford snorted derisively. "Prince Richard *was* with Henry, but he completely undermined and betrayed his father."

Robin tensed but maintained an even demeanor. "What do you mean? What happened?"

"Richard pledged that he would abide by King Philippe's ruling in settling the dispute between Aquitaine and Toulouse. Naturally, King Henry is furious. There is talk that the king plans to name Prince John as his successor."

A stunned Robin was briefly speechless, but he decided not to be deterred by such gossip; he had been around royal courts long enough to know that rumors were often more an attempt to shape reality rather than a reflection of it.

"Bedford, I need to know whether the tavern in Dover is still loyal to the king." Robin's voice was low and urgent.

Bedford reassured him, "The tavern in Dover is still used to dispatch messages to the royal family on the continent. However, I believe that the king utilizes a different method for communicating with Prince John."

"Does Bazile still own the tavern and manage the transmittal of royal missives?" Robin anxiously queried.

"Of course," replied Eustace. "I was there last month and spoke to him personally." He hesitated for a moment before inquiring, "Huntingdon, what is going on here? Why are you waylaying travelers like a forest bandit?"

Robin intently assessed the other man as he counseled, "Have a care around Argentan. He has accused me of nefarious crimes, and I was compelled to seek refuge in the woods until I can clear my name. Do not trust anything he says about me. You know me, Bedford. Do you remember when we were boys in Poitou?"

"I will never forget those days," Bedford affirmed flatly, without any hint of nostalgia.

Robin's intuition sounded a vague alarm at Eustace's frosty reaction. Doubts about Bedford rose in his mind, but Robin was desperate. "I'm asking for your help," he humbly acknowledged. "I must find a way to get word to the king. Henry sent this man, Argentan, to Nottingham, but he is ignoring the king's laws. When will you be returning to London? Do you know of another way to contact the king?"

A triumphant smirk spread across Bedford's face. "This is extraordinary. I would have never imagined that the *illustrious* Robin Fitzooth would need my assistance for anything beyond backgammon lessons."

Robin was irritated by Bedford's feeble jest, but he forced himself to chuckle as he suggested, "Stranger things have happened, I am sure."

"I would be pleased to help you, Huntingdon, just like you helped me in Poitou."

There was an odd glint in Bedford's eyes, and it made Robin pause. He tried to recollect how he had helped Eustace; perhaps it had been during archery practice when many of the other boys had sought Robin's advice and guidance.

Bedford offered, "I will return to London soon. Bazile is not the only way to send messages to King Henry; I will find an alternative, and I promise to be careful in my dealings with Baron de Argentan."

Robin smiled in relief and summoned Allan. "Allan, do you have the message I gave you earlier? The Earl of Bedford has graciously agreed to send it for me."

Allan's face fell slightly, as he enjoyed his excursions to Dover, but he dutifully handed the small rolled parchment to Robin, who passed it on to Eustace.

Robin, Eustace, and Allan rejoined the others, and with an abrupt signal, Robin and his men disappeared into the forest, leaving the Earl of Bedford and his men unharmed. The knights hastily

retrieved their weapons from a nearby pile, and the group continued their journey to Nottingham.

❦

Sherwood Forest was aflame with the colors of autumn, but Guy
was oblivious to the forest's vibrant beauty. He was lingering at
a window in the sheriff's tower room, scrutinizing the crowns of
the trees, as if he might discover Marian perched on some distant
high branch.

For days following Marian's abduction from the castle, Guy
had been in a frenzy, coercing hapless soldiers into sword fights so
that he could crush them and compensate for his humiliating loss
to the Earl of Huntingdon. When the sheriff had put a stop to these
duels, complaining about the expense of bandaging or burying the
soldiers who fell under Guy's blade, Guy's fury had subsided.

His wrath still blazed from time to time, but mostly he was
devastated by his failure to protect Marian; the only woman he had
ever loved besides his mother. He had failed to protect his mother
from Montlhéry, and now he had failed to protect Lady Marian. At
least with his mother, he had the excuse of being a boy, but now he
was an experienced knight. He would always remember Marian's
terrified expression on that fateful night. She had been counting on
him to save her from Huntingdon.

A grim resolve filled him. He would rescue her from Robin
Hood. Guy had lived at the French court from the age of fourteen,
and he knew very well that men like Huntingdon simply took what
they wanted from women. It had been the same with Count de
Montlhéry and his mother. Huntingdon would not hesitate to bed
Marian against her will. Visions of Robin touching and violating
Marian relentlessly circled his mind, and Guy felt white-hot rage
melt and shape his heart like a blacksmith softening and hammering metal into an instrument of death.

He bitterly reproached himself for not bedding Marian,

because surely his rival would have then forsaken her. Now the situation was reversed, and Guy had to decide whether he was still willing to wed Marian. Immediately, he realized the truth: Marian was the woman he loved, and even if Huntingdon had disgraced her, it would not extinguish his devotion to her. Guy vowed that he would still marry her, and he was convinced that the budding affection that Marian had shown him would blossom into love and gratitude for his beneficence and generosity in marrying her even if she were no longer pure.

"Gisborne!" the sheriff's screech penetrated his somber musings. "Are you still crying over that viper? Could you at least pretend that you are a man and attend to me now? My guest has arrived."

Guy reluctantly moved away from the window and assumed his position standing guard on the right side of the sheriff's throne, while Payen glared at him from the left.

An overweight young man dressed in extravagant clothes swept into the chamber and bellowed joyously, "Baron de Argentan! Sir Tancred! It is very good to see you again."

"Lord Bedford," greeted the sheriff enthusiastically, "I am so pleased that you have deigned to visit me out here in the wilderness." Argentan, Payen, and Gisborne all promptly genuflected. Argentan then entreated, "Permit me to introduce the captain of my guard, Sir Guy of Gisborne. He was unable to join me on my recent trip to London." The sheriff leaned forward and winked as he lowered his voice conspiratorially, "He's nursing a broken heart, I fear. His lady love abandoned him for another."

Bedford, Argentan, and Payen all burst into raucous laughter while Guy burned in mortified silence.

Argentan briskly informed his captain, "Gisborne, this is the Earl of Bedford, Eustace Clisson. Payen and I were incredibly privileged to make his acquaintance in London. Prince John holds him in the highest regard, and we are honored and humbled by his presence." His gaze drifted to the earl. "My esteemed Lord Bedford, how was your journey?"

Bedford was preening and posturing, ecstatic to be the object of such effusive praise. "My journey was uneventful until my arrival in Nottinghamshire. It seems that the Earl of Huntingdon has become a forest bandit, and he attacked me and my men, just as you warned me he might."

Argentan feigned shock. "This is unacceptable. Were you hurt? Did they steal…anything?"

"No," answered the earl. "As soon as Huntingdon recognized me, he allowed me to continue on my way. You were right; he did not even search my wagon. I have safely delivered the box you asked me to bring and—"

Guy rudely interrupted, "How many men were with him? Where along the road did he stop you? Was there a woman—"

"Gisborne, do not interrogate my guest as if he were under arrest. You may question the captain of his guard later," scolded Argentan.

A chastened Guy quieted.

Bedford snickered as he disclosed, "Huntingdon begged me to help him. That is a moment I will cherish for the rest of my life." His face darkened, and he whined, "The high-and-mighty Robin Fitzooth, favorite of Prince Richard—I think the prince rigged the contests so that Robin would always win. If Robin broke a rule, people indulged him. If I, uh, I mean, if other people just made a mistake, they were humiliated."

Argentan placed a consoling hand on the shoulder of the distraught young man and spoke in a fatherly tone, "It grieves my heart to hear how Prince Richard and Huntingdon treated you so unfairly. But I am confident that you will have a much brighter future than this renegade former earl. Prince John is very fond of you, and he considers you one of his dearest friends and closest advisors; he revealed this to me during a private audience."

Bedford's eyes had welled with tears at the sheriff's kind words, while Gisborne and Payen glanced at each other and disdainfully rolled their eyes.

The earl beamed gratefully at Argentan. "Prince John will be a great king."

"*King* John will treasure your shrewd mind and loyal heart, Bedford. That is why you are one of his favorites," cooed the sheriff.

Bedford reached into his tunic and tugged out a crumpled piece of parchment. "Huntingdon gave me this message for King Henry." He gleefully handed it to Argentan.

"Excellent, Bedford," commended the sheriff. "I will add it to my collection of increasingly frantic missives from the Earl of Huntingdon to King Henry and Prince Richard. I know you are aware of Richard's betrayal of his father at Châtillon-sur-Inde. Because of this, Henry will be naming Prince John as his successor, and Prince Richard is scheming with Huntingdon to steal the throne from John. When I attempted to arrest Huntingdon for treason, he fled into the forest."

Bedford sighed in satisfaction. "It's such a good feeling to finally have the upper hand over Huntingdon."

Argentan lavished more flattery on him. "When you told me about the tavern in Dover and offered to introduce me to its proprietor, Bazile, I instantly realized that you will be the future king's most important advisor. You are a man of impressive intellect and cunning. Isn't that what I said, Tancred?"

Struggling to suppress his mirth, Payen bowed deeply as he concurred, "My lord, those were your exact words."

The sheriff continued, "Because of your foresight, we can now all work together to protect Prince John from the treasonous plans of Prince Richard and Huntingdon."

Bedford reveled in the glow of the sheriff's fawning admiration. "I am honored to serve Prince John. My mother agrees with you; she says that Prince John will have a glorious destiny, and that I will be his favorite advisor."

"There is not a shred of doubt in my mind," replied an emphatic Argentan. "But first, I am anxious to make you comfortable. I do not wish to incur the wrath of your mother! I promised her I would take very good care of you during your visit." The sheriff's eyes veered to his captain, and all pretense of friendliness vanished. "Gisborne, please escort the earl to our finest guest chamber." Argentan watched as Guy obediently led the plump earl out of the tower room.

As soon as Gisborne and Bedford had departed, Payen complained, "My lord, I do not understand. When we were in London, I could have easily poisoned Prince John. We would have had one less Plantagenet to kill."

Argentan explained, "I do not want to poison Prince John yet. He trusts me, and he will be the easiest to kill. Ideally, I would like to eliminate Prince Richard before King Henry, but the goddesses of fate and opportunity will determine which Plantagenet will die next."

Payen eagerly inquired, "Do you still want these men to sicken and die slowly, as if they were suffering from an illness?"

The sheriff smiled blissfully. "Yes, the emphasis should be on suffering. They must die a miserable, lingering death."

Payen grinned wickedly before sobering as he pondered the difficulties of his master's scheme. "I need to practice with my poisons in order to achieve this. If you could provide me with men who are similar in size to Prince Richard and King Henry, it would be most helpful. I believe that Prince Richard is unusually tall, like Gisborne. Perhaps I could give Gisborne a dose—"

Argentan howled with laughter. "My dear Tancred, I like how your mind works. However, I have plans for Gisborne, and he amuses me. Remember: Gisborne does not know about the plot to kill all the Plantagenets; he thinks we are intending to put Prince John on the throne."

Payen nodded submissively, but frowned in disappointment at being denied the chance to poison Gisborne.

The sheriff then outlined the next steps in their strategy. "Until I find a way for you to get close enough to poison either King Henry or Prince Richard, you will be my contact with the tavern in Dover. I have purchased the loyalty of this man, Bazile, and we will use him to convey dispatches to and from the French court. This will be a vast improvement over our current arrangements."

The two conspirators conversed until Guy returned and declared, "The earl is settled in his quarters. Do you have further need of me? I wish to be excused to attend to my other duties."

His voice dripping with vitriol, the sheriff sneered, "Gisborne, are you organizing another hunt for the fair Maid Marian? Maybe she is happy to be in Sherwood with a *real* man. I can picture Robin and Marian rutting like animals on the dirty forest floor, can't you? Surely, you must realize that if you ever re-capture the no-longer-a-maid Marian, you will have to be satisfied with the crumbs from Huntingdon's table. Are you heartbroken, Gisborne?"

The malicious laughter of Argentan and Payen reverberated loudly in Guy's head as he stomped from the chamber, his heart full of loathing for his cruel master.

Mid November 1188, Lenton Village, Nottinghamshire

Gisborne sat on his stallion and observed while one of his men placed a small chest of coins on a two-wheeled cart harnessed to a single horse. It was time to return to Nottingham with the taxes he had collected. Peering at the sky, he was thankful that the sun had broken through the clouds, and he hoped it would warm the chilly autumn air.

He urged his horse over to the thirteen foot soldiers accompanying him and commanded, "Three men will stay with me and guard the chest. The rest will divide into two groups, one on each side of the road. Just as we have done previously, have your bows ready. Stand facing the trees, watch for bandits, and if you spot someone, kill them without hesitation. When I pass by with the cart, run ahead to the next forward position. Keep advancing to ensure that the road is clear of outlaws."

Guy was quite pleased with himself. He had collected taxes from several villages, and his tactic of constantly shifting his soldiers along the road had kept Robin Hood and his men at bay. The sheriff would be impressed.

After his soldiers dispersed and moved out of sight, Guy glanced back at his remaining men and froze in alarm. They were gone. He was completely alone with the chest of coins. Apprehensively, he turned his horse in a circle, searching for his men. The villagers had also disappeared. He was just about to ride to the cart and take the reins of its horse when a familiar voice sounded behind him, and he spun his horse around again.

In the middle of the road, brandishing Guy's prized sword, stood a grinning Robin Hood. "Gisborne, I hope your soldiers are patient; I fear you might be delayed." Suddenly, the band of outlaws sprang from their hiding places among the thatched buildings of Lenton, arrows nocked and aimed at Gisborne.

"Huntingdon," Guy spit out in disgust. "I see that you are still a thief. You are stealing taxes intended for your king. That is a treasonous offense."

"Well, if anyone would know about treason, I guess it would be the son of a traitor," quipped Robin. "But I am curious about these taxes. Argentan has already collected the king's monies."

"The sheriff has instituted the tallage. These taxes will satisfy that."

His smug grin widening, Robin surmised, "Therefore, these taxes are not for the king, but for the enrichment of the sheriff."

Guy gazed down at Robin from his horse and sarcastically

proposed, "I think we should debate tax law until my men come back to investigate why I have been delayed."

Laughing, Robin motioned to someone as he announced, "I think some of your men are returning now."

Little John then emerged from between a couple of market stalls and shepherded Guy's three soldiers out onto the road and in front of the knight's horse. They were bound, gagged, and blindfolded.

While Robin distracted Gisborne, Will approached the cart horse and calmed it with an apple. At the same time, Kenric and Allan carried a matching small chest packed with rocks and stealthily swapped it for the one filled with coins.

Oblivious to the maneuvers behind him, Gisborne glowered at his nemesis. "What of Lady Marian? Do you care so little for her reputation that you would kidnap her and hold her hostage in a forest camp surrounded by these coarse men? Do the people of Lenton know that you not only killed their lord but also dishonored his daughter?"

Robin's temper immediately flared at Gisborne's accusations, especially since his conscience was still plaguing him for bedding his beloved prior to exchanging marriage vows. "Lady Marian is betrothed to me. She is not your concern."

Guy smirked, pleased that he had unsettled Huntingdon. "When I was visiting her at the castle, she was excited to receive my gifts and affection." He leaned forward in his saddle and reminisced, "I will never forget tasting her honeyed lips—"

At that moment, an arrow whizzed through the air and narrowly missed Guy's shoulder. While Guy calmed his startled horse, a dismayed Robin quickly surveyed his men. Before Robin could discover who was responsible for this disruption of his plan, a few of Guy's soldiers returned, troubled that the knight had not yet appeared on the road to Nottingham.

Knowing that the chests had already been switched, Robin yelled, "Retreat!" and the outlaws scattered into the nearby forest.

Gisborne directed his men to encircle the cart instead of pursuing the outlaws. Relieved that the chest was still there, Guy congratulated himself on his victory over Robin Hood.

∽

The outlaws had relocated their camp to a clearing adjacent to the hunting lodge in order to safeguard Lady Marian, who was living there. The men were subdued as they gathered and watched their leader angrily pace.

As soon as everyone was assembled, Robin glared at Kenric and Allan. "The chest?" he hissed.

Allan fidgeted under Robin's scrutiny as he confirmed, "We put it in the lodge."

Without acknowledging Allan, Robin instructed John, "Tomorrow, we will give the coins back to the people, and you will oversee that."

Little John silently nodded in agreement.

Then Robin ceased pacing and reproached his men. "Since joining you in the woods, I have spent a lot of time training you. You are all demonstrating significant improvements in both weaponry and coordinating as a unit. But now I am wondering: have you forgotten the two most important rules that I taught you?"

He scanned the men as he sought Kenric, Allan, and Will. They were the only ones who could have released that arrow at Gisborne. "Kenric," thundered Robin. "What is the first rule?"

Kenric enthusiastically answered, "My lord, the first rule is: know the plan."

Robin then called for Will.

"Yes, my lord?" responded the youngest member of his gang. Loosely tied around his neck was the scarlet scarf he had worn during the rescue of Lady Marian from the castle.

"What is the second rule that I taught you?" barked Robin.

"The second rule is: follow the plan," Will confidently recited.

Robin was accustomed to leading experienced soldiers, and insubordination could not be tolerated. He castigated his men, "Two rules that are easy to remember and obey. Yet, someone did not follow my plan. I need to know who released the arrow that nearly struck Gisborne."

The outlaws nervously eyed each other, and a hush fell over them until a dulcet voice confessed, "It was my arrow."

The entire group pivoted in unison to find Lady Marian standing behind them. She was dressed in her boyish disguise and holding a bow; a quiver of arrows strapped to her belt, and a bracer wrapped around her arm.

⋘

Basking in the bleak rays of an autumnal sun, Robin and Marian's favorite meadow was an oasis of tranquility in a forest fraught with the menace of an uncertain future. The browning grass was littered with yellow, orange, and red leaves which had previously adorned the trees like fiery crowns.

Robin gallantly removed his hooded cape and spread it on the ground under the sheltering arms of the great oak as he invited Marian to sit. He had brought her here with a heavy heart, knowing that she would not welcome what he had to say. But first, there was the matter of her following him to Lenton and participating in the raid.

Marian smiled tentatively as she settled herself on the thick cloak. They had not spoken since departing the lodge, and she finally broke the awkward silence. "If you had told me the plan, I would have followed it."

Robin harshly condemned her actions. "Marian, you should not have been there. What were you thinking?" he shouted before moderating his voice. "When I was training Allan, and you came to me begging to learn archery and sword fighting, I thought the idea was absurd."

Her cheeks flushed a bit. "Robin—"

"No, let me finish," he insisted, his eyes glittering with displeasure. "But I listened to you. I understood your desire to be able to defend yourself from an attack, so I relented and began to teach you both archery and how to handle swords and daggers." He trailed off and took a deep breath as he repeated himself, "What were you thinking?" Shaking his head in bewilderment, he exclaimed, "You might have killed Gisborne."

Marian grunted in frustration. "He moved, or I would have had him."

Robin sputtered in horrified shock. "Marian, have you lost your mind? Aiming at a man while you are safely hidden from sight is not self-defense. And what if you had injured, or even murdered, Gisborne?"

Struggling to hide her bitter disappointment at missing her target, she looked away and silently swore to redouble her efforts to improve her accuracy with the bow. The despicable knight had nearly told Robin about the kisses and embraces that he had forced on her, and she was sure that he would have made them sound consensual.

Robin continued his stern lecture, "My men are under strict orders to not harm Argentan, Gisborne, or Payen. King Henry sent these men here. I might question the king's wisdom in choosing these men, but it does not change the fact that we cannot kill agents of our king."

Marian's head jerked up at the mention of Henry. "But King Henry ignores your plight. You claim that he is such a wise and just liege lord, yet he does nothing for you. When will the king answer your pleas for help?"

Exasperated by the situation, Robin irately growled, "I have sent four messages to the king and three to Prince Richard through the tavern in Dover. Allan delivered them to the tavern owner. Just a fortnight ago, I sent another dispatch with the Earl of Bedford, a man I have known since my youth. I do not understand why King Henry has not ordered the removal of Argentan. Maybe the messages were intercepted after they arrived in Normandy."

"This tavern, the one in Dover, how can you trust the men there?" queried Marian.

Robin explained, "When I lived in Poitou and Aquitaine, I communicated with my father using this tavern, and many nobles use it to relay information to the king. There are other channels, but this is the one I know best and have trusted for years."

He clasped Marian's hands and was dismayed to realize that they were chilled from the cold November air. "Dearest Marian, I thought that my problems would be resolved before now, and that we would be happily wed, but I was mistaken. I'm sorry, but you cannot remain here in the forest any longer, and I must take you to safety."

Marian paled, and her eyes widened in panic. "Do not send me away! I could not bear to be apart from you. I am very comfortable in the lodge."

Robin regretfully admitted, "I don't want to be separated either, but you must see reason: the lodge was not built to be lived in for weeks at a time, especially not during winter. It does not even have a way to cook meals; the small hearth is only intended to furnish heat."

"I am not starving. Odella and the servants from Locksley have provided all the food I need." Her heart sped and her stomach lurched at the idea of leaving him.

Robin admonished her, "You would expect Odella and the other servants to trudge through snow and winter storms to bring you food?"

Marian felt shame when she saw that he was disappointed in her. She lowered her eyes and contemplated their joined hands as tears blurred her vision. "No, I would never want to endanger them."

Hoping to assuage her anguish, Robin elaborated, "The trees have lost most of their leaves, making it easier for someone to find the lodge, even though it is deep within the forest. And you would need a fire in the hearth day and night for warmth. Until now, we have only been lighting the fire at night for your comfort. A plume of smoke during the day will guide my enemies to your location. I cannot risk that."

Unable to dispute the truth of his words, she asked, "But what about you? How will you keep warm during the winter?"

Robin gently curled his fingers under her chin and tilted her face so that he could gaze into her eyes. "My men and I will not stay near the lodge. We are planning to move to the caves that are near Locksley, but there is no privacy there; it's no place for a lady."

A distraught Marian was determined not to cry. In a tremulous voice, she declared, "I don't want to leave you. I have been so happy here in the woods. I have never felt such freedom…"

Freedom.

Her utterance of that single word caused Marian to stop in astonishment. Like a shaft of sunlight bursting through thick clouds, a bright revelation of how dramatically her life had changed over the past two months pierced her dark fear of being separated from Robin. Although she would forever mourn her dear father, she did not lament the passing of the restricted life that she had previously lived.

Sherwood Forest had once symbolized Robin in her mind, but now it was so much more. During her weeks in the forest with Robin and his men, she had discovered that, like a young bird teetering upon the edge of a familiar nest and facing the broad expanse of an endless azure sky, all she had to do was spread her wings, and she could fly!

For Marian, freedom meant wielding a sword and practicing archery. It meant listening to the men discuss tactics and strategies while sitting around the campfire. It meant closely observing as

Robin drilled the men in military exercises. Her body was growing stronger, and her mind was brimming with new ideas and knowledge heretofore unavailable to her as a sheltered daughter of the nobility. She was thrilled by these transformations in herself.

At last, Marian understood the mystique of Sherwood, which Robin had endeavored to explain to her long ago. She now felt a part of the greenwood, as though the enchantment of the forest was in her blood. How could Robin expect her to abandon this new-found freedom? Once more, tears threatened to spill from her verdant eyes.

Robin's voice intruded into her amazed musings. "Marian? Do you understand why you must leave?" His heart tightened at her obvious distress. He did not want her to go, but he really had no choice. An idea formed in his mind, and he drew his dagger from its sheath at his belt. He was briefly reminded of the dagger that Prince Richard had given him, and he wondered if Argentan still had it. Dismissing that distraction, he stood up and started carving something on the trunk of the great oak.

Marian watched in fascination as Robin carved *R+M* on their special tree. She smiled through her tears at the sweet gesture.

Sheathing his dagger, Robin grinned at her. "Our hearts, represented by our initials, will always be together here in our meadow, even if we must be apart for a short time." He then knelt down next to her and gathered her into his arms, kissing her tenderly.

Marian's kisses became more ardent and demanding, until Robin pulled away and cautioned her, "Marian, no. I have told you: we must wait until we are wed. I regret—"

"You regret loving me?" Marian sharply interrupted him, her eyes flashing.

"No, of course not. But it was wrong of me to allow my body to overrule my mind. Besides, if we surrender to our passions now, we risk creating a child. I cannot disgrace you in such a manner—to leave you unwed and carrying my child. I promise: as soon as my good name is restored, we will marry. You might not care whether or not I am called the Earl of Huntingdon, but I do not want you to be called Robin Hood's wife."

CHAPTER 10
THE BARON OF EMBELTON

Late November 1188, Embelton, Northern England

Constance de Toury shivered despite the luxurious fur cloak that was wrapped around her slender shoulders. Embelton Castle was always cold in the winter, and the light snow outside was a harbinger of a larger storm expected later that night. Of course, the piece of ice in the small earthenware bowl that she was carrying was the primary reason why her hands were so chilled. With practiced stealth, Constance silently crept along the passageway leading to the keep's great hall. Her favorite silk slippers—ones that she had purchased during her family's last trip to London—whispered across the floor.

She had big plans for this piece of ice! It was just the right size to hide in the palm of her hand. She was going to enter the great hall and affectionately embrace her older brother, Lionel, while surreptitiously dropping the ice down his back. Then she would step away from him and watch him struggle to maintain his composure in front of his insufferable new friend as the ice melted against his skin. Constance grinned wickedly in anticipation.

Lionel was deserving of such a prank for inviting the horrid Earl of Bedford, Eustace Clisson, to visit them. It had all begun the previous June. Every year, her father, Edmund de Toury, the widowed Baron of Embelton, took his two children to London. Edmund was training Lionel for his future position as baron, and he hoped that Lionel and Constance might meet prospective spouses among the nobility gathered at court to celebrate Midsummer and the feast of Saint John the Baptist.

Neither Lionel nor Constance were particularly eager to marry, but they both loved the entertainment and shopping available to them in the capital, in contrast to the limited opportunities for such diversions in their remote, northern home. Constance would quickly tire of the noisy, smelly, and crowded city, but she suspected that Lionel would be content to live in London year round.

It was during this most recent London excursion that Lionel had met Eustace Clisson. Constance could tell that her brother was impressed by the man's lofty title, reputed wealth, prowess at backgammon, and close friendship with Prince John.

What Constance could not understand was why Lionel still fawned over this man after hosting him for a fortnight. By now, surely Lionel had recognized that the Earl of Bedford was a conceited braggart with no manners or ability to converse unless talking about himself, his sainted mother, or Prince John. She prayed that he would leave before the upcoming feast of Saint Andrew.

At the imposing double doors that led to the great hall, she hesitated and listened quietly, wanting to ensure that Lionel and Eustace were still there.

Sounds echoed in the cavernous hall, and Lionel's dismayed voice was easy to hear. "Don't be deterred by her age. It's difficult to find a proper husband so far from London. That's why I really appreciate your willingness to travel here to get better acquainted with her. What do you think?"

Eustace whined, "She's older than I thought. And tall. She's too tall and thin."

"She's only twenty," Lionel exclaimed. "Since the passing of our mother six years ago, Constance has assumed all the responsibilities of a baroness. I know it's not the same as being a countess, but the size and wealth of Embelton rivals some earldoms."

This conversation was so unexpected that Constance found it incomprehensible. Was Lionel attempting to convince this man to marry *her*? It must be a joke. Maybe Lionel knew that she was at the door and was playing a trick on her.

Eustace's nasal voice intruded into her musings. "My mother is encouraging me to find a rich wife, even though my earldom is quite prosperous, of course. Mother saw Constance at court and felt that she would be a suitable bride, although I'm worried that Mother did not realize how old she is."

An apparently desperate Lionel emphasized Constance's qualifications to become the Countess of Bedford. "She might be older than some of the other girls, but consider her many valuable skills. In addition to her experience in fulfilling the role of baroness, she is a gifted healer, and she is fluent in French, as our mother was descended from French nobility. Few girls can boast of so many talents."

Constance's heart dropped; this was no prank.

Lionel persisted with his appraisal of her numerous virtues. "Constance is steady and loyal; she's not fickle like some of the younger girls. And she has a generous dowry."

Now Constance was burning with anger. Steady and loyal! It sounded like Lionel was selling one of their prized brood mares.

Eustace reflected thoughtfully, "She seems quiet and biddable. Mother says that's very important in a wife."

At this, she could hear Lionel coughing in a weak attempt to disguise his laughter at Eustace's words. After a moment, he spoke again, changing the subject. "She absolutely adores London and always looks forward to our trips there with Father."

Constance had heard enough. She pivoted to commence a hasty retreat only to come face to face with her father who was observing her curiously, his eyes full of concern.

She brought a finger to her lips, imploring him to be silent as she set the bowl of ice on the floor and ushered him a short distance from where she had been standing.

"Father," she urgently whispered. "Lionel is in there trying to persuade that unbearable, appalling, odious man to marry me. Did you know about this?"

Edmund responded in an equally hushed voice, "Have you just now realized Bedford's purpose in visiting us? I thought it was obvious that he had come here to make an offer for you. Embelton in the early days of winter is not exactly a pleasant destination."

Constance paled as wings of apprehension took flight in her stomach, and her heart began to thrum. Her father had threatened to choose a husband for her if she continued to reject every suitor who sought her hand. She had presumed that he was jesting, but what if he had been serious? She uneasily asked, "Do you want me to marry him?"

Edmund cautiously answered, "He is an earl with a thriving, wealthy estate. He is your brother's age, so he is neither too old nor too young for you."

A low whooshing noise sounded in her ears, and the edges of her vision darkened as Constance wobbled slightly. Edmund promptly reached out and steadied her, and she was thankful for his support. Her wonderful father! He was always there to catch her when she stumbled or fell. But why would he want her to wed Bedford? Nearly in tears, she whimpered, "Please, don't send me away."

Edmund was confused at first, but then his brow rose in understanding. "Constance, I am not telling you to marry this man. What do *you* think of Bedford?"

Constance collapsed into his arms. "Oh, Papa, I could never be happy with that man; he is obnoxious, and…he looks like a toad!"

Tightening his embrace, he murmured, "My dear Constance, I want you to marry for love, but I am worried that you might never find someone and have your own family."

"So, you will not force me to marry that man?" Constance anxiously searched his face.

Edmund tenderly regarded his tall, willowy daughter. She was a constant reminder of his beloved late wife, Jeanne. She shared her mother's expressive eyes and ebony locks, and although he considered her to be beautiful, he reluctantly acknowledged that he was not an unbiased observer. More important than her appearance, she was intelligent and kindhearted, just like her mother.

He endeavored to give her not only his reassurance but also some fatherly advice. "I would never coerce you into any marriage. Truth be told, I don't think I'd allow you to marry him even if you wanted to." He chuckled lightly. "I've never met a man whose character is more incompatible with yours. But, Constance, you should not judge a man by his appearance. There are good men who are not tall, handsome, and dark-haired like the heroes of your girlhood daydreams."

Relief swept through Constance with such strength that she felt a bit giddy. "Well, perhaps I'll marry a tall, handsome, fair-haired hero like my cousin, Robin." She laughed. "But fair or dark, I do not want a man who is balding—especially if I am going to be taller than him and have to look down at the top of his head."

A bemused Edmund escorted Constance into the great hall, where Lionel and Eustace were still conversing. The two men lapsed into silence, and then everyone formally greeted each other. Edmund briefly compared the heavy-set Eustace to his athletic son, whose wavy blonde hair and dark blue eyes were like gazing into a mirror of his youth. Nevertheless, there was one significant difference: Edmund had no interest in fashion; that was a trait both of his children had inherited from their late mother.

"Lord Bedford," Edmund courteously addressed his guest, "I received word that you are preparing to leave today. I'm afraid that a storm is coming."

Constance glanced at her father in surprise; she had not been informed of Eustace's impending departure. Her spirits instantly lifted.

Eustace shrugged, evidently unconcerned. "I have been absent from home too long, and Mother will be upset. My captain tells me that we will arrive at the Durham inn before nightfall."

Lionel interjected, "We are sorry to see you go. We've enjoyed your company. Hopefully, this is just the beginning of a long association between our families."

Constance startled at this bold statement, and her eyes narrowed in annoyance that Lionel was pushing for this match; it was not his place as long as their father was still alive.

Eustace smirked at Lionel and beckoned to someone standing at the periphery of the large hall. A servant approached, dropped to one knee, and gave the earl an ornate wooden box. Eustace then directed his oily leer at Constance, who resisted the urge to recoil as the Earl of Bedford lumbered towards her.

He handed the box to Constance, and she took note of its exquisitely carved and painted exterior. Constance peered at her brother, who was smiling and excited, and her father, whose brow was creased in consternation.

"My mother sent you this gift," Eustace proudly proclaimed.

Constance opened it and was amazed to find a beautiful necklace adorned with colorful gemstones. She nervously eyed her father; she did not want to accept this gift but did not know how to diplomatically decline it.

In a triumphant voice, Eustace declared, "Of course, my mother will retain ownership of the rest of the family's jewels, but she is willing to give you this necklace and allow you to borrow the others when you accompany me to court."

Constance's eyes widened in panic, and she again looked to her father for help.

Edmund was momentarily flummoxed, but he soon managed

to recover his voice. "Lord Bedford, I believe there has been a misunderstanding—"

Ignoring the older man, Eustace kept talking. "We will marry after Easter in the church at Bedford. My mother will supervise all the arrangements and ensure that the wedding is appropriately grand without overspending." He finally paused, grinning smugly.

Before Edmund could resume speaking, Lionel chimed in. "A spring wedding! Won't that be marvelous, Constance?"

"But, I—" Constance was at a rare loss for words, and once more, her eyes desperately beseeched her father with an unspoken plea for salvation. It was the first time that a suitor had just assumed the success of his suit.

At the limit of his patience, Edmund vigorously protested, "Bedford, I do not remember signing a betrothal contract for the hand of my daughter. I think it is premature to start planning a wedding."

Eustace was visibly taken aback by Edmund's objection. "But Lionel told me that you and Lady Constance were enthused about this match." His eyes veered to Lionel, who was suddenly examining the floor at his feet. The young earl huffed in exasperation and refocused on Edmund. "Lord Embelton, I would be happy to sign such a document prior to my departure, if it will put you at ease. I am also willing to wait until the wedding to collect her dowry. But let us sign this quickly so that I can leave before noon."

For an uncomfortable span of time, Eustace and Edmund stood silently assessing each other. Lionel and Constance anxiously observed the two men.

"Lord Bedford," Edmund fought to mask his aggravation as he decreed, "My daughter is an intelligent, thoughtful woman. If you want to marry her, you will have to propose to her."

"What?" A befuddled Eustace again glanced at Lionel, who was still avoiding all eye contact with him.

Constance decided to end this awkward conversation

immediately. "My lord, thank you for considering me worthy of becoming Countess of Bedford, but I am humbly declining your proposal. I prefer to live here, in the north, near my family."

At first, Eustace's expression was impassive, as if Constance had been speaking in a foreign language that he could not decipher. Abruptly, his demeanor transformed as he spoke to Edmund in a highly disapproving voice. "Embelton, your daughter cannot refuse me. Obviously, she is not as intelligent as you claim. She dares to reject me? An earl? An advisor to Prince John? What madness! This is why women cannot be allowed to make crucial decisions. As head of your family, you must tell her what to do."

Edmund's eyes flashed with barely suppressed outrage. "Very well, as her father, I will decide."

Eustace exclaimed, "I'm glad to hear this." Slanting his eyes haughtily at Constance, he sneered, "My mother will teach you how to give me the respect I deserve. You should be grateful for my attentions."

Constance tensed with anger, and a number of sharp retorts hovered on the tip of her tongue, like hounds straining against their leashes and eager for the hunt.

The Baron of Embelton drew himself up to his full height. "Lord Bedford, you have much to learn about women. My Constance is a jewel, and you do not deserve her. I am refusing your offer of marriage on her behalf. Go find some other heiress to live under the thumb of you and your mother."

Eustace was clearly unprepared for this answer, and his face turned bright red. It occurred to Constance that this might be the first time the pampered earl had ever been denied something he wanted.

Lionel struggled to smooth things over. "Eustace, perhaps we could—"

The combined glares of Eustace and Edmund caused Lionel's words to drift into an embarrassed silence.

In a surprisingly swift move, Eustace snatched the box with

the necklace out of Constance's hands and marched to the door where he pivoted, facing the de Toury family and bellowing, "You will regret this. I have the ear of Prince John. I am very important!" With those ominous words, the Earl of Bedford stomped out of the hall.

The family waited quietly as they heard Bedford summon his men and his horses. Lionel stalked to a narrow window that over-looked the bailey, and following a short pause, he announced in a taut, irritated voice, "They are leaving now."

Realizing that the repugnant earl was finally gone, Constance gave her father an appreciative hug while Lionel started restlessly pacing.

Extricating himself from Constance's embrace, Edmund delivered a harsh reproach to his son. "Lionel, it is not your place to arrange a betrothal for your sister."

Lionel spun around and glowered at Edmund. "Father, it is not proper to let her choose. She might be clever at balancing accounts and mixing healing potions, but Eustace is right: key decisions should be made by men." He shook his head in disbelief. "He is an earl. He is a close friend of the royal family."

Edmund attempted to reason with his son. "Lionel, do you care so little for your sister's happiness that you would condemn her to a life of misery with an arrogant, selfish man who does not love her?"

"But she would have been a wealthy countess. It would have elevated the entire family's position in society. Perhaps she is the one being selfish," whined a petulant Lionel.

Constance irately countered, "You think *I'm* selfish? Why don't *you* marry someone to elevate the family? And why do we need to be elevated? Father is a prosperous baron who has the king's favor. I think that means more than having the 'ear of Prince John,' a younger son who is unlikely to ever gain the throne."

Lionel scoffed, "You know nothing about politics. Prince John—"

"Lionel! Constance!" thundered their father. "Enough!" First, he lectured Lionel, "We do not need to sacrifice Constance on the altar of your ambition. It is not selfish for her to want a tolerably happy marriage. And she has a point: why aren't you actively searching for a wife?" Edmund's scrutiny veered to his daughter. "I support your refusal of Bedford, but you must realize that it is high time for you to wed."

Lionel harrumphed and bitterly alleged, "Eustace was her last chance to marry well. At her age, she should consider joining a convent."

Constance gasped, infuriated and insulted, her emotions heightened by the truth of his words. Just as her father opened his mouth to scold Lionel for his tactless remarks, the sound of shouting and running feet disrupted their quarrelling. Anticipating an attack, Lionel and Edmund moved in front of Constance and drew their swords.

At that moment, two beggars in ragged hooded cloaks ran into the great hall with servants and guards pursuing them. One beggar was carrying a third individual, while the other brandished a sword at the people chasing them.

In stunned dismay, Edmund, Constance, and Lionel watched the intruders sprint past them and towards the huge hearth blazing at the far side of the hall. The two men threw themselves down in front of the flames as they tried to place the third person as close as possible to the roaring fire.

Edmund and Lionel sheathed their swords as an apologetic servant rushed forward. "My lord, these men just appeared at the door and demanded entry. I told them that they must go to the church for food and shelter. One of them is sick; maybe they are lepers!"

The assembled servants and guards recoiled in horror, but Edmund and Lionel calmly approached the strangers, who were crowding around the hearth as the snow on their cloaks melted and dripped upon the floor. The individual who had been carried into the hall started coughing, and the frightened servants visibly cringed.

One of the beggars glanced back, and his hood shifted away from his face.

"Robin!" Edmund and Lionel cried in unison, and Constance hurriedly joined them.

Robin looked up at Edmund, his eyes full of anguish and his face grey from the cold. Next to him, Much had laid his sword aside and was rubbing his hands together near the fire. Marian was on Robin's lap; her face was deathly white, and her body shivered uncontrollably as she endured another coughing fit.

Robin fidgeted as he waited in his uncle's solar, slightly uncomfortable to be wearing his cousin's somewhat extravagant clothing. He had always been amused by Lionel's love of fashion, but today he was thankful for the warmth of the woolen bliaut with its ample skirt and long trumpet sleeves. Creaking hinges heralded Edmund and Lionel's arrival.

Edmund admonished him, "Robin, what were you thinking? Bringing Marian north at this time of year? Where is your wagon? Your horses? Your clothes? Were you robbed by bandits?"

With those words, Robin doubled over and laughed until tears gathered in his eyes. Wiping at his face, he finally recovered sufficiently to speak. "No, we were robbed by a sheriff. Haven't you heard the news from Nottingham?"

Edmund and Lionel gazed at each other in confusion before Edmund replied, "I heard about Alfred's passing in late August, but it was during the harvest, and I could not forsake my responsibilities here. I sent word to you, asking if you needed me, but when there was no reply, I dispatched another message to you at Huntingdon, assuming that you had wed Marian immediately after her father's death and would spend the winter there. I was planning to visit you in the spring."

Robin recounted the events of the last three months as the two men gaped at him in open-mouthed shock. Edmund briefly embraced his beloved nephew, his eyes brimming with fatherly concern. "Robin, you should have come sooner, or you should have sent word to me; I would have come to help you."

Robin placed a hand on his uncle's shoulder. "I considered sending a message to you, but I feared for your safety. If Argentan was willing to hang an earl without a lawful trial, he would not have hesitated to arrest you. There is a bounty on my head, so we disguised ourselves as beggars and avoided the customary routes, which resulted in a much longer journey. I was reluctant to furnish my name to the guards at the entrance to your keep because my presence here might endanger you and your family."

Edmund assured him, "My people are trustworthy. I often tried to tell your father: if you treat others fairly and generously, most of them will repay you with steadfast loyalty. You have to give trust to receive it."

Robin nodded; he agreed whole-heartedly with Edmund. Robin's father, Duncan, had been a tight-fisted, suspicious man who had exhibited little compassion for those who served him.

Resuming his account of their travels north, Robin disclosed, "We had a horse for Marian to ride, but it went lame and had to be abandoned. Marian was very stoic and brave, trudging alongside us, but she became sick, and we had to stop more frequently. Eventually, I fashioned a litter so that Much and I could carry her." Robin fretfully dragged his hand through his hair. "I should go to her; I've been so worried, and this is all my fault."

"Robin, I have requested that Constance apprise us of her condition. We will wait here for her. Luckily, Constance has inherited Edith's talent for healing." Edmund's voice softened as he wistfully reminisced about his long-dead sister, Robin's mother.

Lionel changed the subject. "You say that King Henry is ignoring your messages? Is it possible that this man, Argentan, has convinced him of your guilt?"

Scowling, Robin contended, "I do not believe that King Henry would ignore my urgent pleas. My father was one of his favorites; Father even died while performing a service for King Henry. I suspect the messages have been stolen or lost."

Edmund queried, "Have you heard the latest news? I fear your friendship with Prince Richard might outweigh King Henry's fondness for your father."

Robin braced himself as he recalled hearing about a recent conflict brewing between Henry and Richard. "Is this about Richard accepting King Philippe's arbitration of the dispute involving Aquitaine and Toulouse?"

Edmund regretfully reported, "Although that remains a bone of contention between Henry and Richard, the latest development is that Prince Richard has paid homage to King Philippe, aligning himself with the French king against his own father. Your close association with Richard means that Henry considers you an adversary too. That is most likely the reason why he is ignoring you."

Robin began to angrily pace, his nervous energy practically exploding from his body. He was now in an impossible situation: a staunch ally of Prince Richard who was being pursued by an agent of King Henry.

Lionel divulged, "I have heard that King Henry will be naming Prince John as successor. Maybe that would be for the best, if Prince Richard cannot be loyal to his own father."

Edmund's irritation with the royal family's intrigues boiled over into heated words, which his son mistook for a direct rebuke. "That is foolishness. King Henry cannot designate John as his heir as long as Richard lives." Edmund grimly recollected the war of succession between King Stephen and King Henry's mother. "Uncertainty in succession is extremely dangerous. Henry should remember what his mother endured in order to retake the throne from the House of Blois."

Believing that his father had called him 'foolish' in front of Robin, a mortified Lionel snapped, "This situation is nothing like the Great Anarchy. Richard and John are legitimate sons. The nobility will follow whichever son Henry chooses."

Robin endeavored to calm their escalating emotions by acknowledging that both men spoke the truth. "Lionel is correct that the war between King Stephen of Blois and Empress Matilda, Henry's mother, was between competing branches of the royal family tree, and not between two legitimate sons."

Robin paused to collect his thoughts. "But Uncle Edmund is making an important point: an uncertain succession creates a void. Until one side or the other can decisively take the reins of power, the throne becomes like an empty ewer. It is bereft of its purpose, because no one can fill it until a king is crowned. It is vulnerable to breaking, because it is easily tipped over as men fight to control it. Such weakness is a type of provocation. It invites our enemies to meddle in our affairs and perhaps try to seize the throne for themselves."

Edmund moderated his tone, hoping to strike a more conciliatory chord with Lionel. "My son, when Stephen stole the throne from Empress Matilda, we had twenty years of bloodshed and death. Despite the fact that Stephen named Matilda's son, Henry, as his successor, there were nobles ready to champion Stephen's son, William, instead. It was only Henry's strategic cunning and the broad support that he enjoyed among the English nobility that prevented further years of unrest and strife."

Lionel smiled faintly and conceded, "Yes, I have heard that story many times: of how Robin's father, Duncan, helped King Henry defeat the traitors backing William of Blois."

There were still questions plaguing him, so Lionel cautiously suggested, "But shouldn't King Henry have the right to choose his successor? What if the king believes that Prince John would be a better king than Richard? There have been problems between Richard and Henry for as long as I can remember."

Edmund argued, "Prince Richard is Henry's eldest surviving son. It is his right to inherit the throne."

Robin endorsed Richard, with whom he had a brotherly relationship, as a worthy monarch regardless of his birth order. "Prince Richard has governed Aquitaine successfully for many years. I know him well, and he is a strong leader and an excellent military commander. Prince John's attempt to rule Ireland was an utter failure."

Lionel frowned in concentration as he pondered Robin's words. "Maybe we don't need a man whose only experience is fighting and war. People say that Prince John is a good administrator with a keen mind. Besides, everyone knows that his viceroy is to blame for what happened in Ireland."

Robin and Edmund strove to persuade Lionel that a warrior king was critical during these troubled times. Robin also mentioned the need to reconquer Jerusalem; he was certain that only Richard could accomplish such a feat.

A tapping on the door interrupted their debate, and Constance entered. She embraced her cousin affectionately as he impatiently inquired, "How is Marian?"

Constance announced, "Marian is comfortable and warm, but she has a slight fever and is sneezing and coughing."

"A fever?" Robin's voice rose in alarm.

Beaming kindly at Robin, she tried to reassure him. "Be at ease, dear Robin, your lady love will soon recover. This is not a serious illness. I have given her a cough remedy of sage, rue, cumin, and pepper, and she will be fine. She is resting in a cozy bed, and I will give her some hot soup when she wakes. Her phlegm humor will be restored to its proper balance in no time."

"Are you sure?" prodded a dubious Robin.

Still smiling, Constance insisted, "Yes, I'm sure."

Robin noticed that Constance was holding several frayed pieces of parchment. When his eyes lowered to her hands, she offered them to him. "As I was unpacking the few items that Marian brought with her, I found these. I asked her about them, and she told me that she has been meaning to give them to you. She said they might be important, but that you must ignore the poetry. Does that make sense?"

An intrigued Robin eagerly took them.

Constance's eyes gleamed impishly as she teased him, "I think you have a rival for Marian's affections. Some of these verses are quite passionate."

Robin's expression darkened at the thought of Gisborne, and he grumbled, "That's ridiculous. Tell Marian I will come to check on her soon."

Constance departed as Robin shuffled through the pieces of parchment, irritably reading the poems. Annoyance transformed into resentment and unwarranted jealousy that Gisborne had written these romantic, even erotic, odes to Marian.

The men moved to a large table, and Robin laid out the scraps with the poetry face down. They were obviously torn from official documents. Shifting the pieces around, Edmund and Robin fit some of them together, and they were astonished to realize that these documents were from the French court, not London. All three men could read French, so they worked together to translate:

Prince John has agreed—but to what? The remainder of the sentence was missing.

watching Prince Rich—Who is watching Prince Richard, and to what purpose?

King Henry and Prince John will—what will they do?

Signed, Philippe Augustus, King of France—a small remnant from a wax seal left little doubt that this was an official signature.

They stared at each other in bewilderment. The fragments

raised more questions than they answered; it was incredibly frustrating to say the least.

Robin speculated, "Maybe King Philippe is manipulating both sides: accepting fealty from Prince Richard while also establishing a rapport with Prince John behind the scenes."

Edmund was skeptical. "How could Philippe achieve that without John revealing the truth to Henry? John's relationship with Henry is said to be very close." He trailed off as his mind tried to find a logical connection. He somberly added, "I am greatly disturbed by the involvement of King Philippe in our affairs. For nearly six months, we have been teetering on the edge of full-out war with France."

Lionel ventured to advance his opinion. "Perhaps King Philippe is merely monitoring the movements of the royal family without any intention of interfering. Consider this note: 'watching Prince Richard.' Sometimes the simplest explanation is the best."

Humming pensively, Robin remarked, "King Philippe is reputedly an ambitious, shrewd, and self-reliant man. I am convinced that he wants to take complete control of the Angevin lands, especially Normandy. That would explain his recent aggressive maneuvers. I don't trust him."

Edmund concurred. "I don't trust him either. Yet, I think the only conclusion that we can confidently reach is that King Philippe is taking an active interest in the English succession."

Robin stepped away from the table, deep in thought. "Much and I must return to Nottinghamshire. The people are suffering under the brutal reign of this sheriff, and it appears that these Normans have ties to the French court. What if King Henry has entrusted Nottingham to men who are spies for King Philippe?"

Edmund reminded Robin, "Henry has invested heavily in fortifying Nottingham castle with a stone wall, and he has expanded the keep. Nottingham's location is undeniably strategic."

"May I request a favor, Uncle?"

"Of course, Robin," responded Edmund. "What can I do for you?"

Robin earnestly beseeched, "Please safeguard the queen of my heart. Will you watch over Marian until my title and properties are reinstated to me? As soon as this unhappy business is resolved, we will wed. But I fear for her life if she is recaptured by Argentan."

Edmund solemnly vowed, "I promise, Robin, that I will take care of Marian as if she were my own daughter." His face brightened. "I think Constance will enjoy having Marian here with us; she has been lonely for female companionship since the passing of her mother."

A thought occurred to Robin. "Uncle, once I leave here, you must stay away from Nottingham. Do not send any messages to me; they might be intercepted and endanger you, your family, and Marian."

Sighing in resignation, Edmund agreed. "I do not like it, but you are right. I am not afraid for myself, but I must protect my family and my people here in Embelton. And now my family includes the daughter of my dearest friend, Alfred."

Robin smiled, and the relief shining in his pale blue eyes morphed into a twinkle of mischief. "Tomorrow, I would like to put your captain and his men through some drills. Somehow, two beggars successfully invaded your keep unhindered."

Edmund chortled and good-naturedly thumped his impertinent nephew on his back. Just then, Lionel's laughter distracted them.

Lionel was reading one of Gisborne's poems. He gleefully proclaimed, "Listen to this: 'You are more perfect than God's angels; I have worshipped you from the start.'" Lionel gazed at Robin and Edmund, curiosity shimmering in his eyes. "This is a poem about Marian? Has this man actually met Marian?"

Robin ignored the hint of mockery in his cousin's tone and admitted, "Unfortunately, he is acquainted with her. I will have to ask Marian about these verses; some of them are entirely inappropriate."

Still snickering, Lionel asked, "Who is this man writing poetry for the woman you plan to marry, Cousin?"

"He is one of the reasons why I think these Normans are traitors," confessed Robin. "I find it easy to believe that the son of a traitor is also a traitor."

"Son of a traitor?" inquired a surprised Edmund. "Who is this man?"

"It is Guy of Gisborne, son of the traitor, Hugh," Robin clarified.

All the color drained from Edmund's face as he approached Robin and urgently queried, "Do you mean Hugh, the Baron of Gisborne? And his mother is Lucienne de Villeneuve?"

Robin confirmed, "Yes, he is the son of Hugh, the man who attempted regicide in Toulouse, when my father saved King Henry. I do not know the name of his mother."

Edmund peered steadily into Robin's eyes, unblinking and unwavering, as he spoke hoarsely to his son, "Lionel, leave us now. Robin and I will join you later."

"Father—" a perplexed Lionel began.

"Go!" shouted Edmund with an uncharacteristic ferocity, and Lionel immediately exited.

"What's wrong, Uncle?"

Edmund reluctantly revealed a tale of betrayal. "Robin, I cannot allow you to remain in the dark. There is something I must tell you about Guy of Gisborne, and you will not like it."

CHAPTER 11
MORE PRECIOUS
THAN SILVER

January 1189, South of Nottingham

uy's stallion snorted and restlessly side-stepped, clouds of the beast's breath puffing into the chilly morning air. The sheriff's captain was waiting with twenty foot soldiers on the north side of a bridge. On the other side, the road stretched south to Leicester, eventually ending in London itself. The sheriff and Payen had left for London over a month ago, and Guy had received word that they would be returning on this day and would require an armed escort.

Gisborne suspected that the sheriff was transporting another box of silver. The silver arrived periodically from France to fund Montlhéry's scheme. He often felt curious about this mysterious plan; he believed that it entailed putting Prince John on the throne. John would be easily manipulated by the shrewd and formidable King Philippe, particularly if Montlhéry was involved. Guy was convinced that Count de Montlhéry had sold his soul to the devil. That would explain a lot about the man he had known since the age of eight. The only father, really, he had ever known. If only Duncan

Fitzooth had not murdered his father, Hugh. Then his life would have been perfect.

Grumblings from his soldiers interrupted his musings. The freezing men were stomping their feet in an attempt to warm themselves. Guy silently castigated himself; this was no time for daydreams and distractions. Besides, remaining in the dark about Montlhéry's plan helped hide the unpleasant truths of his life and provided a refuge for his conscience. Therefore, he must focus on following orders, because thinking and asking questions was needlessly risky.

Finally, he heard the sound of muted voices and horses' hooves as a company of mounted knights wearing the colors of neighboring Mountsorrel crested the hill at a stately pace. Within their midst, Argentan rode atop an impressive destrier like a conquering king. Behind him, a single horse pulled a small wagon bearing several chests of varying sizes.

When the knights reached the south side of the bridge, they halted while the sheriff and his wagon passed from their protection and into the care of Guy and his soldiers. As soon as Argentan traversed the bridge, the other men turned around and began their trek back to Mountsorrel's keep.

Guy realized that the sheriff was alone. "Where's Payen?" he probed with interest.

Argentan enthusiastically replied, "Payen is now guarding Prince John. When we arrived in London, I learned that the prince was preparing to travel to Saumur to spend Christmas with King Henry. I warned the prince that the royal guard was allied with Prince Richard. John immediately understood the need for a personal bodyguard whom he could trust completely, and he was thankful to accept the services of my best knight—"

Guy bristled at the slur, and Argentan snickered as he corrected himself. "I meant to say, my most *intelligent* knight. Payen will be with Prince John for the foreseeable future."

Guy was just glad that the vile poisoner was somewhere else. He promptly arranged his foot soldiers, placing ten in front of Argentan and ten behind the wagon, while he rode next to the sheriff. The procession soon embarked on their journey through the forest and towards the warmth and comfort of Nottingham Castle.

Mile after mile, they marched without incident. Guy continually scanned the bare limbs that arched over the road. They were nearing Nottingham when he observed a copse of pine trees that loomed ahead. Their thick foliage would offer sufficient cover for bandits, and Guy debated whether to send some soldiers to secure that section of the road. However, he was consoled by the fact that he could see smoke plumes from the hearths and kilns of Nottingham wafting across the horizon. They were only a few miles from their destination, and Guy decided that it would be safe, especially since he had a sizeable contingent of men.

Suddenly, a crow's caw shattered the stillness and startled his horse. It all transpired so abruptly that Guy did not comprehend what was happening at first. Something black was falling from the pine branches above them. It fluttered as it moved through the air, and for an instant, Guy imagined that crows were attacking his men. A cry sounded behind him, and he spun his horse around, only to witness a similar dark shape descending upon the men following the wagon. He quickly realized that his soldiers had been ensnared in large fishing nets.

Guy turned his horse in a tight circle as at least a dozen outlaws emerged from the shelter of the trees, arrows nocked on their drawn bows. At that moment, the bane of his existence appeared, smiling and laughing as he ordered the sheriff and Gisborne to dismount while his men disarmed the soldiers tangled in the nets. One man led their horses a short distance away while a familiar red-headed outlaw approached and nervously took Argentan and Guy's swords from their scabbards. Guy recognized that it was the same peasant who had accompanied Marian when she first arrived at the castle.

His eyes flicked to the trees, and he worried that Marian was nearby and suffering in the miserable cold.

"Baron de Argentan," exclaimed a triumphant Robin. "You've been gone for so many weeks that we were all hopeful that some dire calamity had befallen you. There are many dangers along the roads."

Argentan was evidently more annoyed than afraid as he rolled his eyes. "Your efforts to astonish me have failed. Fishing nets? Obviously, your dirty peasants cannot win a fight against real soldiers."

Ignoring the sheriff's insults, Robin proclaimed, "The Lord commanded His disciples to become 'fishers of men,' and I am merely obeying Him."

The outlaws guffawed as they stood with their weapons trained on the hapless soldiers trapped under the nets. Guy watched as two men, their identities concealed with scarves, climbed into the wagon and started forcing open the chests. Another outlaw unhitched the carthorse; he had a bright red scarf masking the lower half of his face. As always, the color red reminded Gisborne of Marian, and he continued to fret about her welfare.

"Gisborne?" The sheriff's voice was both perplexed and peeved. "Why is Robin Hood carrying *your* sword?"

Guy felt the blood drain from his face. He had not told the sheriff that Robin was in possession of the engraved sword that connected him to Montlhéry. He shuddered to think of the consequences he would endure later. Directing his ire at Robin, Guy spit out, "Because he is a thief. A murderer, a thief, and an abductor of innocent noblewomen."

Robin's eyes narrowed at Gisborne. "It's not an abduction when the lady wishes to be rescued."

His face alight with mischief, Argentan inquired, "Tell me, Robin Hood, where is the fair Maid Marian? I am her guardian, so naturally I'm concerned about her safety and maidenly reputation.

Have you hidden her somewhere in the shadows of Sherwood? How are you keeping her warm at night?"

"Silver!" cried one of the men rummaging through the chests on the wagon. "I found the box of silver!" A cheer went up among the outlaws at the discovery.

Robin's attention was diverted away from Gisborne and towards the wagon.

"Look out!" yelled Much, but it was too late.

Guy leapt onto Robin's back and pushed him to the ground as he knocked the sword from Robin's hand. Robin was briefly dazed while Guy crawled to where his sword lay on the roadway, seized it, and then scrambled to his feet. An arrow whizzed past Guy's hip, and he heard the older outlaw, the big man who had been in Marian's bedchamber with Robin, holler at the others to stop releasing arrows which might accidently injure Robin.

Robin hastily regained his feet as two outlaws rushed forward, each bringing him another sword. He shouted, "Stay back!" just as Gisborne viciously swung his blade and nearly decapitated one of the men. A fountain of crimson blood spurted into the air, and Robin roared, "Edric, no!"

Robin, gripping the sword passed to him from Much, demanded, "Everyone stand back, and keep your arrows nocked." He stalked towards Guy, his weapon ready.

Gisborne smirked in triumph at recovering his beloved sword, and he reverently pressed his lips to the heraldry etched in the blade near the cross guard before facing Robin. Guy had slain one outlaw, and now that he had his sword, he was confident that he would finally vanquish his sworn adversary. Robin lunged at him, and Guy parried. The duel commenced in earnest, but they were hampered by the limited space between the leading group of ensnared soldiers and the sheriff's wagon.

As Robin stepped to the side, his foot found an icy patch, and he slid, landing on his knees. Gisborne took a mighty downward swing at him, and Robin was barely able to block it from his awkward position. When Guy raised his weapon to strike again, Robin punched his opponent in the stomach, using his sword's hilt to increase the force of his blow.

Gisborne doubled over and gasped for breath. Robin then slammed the pommel of his sword into the side of Guy's head, causing him to drop his weapon and collapse. Robin jumped on top of Guy, kneeling on his chest and holding his blade to Gisborne's neck.

Guy stilled; if he made the slightest movement, Robin's sword would slice his throat. He looked at the man who had stolen the woman he loved and would now steal his life. The pale blue eyes of Robin Hood blazed with hatred and bloodlust. Guy's body tensed in fear as he prepared to die. But then, something unexpected happened; Robin's eyes softened into a wistful regret that baffled Guy.

For several heartbeats, they stared at each other, until the sheriff's contemptuous voice broke their strange enchantment. "Well? Why don't you kill him, Robin Hood? He murdered one of your men, and you have defeated him. Kill him."

Guy's heart sped in frightened bewilderment. Why was the sheriff encouraging Huntingdon?

Argentan goaded Robin. "Many times I have heard the story of how your father sent Hugh of Gisborne to the shadows. Yet, you are hesitating. Why is that, Robin? Are you the son of Duncan Fitzooth, or are you a maudlin woman?"

Guy felt the pressure of Robin's knee vanish as the outlaw stood while still pointing his sword at Guy's throat. Robin then reached down and reclaimed Gisborne's weapon. "I will be keeping this sword, Gisborne. I've grown fond of it." Closely watching Guy, Robin instructed his friend, "Much, tie Gisborne's hands so that he cannot attempt another cowardly attack, if I turn my back again."

An apparently disappointed sheriff sneered, "Showing Gisborne mercy demonstrates to me that you are weak. Gisborne is weak too.

It is a fatal flaw that you both share, along with your lust for the same woman. I find it interesting that the two of you have so much in common. What do you think, Robin Hood?"

Intently studying the sheriff, Robin parried Argentan's verbal thrust. "I think I'd like to know why you are communicating with King Philippe." Robin inwardly cheered when he saw the sheriff blanch.

Argentan was actually speechless for several moments, but he soon recovered and coolly replied, "I believe that life in the frozen forest has addled your mind. The King of France would never take notice of a humble baron from Normandy." He frowned and feigned sadness. "You are like a man lost in the twilight of a wintry day; the clouds have obscured the sun, and the abundance of shadows has confused your sense of direction."

Robin barked a short, humorless laugh. "Your riddles are absurd."

Argentan resumed, seemingly unperturbed. "Someday, my young Earl of Huntingdon, the sun will break through the clouds and illuminate everything around you. The truth of the shadows will be revealed."

"You have not answered me: why are you corresponding with the King of France?" Robin repeated while scrutinizing the sheriff's reaction. "Does King Henry know that he sent a spy to Nottingham?"

Suddenly, Argentan started speaking in a high-pitched, singsong voice. "Sire, I have been falsely accused of murder by the sheriff you sent to Nottingham. I respectfully, but urgently, beg for the opportunity to prove my innocence."

Robin paled as he recognized the words of his first message to King Henry, dispatched almost four months ago.

Argentan chortled before continuing in the same falsetto cadence. "Sire, please ask your father to investigate the Norman baron whom he has appointed Sheriff of Nottingham. He conducted an improper trial where I was condemned for a murder I did not commit. I am innocent, and I can prove it."

Once again, Robin identified words which he had sent to Prince Richard months ago.

"I have quite a collection of these pathetic missives to King Henry and Prince Richard," announced an exultant Argentan.

"How?" Robin's voice was slightly hushed as his mind raced to comprehend how Argentan had managed to intercept his messages.

"Does it really matter? Besides, you are not a priority for the royal family at this time. Have you heard the latest news? Your beloved Prince Richard has joined forces with King Philippe. They are battling King Henry in an effort to compel the king to name Richard as his successor." Argentan grinned maliciously. "Poor Robin Fitzooth. So closely allied with Prince Richard that King Henry will not want to help you. And Prince Richard is so preoccupied with securing his inheritance that he could hardly be expected to come to your rescue."

Robin glared at the sheriff before shifting his attention to Little John. "Ready?" he tersely queried.

"Yeah," grunted John.

Following Robin's plan, the outlaws had put the silver into leather bags which were tied to the carthorse. Meanwhile, one of the men had wrapped a cloth around Edric's mortal wound so that they could carry his body into the woods without leaving a trail of blood.

"Much," summoned Robin.

Much scurried over. "Yes, Lord Robin?"

Robin swung his gaze back to the sheriff. He was still disturbed by the gleeful malevolence shining in the man's dark eyes, but he forced himself to focus on Argentan as he gave his men their instructions. "Little John, you take the horse with the bags of silver. Much, you will take Gisborne's stallion, and I will ride the sheriff's fine destrier." Robin then raised his voice so that everyone could hear him. "Men, you know the plan. Now, follow it."

With those words, Robin's band of outlaws dispersed into the sanctuary of the woods, each traveling in a different direction to confound anyone tracking them. Little John, Much, and Robin mounted the horses and prepared to depart.

Argentan stepped forward and proclaimed a somber warning. "You are doomed, Robin Hood. You cannot defeat me."

Robin's lips stretched into a lethal smile as he sat atop the sheriff's horse. "I easily defeated you today." Without a backward glance, Robin rode away.

Guy observed the sheriff reach under his cloak and retrieve Robin's prized dagger. Luckily, the peasant who had confiscated their swords had not thought to take their daggers as well. After the sheriff cut the rope binding his wrists, Guy hurried to free the soldiers beneath the nets. Soon they were ready to leave. Several men were clutching the wagon's shafts in order to pull it the rest of the way. Guy fumed that he and the sheriff would have to walk to Nottingham.

"Gisborne!"

Guy warily approached his enraged master, who was standing next to the wagon.

Argentan reverted to French, snarling, "You knew that Robin Hood had that sword with the seal of Montlhéry, yet you failed to notify me. Your incompetence has endangered my plan." The sheriff's wrathful glower caused a chill in Guy's heart that rivaled the icy January air. He braced himself for a painful punishment as the sheriff screamed, "You fool! You stupid, worthless, blundering fool! Do you realize the potential risk of Huntingdon having that sword?"

Guy remained silent, unsure of what to say. He recognized that the blade furnished clues about their association with Montlhéry, and thus, the French court. Robin Hood might discover that they were not actually from Normandy.

"Tell me now; if your tiny brain knows, why does Huntingdon think that I am communicating with King Philippe?"

"My lord, I have no idea," Guy honestly answered.

Argentan took Robin's dagger and sharply poked Guy. "If I stab you in the stomach, it will be a slow, agonizing death. And remember, I always know when you're lying. Did Maid Marian use her considerable charms to loosen your tongue?"

Guy's eyes widened in shock, and he desperately tried to reassure the sheriff. "I would never jeopardize the plan in such a way. My future is dependent on your success."

"No, Gisborne." The sheriff sheathed his dagger as he emphasized, "Your *life* depends on the success of the plan." Argentan then pointed to the ground next to the wagon. "On your knees," he demanded.

Guy apprehensively gulped, "My lord?" He could not withstand the intensity of the sheriff's evil, dark eyes, so he obediently dropped to his knees.

"Down on your hands and knees," amended Argentan. "Now."

Guy's heart was still pounding in dread as he moved to his hands and knees, only to feel the sheriff's foot on his back as Argentan clambered into the wagon. Guy burned in mortification to be humiliated in such a manner in front of the other soldiers, but it was not as severe a punishment as he had anticipated. As soon as the weight of the sheriff lifted from his back, Guy promptly rose to his feet and watched as the sheriff settled himself on the boards where the wagon driver normally sat.

Gisborne stared at the sheriff, his heart filled with loathing and fierce yearnings for revenge against this man who governed his life and controlled his future. Impulsively, Guy asked a question that had been plaguing him, and his words tumbled out in an accusatory tone that invited further abuse and degradation from his master. "My lord, why did you tell Robin Hood to kill me?"

Argentan laughed in his face. "Did I hurt your feelings? Grow up, Gisborne. I was just taunting him. I knew he wouldn't kill you."

"I don't understand why he spared me," Guy confessed. He had seen the hatred in Robin's eyes and did not doubt that the outlaw *wanted* to kill him. Instead, Robin had shown him mercy.

The sheriff shrugged and alleged, "He's a sentimental, weak fool. And that is why I will prevail in the end." He then commanded the men who were prepared to tow the wagon, "Make haste! I'm cold and hungry." He scowled at Guy. "Gisborne, go help them pull the wagon. A knight without a sword or a horse is little better than a foot soldier."

With a thunderous expression, Guy took his place with the other men, and they towed the wagon towards Nottingham.

February 1189, Locksley Manor, Nottinghamshire

Leofric and Elvina shared uneasy glances before he cautiously entered the dining hall of Locksley where the new, self-proclaimed 'Lord of Locksley' sat morosely contemplating the roaring fire in the hearth while drinking the manor's best ale.

Leofric politely suggested, "My lord, should we serve the midday meal? This is the usual time when–"

Guy of Gisborne's icy glare swung to the elderly servant, who immediately stilled, wondering what he had said to provoke the volatile knight.

Gisborne sprang to his feet and towered over the older man as he menacingly growled, "The usual time when *Lord Robin* ate? Is that what you were planning to say?"

"Of course not, my lord." Leofric nervously swallowed. "We haven't forgotten your rules. I was going to say that it is the usual time when we serve the midday meal."

Guy surveyed Leofric's weathered face, searching for signs of deception. Then he harshly scolded, "The next man who either mentions *Lord Robin* or does not give me proper respect will end up with a dagger in his gut and spend his last hours apologizing to me, just like that stable hand who dared question my authority as Lord of Locksley." He then bellowed, "Do you understand?"

"Yes, my lord, we all understand." Leofric was desperate to calm this cruel man who had already slain two servants and seriously wounded a third. He veered his anxious gaze to Elvina. "Ain't that right, Elvina?"

Elvina nodded wordlessly, but her eyes glimmered with defiance. She refused to show fear in front of this usurper, this sham Lord of Locksley. Behind his back, everyone called Gisborne 'Lord Sham.'

Just then, Odella came into the hall and set a large platter of food on the table.

Guy jabbed his finger at her. "What are *you* doing here? You are Lady Marian's maid." In three strides, his long legs carried him across the floor until he was inches from the frightened girl. He grabbed her by the upper arms and shook her. "Where is Lady Marian? You know where she is, don't you!"

Leofric and Elvina frantically rushed to Odella's defense. Elvina explained, "My lord, with the death of Lord Lenton and the disappearance of Lady Marian, there is little work at Lenton Manor. I have hired her to help me in the kitchens."

Guy did not let go of Odella. "Where is Lady Marian?" he angrily repeated. "I have ways of getting the truth from people, and they are very painful. Tell me everything you know."

Odella was swamped with conflicting emotions of terror and resentment. No one had ever handled her so roughly or threatened her in such a manner. But she had a brave spirit, so she boldly spoke up, "How should I know? I wasn't at the castle when she escaped, and I ain't important enough to be told anything."

Guy frowned in disapproval. "Lady Marian didn't escape. She was abducted by the criminal who murdered her father."

Odella shrugged, struggling to assume an air of nonchalance. "I don't know about that. I'm just a servant."

Gisborne maintained a tight grip on her arms as his eyes slowly drifted down her body before returning to her face. Her curly blonde hair was much darker than Marian's flaxen locks, and her figure lacked Marian's generous curves. Although her chin was raised defiantly, he recognized the panic in her eyes.

He released her and took a seat at the table. The girl was a peasant, and she was evidently not interested in his attentions. Guy had principles; he did not bed women who were unwilling, and he only bedded servants who approached him first, otherwise he could never be sure if their consent was sincere.

However, Guy was tense and in a foul mood; it had been several weeks since his needs had been satisfied. He vowed to arrange a tryst with his favorite blonde widow during his next trip to Nottingham, but for now, he would partake of a hearty meal. Maybe it would clear his mind, which was fogged from the copious amounts of ale that he had consumed.

✧

Locksley was a small, prosperous estate, and Guy was quite pleased to have it. The servants and peasants were finally showing him the deference he deserved as their new master. All heraldry and symbols of the Huntingdon family had been removed from the manor and replaced with the Gisborne coat of arms, a white chevron on a blue field, as well as one of the sheriff's scarlet banners, which featured a bright yellow rising sun embroidered near the top.

Guy was standing by the hearth, staring into the flames and thinking about Marian, when he heard the sound of horses in the distance. After a short wait, he watched as Leofric opened the door to welcome the sheriff, who was wrapped in an expensive cloak lined with squirrel pelts.

The sheriff greeted him in an excessively cheerful voice.

Guy apprehensively sank to one knee and rose again. Whenever the sheriff affected such happiness, it was an ominous forewarning.

"Locksley Manor is so cozy and warm. Look at your blazing hearth! On this freezing February morning, it must be incredibly pleasant to enjoy such a fire." Argentan's broad smile did not reach his eyes.

Guy humbly replied, "My lord, I am very grateful for your gift of this estate. Is there a service that you require today?"

Without acknowledging Guy's words, Argentan switched to French and revealed, "I have received some unhappy news from London."

Guy's hopes soared. Maybe Payen had met some unfortunate, painful end.

The jubilant sheriff could barely contain his excitement. "My dear Tancred returned to London last month with Prince John. He tells me that King Henry developed a stomach ailment of some sort over Christmas while Prince John and Payen were there with him; he is very sick. How sad. The prince and Payen are planning to visit him again at Easter; I wonder if he will recover by then."

Unexpectedly, Argentan's grin morphed into a grimace. "But that is not why I am here today. This morning, I went to my tower room, and there was no fire in the hearth."

Puzzled by this odd statement, Gisborne waited for the sheriff to elaborate.

Argentan disclosed, "When I requested a fire, I was informed that Robin Hood had stolen the firewood intended for the castle. As I traveled here, I noticed that all the peasants in the villages that I passed through seemed to be enjoying cozy fires, yet I am shivering in my cold chambers."

Guy sighed in aggravation. As usual, Robin Hood was causing trouble.

"What are you going to do about this, Gisborne?" demanded the sheriff.

Guy briskly offered, "My lord, I will lead a group of men to gather firewood for the castle."

Argentan tapped his chin thoughtfully. "Well, that would be a start, but it's not enough. First, Robin Hood takes my silver, and now he has taken my firewood. I think it is my turn to take something."

"My lord, I don't understand." Guy gazed curiously at the sheriff.

"Gisborne, I have already sent a contingent of men to the forest to cut additional firewood. I want you to organize the remaining men and send them into each of the local villages: Locksley, Lenton, Carentune, Ernehale, and any of the other insignificant hamlets whose names I've forgotten. Go into every hut, hovel, and cottage. Confiscate all the barley and oats that you can find, and bring it to the castle granaries."

Guy's forehead creased in confusion. "My lord, what will the people eat? It is mid-winter, and there is little besides barley, oats, and dried beans to feed the peasants." He paused and worriedly asked, "Are you taking the food from Locksley Manor as well?"

Argentan scoffed, "Of course not, but fail me in this task, and I might change my mind. Go, *now*, before word spreads among the peasantry; I don't want to give them time to hide their stores of food. I have brought extra men with me today whom I place at your disposal. Do not disappoint me, Gisborne."

Late February 1189, Sherwood Forest

It was no longer snowing, and a stillness had settled upon the ancient woodland. Robin listened to the soft hush of the wind, the creaking of snow laden limbs, and the crackling of campfires as he sat near the entrance to one of the caves where the outlaws lived during the bleak winter months. He held his palms towards the fire before rubbing them vigorously together and tucking them back inside his cloak. Although grey clouds masked the sun, Robin knew that it was almost midday, and he was impatiently awaiting the return of his spies from their reconnaissance into several of the local villages.

Robin was in a bad temper, and he had no one to blame except himself. With consternation, he recalled the cheering people who had welcomed him into their villages when he delivered free firewood to them, courtesy of the supply originally meant for Argentan and the castle.

He had basked in their adoration, while relishing the idea of a miserable Argentan shivering in his tower room. However, there had been unforeseen consequences to his scheme: shortly afterward, Gisborne and his soldiers had ransacked every home in the villages surrounding Nottingham, seizing the oats and barley that formed the mainstay of the people's winter diet. Only Locksley Manor and the estates of nobles who were supportive of the sheriff had been spared.

Peasants throughout Nottinghamshire were on the brink of starvation. And it was Robin's fault.

The crunching of snow underfoot heralded the arrival of Kenric, Allan, and Will as they trudged towards him. Kenric had become Robin's eyes and ears in Nottingham; Will Scarlet was his contact with the people of Locksley and Lenton, while Allan-a-dale frequently ventured further afield, reporting news from larger towns. Robin was thankful for these young men and their willingness to perform the dangerous role of spy. Therefore, he carefully safeguarded their identities by stipulating that they cover their faces whenever they participated in raids with the other outlaws.

As the three scouts drew near, everyone gathered to hear their news.

Will spoke first, and he was clearly upset. "The people of Locksley and Lenton have no food. Without their oats and barley, they have already depleted their supplies of turnips, carrots, onions, dried peas, and beans. They are begging for help."

Robin detected deep resentment shimmering in the youth's eyes. "What is it, Will?"

Will angrily divulged, "There are people who are complaining that the Locksley servants have food. They believe that you are providing food to them and letting everyone else starve."

A wave of indignation swept over Kenric. "That is nonsense. Gisborne is living there now. He is not going to starve, and he certainly will feed those who are serving him."

"That's what I told them," snapped Will.

A frustrated Much argued, "How can they criticize Lord Robin? Because of him, they are warm this winter."

Robin endeavored to soothe everyone's escalating emotions. "Let's direct our anger where it belongs—not against starving people, but against the devil in his tower who took their food. Even the most sensible man will become agitated and irrational when his belly is empty, and his children are crying from hunger." He peered at Kenric and inquired hopefully, "Have you determined where they are keeping the grain that was stolen from the people?"

Kenric opened a pouch tied to his belt and pulled out a wrinkled piece of parchment. "The sheriff posted this proclamation, and there was no one around to read it to me, so I snatched it and brought it to you. Whatever it says, it will be posted and announced in all the towns and villages by tomorrow." He handed the parchment to Robin, who immediately read it.

Little John urgently questioned Kenric, "Is the grain stored in the granaries near the castle mill? Perhaps we could conduct a midnight raid."

An exasperated Kenric delivered more dismal news. "There are as many men-at-arms surrounding the granaries as there are guards defending the castle gates. I was told that a peasant tried to walk up to one of the granaries to beg for food, and he was struck down by an archer."

"Is he...?" gasped Much.

"No, I'm told he will recover," replied Kenric, to everyone's relief.

Robin looked up from the parchment and asserted, "We cannot rob the granaries. They are between the cliffs and the river. An attack on them would be foolhardy." He paused. "Thankfully, that will be unnecessary because the sheriff is willing to return the grain—"

Excited murmuring from the men interrupted Robin, who brusquely demanded, "Let me finish." As soon as everyone quieted, Robin resumed, "The sheriff is offering to sell the grain to the people. Anyone who has the price—in silver—will be allowed to buy grain."

An eruption of irate voices echoed within the walls of the cave. "The sheriff wants his silver!" exclaimed an outraged Much.

John gruffly insisted, "We cannot surrender that silver. We must find a way to take the grain. When the sheriff transports it—"

Robin shook his head and gestured at the parchment. "It says here that people will be required to come to the castle granaries to purchase grain. Only silver will be accepted as payment, and if there is an attempt to steal the grain, then it will be set on fire."

Much lamented, "Robin, what will we do?"

Robin shrugged; in his mind, the answer was obvious. "We will give the sheriff's silver to the people so that they can buy the grain."

"No!" John exploded. In a voice filled with bitterness and grief, he contended, "Edric gave his life for that silver. And I still don't understand why you let that Norman bastard live."

Robin bristled as he confronted John. "I had a very good reason for sparing Gisborne's life. However, I do not owe you an explanation beyond the fact that he and Argentan are agents of King Henry, and they have the king's protection."

Little John scowled and grumbled under his breath, reluctantly yielding to Robin.

Facing his men, Robin bluntly asked, "I did not know Edric as well as you, so tell me: would Edric want us to keep the silver while people starve?"

With these words, the outlaws, including John, lowered their eyes in shame. Of course, Edric would not have wanted that; they knew it, and so did Robin.

Without any further discussion, Robin decreed, "We will each take a supply of silver to the affected villages. Give the families whatever they need in order to buy enough grain to last until spring. No one will starve. The lives of the people are more precious than the sheriff's silver."

CHAPTER 12
THE HERO OF ENGLAND

Early May, 1189, Ernehale, Nottinghamshire

Our noble and clever Robin Hood,
He leads a band of brave and merry men.
From deep in the heart of the great greenwood,
They laugh at the cruel Sheriff de Argentan!

Wood and wealth, they will boldly pilfer,
And then merrily give it to the poor.
Greedy Argentan loves only silver,
Our hero, Robin Hood, loves people more!

Allan-a-dale's strong tenor voice had drawn a crowd near a tavern in the town of Ernehale. Some of the onlookers tossed coins into a cup at Allan's feet, and everybody was smiling and happy to hear his songs about Robin Hood. Ballads and stories about Robin's courage in defying Argentan, and his unwavering devotion to those who were suffering at the hands of this ruthless sheriff, had spread across England. There were reports that these ballads were popular in faraway places like Normandy, Poitou, and Aquitaine, where they were merged with tales of Robin's legendary prowess with a bow and his past victories at tournaments. People everywhere were calling him, 'The Hero of England.'

On this beautiful spring day, Allan was graciously accepting applause and coins from his audience when the sound of approaching mounted men-at-arms caused everyone to swiftly disperse. With practiced stealth, Allan retreated into the shade of an alleyway as the soldiers came to a halt nearby. He observed the Earl of Bedford awkwardly dismount and enter the tavern. Concealing his lute behind a barrel, Allan adjusted the hood of his cloak to hide his face. He then followed Bedford, purchasing a tankard of ale and sitting at a table adjacent to the earl.

Another man, his face shadowed by a hooded cape, sat down with Bedford. Allan's interest was immediately roused; this appeared to be a clandestine meeting. He subtly shifted on his stool, turning an ear towards the two men. Thankfully, this tavern was both darker and quieter than some he had visited recently.

"...to meet here. The king fell ill during Easter celebrations. Prince John says it's the same stomach ailment that afflicted him at Christmas." Bedford's voice was hushed but distinct.

The stranger harrumphed, "It's probably God's punishment for his wicked, blaspheming ways."

Bedford grunted in agreement. "I don't think that King Henry fears God, but it's not too late to repent. If he..." The earl further lowered his voice, almost certainly realizing that it was not prudent to criticize the king so openly.

"You mentioned that Prince John was with him at Easter. The succession..." The stranger's voice was briefly drowned out by raucous laughter from several men seated at a neighboring table.

Allan noted that the mysterious stranger spoke like an educated nobleman despite the fact that he was dressed as a merchant.

Bedford confidently asserted, "Yes, the king is still planning to announce..."

The earl's voice faded amid the hum and clatter of the tavern, and Allan leaned towards the men's table.

"...as soon as Richard and Philippe are defeated," the earl finished.

The other man countered, "These skirmishes began nearly a year ago. Prince Richard is a talented military leader. What if..."

Once more, the conspirators' voices morphed into jumbled sounds until the stranger bitterly grumbled, "Women! They forget that God created them to serve men."

A sympathetic Bedford concurred. "I agree. My mother always told me..."

Allan swallowed the rest of his ale and left. The conversation had deteriorated into grousing about women, and Allan was anxious to leave before the two men noticed him. Besides, although Allan had not been able to identify the stranger, he had collected important news for Robin: King Henry was sick again, and the supporters of Prince John were as determined as ever.

As Allan hiked to a prearranged rendezvous point, he pondered how much he enjoyed sneaking around and spying on people. It was much more diverting than sword fighting and archery. Of course, it was not as gratifying as performing for an enthusiastic audience, like the one he had entertained earlier. Allan could not help but congratulate himself; joining Robin Hood's band was a stroke of good luck, without a shadow of a doubt.

The Earl of Bedford and his heavily laden wagon were protected by a contingent of ten mounted knights. Hidden between the trunks containing the earl's lavish wardrobe was a small, unadorned wooden box filled with silver. Eustace had happily offered to transport it for his friend and mentor, Baron de Argentan. He smugly reminisced about tricking Huntingdon, or Robin Hood as he was now called, when he slipped a similar box past the renegade earl in January.

As he continued south towards Nottingham, Eustace was relieved to see that the trees had been cleared a fair distance from each side of the road, making it difficult for bandits to attack. The road itself was scarred by well-worn grooves running parallel down its center, and as long as the wagon's wheels were settled into these ruts, steering was unnecessary. The driver was barely clasping the reins as the rhythmic rumbling of the wheels and the comforting warmth of the midday sun had lulled him into a light doze.

Suddenly, a deafening crack shattered their peaceful progression. Eustace spun his horse and was flabbergasted at the sight before him: the wagon's front wheels had sunk so far into the ground that their axle was touching the road. The dazed driver had been thrown from his seat, and he hastened to calm the wagon's two horses. Eustace and his soldiers dismounted and gathered around the wagon.

The captain of the guard apprehensively surveyed the tree line on either side of the road. This accident had all the hallmarks of a trap, for the seasoned knight could plainly see that the ruts had been purposefully dug deeper at this spot and covered with burlap to disguise the danger. He implored Eustace, "My lord, we need to empty the wagon in order to lift it out of these furrows. But we have to hurry; I fear a trap."

Now it was Eustace's turn to nervously examine their surroundings while his men started unloading the wagon and stacking its cargo on the ground.

⚜

Perched in the branches of a nearby tree, Robin and his outlaws silently observed. Robin whispered to Kenric and Will, "It will not be one of those bigger trunks. Watch for a chest that is heavy for its size."

Just then, they witnessed a man straining to carry a small, non-descript box from the wagon.

Robin triumphantly declared, "It's the silver." He quickly released a volley of arrows and pinned Bedford to the side of the wagon by spearing the wide sleeves of his bliaut without nicking his arms. Robin then whistled to his men, and they loosed a hail of arrows, intending to intimidate without actually harming anyone.

When the earl's captain recognized the expert marksmanship required to ensnare Bedford without injuring him, he shouted, "It is Robin Hood! We must yield!" It was no secret amongst the soldiers and knights who traveled through Nottinghamshire that Robin and his band of outlaws took great care to avoid killing, or even wounding, their adversaries. A prompt surrender would ensure that no one was hurt.

All the soldiers dutifully dropped to their knees and submissively raised their hands over their heads.

Bedford shrieked at them, "What are you doing? You cowards! Fight!"

"My lord," replied the beleaguered captain. "Robin Hood could have easily murdered each and every one of us. Instead, his arrows were meant as a warning; he is offering us a chance to live if we surrender."

At that moment, the outlaws emerged from the trees, their bows trained on the kneeling men. As Robin lowered his weapon, he brazenly proclaimed, "A wise captain is more valuable than a box of silver."

All the color drained from Bedford's face.

While the outlaws bound the hands of the knights and wagon driver, Will and Kenric, their faces concealed behind scarves, forced open the box and began transferring the silver into leather pouches.

Robin approached Eustace Clisson and assessed him with a mixture of annoyance and amusement.

"Huntingdon," Eustace's voice had risen an octave, revealing the extent of his panic. "You cannot rob me. I am under the royal protection of Prince John. You will hang for this!"

Robin chortled contemptuously. "Haven't you heard? I've already been hanged for my crimes." Sobering, he probed, "Do you really believe that King Henry will bequeath the throne to a weak, ineffectual man like Prince John? A man who has never tasted victory in battle?" He shook his head. "Henry is not a fool. He might not feel fatherly affection for Prince Richard, but I assure you that Prince Richard *will* be our next king, and he will be pitiless when he takes his vengeance against those who conspired to deliver his birthright to John."

Eustace blanched, and his eyes widened in fright.

Hoping that Bedford would heed his counsel, Robin went to check on the progress of his men.

Everything was proceeding smoothly: Kenric and Will had placed the silver in the pouches, the soldiers were bound, and Much was tying Bedford's wrists. The outlaws' horses were secured nearby; they would ride their own mounts back to camp while escorting the other horses a few miles away before releasing them. This would confuse their trail and provide additional time for their escape.

An inspiration struck Robin, and he directed Much and Kenric to open all of Bedford's trunks. They were overflowing with clothing and other items typically transported during an extended journey. Robin signaled to Little John, and in a low voice, he instructed, "Set aside two horses for Much and me. Then, light a torch, and give it to Much. Everyone else will follow the original plan."

All the outlaws left, except for Robin and Much. Robin went to one of the trunks and pulled out a length of fabric, stretching it from the chest to the middle of the road. He then tore a small strip of cloth and tied it to the shaft of an arrow.

Observing Robin's puzzling actions, Bedford finally found his voice, "Huntingdon, this isn't over. My men will hunt you down."

Robin smirked at Eustace. "First, you have a decision to make."

Holding his nocked arrow close to the torch until the cloth at its tip burst into flames, he clarified, "Either send your soldiers to capture me, or order them to put out the fire."

Bedford gasped, "What fire?"

Without answering, Robin loosed his flaming arrow, effortlessly piercing the edge of the fabric on the road, and the cloth became a fuse leading to the earl's chests. The blaze eagerly advanced towards the expensive clothing.

"No!" screeched a horrified Bedford.

Laughing, Robin cut the ties around Bedford's wrists. "Now, when you free your men, you must choose whether they will save your fancy clothes or pursue Argentan's silver." Still snickering, Robin and Much mounted the two remaining horses and departed.

Behind them, the flames had engulfed the nearest trunk, and Eustace hastily slashed the bindings on his captain's wrists while demanding that he immediately rescue the remainder of his belongings from the rapidly spreading blaze.

June 1189, Locksley Village, Nottinghamshire

It was Sunday Mass in Locksley's church, and Guy proudly sat in the place reserved for the lord of the manor. He was delighted with Locksley despite its small size, and he was certain that his success in managing it would eventually result in him regaining the Barony of Gisborne after Montlhéry elevated John to the throne.

The priest's homily was recounting the story of Abraham and his two sons. "...and so Abraham cast out his illegitimate son, along with the boy's foreign mother. Only the son of his wife, Sarah, would be given the fullness of the inheritance that God had promised Abraham. Even though Hagar and Ishmael were banished and sent to another land, the Lord, our God, was benevolent and..."

Guy's mind wandered from the familiar Bible story. Sitting in church led to thoughts about his mother and hazy, distant memories of attending Mass with her. When he was a young boy, she had zealously urged him to dedicate his life to God and become a monk or a priest.

As much as he enjoyed pleasing his mother, Guy doubted that he would have ever pursued a religious vocation. Instead, it was Lucienne's stories about Hugh of Gisborne's heroism in supporting William of Blois, the true King of England, and Hugh's murder at the hands of Duncan Fitzooth that had truly excited her son's imagination in a way that theology never could. The seeds of his desire for revenge had been planted at a very early age and diligently nurtured for as long as he could remember.

Guy wished he knew more about the sequence of events that had brought Montlhéry into their lives. They had been residing with his mother's sister and her husband in the bustling town of Montlhéry when the Queen of France bestowed the title, Count de Montlhéry, upon her favorite courtier, Ambroise de Limours. After the death of his aunt, he vaguely recollected heated arguments between his mother and his uncle. Suddenly, his uncle vanished. Later, Guy learned that the newly arrived Montlhéry had ordered his uncle's execution.

From that time forward, their lives were ruled by the whims of this ruthless man. Soon, Lucienne and Guy were shunned by society and forbidden to attend Mass. Guy's world simply collapsed; he was no longer welcome to associate with his boyhood friends, so eight year old Guy was relegated to a claustrophobic existence inside his home with only his mother, Montlhéry, and a few servants as companions. But even the servants seemed to hold him and his mother in contempt. He would never forget the cruel taunts of his erstwhile friends, who started calling his mother, 'Montlhéry's whore.' People considered her responsible for the death of his uncle, who had been well-liked and respected.

As a boy, Guy had often felt angry at his mother, blaming her for their fall into disgrace and for her inability to protect either of them from Montlhéry's bouts of rage. As a man, he had to concede that Lucienne did not have a choice; Montlhéry was an incredibly powerful advisor to the Queen of France. Guy guiltily acknowledged that his mother had bartered herself to this man in exchange for promises of a better future for her landless, fatherless son. She had never hesitated to take beatings for him. For Guy's sake, Lucienne had endured the brutal affections of an iron-hearted beast.

Over the years, Guy's feelings for his mother had become a complex mosaic of love, resentment, gratitude, guilt, and wistful yearning. *If only we had not quarreled before she sickened and died...*

Guy realized that the service was ending, so he genuflected towards the altar, crossing himself reverently and rising to leave. Reminiscences of his mother were replaced by thoughts of the many duties which awaited him. The sheriff was on a secret mission to France and had left Guy in charge of Nottinghamshire. Of course, everyone believed that Argentan was in London. Guy was thankful to have some freedom from his master, who would have harshly berated him for attending Mass when there were tasks that needed to be done. The sheriff's disdain for God and all things holy frequently filled Guy with dread.

As the highest ranking person in the church, Guy exited first. He was contemplating his obligations at the castle when he glanced back, intending to find Leofric and notify him of his plans to travel to Nottingham.

That was when a flash of scarlet caught his eye. He was stunned to see a youth, no longer a boy, but not fully a man, wearing a red scarf around his neck. Guy promptly recalled the bandit who had concealed his identity using such a cloth. He stalked towards the young man, convinced that this was one of Robin Hood's outlaws.

Will's heart was buoyant and carefree; Mass had finally concluded, and he was with his friends, debating what to do next. It was a perfect day, and not a single cloud blemished the bright blue canvas arching over them. They were joking and laughing as they strolled away from the church, heedless of the coming storm; for although the June sky was sunny, the turbulent clouds on Guy's face threatened a perilous tempest.

Guy strode across the village square, grabbing Will's arm and spinning him around. "What's your name?" thundered Gisborne.

Swallowing hard, he whispered, "Will, I'm called Will."

"Where did you get this?" Guy's long fingers tugged at the scarf so forcefully that Will began to choke and sputter. Gisborne eased his grip to permit the boy to talk.

Will's face turned deathly white, and he stammered, "I, uh, don't remember; I, uh, think I found it; I, uh–"

"Liar!" roared Guy. "You're one of Huntingdon's outlaws. I recognize you."

"No, no…" A terrified Will wagged his head in denial.

Gisborne released his tight hold on the young man, only to viciously punch him in the face, sending Will to the ground, unconscious and bleeding from his mouth and nose.

⁓

The shadowy world of a dreamless stupor abruptly disintegrated as a deluge of frigid water cascaded over Will's face. He gasped in shock and tried to move, but he was trapped. For several agonizing heartbeats, he worked to clear his mind. His head was pounding, his jaw was aching, and his arms were hugging something and bound at the wrists. Gingerly opening one eye, he saw weathered wood…

Holy Mother of God! Will instantly grasped the severity of his situation: he was tied to the whipping post near Locksley Manor, and he was practically naked, since he was only wearing his braies. His pale features darkened into a deep blush that rivaled his beloved red scarf. Surprisingly, it was still around his neck. A part of him— the part that was still a boy—wanted to cry for help, but the brave and capable man who now governed his boyish impulses took control, and Will opened his eyes.

The sheriff's captain stared at him from the other side of the post, intimidating Will with his fierce glare. Will cowered, but then he recollected Lord Robin's courage at the gallows, and he drew strength from that memory.

"Where is Lady Marian?" demanded Gisborne, his words thickly accented by his native French.

Will was dumbfounded; he hadn't expected this question. Will's perplexed silence was taken as intransigence, and he watched as Gisborne's eyes flicked to the side. He heard a whistling sound, and then his back exploded with pain. For a moment, his vision dimmed, and he couldn't breathe.

"Where is Lady Marian?" Gisborne repeated.

Will panicked; he had no idea where she was, and even if he had been told her hiding place, Lord Robin was counting on him to protect her. "I don't know," Will insisted.

Once again, Will heard the whistling of the whip, and his body tensed in preparation for the next strike. Unfortunately, the second stroke was even more excruciating. Bile rose in his throat, and he frantically swallowed to avoid the humiliation of vomiting on himself.

"Stop lying to me. Where is Robin Hood holding Lady Marian prisoner? In his camp?" Gisborne growled.

With trepidation, Will decided to reveal a little information, and perhaps that would placate this Norman dog. Obviously, the man thought that Robin was keeping Lady Marian in the woods. Just as Gisborne signaled the man with the whip, Will urgently begged, "Wait! Let me explain—"

A triumphant smirk lit Guy's face, and his eyes glittered with satisfaction. "Tell me everything."

Will reluctantly disclosed, "Lady Marian is not living in the woods. Lord Robin took her somewhere safe, but he didn't tell any of us the location because it's a secret."

"When?" hissed Gisborne.

"Months ago," admitted Will. "Last November." Will was astounded to see the other man visibly deflate; Gisborne seemed more concerned about Lady Marian than Robin Hood.

Guy swiftly recovered, and he resumed his interrogation. "Where is the outlaw camp?"

Will's heart sank. Throughout the past year, Will had been enthusiastically stepping into the role of an adult, and now he was confronting the ultimate test of his manhood. Determination filled him, and he was absolutely confident of his path; he would not divulge anything else to the sheriff's brutal captain. Peering into Gisborne's icy blue eyes, he boldly affirmed, "You can flog me, beat me, or torture me unto death, but I will never betray Lord Robin. I am proud to die for such a great man!"

Gisborne's eyes widened in disbelief; then his face darkened with rage. He stomped past Will, and barked, "Give me that whip."

Will peeked over his shoulder and beheld a throng of spectators murmuring disapprovingly. He heard the portentous whine of the lash and braced himself; the pain stole his breath, and his head swam as the world faded. With Gisborne wielding the whip, its bite was sharper. After two additional strokes, Will lapsed into unconsciousness.

❧

When the boy fainted, Guy ceased flogging him and threw the whip down in disgust. He was frustrated and furious. Marian could be anywhere. How would he ever find her? What if Huntingdon had smuggled her to Poitou or Aquitaine? She might be lost to him forever. His heart was rent with worry and grief.

He pivoted to the crowd congregating around the whipping post. When he looked into their faces, he recognized the familiar derisive gazes that had greeted him and his mother whenever they ventured outside their modest home. How dare these people sneer at him? He was their superior in every way! At that moment, he longed to draw his sword and slaughter every single person who presumed to judge him and his mother. That thought made him take a deep breath and briefly close his eyes. His mother had been dead for fifteen years, and he needed to gain better control over his emotions.

As he reflexively put his hand on the hilt of his weapon, an idea occurred to him. Haughtily addressing the group, he announced, "This boy *should* be executed, but I am willing to offer mercy. Robin Hood has something I want. Now I have something that he wants. I know you worthless peasants can get word to him." Guy watched as the people nervously averted their eyes. "Tell Robin Hood to return my sword to me, and I will give him this boy." Squinting at the sky, he vowed, "It is midday. If I do not have my sword by sunset, I will kill him."

Everyone scampered away, except for Leofric and Elvina. The elderly woman fearlessly approached Guy and suggested, "My lord, allow me to tend to him. If he sickens with wound fever, he could die. And if Will dies, Lord Robin will not give you that sword."

A seething Guy scowled at the old woman; she knew that it was forbidden to mention 'Lord Robin.' Nevertheless, he could not dispute the wisdom of her words, so he cautioned her, "The boy must stay tied to the post. You can clean and dress his welts where he stands."

Elvina opened her mouth to argue, but Leofric hastily pulled her away from the dangerous and volatile Sir Guy of Gisborne.

It was mid-afternoon when Guy received an answer from Robin. Secured to an arrow embedded in the front door of Locksley Manor was a note outlining the terms of a parley between Robin and Guy. Guy was instructed to bring Will, but no one else, to the back of the wheelwright's shed, which was adjacent to the stables. Robin would be accompanied by one man of his choosing, and he promised to give Gisborne his sword. The exchange would happen at sunset.

The summer sun was leisurely descending towards the horizon as Gisborne marched Will to the designated meeting place. The boy was stumbling, so Guy grudgingly picked him up and slung him over his shoulder. Upon their arrival, he unceremoniously dropped Will on the ground, and the boy started retching from the pain of his welts as tears rolled down his cheeks.

"Huntingdon," summoned Guy. "I brought the boy. Show yourself." The shed and stables were only a few yards from the forest, and Guy anxiously scanned the tree line until he was startled by a sound behind him.

Robin and Little John emerged from the narrow gap between the shed and the stables. Robin was holding his bow, an arrow at the ready, as he calmly stipulated, "This is how we will proceed. Little John will carry Will, and as soon as they are out of sight, I will return your sword."

Guy reluctantly agreed. Although he resented Robin's self-assured command of the situation, he was beyond desperate to reclaim the sword that linked him to Montlhéry and the French court.

John gently lifted the injured Will, cradling him in his strong arms. The fatherly affection and concern on the big man's face caused Guy's heart to twist in his chest as feelings of yearning and envy fought for supremacy. He had never known the love of a father, and he grieved for what might have been and what would never be. Guy hurriedly glanced away, embarrassed to have such sentimental longings.

When Little John and Will had disappeared into the safety of the trees, Guy coldly eyed Robin and snarled, "My sword. Now."

Robin tilted his head in the direction of the shed. "It's in there, Gisborne. Look into the window, and you will see it."

Guy grumbled in exasperation. The small window was

positioned under the eaves of the thatched roof. It was high enough that even with his great height, he had to raise up on his toes to see inside. With relief, he glimpsed the hilt of his beloved sword gleaming in the shed's low light as it protruded from a burlap sack.

When he looked back at Robin, the outlaw was gone. Guy decided that he would retrieve his sword before leading a contingent of mounted men-at-arms in pursuit of Robin, even though it was a violation of the terms and spirit of the parley.

Guy entered the wheelwright's shed, a disorderly space cluttered with spare wagon parts and tools as well as tack for the horses. Without warning, the door slammed shut behind him, and he heard an ominous thud. He spun around and pushed against the door, only to discover that it was blocked.

"*Merde!*" cried Guy in outraged frustration.

He should have anticipated this. The windows were too small to accommodate his large frame. Unsure of how he would escape, Guy resolved to finally be reunited with his sword. As he approached the bag, he paused with uncertainty when he thought he saw it move. Ignoring his increasing unease, Guy withdrew his sword with a grand flourish, and he gazed lovingly at the elaborate designs etched into its blade.

Suddenly, he was cognizant of a loud buzzing, and his eyes slowly drifted down to the floor. When he had removed his sword, the rough sack had fallen open, exposing the rest of its contents: a broken honey comb and an angry swarm of bees which were surging out of the bag like a plague of Biblical proportions.

᠆ᢒ᠆

Standing just within the tree line, Robin, Little John, and Much listened to Gisborne yelling for his men and cussing in French. Much, who was clutching their horses' reins, asked, "Do you think the soldiers will come to Gisborne's aid?"

Robin was very pleased with the success of his scheme. He

explained, "Gisborne has them hidden on the far side of Locksley Manor, so they can't hear him. Besides, Elvina prepared some honey biscuits earlier today, and she planned to distribute them to Gisborne's men during the parley. They are probably distracted right now."

Much and John chuckled, and Will, who was still cradled in John's arms, stirred. Hearing Gisborne's shouts, he groggily queried, "Are they flogging someone else?"

The other men laughed even harder. Sporting a devilish grin, Robin answered, "No, it's not that. We're merely inflicting a little revenge on Gisborne. I know it's not equivalent to a flogging, but it was the best plan I could devise on such short notice." A glint of mischief in his eyes, Robin snickered, "At long last, Gisborne has his precious sword. Maybe he is screaming for joy."

It was time to leave, so they mounted their horses, and John held Will as they rode to the outlaw camp. Behind them, Gisborne was still howling in pain as he tried to escape Robin's stinging rebuke.

22 August 1189, Sherwood Forest

Robin sat on the banks of the River Trent, absent-mindedly tossing pebbles into the water as it rushed past him. On this day, the anniversary of his father's death and Alfred's murder, he was thinking about Marian. In truth, he was missing her terribly. As weeks became months, Robin's loneliness for Marian only grew sharper and more persistent. It had been almost nine months since he had left her with his uncle Edmund, and Robin often fantasized about their reunion and the marital bliss that he would find in her arms. Tonight, he decided to go to their special meadow and sleep under the great oak that bore their initials—that always made him feel closer to her.

"Lord Robin!"

In a voice tinged with melancholy, Robin joked, "Much, you

have found my secret hideout. I'm glad that the sheriff does not have your tracking skills."

Much hesitated as he inquired, "Do you wish to be alone?"

"No; I welcome your company," Robin honestly replied.

"You miss her a lot, don't you?" Much perceptively observed as he sat next to Robin.

Robin smiled wistfully at his best friend and confided, "More than I ever could have imagined. I assumed that I would eventually grow accustomed to our separation, but I was wrong."

Much proposed, "Why don't you visit her? Everyone is busy with the harvest, and the sheriff sometimes disappears for weeks at a time."

Robin stared at Much in surprise. With a few simple words, he had helped Robin focus his yearnings into a workable strategy. "My friend, that's an excellent idea. The next time Kenric reports that Argentan has gone to London, we will disguise ourselves and travel north. Little John is certainly capable of managing everything for a fortnight." Realizing that he would soon be reunited with Marian, Robin's mood instantly brightened, and he felt euphoric.

They sat in companionable silence for a while until Robin admitted, "I've been thinking about Gisborne's sword."

"The one with the fancy, engraved blade?"

"Yes. He was so obsessed with it. I remember when Argentan noticed that I had Gisborne's sword—do you recall that time when we used the nets?" Robin looked for Much's nod before continuing, "I swear that I thought Gisborne was going to faint. I didn't see that much fear in his eyes when I held my blade against his neck. There is something about that sword..." Robin's voice drifted off.

Much's brow creased in concentration as he considered Robin's words. "What did Baron Embelton think about it?"

An annoyed Robin slapped the ground. "I forgot to show it to him. I was so worried about Marian—she had become so sick during our journey north—and then we were studying those scraps of parchment with Gisborne's poems…This is another reason why we must go to Embelton. Perhaps Uncle Edmund will recognize the heraldry: a rising sun over two *passant* lions."

"And that odd inscription," Much reminded him. "It seemed blasphemous."

Robin agreed as he quoted it from memory: "'From Shadows to Glory: I am Immortal and My Kingdom Awaits.' Argentan is always talking about shadows; he loves his ridiculous riddles. But now I believe that this is a vital clue. I keep thinking that I am overlooking something that is right in front of me."

Just then, Will Scarlet, recovered from his flogging and now a full-time outlaw, jogged up to them and breathlessly announced, "Kenric has arrived from Nottingham. He says he's got important news."

When they joined the assembled outlaws, Kenric eagerly handed Robin a parchment that he had pilfered. He declared, "Copies of this were posted throughout the city of Nottingham, so I stole one from the tavern door."

Robin took it and read aloud. "Alaric de Montabard, Baron de Argentan and Sheriff of Nottingham, hereby proclaims that the vile murderer of Alfred Fitzwalter, Baron of Lenton, has been captured and has given a full confession."

Much whispered in amazement, "Could it be true?"

Robin shrugged and resumed reading, "With a contrite heart, Baron de Argentan regrets the misunderstanding that led to the false conviction of Robin Fitzooth, Earl of Huntingdon. Lord Huntingdon is absolved of all crimes, and the sheriff invites the earl to Nottingham Castle where he will receive an official pardon."

This unexpected news resulted in a chorus of protests from the men.

"It's a trap!" exclaimed Little John.

Robin scoffed, "Of course, it's a trap, but I find it very curious. He must be quite desperate to attempt such an obvious ploy."

The outlaws were still debating the significance of the sheriff's audacious new tactic when Allan-a-dale ran into the camp; he had been sent to Mountsorrel to gather information from the outside world.

"Robin," Allan gasped. He then bent at the waist as he wheezed and coughed, struggling to catch his breath.

Robin had never seen Allan so flustered. He teased, "What is it, Allan? Did you have a big crowd of admirers throwing coins at you in Mountsorrel?"

Allan shook his head vigorously, "No—well, yes actually—people love my ballads, but that's not why I've been running since this morning to get here." When everyone quieted, he dramatically revealed, "King Henry died from a stomach ailment on the 6th of July. He named Richard as his successor, and the coronation will be in London on the 3rd of September."

CHAPTER 13
FATEFUL DECISIONS

The end of September 1189, Tower of London

As soon as Robin arrived at the royal court in London, Richard the Lionheart, the newly-crowned King of England, proclaimed him innocent of Baron Lenton's murder and reinstated his titles and lands with a jaunty wave of his royal hand and a bold flourish of the royal quill.

London was settling back into its normal routine following the coronation celebrations, and the autumn sky rumbled as storm clouds gathered above the city. King Richard and Robin were renewing their long-standing friendship in a brightly illuminated royal chamber extravagantly decorated by the king himself. Two walls were covered with expensive tapestries depicting the Crucifixion of Jesus Christ, the Annunciation of the Virgin, and the Capture of Jerusalem during the First Crusade; the other walls were whitewashed and adorned with heraldry. Elegantly carved chairs stood like sentinels along the table, while a massive, ornate throne imposingly presided over the chamber from a dais in the far corner.

Richard and Robin were slowly drinking wine that glimmered red like the rubies embellishing their jeweled goblets. The king could not abide English wine and had arranged for a supply of his favorites to be delivered from Aquitaine. The rare, exquisite wine was fueling the king's animated ramblings about his triumphant coronation and the amusing foibles of his brother, John. Richard often lamented John's shortcomings, while praising Robin as the younger brother of his heart. John and Robin had been born in the same year, but their dispositions could not have been more different.

Robin tried to listen closely, but his mind was wandering, and it occurred to him that Richard hadn't changed much in the three years since their last meeting. Dressed in a dazzling white tunic embroidered with silver thread and matching chausses, the king still possessed a youthful vigor and had recently marked the 32nd anniversary of his birth. An attractive man of fair complexion, red-gold hair, and an athletic, muscular build, he was so tall that he towered over most of his subjects; Richard joked that he could stride across the bottom of the sea with his head above the waves.

The king's demeanor was typically aloof and proud. However, Robin knew him well and had seen many facets of his personality: his short temper, his frequent flares of high spirits, and even his blasphemous humor. Sometimes, the king ignored royal etiquette, laughing and carousing with his soldiers and courtiers. Regardless of his mood, Richard had a majestic manner about him; an air of command that dictated an immediate surrender to this man who was at the height of his power.

Richard's innate charisma and confidence had been on full display when Robin appeared at court after the grand coronation. With apprehension, he had approached the new king, only to be welcomed by Richard with the same brotherly affection that had always characterized their long acquaintance. Soon afterwards, Robin had revealed to his liege the story of how he became a fugitive in the forest. Trusting Robin whole-heartedly, Richard had declared him innocent without launching an investigation.

Since then, Robin had become the second most discussed topic at court; only the king's Crusade generated more excitement. The dashing Earl of Huntingdon received a constant flow of flattery and admiration from his peers and numerous ladies who adored the handsome and heroic Robin Hood.

"Sultan Saladin and the heathens," grumbled King Richard. His eyes were blazing with wrath at the state of affairs in the Kingdom of Jerusalem, or Outremer, as it was often called. "In the shameful Battle of Hattin, Saracens defeated the Crusader armies, and we must decisively reassert our God-given right to rule the Holy Land." The king's conversation once more focused on his plan to recapture Jerusalem.

King Henry and King Philippe had both responded to the pope's call to arms by taking the cross, but the two kings had lacked the zeal to proceed; they were too consumed with conflicts and threats pertaining to their own domains. In contrast, Richard was impatient to lead the next Crusade, and he began weaving captivating tales about his glorious future conquests in the Holy Land.

Talk of battles promptly seized Robin's complete attention. He firmly believed that, even though the situation in Outremer was dire, Richard would quickly set it to rights.

The king's voice became a crescendo of blustering outrage. "The Saracens destroyed the capability of Christians to wage war in the Holy Land. We lost Jerusalem, Acre, Jaffa, and other towns and villages. This affront cannot remain unanswered: the Holy Land belongs to Christians. Pope Gregory decreed that the fall of the holy city was a punishment for our sins. And it is true."

Robin was stirred by the king's speech. "The pope is holy, and he is never wrong, Sire."

The lion drained the contents of his goblet and slammed it on the table. "It is our duty to reclaim the Holy Land from the infidels. I vowed to liberate Jerusalem when my father was still alive, and now I'm determined to crush Saladin and the Saracens." Vehemence colored his words, and he was scowling fiercely.

"It is the most sacred mission of all Christians," Robin exclaimed;

the potent wine had lowered his inhibitions and intensified his fervency.

"I will reconquer what is rightfully ours," proclaimed a cocksure Richard.

"My liege, you will utterly vanquish Saladin."

The overweening monarch boasted, "It will be the greatest Crusade of two powerful kings and my most magnificent triumph. Of course, my contribution to our victory will be more significant than Philippe's, as his military experience cannot rival mine."

"King Philippe is definitely not a military man," Robin observed.

Richard's booming laugh reverberated throughout the chamber. He insisted, "Philippe is my dear friend, but he will be my apprentice at war."

"Sire, you are the greatest warrior in Christendom," cried Robin admiringly.

The king smiled warmly, appreciating Robin's sincere, if slightly inebriated, enthusiasm. He continued to brag, "I will reclaim the Holy Land and Jerusalem within a year. I will show Saladin the power of a Christian with the heart of a lion, and he will witness the courage and daring of God-loving Christian knights who serve Jesus Christ, the pope, and me. Saladin's troops will flee into the desert at the sound of my roar."

Robin emptied his goblet and set it aside. "We cannot lose the war because we will fight for the Lord, the Holy Father, and for England."

Richard's expression grew serious as he crossed himself. "We will draw strength from our sacred faith in Christ. God is on our side, and He has preordained our ultimate triumph."

"God will guide us to victory," affirmed Robin as he crossed himself.

"I thank God that you will be there with me, Robin. I have very high expectations of you. The strategies you devised while serving me in Aquitaine were brilliant. Your military genius is nearly equal to my own."

Robin beamed to receive such praise from his king. "Thank you, my liege."

"You will be one of my principal generals in this campaign," announced Richard.

Robin was elated by this news. "Sire, I will labor tirelessly to be worthy of your faith in me."

A bright flash of lightning, swiftly followed by a deafening crack of thunder, interrupted their conversation. The sudden downpour that descended upon the Tower of London did more than dampen the previously sodden soil; it drowned Robin's ebullient mood in a tempest-tossed sea of reality by reminding him of his conflicting promises to Richard and Marian.

Like a splintered branch struck by lightning, Robin was fractured by divided loyalties. He was thrilled by the idea of going on Crusade; he was so excited that he was already picturing himself on the deck of a ship threading its way towards an exotic Eastern land. But then, a sharp edge of regret would pierce him. What about his vow to Marian? He had assured her over and over that he would wed her as soon as he was restored to his titles and lands.

These guilty thoughts created uncertainty in his mind, but memories of other oaths long ago made to Richard, and most importantly, to God, seemed to overshadow the words he had spoken to Marian.

And what about his own wishes? Robin had inherited his wealth and privilege, and it was not until he began training in Poitou that he discovered the exhilaration of achieving something on his own. His successes on the battlefields of Aquitaine had only fueled his desire to be celebrated for his own accomplishments.

Going on this Crusade would allow him many opportunities to prove himself to the world. The people of Nottinghamshire had called him 'The Hero of England' for his adventures as Robin Hood.

But success in the Holy Land would earn him the title, 'The Hero of Christendom.'

Robin was convinced that Marian would burst with pride to be married to such a great hero. This Crusade would also make him a better man and more deserving of everything he had: titles, wealth, and most of all, Marian. All he needed to do was help Richard recapture Jerusalem from the infidels. Marian would not only be proud of him—she would love him even more.

Despite these optimistic notions, a cloud of misgiving swirled around his heart, like the fog that often enveloped London. Although the choice between duty and love was not as clear as he would have assumed, he resolved to go on this Crusade: for his king, for God, for Marian, and for himself.

However, the prospect of extending his separation from Marian was almost unbearable. Would she understand the need to postpone their wedding so that he could fulfill his obligations to his liege? His heart tightened in his chest at the possibility that he might disappoint her or bring sorrow to her beautiful, sweet face. But Marian was the most compassionate, intelligent woman in the world, and she would support him. After all, he was her Odysseus, and she was his Penelope.

"Robin, did you hear what I said?"

Robin was embarrassed that he had been lost in his thoughts. He smiled ruefully. "Yes, of course, Sire."

If the king had been offended by Robin's lack of concentration, he didn't comment. Instead, he outlined his strategy. "Robin, you will journey to Aquitaine in a fortnight. I want you to start training my men for the Crusade."

Robin's mind churned with plans for a brief trip to Embelton to visit Marian. A fortnight would give him sufficient time to travel there and back before the king sent him to the continent.

Richard was refilling his goblet as he continued. "In the meantime, I need you to raise money and men-at-arms from the nobility who have gathered in London for the coronation." Grinning playfully, he asserted, "As the Earl of Huntingdon and the famous 'Robin Hood,' many people are eager to meet you. They find your escapades in the woods fascinating. We can use this to get their attention, and then you can persuade them to support my Crusade."

Robin's heart sank; he would have to leave England without seeing Marian first. Obviously, Richard had plans for Robin that would keep him in London until his departure for Aquitaine. His only option was to dispatch a message to Marian tomorrow.

"This Crusade will be an expensive undertaking," explained Richard as he took a hearty swig of wine. "I am implementing a special tax, and I have been working with my advisors to sell whatever can be sold. If I could find a buyer, I would sell London itself."

If Robin had been crestfallen by the realization that he would not be able to visit Marian, he was utterly deflated by the knowledge that the people of the kingdom would have to bear even more burdens. Didn't the king understand that many peasants barely had enough to feed their families and pay the existing taxes? Richard's energetic voice intruded into Robin's somber musings.

"I will also appoint a Council of Regency, consisting of my most trusted nobles who will govern England in my absence. It goes without saying that my mother will be acting as regent." Richard trailed off, collecting his thoughts. "We will spend several months in Aquitaine, where you will assist my cousin, André, in improving the fighting skills of our men. We will take the cross there as well."

"I am honored that you want me to help train your men," Robin tonelessly replied as he gazed at the empty goblet in front of him. He was again distracted by conflicting emotions. The king was bestowing a great distinction upon him, but Robin's enthusiasm for his liege's grand predictions of battlefield glory and impressive conquests had been tempered by the sober reality of how this Crusade would affect not only his relationship with Marian but also the people of England.

Richard was quiet for a few moments as he tried to unravel the reason for the worry so evident on Robin's face. "What is bothering you, my friend?" the king bluntly asked.

Robin was apologetic for his lapse in manners. He confessed, "I am betrothed to Lady Marian of Lenton, and I vowed that we would wed as soon as my good name was restored."

The lion perceptively remarked, "I have heard about the fair Lady Marian of Lenton, may God rest the gentle soul of her father."

"May Lord Alfred rest peacefully," Robin solemnly beseeched.

Robin and Richard crossed themselves and silently gave tribute to Alfred.

As an image of Marian resurfaced in his mind, his sadness retreated, and Robin smiled blissfully. "Marian is clever and kind. I'm sure she will understand."

Richard chuckled good-naturedly. "The future Countess of Huntingdon must be an extraordinary woman, if she has captured the heart of the valiant Robin Hood. You are indeed smitten."

Robin blushed slightly when he realized that his adoration of Marian was so apparent. "I will always strive to be worthy of my Lady Marian, and I believe that our victory in the Holy Land will be a source of immense pride for her. But I fear to begin our future with a broken promise."

Finally identifying the cause of Robin's growing anxiety, the king soothingly proposed, "I have no doubt that such a fine flower of English nobility will perfectly understand that this is not a promise broken, but a promise delayed. Remember, your oath to me was made prior to your betrothal. Be at ease. Neither time nor distance can erode or weaken true love. This short separation will strengthen your feelings for each other."

Robin smiled with gratitude. "I pray you are correct, Sire."

Soon dinner was served, and an orgy of delicious food was brought to the table. The king resumed his boastful tirades about their inevitable victories on the Crusade while he castigated the evils of the world; Richard was convinced that God's wrath had led to the loss of Jerusalem.

Robin feigned interest while he dreamt of Marian. For so many months, he had anticipated their reunion, and now it would be postponed. It was regrettable that the Holy Land was so far away; they would probably spend more time traveling than it would require to defeat the Saracens. He just hoped that the time would pass quickly.

October 1189, Tower of London

In the luxuriously appointed quarters reserved for the distinguished Earl of Huntingdon, a subdued Robin sat nervously clutching a rolled parchment, gazing intently at the seal. It was a letter from Marian, personally delivered by Baron Embelton. At first, Robin had been excited to greet his uncle, but Edmund's somber demeanor had instantly dulled his bright spirits and filled him with foreboding.

Edmund had proceeded to his nephew's chambers upon his arrival in London, and now he sat beside Robin, closely observing him. Also present was one of Robin's best friends, Sir André de Chauvigny. André was a handsome man with chiseled features and a careless smile. At age forty, he had recently become Lord of Châteauroux as a result of his marriage to the widowed heiress, Countess Denise de Deols. After the death of King Henry, Richard had promptly secured this valuable fiefdom for André, his second cousin and a loyal knight with impressive military skills.

Robin sighed loudly, and with an apprehensive heart, he split the seal and unrolled the parchment. As he read, bewilderment clouded his expression; then his face turned marble white as a wave of shock passed through him.

Lord Huntingdon,

I am very pleased that your lordship was happily reunited with our gracious King Richard the Lionheart. I pray that my letter is not taking too much of your precious time which should be dedicated to England, our king, and your glorious Crusade.

I beg of you: do not be concerned about my humble self; I don't deserve the notice of such a devoted and obedient servant of his king as you. I'm doing just fine, and I don't need anything, but I'm eternally grateful for your interest in my welfare.

I release your lordship from your promise to marry me, which you gave my esteemed father and me. With a heavy heart, I question whether you ever truly loved me as you professed several times in the past. If you lied to me, then it is on your conscience.

I will not be waiting for you, and I will destroy our official betrothal document when I next visit Lenton.

I hope and pray that you will find another woman who will be more mindful of your staunch loyalty to England and of your insatiable need for glory.

I wish your lordship all the best in your honorable mission in the Holy Land.

Warm regards, Lady Marian Fitzwalter of Lenton

Robin kept staring at the parchment, shaking his head in disbelief. His devastated heart was stricken with anguish as he struggled to comprehend this cold and sarcastic letter. He had seen many facets of his beloved, but never had he seen an acrid Marian. He could not believe that she had rejected him. He sprang to his feet and paced across the floor like a caged panther.

Questions ceaselessly circled his mind. Was their love really dead? Was their union so irrevocably shattered that the troubadours of Aquitaine would be composing funeral dirges instead of jubilant odes to the story of Robin Hood and his Lady Marian?

A tense silence ensued, threatening to lengthen into a lifetime. Edmund and André worriedly glanced at each other, and Edmund finally asked, "Did Marian end your betrothal?"

The curtain fell from Robin's innermost world. His eyes were full of pain, and his face was unadorned by his usual cheerfulness. He swallowed before admitting in a taut voice, "Marian has notified me that she no longer wishes to be my wife."

"That is impossible," André argued. "You told me that she eagerly accepted your marriage proposal. Are you certain? Perhaps it is a misunderstanding."

Edmund had watched Marian write that letter, and he had endeavored to provide some fatherly advice by cautioning her against making a hasty decision driven by injured pride and resentment. He had not been surprised by Robin's enthusiasm for the Crusade, and he was debating whether he should reveal more about the reasons for Marian's sharp words.

Regaining control over his emotions, Robin paused near the window and surveyed the darkening sky. "Church bells will not be ringing for my wedding to Marian," he commented.

The day was ending, and the clouds rolling along the horizon heralded a storm. Robin pivoted and eyed André, a sardonic smirk on his lips. "Women are as mutable as the clouds blowing across the sky. We men must acknowledge this truth."

André stood up and approached him. "You would put men at the mercy of a woman's whim? Perish such thoughts! If women are clouds, then men are the wind. We are responsible for the protection and care of women. And if men are the wind, then you are a whirlwind."

Robin frowned in confusion at the metaphor.

André ventured to explain, "Robin, you are a whirlwind because you are England's hero, and every sensible woman desires you. You have wealth, a title, and the friendship of the king. All you have to do is give a woman a look or a wink, and she will be yours for a night or a lifetime." He snickered. "Years ago, at the courts of Aquitaine and Poitou, women swarmed around you like bees to honey. Do not pine for one distant flower when you are surrounded by a garden of delights."

Robin grinned feebly as he attempted to jest. "As Earl of

Huntingdon, it is a challenge to elude all the women who aspire to become my countess. Women are drawn to my title and wealth like moths to a flame."

Edmund was disturbed by the increasingly flippant nature of their banter and sought to refocus Robin's attention. "Robin, you need to meet with Marian."

Robin swung his gaze to Edmund. With trepidation, he asked, "Uncle, has Marian met another?"

Edmund asserted, "Nothing of the sort, Robin."

"Are you sure?" Robin needed this reassurance as much as he needed his next breath.

An enigmatic smile crept onto Edmund's face. "Marian still loves you, Robin. Now more than ever."

Robin threw his hands up in aggravation. "But she ended our betrothal."

"And what reaction did you expect? You broke her heart when you broke your promise to marry her after being reinstated to your title and lands," accused Edmund. "If you don't mind telling me, what did you write her?"

Robin returned to his chair and disclosed, "I wrote Marian that I would join the Crusade and would be absent from England for a year or so. I told her that I have an obligation to England and my king. Also, I explained that this was an opportunity for me to test my military prowess in an all-out campaign against a truly formidable foe instead of the relatively minor skirmishes that I fought in Aquitaine." He scoffed bitterly, "I was confident that Marian would support me. Did she even try to understand my position? I'm a man of duty, not some pampered, effeminate boy who stays at home and fulfills his oath of vassalage by sending men-at-arms as surrogates."

André also sat back down. Looking between Edmund and Robin, he declared, "Men who don't follow their king into battle are cowards."

Edmund sighed; as a young man, he had followed King Henry

with the same exuberance, and Robin's fervor was an echo of his own youthful zeal. He conceded, "I know that you are honor and duty bound to go to war."

"Exactly," Robin and André chorused, their heads bobbing in synchronized agreement.

"Robin, did you tell Marian that you *want* to go to war?" Edmund anxiously inquired.

Robin gave another nod. "Of course, I did; I was very frank with her."

A disheartened Edmund admonished, "My intrepid and honorable nephew, you have nobody to blame but yourself for Marian's rejection. You know her well, and you should have foreseen how she would respond to such a pronouncement from you. You made a fatal mistake by informing her that you want glory more than you want to wed her. Did you really think that she would be pleased by this?"

An indignant Robin countered, "It's not just glory. Holy war is the most sacred duty of every God-fearing, Christian knight. I am answering the call of the Lord, the pope, the king, and my conscience. We must reclaim Jerusalem."

Edmund climbed to his feet and walked over to the table in the farthest corner, where he had left his travel bag. He rummaged through his belongings until he located a black velvet pouch. Retracing his steps back to Robin, he divulged, "Marian requested that I give this to you."

Robin dipped his fingers into the pouch and extracted the silver ring that he had given to her. He blanched and gaped at it in shock. Sending this ring back to him was unexpected, cruel, and beyond his imagination.

He stared fixedly at the ring. An ebony veil of melancholy enveloped Robin, and despair burrowed into his heart and soul. A sense of chasmal loss—the loss of his only true love and their future together—was so profound that for a moment, he couldn't breathe. Abruptly, a surge of intense, righteous fury overwhelmed him. In

Robin's judgment, returning this ring was so disrespectful that it bordered on contempt. How could she treat him in such a manner? How could she so utterly disregard *his* feelings?

Robin's mouth twisted into a grimace, and his usually merry features morphed into something almost feral. The unappeasable ferocity of his temper pushed him to explode. "Marian has crossed a line. This ring belonged to my mother, and she dares to hurl a part of my legacy into my face? Her behavior is shameful."

"Calm down, Robin," Edmund begged.

"My friend, settle yourself," advised André.

Robin glowered at the two of them and fumed, "She has evidently forgotten that I am a man and a knight. She cannot force me to stay in England merely because it is her wish to always have me by her side." Holding the ring tightly in his fist, he lowered his voice. "As God is my witness, I love Marian with all my heart, but I will not bow to her whims or submit to her manipulations."

Edmund scrutinized Robin, his face impenetrable. "Is this your final decision? Are you choosing your pledge to Richard over your vow to Marian?"

Robin glanced away as his love for Marian and his avid sense of duty warred for dominance in his heart. But she had spurned him, and now there was nothing that tethered him to England. "I cannot ignore my duty," he averred.

Edmund forewarned him, "You might die in Outremer and never see Marian again."

A startled Robin looked at Edmund as if his uncle had lost his mind. "I won't die. I am a skilled warrior, and I am fighting for a righteous cause."

"The king is depending on you, Robin," intoned André.

Edmund insisted, "Robin, come with me to Embelton and talk to Marian."

Even though it was impossible, Robin longed to be reunited with Marian. Yearning was fleetingly reflected in his eyes before his expression hardened into bitterness. His nostrils flared, and his temper spiked yet again. "I refuse to meet with Marian. She is so blinded by anger that she will be deaf to my words. I will marry her after my return; by then she will be thinking more clearly, and she will be proud of my triumphs on this Crusade and appreciate that I made the right choice."

Hoping to reason with his nephew, Edmund implored, "Robin, listen—"

"This is my final decision. This conversation is over, and I wish to be alone." Robin rudely interrupted. He resumed pacing until the sound of the door latch signaled that he was alone.

Uncurling his fingers, Robin stared in dazed fascination at the ring in his palm. In the torchlight, the silver gleamed like a blade, and he felt that Marian had pierced his heart by annulling their betrothal. He kissed the ring reverently and held it to his lips. Her rejection had turned his world to cinders, but this silver circle would forever be a symbol of Robin's eternal devotion to her. Memories of his beloved would never be completely obliterated from his mind, but he had to restrain his grief; otherwise, it would become the determinant of his existence.

Following a sleepless night and a morning spent in prayer, Edmund returned to Robin's quarters, full of resolve. He would break his promise to Marian and explain everything to Robin. Tapping on the heavy wooden door, Edmund was greeted by a servant who notified him that Robin and Much had left for Dover at dawn. He was probably already on a ship bound for Normandy. Edmund realized that his broken-hearted nephew had simply run away, and he made plans to travel home at once.

The end of October 1189, Nottinghamshire

Rain had forced Sir Ferrand Crawford and his men to take shelter overnight at Locksley Manor. Crawford, the new Sheriff of Nottingham, was frustrated by the delay and impatient to secure the castle, so he had sent his captain and a dozen men-at-arms to brave the inclement weather and proceed to Nottingham before Argentan and his henchmen could escape. When the captain returned early the next morning, he reported that Argentan, Gisborne, and Payen had fled several days ago. A disappointed Crawford then commanded his men to march to Nottingham Castle.

The cortege was slowly moving along the slushy roads with Sir Ferrand surrounded by his personal guard. People lined the road, clapping and shouting boisterously. Astonished to see so many welcoming him, Crawford calmed his skittish horse and gaped at the peasants in wonder. As his initial amazement receded, he grinned widely and waved.

When they entered the castle's bailey, it was difficult to navigate through the assembled populace. Crawford's soldiers urged the audience to make way, and the crowd obediently parted.

The new sheriff halted near the front steps of the stone keep and dismounted. A hush fell over the courtyard, and everyone's attention was riveted on Crawford. He was a middle-aged man with grizzled hair and a short tuft of silvery beard. Despite his age, he appeared fit and strong as he briskly strode halfway up the stairs where the multitude could hear and see him better.

With a sincere smile, Sir Ferrand addressed them in perfect, unaccented English. "Good subjects of King Richard the Lionheart, I was appointed Sheriff of Nottingham by our king and sent here to govern the shire and arrest Baron de Argentan. Our liege knows about your sufferings under the tyranny of the former sheriff." He paused to let his words sink in. "Argentan's regime of brutal violence and injustice has ended!" The throng roared with approval, and Crawford was delighted by their enthusiastic response to his speech.

"Long live King Richard!" exclaimed an ecstatic Allan, his gaze fixed on the sheriff as he stood with Little John and the other outlaws in the crush of people.

"Long live King Richard!" echoed the crowd.

Robin's band of men had journeyed to Nottingham after Kenric reported that a new sheriff would soon arrive at the castle. Their mood was buoyant, and they started making silly jokes at which they all laughed for no particular reason. John scowled at them, irritated by their frivolous gaiety.

Crawford was euphoric to receive such a greeting. He gestured for silence, and in a loud voice, he continued, "King Richard has declared Robin Fitzooth, the Earl of Huntingdon, innocent of Baron Lenton's murder, and he restored his titles and lands."

At this news, the gathering exploded with thunderous cheers. Crawford could see the tremendous popularity of Robin Hood and the people's great love for him.

"Robin Hood is our hero!"

"Lord Robin didn't kill Baron Lenton!"

"Long live Robin Hood!" Allan's voice resonated, and the other outlaws joined in the clamor.

Only a thoughtful John was quiet, as foreboding crept into his consciousness. John's many years of living in the wilds of Sherwood had given him a keen sense of the world around him. In the forest, predators had an uncanny ability to remain hidden until the moment of attack. Survival in the woods often meant anticipating threats that could not be seen or heard; perils that had to be felt along the hairs on the back of a man's neck.

Meanwhile, Crawford and his men were astounded as they observed the crowd. They knew of Robin's fame amongst the peasantry, but they still struggled to grasp the mystique of Robin Hood—a noble outlaw helping the poor and standing against tyranny with the assistance of his band of merry men. Besides, they had all met Robin in London where he was a dashing courtier, and it seemed impossible that this young man—a wealthy earl and the king's favorite—could be the hero of the many ballads circulating in England.

As the cheering subsided, the new sheriff resumed his speech. "The men who followed Lord Huntingdon and opposed Baron de Argentan will not be prosecuted by King Richard. All of the men from Sherwood Forest have been pardoned by our benevolent and just king." Then he unrolled a parchment and read the official pardons for each of the outlaws.

The people burst into noisy acclamations. All of the former outlaws applauded and laughed while John warily surveyed the courtyard.

An animated Allan beamed at his smiling friends as they gave each other good-natured nudges and backslaps. Then Allan began to sing one of his most popular ballads:

Our great hero, we praise and honor Robin Hood!
A devoted lord, he humbly lived among the forest men.
A valiant knight, he merrily ruled vast Sherwood.

Our great bane, we curse and scorn Sheriff de Argentan!
A cruel lord, he nested in a tower above the trees.
A lawless sheriff, he harshly ruled our fair Nottingham.

Our brave hero, we summoned him with a loud lament!
A fierce champion, he fought the wicked sheriff.
Our own St. George, Robin Hood slew the wily serpent.

The people joyfully recited the verses, while Crawford listened attentively, smiling and pleased to see the populace so happy.

"Long live King Richard and Robin Hood!" Allan cried.

"Long live Robin Hood!" repeated the crowd.

"Long live me!" proclaimed a familiar voice, mocking and

deep, in highly accented English. "Long live the only rightful ruler of Nottinghamshire."

CHAPTER 14
HEARTS IN DARKNESS

25 October 1189, Nottingham Castle

"Long live me!" proclaimed a familiar voice, mocking and deep, in highly accented English. "Long live the only rightful ruler of Nottinghamshire."

An anxious stillness spread throughout the courtyard, as Crawford pivoted and beheld Alaric de Montabard, Baron de Argentan, at the top of the stairs, where he was leaning casually against the massive doors of the keep. Guy of Gisborne and Tancred de Payen stood on either side of him, tensely monitoring the crowd.

As usual, Argentan was dressed in austere, somber clothing. He regarded Crawford with a contemptuous, triumphal gaze and announced, "The reign of Sir Ferrand Crawford has ended before it could begin."

Panic clutched the hearts of the people, while Crawford frowned in confusion. Abruptly, he recognized that this man was the nefarious former sheriff, and his puzzlement morphed into outrage. "You speak treason; the king himself appointed me sheriff."

Argentan smiled nastily. "The king granted Prince John dominion over Nottinghamshire, and Prince John has decreed that I am sheriff."

"I am Sheriff of Nottingham!" roared Crawford, his hand on the hilt of his sheathed sword.

"I would rather die of anything but boredom," chanted Argentan smugly. Pointing at the new sheriff, he taunted, "And you are boring me, you soon-to-be sheriff of the underworld."

In the midst of the terrified assembly, Kenric was the first to find his voice. "It is Argentan!" he shrilled. "He has returned to Nottingham!"

Crawford immediately drew his weapon. Looking at the captain of his guard, he ordered, "Seize Baron de Argentan. He is a traitor to England and King Richard."

With a deliberate flourish, the captain unsheathed his sword and aimed it at a stunned Crawford. More of his soldiers joined their captain, and the new sheriff found himself in a circle of his erstwhile guards.

Sheriff Crawford leveled a withering glare at his captain and simply asked, "Why?" The impudent man smirked without replying.

Argentan cheerfully declared, "Sir Ferrand, I congratulate you on hiring these astute men. They wisely chose to align themselves with the strongest and wealthiest Sheriff of Nottingham. That would be me—not you. I have bought their fealty, and now they serve me and my liege lord, Prince John."

Unbeknownst to Crawford, when his men had arrived at the castle the preceding day, Argentan had surreptitiously observed them from the shadowy balcony that overlooked the great hall. The men had been in awe of the keep's luxurious furnishings. Argentan had listened with glee as the men grumbled resentfully that they had been sent to Nottingham in pouring rain while Crawford enjoyed the warm hospitality of Locksley Manor. When he heard the captain bitterly grouse about the unfairness of being passed over for a better post in London, he greeted the weary, rain-soaked men with a bag of silver and an extravagant feast in the great hall. The unscrupulous captain and his men had scarcely hesitated before accepting Argentan's generous bribe.

With the support of Crawford's men, Argentan's victory was assured. He sneered, "Sir Ferrand, it is time for Gisborne to make you choke on your own blood."

Guy ripped his blade from its scabbard and hastened down the steps to challenge the older man.

"Those men who are loyal to me, prepare to fight," appealed the new sheriff, his eyes darting from man to man. "We must defend King Richard's sovereignty."

Crawford's few remaining trustworthy men-at-arms rushed to assist their master, and the battle commenced. The clanging of swords and the cries of frightened people echoed within the courtyard.

As Gisborne and Crawford began dueling in earnest, Little John yelled, "Retreat to the gate!"

John's booming voice had carried across the bailey, and Argentan screeched, "The forest bandits are here! I want them alive." He then directed Payen to lead a group of men into the crowd and arrest the outlaws.

The wide, broad steps of the keep became a bloody battlefield as men who were previously brothers-in-arms fought to the death. In the courtyard below, men and women were pushing and colliding with each other as they surged towards the portcullis, which was still open.

In the heart of the dreadful horde, Little John, Allan, and Will were separated from their friends. They could see the others trapped in the writhing throng, and Kenric waved wildly at them as though he were drowning in the swift currents of the River Trent. Suddenly, Payen and his soldiers appeared, and everyone fell back as the outlaws were promptly surrounded and apprehended.

Allan and Will were frantic to save their friends, but John knew that the only prudent option was to flee. The big man prayed that he would be able to devise a rescue plan later as he grabbed Allan and Will and hauled them to the gate.

∽

Guy lunged at Crawford and savagely growled, "You will never be sheriff. Surrender now."

Crawford retorted, "Argentan is committing treason." He deflected a strike and revealed, "I remember Hugh of Gisborne. He was a traitor, and you are following in his shameful footsteps."

"My father was loyal to William of Blois, the true King of England. He was a patriot!" bellowed Guy as he swung his sword in a quick succession of assaults, aiming for his adversary's neck and face.

Crawford was no match for Guy's youth and vigor, and he was rapidly tiring as he strove to parry Guy's vicious blows. The new sheriff's despair at the hopelessness of his situation transformed into fury as he shouted at Gisborne, "A father and son: two wretched, dishonorable traitors!"

Chaos continued to reign in the courtyard, as the people fled through portcullis. The sentries were befuddled and uncertain; Argentan was screaming at them to secure the gate while the sheriff sent by the king had stipulated that it be kept open.

While Payen was instructing his men to escort the captured outlaws to the dungeons, the new sheriff was losing his duel. Crawford's blows were deftly blocked by Gisborne who responded with formidable counterstrikes. The older man's strength was fading as he sidestepped and attempted another thrust. Guy parried and countered, managing to shallowly slice Crawford's arm. The minor injury distracted Crawford, and Guy plunged his sword into him.

Crawford, impaled by Guy's blade, blinked in disbelief and groaned, "A damned traitor...just like your father." A trickle of blood seeped from one corner of his mouth and dribbled down his chin, and then he went still.

"My father was a hero," insisted Guy in a hushed voice, visibly affected by Crawford's denunciations. He withdrew his weapon with a grim scowl as the lifeless body of the new sheriff slumped to the smooth stone steps beneath his feet.

Even though Guy had triumphed, he felt utterly defeated. Crawford had displayed remarkable courage in facing a much younger rival, and Guy's guilty conscience trembled. He snatched the dead man's cloak and wiped the blood from his beloved sword before sheathing it and surveying the bailey. The melee had ended, and the crowd had dispersed. All of the men faithful to Crawford had been slain, and their bodies littered the area around him.

Searching for the sheriff and Payen, Guy learned about the arrest of the outlaws, and his spirits instantly lifted. *Marian!* It was likely that one of them knew where Huntingdon had taken her. He would interrogate these men and compel them to talk. His heart brightened with hope.

When Guy approached the cell where the outlaws were being held, he froze in stunned dismay. Nearly a dozen men lay motionless on the stone floor. One of them was moaning, his body shuddering in the throes of death.

A bewildered Guy assessed the scene and cautiously asked, "What happened to them?"

Payen, his eyes alight with giddy enthusiasm, stepped forward and excitedly disclosed, "Lord de Argentan gave me these forest rats so that I could test my new poison. It is a great success." He tittered malevolently as his gaze oscillated between the corpses and Guy. "Look at how it exterminates so beautifully."

Argentan emerged from a murky corner. "It is such an exquisite poison. It is like Circe's cup of enchantment: those who drink it feel a pleasant drowsiness before a web of ruin ensnares them." He pointed at the convulsing man. "Behold this dirty peasant: he is young and robust. Yet, he is wilting like an irksome weed that has been plucked from its place in the sun and left to wither in the shadows."

"He was not as thirsty as the others," observed Payen. "But death will claim him soon."

"Tancred, your father would have been so proud of you," Argentan commended, an affectionate gleam in his dark eyes. "You are an artist. The troubadour of apothecaries!"

Guy gulped for air as nausea stirred in the pit of his stomach and revulsion overcame him. His brow creased, and his hands became clammy. "My lord, I assumed that you were going to make an example of them with a public execution."

"That is true," confirmed Argentan. "But then I decided to give them to my dear Tancred."

Payen bowed low to the sheriff. "Thank you, Lord de Argentan." He studied the dying outlaw whose limbs were feebly twitching. "It is a pity that three of these forest parasites eluded capture. I am sure they were thirsty too. This sweet poison quenches your thirst for all eternity."

"Poisoning is not honorable!" Guy was so shaken and full of disgust that he recklessly divulged his private thoughts.

Argentan cackled venomously. "When did you become such a paradigm of virtue, Gisborne? What do *you* know of honor? A traitor's son preaching about honor. You are not honorable; you are merely weak—like a useless, pathetic woman. Your newfound righteousness is highly amusing, but you cannot compete with the entertainment of watching Robin Hood's merry men die from Payen's poison."

The remaining outlaw whimpered, and Guy hurriedly advanced to crouch next to him, demanding harshly, "Where is Lady Marian? Where did Robin Hood take her?"

Behind him, Guy could hear the sheriff and Payen snickering; they never tired of ridiculing his love for Marian.

The man's lips quivered, and he hoarsely declared, "Kenric... My name is Kenric..."

Guy gripped Kenric's shoulders and shook him. "Where is Marian?" he repeated.

Glaring at Guy hatefully, Kenric uttered his final words. "You, Argentan, and Payen are soulless beasts. God is all-seeing and all-knowing, and you will not escape His wrath." Then he closed his eyes and drew his last, ragged breath.

Gisborne scrambled to his feet awkwardly and staggered back, as if he had been buffeted by invisible fists. Driven by fear and horror, he stormed out of the cell and ran to the rickety stairs that led away from the sheriff's abyss of hell and towards the faint light of a waning autumnal sun. Guy knew that God was somewhere above the sky, seated upon His judgment throne and sentencing him to spend eternity serving demons like the sheriff. Gasping, he stumbled into his quarters, where he dropped heavily onto his knees and buried his face into his hands.

Guy was seized by an overwhelming dread, and he feared that his service to his master had irrevocably darkened his heart and condemned his soul.

20 July 1191, Crusader camp, City of Acre, Kingdom of Jerusalem

After twenty-one months of delays, distractions, and near-disasters, Robin had finally tasted his first victory in the Holy Land. King Richard had conquered Acre in 35 days, decisively ending a siege that had begun two years prior to their arrival. Robin was ebullient, and he had no doubt that Acre would be the first of many such triumphs.

The king was meeting with his most trusted commanders as they reported on the subjugation of the city. Sir André de Chauvigny happily announced, "The churches have been re-consecrated, and the royal palace is ready to accommodate your wife and sister, my liege. King Philippe will be lodging in the mansion of the Templars."

This news greatly pleased Richard, who effused, "I am impatient to be reunited with my bride. Perhaps my son will be conceived here, in the Holy Land. It is very likely that, by the time of his birth, my son will be born in Jerusalem—maybe even Bethlehem. I cannot imagine a more fortuitous beginning for my future heir."

The men chuckled indulgently at Richard's impious remarks. The king was unreservedly ecstatic to be free of his long-standing betrothal to King Philippe's sister and wed to a woman of his own choosing and not his father's. Robin mused that an argument could be made that Richard had instead married a woman of his *mother's* choosing, as marriage to Berengaria provided an important alliance with the Kingdom of Navarre on the southern border of Queen Eleanor's beloved Aquitaine.

Sir William de l'Etang, a popular, esteemed knight, gave his account next. "We have captured nearly 3,000 prisoners, and we've separated the high-ranking men from the common soldiers. However, the Saracens have torched much of the land adjoining Acre, and there's not enough food for both our men and these prisoners."

At this news, Richard waved his hand dismissively. "Saladin has agreed to pay a ransom for these men within thirty days. Feed them half-rations on alternate days." The king's eyes then slid expectantly to Robin.

Robin dutifully advised, "Sire, security around the breached walls has been re-established." He hesitated, realizing that it was time to broach the king's least favorite subject. "Regarding your personal security, I have replaced the kitchen staff with our own people. All the guards at the palace will be men whom I know and trust."

Richard bellowed heartily and teased Robin, "You are worse

than my mother. Or my new wife. You have become quite the mother hen."

All the men laughed at Richard's protests, but Robin was unperturbed. He reminded the king, "We still do not know who poisoned the de Châteauneuf sisters before we left Poitou. That poisoning was undoubtedly an attempt on *your* life; the tainted English wine had been specifically sent to you. It is only your dislike of such wine, and the girls' curiosity about it, that spared your life."

Sobering as he recalled the suffering endured by the fatally poisoned young women, Richard conceded, "My love of Poitevin wine saved my life."

Robin concurred. "We must remain vigilant." Moving to a more pleasant topic, he apprised, "I will start the preparations for our march to Jerusalem. I need to explain your plans to King Philippe's commanders as well as the Templars and Hospitallers."

"Philippe and his cousin, the Duke of Burgundy, are due to arrive at any moment," responded Richard. Aggravated, he sighed noisily. "I have devised a brilliant strategy, but I must consult with Philippe, an amateur distinctly lacking in skill on the battlefield. Thankfully, Burgundy is a talented military man."

Sir Baldwin de Béthune had not yet spoken, and he took this opportunity to disclose some distressing news. "Sire, I'm hearing ugly gossip from the French knights. They are blaming your belated arrival for the death of Philip of Alsace, the Count of Flanders. He died without an heir, so there is considerable anxiety amongst his vassals. And..." His voice faded into uneasy silence.

"Tell me everything," Richard frostily instructed.

Baldwin reluctantly confessed, "They are criticizing your refusal to partition Cyprus with King Philippe and grumbling that your decision to winter in Sicily has forced us to fight in the blistering heat of summer. Also, the French are claiming that you have been deceitful and uncooperative towards King Philippe."

Richard exploded in outrage. "Philippe is spreading these

rumors. His temper tantrums and meddling have caused me nothing but headaches and delays. It is like dealing with a child who has never been denied."

All the men murmured in agreement, indignant and frustrated on Richard's behalf.

When the group had quieted, Richard commanded, "Robin, I want you to stay with me; everyone else is dismissed. We will meet with Philippe and the Duke of Burgundy in order to resolve these disputes."

Presently, Robin and Richard were alone in the tent as they waited for Philippe. The king reminisced, "I remember Philippe accusing my father of treachery, and now he is circulating the same lies against me. I suspect that is his scheme: to divide and conquer. But my eyes are at last open, and his manipulations will no longer sway me."

As Robin contemplated the king's words, he recollected his first encounter with King Philippe. The French monarch had scornfully called him Robin Hood. It had been an unanticipated and disconcerting moment. Had Allan's ballads been performed at the French court? That seemed unlikely. Or, was this proof of a connection between Baron de Argentan and the French court?

Furthermore, there was something about Philippe that was troubling. When interacting directly with Richard, he was usually civil, although a bit aloof. But when Richard's attention was diverted away from Philippe, Robin frequently noticed glittering, unambiguous hate shining in the eyes of the French king as he observed the King of England. It was unsettling, even disturbing, in its naked fervor.

Cautiously, Robin mentioned a subject he had long pondered: his suspicions that the Sheriff of Nottingham had been in contact with King Philippe. "Sire, do you recall the Norman baron who was Sheriff of Nottingham? The one who falsely prosecuted me for murder?"

Richard was briefly perplexed by the apparent change of topic but promptly recovered. He acknowledged, "Vaguely. However, I sold that post to another man after my coronation. What was the baron's name?"

"Alaric de Montabard, Baron de Argentan," replied Robin.

The royal brow frowned in concentration, and Richard admitted, "I am familiar with the Barony of Argentan, but not the de Montabard name." The lion shrugged. "I don't remember anyone from this family, but it signifies nothing. Argentan is a small fiefdom, and I have numerous vassals who have sworn fealty to me. Of course, I cannot remember everyone."

Robin fell into thoughtfulness. "I wonder if this family is somehow affiliated with the French court. There is something that I saw—perhaps it is meaningful; perhaps not."

"What did you see?" Richard probed.

Robin divulged, "I saw some scraps of parchment which indicated that Argentan was communicating with the French court, possibly even King Philippe himself."

Shaking his head in disbelief, the king insisted, "It would be most surprising if a minor vassal from an inconsequential barony had ties to the French court. Are you certain?"

"I cannot be sure, my liege. Yet, my watchful heart warns me that it might be important. Only time will tell." A gloomy wariness pervaded Robin's mind, but he did not say anything else on the matter.

Soon, a page heralded the entrance of King Philippe and his courtiers, and Richard declared his intention to restrict the meeting to Robin, Philippe, and Hugh, the Duke of Burgundy. While the rest of the French entourage left Richard's tent, Robin studied King Philippe with interest.

Philippe, a man of above-average height, was only a few months older than Robin. He had lost weight since disembarking at Acre and succumbing to an illness, so his ornately embroidered dark blue tunic hung loosely on his lithe frame. His skin was pale and unblemished, and he was undeniably handsome despite his prominent nose and somewhat long face. There was a regal aura about Philippe, and there was also an air of cunning and guile which seemed to be intensified by his sharp, ever-penetrating gaze.

The King of France haughtily stared at him, and Robin hurriedly glanced away when he realized that he had been gawking at Philippe longer than appropriate.

Richard explained the plan for moving the army south. They would advance along the coast in a tight formation with the mounted knights safeguarded by the infantry. The fleet would carry their supplies and siege engines, hugging the coastline and sailing parallel to the army.

Hugh of Burgundy had many intelligent questions, primarily relating to the challenge of maintaining the infantry's configuration during the march. He also described the difficulty of restraining the knights; they were susceptible to taunts from the enemy, and the Saracen light cavalry often lured them out of formation. Once the knights were drawn away from their protected position, they were swiftly surrounded and defeated. It had been a recurring problem.

Robin enjoyed discussing strategy with Burgundy and Richard, and he was relieved that King Philippe was strangely quiet. Maybe the French monarch would simply defer to Richard's approach. When Burgundy asked about the timing of the campaign, Richard reminded him that they must await the ransom for the prisoners; it would be at least a fortnight before the march could commence.

Richard then addressed Philippe, "We need to show a united front to both our men and the Saracens. Therefore, I propose that we sign a pact pledging to remain here for either three years or until Jerusalem is reconquered, whichever comes first."

Robin watched as all the blood drained from Philippe's face. He was evidently horrified by the idea of making such an oath.

The silence in the tent stretched uncomfortably, as Richard

continued his relentless scrutiny of Philippe, while Robin and Hugh of Burgundy observed the two men with bated breath. Finally, Richard demanded a reply. "Well? Tomorrow we could stand together and proclaim this covenant to our men."

Philippe's eyes narrowed in a mixture of annoyance, anger, and the hateful gleam that Robin had seen so many times in the past. The French king lifted his chin, and defiantly averred, "I will give no such oath."

"Surely, you recognize that this pledge will inspire our men while demoralizing the enemy," suggested Richard.

Rudely ignoring his most powerful vassal, Philippe's glare veered to Burgundy. "Are you satisfied with this plan for the march south?"

Hugh of Burgundy's eyes nervously flitted between the two kings, and he conceded, "Yes, Sire, it is a brilliant strategy."

Philippe scoffed, "Of course, it is." No longer attempting any pretense of politeness, he announced, "We are leaving to attend to other business; I will enter the city later today and reside with the Templars." He started to follow Burgundy, who was already exiting the tent.

Before Philippe could depart, Richard called after him and inquired, "Philippe, what word have you received from Baron de Argentan?"

An irritated Philippe spun around to confront Richard and Robin. He sneered, "He is not your concern–" Suddenly, Philippe's eyes widened in absolute shock, and he glanced at Robin. The King of France hastily regained control over his emotions and admonished Richard, "I do not know this man of whom you speak. This is a *Norman* barony, no? Why do you speak such nonsense to me?" Philippe again glowered at Robin before pivoting and stomping from the tent.

Robin and Richard stared at each other in amazement. Richard spoke first. "That was quite informative, Robin. Did you notice his reaction?"

Robin nodded. "He damn near answered you. If he truly did not know Argentan, he would have been confused and said as much."

Richard concurred. "And consider this: he immediately looked at *you,* as if he knew about your association with Argentan, even though I did not mention you."

It was hard to fathom, but the King of France was not only acquainted with Baron de Argentan, he also knew that the man had a connection to Robin Hood.

22 July 1191, the Royal Palace, City of Acre

Robin stood quietly with André, William, and Baldwin. A delegation from the French king, led by the Duke of Burgundy, had just arrived for an audience with King Richard.

The men were ashen-faced and hesitant as Hugh of Burgundy cleared his throat and recited his memorized speech. "Sire, we have come to notify you that King Philippe's physicians are very worried about his recent grave sickness and persistent ill health. His kingdom and his many vassals are dependent upon his benevolent and wise rule. Now that the conquest of Acre has been accomplished, the King of France will begin his journey home within a fortnight."

The men anxiously awaited Richard's response; some dreaded an explosion of his legendary temper, while those closest to the king, including Robin, suspected that Richard would welcome the opportunity to assume sole command of the Crusade.

Richard rose and surveyed the men. "Are you departing as well?"

Hugh of Burgundy's courteous reply was accented by an unmistakable note of eagerness. "King Philippe has directed me and my men to stay here. With your permission, we would be honored to continue this Crusade under your leadership."

A smile tugged at the corners of Richard's mouth. The willingness of these men to serve him was a slap at Philippe. Moreover, with so many of his top military men remaining in Outremer, Philippe's ability to cause mischief in disputed territories back home would be hampered. In a spirited and faintly amused voice, Richard decreed, "It will be a shame and a disgrace if King Philippe leaves without completing our sacred mission. However, if he finds himself ailing, and he's afraid that he might die here, then we shall submit to his will."

20 August 1191, the Royal Palace, City of Acre

A funereal silence reigned in the quarters shared by King Richard's commanders. The four men, Robin, André, Baldwin, and William, were seated on cushions around a Saracen-style low table. It was late, but no one was thinking of slumber. The table was laden with platters of fruit and cheese, and their goblets were filled with wine, but no one was thinking of eating or drinking.

Robin reached up and wearily rubbed his face as he wondered if he had ever felt so fatigued, yet so reluctant to sleep. Would he dream of Marian or rivers of blood?

An unexpected realization dawned. Before this day, if someone had asked him when he had left childhood behind, he would have opined that it was when he became a squire in Poitou at age thirteen. If they had asked when he had become a man, he would have suggested that it was when he attained knighthood at eighteen. Or perhaps, when he became the Earl of Huntingdon at the age of twenty.

But now, he would answer that his childhood had ended today on a small hill near the City of Acre named Ayyadieh. In this accursed place, his mind, his heart, and his very soul had been permanently altered in such a way that his life would be forever divided into two chapters: his life before he commanded his soldiers to decapitate almost 3,000 unarmed men, and his life as a man who, although acting on the orders of his king, considered himself guilty of such an atrocity.

Robin closed his eyes, not wishing to see anything, only to discover that his mind was teeming with images of the day's bloody events. Maybe if he focused his thoughts on Marian, he could forget these other macabre visions.

A slow, dazzling smile intended only for him. Soft lips pressed against his; the honeyed warmth of her mouth welcoming him.

Men on their knees, their lips moving in hushed prayers as they awaited certain death.

Silky strands of long, flaxen hair shining in the glow of the hunting lodge's firelight.

The fountain of blood that always spurted from a man's body after decapitation.

Fathomless green eyes full of both gentle longing and heated, passionate hunger.

Heads scattered on the ground like gruesome stones; their eyes bulging unnaturally from their sockets, as if they were in the thrall of an abject, unmitigated terror.

A musical laugh, her mellifluous voice affirming her everlasting love and devotion to him.

The pitiless laughter of Hospitaller knights who were celebrating and loudly asserting that sending all these infidels to hell was a glorious revenge for the massacre of *their* comrades after Saladin's victory at Hattin.

Robin bitterly contemplated these "holy" warriors and their merciless antipathy for the Saracens. Robin did not share the religious beliefs of the Saracens, but he could not ignore their humanity. In battle, it was kill or be killed, and there was no shame in striking down an enemy. But to butcher so many men—all unarmed, all common soldiers who surely had families—Robin could not reconcile this with either his code of honor or his Christian faith. His despondent musings were interrupted as he heard someone enter the chamber.

"Who are you?" demanded an annoyed André as everyone jumped to their feet.

Robin recognized the intruder and revealed, "This is Sir Juan de la...I'm sorry; I can't recall the rest." He apologetically gazed at the man, embarrassed to admit that he had forgotten his long and cumbersome Spanish name.

Sir Juan was an older knight, and his curly black hair was streaked with grey. He was short, yet muscular, with brown eyes and skin, although he was not as dark as the Saracens. Upon their initial meeting, Robin had instantly liked the friendly and plain-spoken man whose eyes sparkled with carefree humor. But tonight, even the jovial Sir Juan was as sober as a monk during Lent.

Sir Juan rescued Robin from any further discomfiture by introducing himself. With an indifferent shrug, he declared, "I am content to be known simply as Juan of Navarre."

Robin was grateful that the man had not been insulted, yet too down-hearted to muster much enthusiasm for a visitor on this night of sorrow and regret. He enlightened his friends, "Sir Juan is Queen Berengaria's vassal, and he always travels with her as her personal guard." After presenting the other men to Juan, Robin invited him to join them.

Once everyone was seated on their cushions, the Spanish knight elaborated, "From the time when Princess Berengaria was a young girl, I have faithfully served her and devoted my life to her protection. Now, she is the Queen of England, and I am a vassal of King Richard. Tonight, I come to you with a question: what kind of man has my princess married? A man who would slaughter defenseless prisoners? This was not the action of an honorable king."

For the space of several heartbeats, the men stared in shock at Sir Juan's bold challenge to their liege lord. The first to recover was Sir William, who sputtered as he tried to explain, "There was no food. Saladin burned the surrounding fields and failed to ransom the prisoners. Would you have the Christian army starve in order to feed heathens?"

Sir Baldwin regained his voice, and he angrily remonstrated, "Watch your words! King Richard is our liege lord, and we owe him our unwavering allegiance. Besides, would you have us leave soldiers here, to guard all these infidels, when they are needed to reconquer Jerusalem? We must begin our march south as soon as possible."

As the king's second cousin, André felt that he was best qualified to help Juan understand. He raised his hand to silence the others. "Sir Juan, this was regrettable, but King Richard really had no other option. Saladin had reneged on his promises—only remitting one payment and allowing the deadline to pass. Surely, you realize that if we had released these men without the entire ransom, it would have been both an affront to our king and a threat to our campaign, for we would have likely encountered these soldiers again in forthcoming battles. Remember, Saladin butchered many Templars and Hospitallers after the Battle of Hattin." André shrugged. "Such carnage is common in the land of the Saracens."

Robin listened as his companions defended the indefensible. He had already heard all these arguments, and he understood the rationale behind Richard's actions, yet he was profoundly unsettled. Even now, hours after the deed had been done, he was still searching his mind for another alternative that might have spared the lives of the prisoners while preserving Richard's pride.

It was the first time in Robin's life that he had been confronted by choices which were not easily sorted into tidy buckets of *right* and *wrong*. There were compelling reasons why the prisoners had been killed, but in his heart, Robin believed that these justifications were not sufficient to overcome the moral travesty of the massacre.

Sir Juan queried Robin. "Lord Huntingdon, what do you think of the king's decision to murder those men?"

The others muttered sullenly about his use of the word 'murder' but hushed as they were impatient to hear Robin's opinion, especially since the Earl of Huntingdon was the highest ranking man in the chamber.

Robin met Juan's curious scrutiny before his eyes shifted to his friends' apprehensive stares. He knew that they were beset by remorse and hoping that he would ease their conscience by endorsing the king's decision. He loved his friends and was grieved that he would have to disappoint them.

Solemnly, Robin gave his assessment. "This was a political move; Saladin did not pay the ransom, and Richard could not risk appearing weak to the enemy. Also, executing the prisoners created a military advantage. Therefore, this was implemented for both military and political purposes." Robin paused while his friends nodded vigorously, gratified by Robin's evident support.

But Robin was not finished. Returning his gaze to Juan's troubled eyes, he acknowledged, "This was a shrewd political strategy and an effective military tactic, but it was morally wrong, and no one here can convince me otherwise. Not one of the excuses I have heard could possibly justify what we did today. We will never be able to make this right, and I will bear the burden of this day for the rest of my life. May God have mercy on my soul." Robin reverently crossed himself.

Juan's expression softened with compassion. "I agree. However, if King Richard has chosen a man with your wisdom as one of his favorites, then I feel hope for the future." With a dramatic flourish, Juan retrieved the dagger from his belt, and all the men tensed at his unexpected action. He laid it on the table in front of Robin.

Robin viewed it with interest. It was completely covered with intricately etched motifs, and there were crimson jewels in the hilt. The tip of the blade had been broken.

"Lord Huntingdon, do you notice anything about this dagger?"

Robin examined it until a startling insight emerged. "The

designs, they look Saracen, like some of the decorative patterns I have seen here in Acre."

Juan's eyes brightened with approval, and the knight from Navarre grinned. "You have a good eye, my lord, but these patterns are not Saracen—they are Moorish. Do you know the history of my people? We have been fighting the Moors, who are descended from Saracens, for centuries. But we have also been living side by side with the Moors for generations. This dagger was given to me by my grandfather, a Moor who wed a Christian lady."

At this scandalous revelation, André stridently accused, "You are a Saracen! Maybe you were sent here as a spy."

Baldwin suspiciously alleged, "No wonder you slander our king and mourn the death of those infidels. You are one of them."

"Enough!" Robin thundered, as he studied Juan.

Juan did not seem to be distressed or offended by the other men's words as he asserted, "I have sworn fealty to King Richard, and he has my loyalty. But I know that most Moors and Saracens are just people who love their families and yearn for a better future. Make no mistake: I am a Christian, and I will zealously defend my faith against the Saracens, but I fear that God will deny us Jerusalem as a punishment for murdering those men in His name."

Robin had the same misgivings. Were they worthy of winning the holy city after committing such an atrocity? Regardless, he had no doubts about Juan's fidelity, and he declared, "I want to defeat the Saracens, but I do not hate them." Handing the dagger back to Juan, he inquired, "What happened to the point?"

Juan smiled broadly as he sheathed his dagger. "That is a story you will never forget. Someday, you will tell your grandchildren the tale of Sir Juan of Navarre and how his Moorish blade was broken. I propose that when we return to England, you will buy me large quantities of ale, and I will entertain you with the true story of this dagger."

Juan's affable humor helped everyone relax, and the men

chuckled wistfully at the idea of going home. Finally, they began to eat, determined to banish all thoughts of the day's events from their minds. Robin was quiet as the conversation wandered from one frivolous topic to another, and he absent-mindedly put food in his mouth, perfunctorily chewing and swallowing as a somber, relentless foreboding haunted him.

Robin was seized by an overwhelming dread, and he feared that his service to his king had irrevocably darkened his heart and condemned his soul.

CHAPTER 15

REUNIONS

15 October 1191, North of Nottingham

"Slow up, Marian; this is not a race," scolded Lionel de Toury as he maneuvered his horse alongside Marian's.

Marian resisted the impulse to roll her eyes. She was impatient to return to Lenton after receiving word of a devastating fire at the mill. However, she had to admit that the desire to escape Robin's cousin was also spurring her onward. Lionel was constantly advising her about what to do, think, and wear. Earlier, he had been droning on and on about the new narrow sleeves that were becoming popular. Regardless of his condescending manner, Marian was determined to get along with Lionel because she loved Robin's uncle Edmund and his cousin, Constance.

"If you maintain this pace, we'll reach the rendezvous point too early, and we'll have to wait for your escort," Lionel whined.

Marian gave him a withering look, but he was not deterred.

He then snickered, "Perhaps you don't require guards considering all the time you've spent with my father, practicing archery and sword fighting."

Marian could no longer restrain her tongue. "You should be pleased that I can defend myself, if we're beset by bandits."

Lionel laughed in her face and retorted, "You can pretend to be a knight if you want, but you'll never be one, *Sir* Marian. I can't believe how Father indulges you and Constance. It's ridiculous."

Trying to control her temper, Marian spoke between gritted teeth. "I think every woman should be capable of defending herself from attack. Men aren't always around to provide protection."

"You're right. They go on Crusade instead of honoring their promises." Again, Lionel chortled loudly, as though his comments were brilliantly hilarious.

Marian could not refute his cruel remarks, so she quietly seethed. It had been two years since she had penned that irate, sarcastic note to Robin. Mercifully, Edmund kept her informed whenever he received word of his nephew, so she was aware that Robin and the king had safely landed in Outremer in June.

Two years! She still had his letter where he had excitedly written that he'd be gone for a year to seek glory on Crusade. Huffing in frustration, she resentfully thought, *I hope he's enjoying himself. Him and his beloved king.*

She endeavored to focus on the present. Just a few days ago, an urgent dispatch from Lenton had been delivered. The mill had caught fire and burned down, and the people needed her assistance. Marian immediately made plans to journey home. Unfortunately, Edmund was supervising the harvest at one of his other estates, so only Lionel was available to chaperone her. And Lionel could not travel all the way to Nottingham, as he had a prior engagement in neighboring Lincoln. Constance had begged Marian to delay her departure until Edmund returned, but Marian was resolute, and she was also secretly homesick. Constance had questioned how the Lenton steward knew to send his report to Embelton, and that had elicited a prickle of unease in Marian's mind, but Lionel was not worried, so they had left.

Finally, they were approaching a fork: one path led to Lincoln and the other to Nottingham. Marian observed at least a dozen men-at-arms on the road, waiting for them. She apprehensively scanned their faces, searching for someone familiar. Her qualms were dispelled when she identified the captain of the guard from Lenton. The rest of the men were strangers.

As soon as they drew near, Marian called to the Lenton knight, "Sir Giles, how is your family?" She smiled cordially at this man, whom she had known for years, but she was surprised to see him blanch and timidly look at the man next to him, as if he needed permission to speak.

The other man's lips curved into a smirk that did not reach his eyes. "My lady, I am Sir Wilfred, the captain of the guard for Sir Ferrand Crawford, the Sheriff of Nottingham appointed by King Richard. I am here to accompany you to the castle, where the sheriff would like to celebrate your homecoming with a feast before we escort you to Lenton tomorrow."

Marian countered, "I want to go directly to Lenton. I'm concerned about rebuilding the mill—"

"My lady," the captain interrupted, "the sheriff will explain how he can help you with that."

Lionel inserted himself into the conversation. "Marian, let the sheriff make all the decisions. You don't know anything about building a mill."

Marian had had enough of Lionel's patronizing tone. She ignored him and crossly addressed Sir Wilfred. "If the sheriff wishes to *help*, then I will be pleased to hear his suggestions. Let's proceed to the castle."

"Marian, send word when you are ready to return to Embelton," instructed Lionel.

Without a backward glance, Marian spurred her horse towards Nottingham.

～

When Marian entered the great hall of Nottingham Castle, she was shocked by its transformation: it was draped with massive scarlet banners, the high table was covered by a red cloth, and the chairs were painted crimson. A strong perception that something was wrong overwhelmed her, and she hesitated.

"Welcome home, Maid Marian," Sheriff de Argentan proclaimed as he emerged from the shadows. He was joined by a somber Guy of Gisborne and the sinister Tancred de Payen.

"No!" Marian squeaked as she spun on her feet and tried to run out the door.

Sir Wilfred seized her roughly by the arm, and Gisborne barked, "Unhand her!" Guy wrenched Marian from the man's grasp and furiously shoved him away.

Wilfred's eyes narrowed in contempt, but he submissively retreated while Argentan and Payen laughed at Guy's overprotective reaction.

"My lady, are you all right?" Gisborne's ardent stare and possessive grip made Marian's blood run cold. She nodded and stepped away from him. Thankfully, he released her, although he lingered at her side.

"Such a touching reunion," cried Argentan. He dramatically placed a hand over his heart, and his bulky red and gold ring glimmered in the sunlight streaming into the hall.

Marian had not been so terrified since the last time she had been ensnared in the sheriff's web. She sputtered, "But…I was told that you were gone."

Argentan willingly explained, "Prince John was granted dominion over several shires during King Richard's absence, including Nottingham. The prince trusts me and stipulated that I remain here as sheriff."

A disquieting notion occurred to Marian. "The mill—did you burn it to lure me here?"

Argentan scoffed, "And lose the tax revenue that I collect for every bag of grain ground into flour? Absolutely not."

Marian was relieved to hear this, but she was distressed that her people in Lenton had been suffering from the ruthless taxation of Argentan. Another realization dawned, and she blurted, "How did you know where to find me?"

"When my dear friend, the Earl of Bedford, recently mentioned that Robin Hood has an uncle in the north, I easily found you." The sheriff was openly savoring his success. "And now you will compose a message for the Baron of Embelton describing how happy you are to be back in Lenton, and that you will reside here for the foreseeable future."

"I will not!" challenged an indignant Marian.

Argentan grinned as Sir Wilfred pushed the captain from Lenton towards Marian.

The distraught man sank to his knees and implored, "My lady, please; I beg you. Not for myself but for my wife and children. He will execute them!"

Marian gasped in horror as her gaze veered to a smug Argentan who confirmed, "You can save this man's family by writing a simple note." He then pointed at a table bearing everything she required to prepare a letter for Edmund. A defeated and discouraged Marian promptly complied, convinced that Edmund would doubt the legitimacy of the message and come to her rescue as soon as he received it.

Argentan perused the letter and was apparently satisfied. He announced, "How sad for Gisborne. At long last, he is reunited with his lady love, but only for one night. Maid Marian, until we meet again, I bid you a fond farewell. Gisborne, show her to her chamber."

Marian had no choice except to obediently follow Guy; she was trapped and at the mercy of these despicable men. As they exited the great hall, Argentan spoke to Guy in French, and Marian listened carefully. She had worked diligently with Constance, who was fluent in the language, to increase her skills, and she silently translated the sheriff's comments: *we will depart at sunrise; Wilfred will take her;* and *we will begin our lion hunt.* Trailing after Guy, Marian became annoyed with herself. She had imagined her French much improved, but obviously she had misinterpreted the part about a lion hunt. That made no sense.

She shuddered in trepidation as Guy ushered her into the same chamber where he had nearly raped her three years ago. Her heart was pounding, and she felt dizzy as they entered. The latch of the door clanked ominously.

"Marian, I'm begging for your forgiveness." Guy's voice was earnest and beseeching, and his words tumbled forth, as if they had been set free after a long imprisonment. "I apologize for failing to protect you from Huntingdon when he abducted you from the castle—"

"What?" Marian was momentarily bewildered, since that was not how she remembered that fateful night when Robin had rescued her from the castle.

"I have spent all this time searching for you." He clasped her hands, and she struggled to tug them away.

"No, don't—" Marian started to plead.

"Let me finish," he insisted. "I must leave tomorrow, and I'll be gone for many months. But when I return, we will renew our courtship."

Marian's skin crawled with revulsion at his touch. She wanted to scream that she would never belong to him, but she feared his volatile temper.

Guy continued his declarations. "I have never stopped loving you, and I don't care if Huntingdon disgraced you before he went on Crusade. He never loved you; instead, he cruelly discarded you. We will marry, and I will devote my life to your happiness." He glanced down, letting go of her hands to untie a small bag from his belt, so he didn't notice the flash of fury in Marian's eyes at his stinging reminder of Robin's abandonment.

He deftly opened a velvet pouch and withdrew her red brooch and an extravagant necklace. "I have kept this brooch all these years, recalling how you treasured it and anticipating the day when I could restore it to you. I also purchased this necklace. When I saw the ruby stones, I was eager to buy it for you. Put them on," he demanded. "I want my last memory before leaving to be of you wearing these gifts from me."

Her trembling hands fluttered as she pinned the brooch to her bliaut while Guy stepped behind her and fastened the necklace. "Where are you going?" Marian nervously asked as she moved away from him.

He grimaced, and Marian deduced that he had no enthusiasm for his upcoming journey. "I cannot divulge that to you. In the meantime, it is not wise for you to stay here; Huntingdon's family might try to kidnap you. Sir Wilfred will escort you to London tomorrow, where you will be safe pending my return." He then gathered her into his arms and sighed contentedly.

Her whole body stiffened in protest, and bile rose in her throat to be embraced by this man whom she loathed with every fiber of her being, so Marian squirmed and entreated, "Please, let me go… don't hurt me."

Guy reluctantly released her, his expression chagrined. "Marian, I won't hurt you. I'm not like Huntingdon; I will wait. Don't you remember? I promised you that I would never force you to my bed."

Marian vaguely recollected him saying something like that, but she didn't trust him. She distanced herself from him and hoped to encourage him to depart by offering, "Godspeed on your voyage."

Guy gazed at her with heated, lust-filled eyes. Marian observed him clench and relax his fists as she remained stonily aloof. She wondered if he could hear the frenetic beating of her heart, and the time lengthened uncomfortably.

Eventually, he relented. "I love you, Marian. When we are wed,

I will give you anything you desire, and you will be very happy. You will not regret joining your future to mine."

She held her breath until he left, exhaling thankfully at the sound of the latch.

16 October 1191, Sherwood Forest

Marian anxiously surveyed both sides of the road, peering into the shadowy forest and praying that the outlaws would appear and rescue her from Sir Wilfred and a second soldier as they shepherded her to London.

"Don't worry about bandits," the younger soldier reassured her. "Sheriff de Argentan executed them two years ago."

This news was so unexpected that Marian was silent as tears welled in her eyes. In a tremulous voice, she asked, "Are you certain?"

Wilfred nodded. "Payen poisoned them, and then Argentan hung their bodies from the castle walls as a warning to all followers of Robin Hood."

Marian surreptitiously dabbed at her watery eyes. Her heart broke at the memory of those coarse, uneducated men who had been so brave and steadfast in their loyalty to Robin. Their deaths would devastate him. Marian knew that Robin would blame himself for not being there to rescue them. There was no one to save her either, so she resolved to save herself.

But first, she was duty-bound to discover more about Gisborne and Argentan's mysterious expedition. She boldly inquired, "Sir Wilfred, do you think Sir Guy and Sheriff de Argentan will have a successful...lion hunt?"

Wilfred regarded her suspiciously. "Gisborne told you about that?"

Marian widened her eyes in feigned innocence and sweetly replied, "Sir Guy intends to marry me, so he revealed everything to me, but I am concerned; will the lion hunt be…dangerous? What do you think about their plan, Sir Wilfred?"

Luckily for Marian, Sir Wilfred was something of a gossip. He chortled. "Dangerous? You women have no comprehension of such things. It doesn't get more dangerous than traveling to Outremer to kill King Richard so that Prince John can take the throne. But I believe that they will succeed because, if anyone can slay the lion, it will be Lord de Argentan."

Marian was aghast. She frowned as she contemplated Argentan's audacious plot. Then, with dread, she recognized that Robin would be at risk too. Most likely, wherever the king was, Robin would be there too. Robin might be murdered defending the king!

She was riding through a familiar section of the greenwood, and Marian was confident that she would be able to locate the hunting lodge as soon as she escaped from these men. She slowed her horse, and the two men, who were discussing their favorite foods, progressed ahead of her. When they realized that she had fallen behind, they curiously looked back to see her stopped in the middle of the road.

"I think my horse is going lame," she lied.

"Shit!" bellowed Sir Wilfred, who evidently did not care whether it was appropriate to use such language in front of Lady Marian. "Go check on her horse," he commanded the younger man.

While Wilfred waited, the soldier rode to Marian and dismounted to inspect her horse's legs. Marian politely bade him, "Please, help me down." She put her left hand on his shoulder as he lifted his arms towards her. With her right hand, Marian reached down and seized the hilt of the dagger sheathed to his belt. Before he could react, she took her horse's reins and jerked them hard. The large beast reared up and twisted sideways, knocking the hapless man unconscious with a flailing hoof.

Marian then spurred her horse away from a stunned Sir Wilfred. Unfortunately, the seasoned soldier instantly understood what was happening, and the chase commenced. Marian coaxed her horse into a gallop and sought a gap in the trees. If she could enter the forest, she was convinced that she could elude her captor by employing the skills she had learned from Robin. But with her horse charging at a breakneck speed, the trees became a blur. With increasing panic, she glanced over her shoulder and saw the older knight steadily gaining on her.

Suddenly, Wilfred was alongside her, clasping her horse's halter and bringing the two horses to an abrupt halt. He snatched the reins from her hands and swung his horse around until he was facing Marian as they sat on their mounts. "You bitch!" he screamed. "What the hell are you doing? Give me that dagger now."

Holding the dagger so that the blade was parallel to her forearm, Marian raised the weapon up over her head. Wilfred stretched to grab her wrist, but Marian evaded his grasp and plunged the dagger deeply into his inner thigh. Wilfred howled in pain, and he released his grip on her reins, pulled the blade from his leg, and tossed it away. To Marian's horror, blood began to spurt from the gash. He pressed against the injury, but the blood gushed out between his fingers, spreading across his saddle and dripping onto the ground beneath his horse. Marian gawked at him in an appalled hush as nausea overcame her, and she fought the urge to retch.

"Bitch!" he shrieked again. "What have you done?" He clumsily dismounted, and Marian watched as he staggered several steps before collapsing. The blood continued to pour out of his body at a lethal rate. "Fetch me a cloth!" he hollered, still clutching his wound.

Marian slowly got down from her horse and hesitated. She knew that she should flee at once, yet a part of her felt compelled to aid this man whom she had gravely injured. As she dithered, he slumped to the side, lying motionless on the road.

"Sir Wilfred?" she hoarsely called to him. There was no response. Tentatively, she moved closer. There was a substantial pool of blood encircling him, and his eyes were open and staring into the distance, but they were no longer seeing anything.

Marian gasped. She had killed him! She vomited, stumbled to her horse, and unsteadily hauled herself up into the saddle. Soon she was on a familiar path, determined to rescue Robin and desperately trying to forget what she had just done.

⁓

R + M

Marian lovingly traced the letters with her finger. For three years, they had endured, and she was gratified to see them on the trunk of the great oak, although they had become weathered and worn over time. Using a dagger that she had found in the old hunting lodge, she painstakingly re-carved them. In the lodge, she had also found her boyish clothes, and despite their musty and moth-eaten condition, she had happily donned them. From the lodge, she had located the meadow without difficulty.

She knew that time was of the essence; Argentan and Gisborne were already a day ahead of her, and she dreaded the possibility of disembarking in Outremer one day too late to save Robin. *And the king*, she reminded herself.

Closing her eyes, she allowed memories of Robin to fill her mind: his pale blue eyes, sparkling with mischief and then aflame with passion. His sandy hair, tousled from a wild horseback ride and then softly sliding between her fingers. His lips, grinning playfully and then pressed firmly against her mouth. His deep voice, laughing out loud and then murmuring promises of eternal love and devotion.

"Oh, Robin," she tenderly whimpered as tears rolled down her cheek. Again, she caressed the carving on the tree. "I'm so sorry that I wrote that letter." She wiped at her damp face. "I was so confident that your message was announcing your imminent arrival, and I was aching for you, but then you tell me you've got more important things to do than marry me. I was so angry, but now, I'm so sorry..." Sobs briefly drowned her words. Once more, she wrestled to contain her emotions, and she resolutely vowed, "Robin, I will come and save you. I'm really afraid and all alone, but knowing that you need me will give me strength."

"Lady Marian?" a friendly voice called across the clearing.

Marian spun around to behold three men jogging towards her. She recognized them but wavered. Weren't they all dead? She cautiously speculated, "I must be having a vision. They said you had been poisoned!"

Little John, Allan, and Will were standing in front of her, their expressions anguished. John confirmed, "Everyone was arrested and poisoned, except for the three of us. You must go back into hiding, because Argentan still rules Nottingham."

Marian described how she had been lured to Nottingham and apprehended. She did not disclose that she had killed a man, only that she had tricked her guards and fled into the woods. They listened attentively and did not question her account. She then revealed, "Robin is in danger, and I must go and forewarn him."

The surprised men stared at her. John asked, "Did he return from the Crusade?"

"No, he's still in the Holy Land, so I'm going there." Marian replied matter-of-factly. She then told them what she had learned about Argentan's scheme to murder the king.

There was a baffled silence before Will clarified, "You're going to journey to the Holy Land by yourself? How?"

Marian shrugged as she endeavored to hide how frightened she truly was. "I have this jewelry." She showed them the brooch and necklace from Guy. "I will sell it to buy passage to Outremer, and I will wear these clothes to disguise myself as a boy."

Again, there was an awkward hush as the flabbergasted men gaped at her while they visualized one perilous scenario after another. John attempted to reason with her. "My lady, if someone discovers that you're a woman…" His voice faded as he struggled to find a delicate way to communicate his worries.

"I can take care of myself. I'm going, and no one can stop me." Marian lifted her chin defiantly.

Allan helpfully advised, "It's always best to travel with a companion, and since I've spent most of my life on the road, I know how to avoid some of the dangers that you will face." He then suggested, "I can also ensure that you're not cheated or robbed when you sell your jewelry. Let me go with you. We'll tell people that you are my younger brother."

Profound relief swept over Marian as she impulsively hugged Allan. Releasing him and wiping an errant tear from her cheek, she insisted, "There is no time to waste. I want to leave *now*."

22 February 1192, Mansion of the Templars, City of Acre

Robin and Much rode through the gates of the Templar compound and swiftly made their way into the elaborate structure that housed the elite of the holy order. Robin distractedly followed a servant along the corridor with Much close on his heels while he pondered the bizarre missive that had been delivered to him: *Lady Marian of Lenton has disembarked from England. She requests that the Earl of Huntingdon come at once to discuss an urgent matter.*

When they entered a chamber, Robin froze in astonishment as he came face to face with the woman who haunted his dreams and had broken his heart. Marian was as lovely and elegant as ever, even dressed in an exotic, Saracen-style gown. Her green eyes were wide, and her lips were parted in a gasp of wonder. She seemed both the same and much changed. It occurred to him that three years ago, she had been a dainty rosebud, but now she was a woman in the full flower of her beauty. He was consumed by his fervent desire for her, and it irked him that she still had such power over him.

Scowling fiercely, he yelled, "What in God's holy name are

you doing here, Marian? Have you gone mad?" The instant the words left his mouth, he regretted his harsh tone, especially when he detected an increased shine in her eyes, which he feared might be tears.

He then spotted Allan, and he focused his wrath on him. "Allan, I'm holding *you* responsible for this. I assumed you had better judgment. You bring my–" At this, he faltered; did he have the right to call her his betrothed? Not according to that note she had sent him. Instead, he repeated, "What are you doing here?"

Allan swallowed nervously. "Lord Robin, this was her idea; I'm only here to protect her."

"My lady," Much effused as he stepped forward and briefly went down on one knee. "I am so happy to see you!"

Marian had recovered from the shock of seeing Robin, and her feelings had shifted from elation to resentment. "I'm glad someone is pleased to see me," she snapped.

For an uncomfortable stretch of time, Robin and Marian glared at each other. Robin's emotions were a writhing morass. He wanted to grab her and kiss her. No, he wanted to grab her and shake some sense into her. He couldn't bear to contemplate the perils that she must have encountered on the long, hazardous voyage from England to the Holy Land, yet here she was, safe and sound. His heart wanted to leap for joy, while his mind kept echoing phrases from her letter: *I release your lordship from your promise to marry me...* Robin could feel the weight of the ring she had returned to him; it hung from a chain around his neck, under his tunic and over his heart.

Marian was also battling conflicting emotions. She wanted his embrace. No, she wanted to grab him and shake some sense into him. There he was, arrogantly chastising her for coming and evidently angry at her. He seemed much the same, yet vastly different. His face was thinner and less boyish; maybe it was the short beard that he now wore. His skin was tanned from the blazing sun of the

Holy Land, and that made his pale blue eyes even more striking. How could he be so handsome, and so infuriating, and still be the only man she would ever love? She became aggravated that he had such power over her after all this time.

Allan cleared his throat and disrupted their enchantment. "Marian, isn't there something you need to tell Lord Robin?"

Marian was grateful for Allan's reminder, and she divulged, "Argentan never left Nottingham; he's been sheriff all this time, and he is traveling here with Gisborne to kill the king."

Robin was visibly stunned by her news, and he inquired, "Do you know when they will arrive?"

She frantically shouted, "You don't understand! They departed at least a fortnight before Allan and I could arrange for passage and leave England. *They are already here!* The king is in danger, but I believe that they are also planning to murder you. I heard from one of their men that they plan to kill Richard so that John can be crowned king."

An alarmed Robin hastily instructed Much, "Send a dispatch to the king warning him that there is a credible threat against his life and that he must remain at the royal palace until I return. There is no time to lose; the king has been invited here to attend a feast later today." He glanced at Allan and added, "Go with Much."

Much and Allan bobbed their heads and rushed from the chamber.

Finally alone with his former betrothed, Robin gentled his voice, feeling remorse for his earlier disapproving words. "Marian, why are you here with the Templars? This is the southwestern part of the city, and the king's palace is on the other side of town."

Marian bristled at what she perceived as more criticism from Robin. She grudgingly answered, "When we came ashore, the captain of the boat said there had been violence in the streets amongst the Genoese and Pisans, and that the Templars would keep me safe."

Robin was not surprised by this; the unrest between the

Genoese, who were allied with the French, and the Pisans, who were loyal to Richard, was the reason why the king was in Acre at this time. He observed her Saracen robes and chuckled lightly. "Why are you dressed like that?"

Once more, Marian tensed. She didn't like having to explain herself to him. "I traveled disguised as a boy. The Templars were scandalized by my attire and gave me these clothes." She narrowed her eyes and retorted, "Don't they have razors here in the Holy Land? What is that all over your face?"

Robin laughed heartily. "I'll gladly shave, if it would please you." Immediately, he felt embarrassed and exposed by his offer. Why had he disclosed that he still cared what she thought?

Marian beamed in delight, nostalgic for the verbal jousting the two lovers had enjoyed in the past, but before she could respond, Much and Allan appeared and summoned Robin, who joined them in the corridor. She could not hear what they were saying, so she walked towards them, only to have Robin solemnly request, "Marian, remain here. I must go and organize your removal to the royal palace." Without pausing for her reaction, Robin, Much, and Allan left.

Marian grumbled in annoyance to be abandoned so soon after their reunion. She sat on a cushion and irritably awaited his return.

⟡

Marian must have dozed off, for she startled awake at the sound of a booming voice.

"Where is she?"

The door flew open, and Marian jumped to her feet, grabbing a small knife from a table and preparing to defend herself. A remarkably tall man with reddish blonde hair stormed into the chamber with Robin and another man in close pursuit.

"Ha!" the man snorted in amusement. "She's a feisty one. Is she intending to stab her king? Robin, is this girl the reason why you are fretting and fussing like an old woman?"

Marian suddenly realized that this was the legendary King Richard the Lionheart, so she lowered the blade and respectfully curtsied.

Robin was noticeably exasperated by the king's flippant attitude as he presented her. "Sire, this is Lady Marian Fitzwalter of Lenton. She journeyed here from England to warn us of a threat on your life."

"My lady, it is a pleasure to meet you," exclaimed the king. "Your timing is impeccable, for today the Templars are hosting a grand feast celebrating my impressive success in reconciling the Genoese and the Pisans. You must join us. But first, enlighten me about this supposed threat."

Before Marian could reply, a perplexed Robin interjected. "Sire, I sent word for you to *wait* at the palace; why are you here?"

Richard regarded him curiously. "The missive begged me to come here as speedily as possible. Upon my arrival, I was informed that Lady Marian was also here."

Robin rubbed his face in agitated frustration; Marian recognized the familiar gesture at once. "Sire, my message must have been intercepted and altered. We should retreat to the palace forthwith. The Templars could provide men to supplement your usual guard."

"Robin," the king chided, "you are constantly imagining perils in every shadow. In all likelihood, the messenger was confused. Besides, I cannot risk offending the Templars by refusing to attend this feast being held in my honor."

Sighing in resignation, for arguing with the king was a futile exercise, Robin then introduced Marian to Sir André de Chauvigny, the king's second cousin, before asking her to apprise the king of Argentan's lion hunt.

The king was attentive, and when she had finished, he smiled amiably at her. "Lady Marian, you have the gratitude of your king.

Your loyalty to me and your bravery in traveling so far from home for my sake do you great credit. We will make arrangements for you to reside with my queen and my sister. They will be very pleased to have your charming company."

"Thank you, Sire," Marian politely answered. Her mind wandered as she deliberated whether to linger in the Holy Land or return home without delay. Did Robin want her here? He seemed so distant. Her musings were interrupted by raised voices.

"—and that's why this war has become pointless. Even if we capture Jerusalem, we'll never be able to hold it; significant numbers of our men will deem their pilgrimage complete, and they will simply go home. We cannot force them to stay." Robin was quarreling with the king, and Marian was troubled by his lack of decorum.

André candidly opined, "You've seen the lay of the land; a siege of Jerusalem will be a daunting undertaking, and its inland location will make our supply lines vulnerable to attack."

Richard waved his hand dismissively. "After we refortify the city of Ascalon, it will serve as a support base for our siege of Jerusalem. I'm still considering an Egyptian campaign; if I conquer Egypt, then the wealth of the Nile will fund our efforts here. In the meantime, Robin will meet with Saladin's representative to stall for time with peace negotiations."

Robin boldly asserted, "Our coalition is splintering; this hostility between the Genoese and the Pisans is merely a symptom of a larger crisis between the French and English forces. The men only want to enter Jerusalem and then go home. How will you conquer Egypt without an army? How will we hold Jerusalem? Are you prepared to spend every coin in your treasury for a fleeting victory?"

Richard seized a nearby ewer and hurled it against the wall where it shattered into countless wet fragments. Marian cringed in fear as the lion roared, "It's my treasury, and I'll spend it however I want!"

An irate Robin contended, "A treasury funded by the sweat and toil of peasants who barely have enough food to eat."

André paled as he anxiously intervened. "Sire, Prince John is behind this plot to murder you. And King Philippe is actively scheming to annex your Norman and Angevin lands. Maybe it is time to seek peace and go home."

Richard's face was flushed with fury. He bellowed, "You both need to watch your words. I am king, and I decide! Perhaps Huntingdon would prefer to fight as a member of the infantry alongside the peasants he loves so well."

Marian was terrified by Richard's threats and appalled to witness the king speak so scornfully to her Robin. He was the king's most devoted, honorable, and trustworthy subject! She was filled with resentment towards the blustering, overbearing monarch.

At that moment, a servant arrived and summoned them to the great hall, where a sumptuous feast had been laid out. The king himself escorted Marian, and when they were seated, the Grand Master of the Templars stood and saluted the king in a speech layered with pomposity and fawning admiration, "Now we will drink a toast to the magnificent, incomparable King Richard the Lionheart! His glorious, God-given supremacy settled the dreadful conflicts which have been beleaguering this city. Today, we celebrate his brilliant resolution of the dispute between the Genoese and the Pisans."

Richard beamed at the lavish praise as a short, fidgety man poured wine into his goblet. The king boisterously joked, "I hope this is not English wine; I cannot abide it."

To Marian's bewilderment, Robin leapt to his feet and confiscated the bottle from the man, whose hands had been shaking so badly that he had accidently overfilled the king's goblet and soiled the tablecloth. Marian wondered why Robin was so incensed at the man for making a mess.

"Wait," cried Robin. "Sire, do not drink this until it has been taste-tested."

The king was still furious with Robin, so he sneered, "Sit down, Huntingdon. You are embarrassing me and insulting the Templars."

A suspicious Robin ignored Richard; he was intently studying the man. The servant tried to run away, but a signal from Robin caused several soldiers to block his escape. The man slowly pivoted and stared in wide-eyed panic at Robin.

"Where is this wine from?" Robin sternly queried.

"From the Pisans, my lord," he claimed. "It's a gift for King Richard."

Robin evenly proposed, "Then you will not object to having the first cup."

Richard indignantly protested, "I am not in any jeopardy from the Pisans; they are loyal to me."

Robin set the bottle aside and appropriated Richard's goblet while calmly reminding him, "Sire, you gave me the responsibility of ensuring your personal security. I am merely obeying your orders." He then carried the ornate cup to the man who was quaking in terror.

"Drink it," demanded Robin.

"No!" the man screeched. "It's poison!"

Robin nodded in grim satisfaction. "You might receive mercy from the king if you reveal who sent you."

The man blanched. In a taut voice, he avowed, "I'll never tell you."

André and a glowering King Richard were now standing next to Robin, and the servant was trembling like a leaf in a windstorm. The king thundered, "Tell us the name of your master."

André coolly remarked, "I have very persuasive techniques for loosening your tongue."

Unexpectedly, the man lunged at Robin, snatching the king's goblet and drinking the adulterated wine. As he dropped to his knees, he stuttered, "You won't...torture...me..." He began to gag and foam at the mouth.

Robin gripped him by his tunic and growled, "Who is your master?"

The man's body was beset by convulsions until he abruptly stilled, and all the knights attending the feast crowded around, straining to see what had happened and buzzing with morbid curiosity, while Marian averted her eyes.

The Templars' Grand Master screamed for silence, and as everyone quieted, he yelled, "Where did this man come from? Who allowed him to bring wine to the king?"

Amid the turmoil, Robin urged Richard, "Sire, Argentan is cunning, and he must not be underestimated. He is a stranger in this land, yet he smuggled this bottle of tainted wine into the formidable, closely guarded Templar fortress. What else is he capable of? Before we return to the palace, we must send for reinforcements and stipulate that the Templars furnish extra men for your protection as well."

Richard disagreed. "After days of factional fighting in the streets of Acre, a sizeable force of men-at-arms moving through the city could incite more violence. We will leave as soon as possible with my usual guard, led by you and André. Arrange for a few Templars to supplement our numbers. Truthfully, I'm not concerned; the attempt on my life has failed."

Robin reluctantly submitted to Richard's decision. He spotted a Templar commander who had just entered the great hall, so he approached the man and insisted, "The king requires additional men to accompany us to the palace. We need to depart immediately."

The Templar knight regretfully explained, "I apologize, my lord, but we don't have any men available. I just received word that many of our men have fallen ill with a stomach complaint. We are worried that they might have eaten some spoiled meat, but many claim that they have not had a meal recently, although they have been drinking ale."

An alarmed Robin recommended, "You must discard any open containers of ale. Someone tried to poison the king, and I'm certain that your ale has been contaminated too."

CHAPTER 16
THE LION HUNT

22 February 1192, City of Acre

uy yawned as he stood at an upper floor window. Below him, a sun-drenched plaza led to the heavily guarded gates of the Templar compound, where King Richard was attending a feast. As soon as the lion was dead, they would return to England, and Prince John would seize the throne. Officially, Richard's young nephew was his heir, but he was only a child and in the custody of King Philippe, so he posed no serious threat.

Shaking his head and stomping his feet, Guy fought the drowsiness that clouded his mind and dulled his senses. A bead of sweat slid down the side of his face, and he roughly wiped it away. In an effort to stay awake, he thought about his upcoming marriage to the woman he loved.

It had been nearly three and a half years since Huntingdon's abduction of Marian, but Guy had never stopped desiring her. He planned to shower her with gifts and affection, and then she would surely fall in love with him. Gisborne smiled wistfully as he envisioned his future: King John would restore the Barony of Gisborne to him, and he would become Baron of Lenton by right of wife while still retaining the Locksley estate. Guy would have wealth, titles, and the most beautiful, perfect woman he had ever known. A noise startled him out of his reverie.

"Any developments?" Argentan probed as he joined him at the window.

"No change, my lord." Guy squinted at the sky. It was past midday, and he cursed the blazing sun that hurt his eyes and blistered his skin. He yearned for the cool breezes and green woodlands of Nottinghamshire. After living in crowded, hectic Paris for so many years, he had grown quite fond of the bucolic English countryside. It had begun to feel like home.

Argentan grinned broadly and rubbed his hands together, full of anticipation. "Today, a lion will be slain by a shadow." He snickered. "Oh, I can just imagine the lamentations. The great Lionheart, dead from a digestive ailment. These Plantagenet men have such delicate stomachs."

Guy tried not to roll his eyes at the sheriff's sarcasm and peculiar jests. "My lord, I thought the fast-acting poison would make it obvious that the king had been killed."

Argentan shrugged his shoulders. "It does not really matter. If they realize that their liege was poisoned, there are many potential suspects: the Saracens, the Genoese, or perhaps Conrad de Montferrat, whose claim to the throne of Jerusalem was denied by Richard. Regardless, we will be on our way back to civilization and beyond suspicion."

At the risk of ruining the sheriff's cheerful mood, Guy cautiously asked, "What about the men who have seen us here? I mean, there is the Duke of Burgundy, and all these soldiers..."

Argentan scowled at Guy, irritated by his lack of enthusiasm. "Burgundy is Philippe's first cousin, and he knows that divulging my presence here will implicate him because of our mutual ties to the French court. Besides, I have sent him north to Tyre so that he can profess ignorance of the plot to snare the lion. He is in my debt and will diligently control the tongues of his men and the Genoese; if anyone betrays me, their life is forfeit."

Just then, the captain of the Genoese guard and a boy rushed into the chamber. They genuflected to Argentan, and the man hastened to disclose, "My lord, my squire has brought word from the feast."

The anxious youth bravely reported, "My lord, the poisoned wine was discovered before the king drank it. The English king and his men are organizing their return to the palace as soon as possible."

"The Templars?" Argentan curtly inquired.

"Most of them are sick from the tainted ale, and they won't be able to escort the king when he leaves the Templar fortress." It was the only good news the boy could offer.

Argentan dismissed him with an imperious wave of his hand. Noticeably disappointed that the attempt to poison King Richard had failed, the sheriff resolutely prepared to implement his contingency plan. He bade the Genoese captain to gather the twenty men who had previously been chosen for his secondary plot. Argentan queried the knight, "Have you readied the trap?"

The captain nodded as he replied, "The king's customary route includes a street on the border between our quarter and the Venetians. There is a segment where the road narrows significantly, and the buildings are vacant and in disrepair. We have barricaded these structures, and this will allow us to surround the king and his men. The lion will be cornered."

Contemplating his strategy, Argentan stipulated, "I must verify the death of the king, and I want his ring as proof. Is there a location nearby where I can watch? Also, how close will I be to the harbor? I have a ship waiting."

The captain proposed, "My lord, there is a suitable place at the end of the street; I will take you to it. You can easily travel to the harbor from there."

Satisfied with the scheme, Argentan announced, "It is time for our lion hunt. Go now, and do not fail me."

The Genoese captain cleared his throat and nervously explained, "My lord, my people have just accepted a truce with the Pisans and the English, pledging to cease hostilities. We are honorable men who stand by our promises. I don't understand..." His voice faded as he sought to articulate his trepidation without offending Argentan.

Eyes narrowing in contempt, Argentan growled, "Your liege lord, Hugh of Burgundy, put me in command while he is in Tyre." He then sneered, "I don't answer to *you,* but hear my words: who is truly dishonorable? The Genoese and French? We came here with one purpose: to liberate Jerusalem. Who has hindered us from achieving this goal?"

Argentan surveyed the assembled men as he reminded them, "King Richard was twelve miles from Jerusalem. Did he use his vaunted military prowess to recapture the city for Christendom? No! Instead, he retreated like a beaten dog. Was that the action of a lion-hearted warrior for Christ? Does King Richard deserve your loyalty?"

Like a troubadour who could make his audience weep with despair or soar with joy, Argentan's words sounded all the right chords among the dedicated, pious men who had forsaken their homes in Genoa with dreams of recovering the Holy Land for Christendom. Many of them hoped to build a new life here, in the Kingdom of Jerusalem, and their zealous support of the Crusade outweighed any loyalty to distant European kings who arrived and departed like birds on a migratory path.

As usual, Guy was impressed with the sheriff's uncanny, diabolical way of manipulating men to do his bidding while convincing them that it was in their own best interest. That notion caused Guy to wince slightly; he was just as ensnared by the sheriff as these men.

❧

As he led the royal procession, Robin worriedly looked back at the litter carrying Marian. Her flaxen hair was concealed beneath a Saracen-style headscarf, and her litter had a fabric canopy to hide her from view. Marian was oblivious to the perils she faced in this land, where great wealth could be obtained by selling such a fair-haired beauty to the highest bidder. Although she had scoffed at Robin's orders that Much and Allan march beside her litter with their swords drawn, the two men had obeyed Robin's stern directives without hesitation.

Next to Marian's litter rode a sullen King Richard; he was still furious at Robin for his criticisms of their stalled Crusade. The fact that Robin was right had only fueled the king's temper, which burned hotter than the accursed desert sun. André followed Richard, and there were eight mounted knights protectively situated around the king and Marian.

Robin sighed loudly as he resumed his forward scrutiny of the road. He didn't have enough men to properly guard the king, but Richard, who was supremely confident in his fighting skills, had flatly refused to wait for reinforcements. Robin deeply resented the king's willingness to expose Marian to danger. It was inexcusably selfish and thoughtless in Robin's opinion, but he had no choice but to acquiesce to the king's demands. Because of the threat to Richard, Robin had instructed his men to wear helmets and chainmail hauberks under their surcoats. Additionally, they carried Norman-style kite shields, which had both neck and arm straps.

Robin had traveled too far ahead of the group, so he stopped and examined his surroundings with care. They were on a road flanked by the Genoese and Venetian quarters, and the harbor was a short distance away. Like many areas in this war-torn city, the buildings were heavily damaged. Removing his helmet to wipe the sweat from his brow, Robin observed that the street was strangely deserted, and he felt a stirring in the pit of his stomach. He signaled for the procession to halt. In the resulting eerie stillness, Robin concentrated all his senses.

"What is the problem?" the king gruffly complained with unmistakable impatience.

Robin did not respond; something was wrong, and he could feel it. Suddenly, a small rock fell from the heavens and rolled across the street. At first, he gave it little consideration as he put his helmet back on, but then his mind was filled with the awareness that stones do not drop from the sky like rain.

His eyes darted upward, and fear seized him as he recognized the familiar shape of a bow. Urgently, he yelled over his shoulder, "Shields up, left!" The well-trained knights, including the king, promptly raised their shields as the archers released a volley of arrows.

Robin turned his horse and sped to the king. He had seen three archers, and they were clearly targeting King Richard. Rejoining the others, Robin saw ten men brandishing swords and riding towards the royal party from a forward position, while another eight were approaching from the rear. There was no avenue of escape, and the king's elite guard arranged their horses in a defensive semi-circle around Richard and Marian, using the façade of an adjacent structure to prevent the enemy from completely surrounding them.

Robin continued to assess their situation. Marian was crouching behind Much and Allan as they stood in front of her with their swords ready and shields up; the litter bearers had abandoned her and fled. He grimly noted that King Richard had been struck; an arrow was shallowly implanted in the king's leg, just above his left knee. The archers were employing long, narrow bodkins—lethal arrowheads designed to slide between gaps in chainmail. While holding his shield aloft, a visibly annoyed Richard pulled the arrow out and tossed it aside before drawing his sword.

The archers on the roof were focused on the king, so Robin

took a chance that they would not notice him as he lowered his shield and reached for his prized Saracen-style bow, which was hanging from his shoulder. Grabbing three arrows from the quiver at his belt, he took aim and loosed them in rapid succession at the archers' unprotected necks and faces. His missiles found their marks, and the men fell from their perches, landing with dull thuds on the road below.

Meanwhile, the mounted attackers had arrived, and a brutal battle commenced. Robin could not safely use his bow in such close quarters—the risk of harming one of the king's men was too great—so he slung his bow over his shoulder and drew his sword.

Abruptly, King Richard bellowed, "Retreat right!"

Robin ventured a glimpse back and instantly understood the king's intentions. At the end of this desolate street there was one house that was relatively untouched, and its door was not obstructed by rubble like the others. "Retreat right!" Robin echoed the king.

From the corner of his eye, he could see Much protectively shepherding Allan, who was now cradling Marian, towards the dwelling. Marian's shrill screams could be heard over the clamor of the melee, but Robin banished any thoughts of her from his mind; such distractions were fatal during combat. He was simply grateful for the enemy's indifference to Much, Allan, and Marian's escape.

Robin then ceased thinking about anything except the swing of his sword and the need to find refuge down the street. The elite knights guarding the king began to shift to the right, putting added pressure on those attackers between them and their destination. Their opponents' numerical advantage was being steadily eroded by the discipline and expertise of King Richard's men.

Despite the din of the battle, Robin heard Much's frantic voice. "Lord Robin, don't–"

Robin glanced back; they were almost to the building, and he spotted Marian standing in the window. She was waving at him, and her eyes were wide with panic. She shrieked, "—not safe—," but the intensity of the fight was all-consuming, and he could not stop to listen. After dispatching another man, Robin looked back again, but Much and Marian were no longer there. However, that fleeting distraction nearly cost Robin his life; fortunately, André managed to block what would have been a killing blow.

The road was littered with fallen horses, the dead, and the dying. Both sides were on the brink of exhaustion, and the aggressors' fervor was fading fast. At that moment, the Lion of England roared a ferocious battle cry as he rallied Robin, André, and his remaining two knights in a charge against the enemy. The unexpected counterattack by the legendary and fearsome monarch caused the surviving seven adversaries to turn tail and ride away at full speed.

As soon as the assailants vanished from sight, Robin ordered the two unscathed knights to ride for help; one was to go to the palace for reinforcements and the king's physician; the other was instructed to return to the Templar compound for additional men-at-arms. Robin demanded, "I don't care if the Templars are puking and shitting themselves. They must come at once!"

The two men immediately rode away, while Robin and André moved the king and three injured knights into the vacant residence. Although in disrepair, it would be much safer than the street, since the enemy might return with more men. When everyone was settled, André and Robin peered out the window while lingering in the shadows. The only sounds were the cries of several attackers as they lay dying in the cluttered road. He assumed that Much had taken Marian and Allan to the rear of the home, as far from the fighting as possible.

Richard was reclining on the floor, stoically bearing the pain with his eyes closed. As the primary target, the king had sustained a number of injuries, and he was much too pale for Robin's comfort.

Robin and André were exhausted and thirsty, but they had gladly given their canteens to the wounded men and the king. Encumbered by their chainmail and sweating profusely, they wearily removed their helmets and hauberks, placing them in a pile next to their shields and weapons.

Just then, Robin noticed that the sleeve of André's sword arm was soaked in blood, and he appeared pallid and unwell. Alarmed, he persuaded the older knight to sit beside the king as he tore a strip of cloth from his surcoat to bind a jagged slash on André's forearm.

"What happened, André?" Robin gently asked.

"That damn bastard almost cut your head off," André grumbled, "and I had to save your pretty head...for the fair Lady Marian." He smiled feebly before leaning away from Richard and vomiting on the floor.

Robin frowned as he remembered André rescuing him during the battle. At the time, he hadn't realized that his friend had been hurt. King Richard then insisted that André drink the remaining swallows of water in his canteen.

"Who were those men? Did you recognize them?" the king hoarsely questioned.

André observed, "They were not Saracens, but they were not displaying heraldry either."

"Sire, maybe they were Genoese," Robin suggested. "They were fleeing in the direction of that quarter."

Richard growled between clenched teeth, "Find Lady Marian, and establish whether this building is secure. We cannot return to the street and risk another confrontation, and I do not want any more surprises."

Robin nodded; he had been thinking along the same lines. He considered putting his chainmail back on, but he didn't have the energy for such a task. Instead, he grabbed his sword and absent-mindedly swung his bow over his shoulder as he reluctantly left Richard in the custody of a weak and wounded André. Walking into an adjoining chamber, he discovered the Saracen headscarf that Marian had been wearing and cautiously opened a nearby door.

It led to a walled courtyard that was littered with stones,

potsherds, and crumbling mud bricks. An old table, its rotting wood marred by the destructive power of time and nature, seemed oddly out of place. Robin startled when he spotted Much and Allan lying on the ground on the far side of the table. Sprinting to them and kneeling, he shook Much's shoulder and breathed a sigh of relief once he discerned that they were alive.

A malicious chuckling caused Robin to rise and pivot. His nemesis, the Sheriff of Nottingham, was standing behind him and restraining a terrified Marian. She was facing Robin, but Argentan had one arm firmly wrapped around her waist, while the other was draped across the front of her shoulders as he pressed a blade to her throat.

With horror, Robin recognized his own dagger; the gift from Richard that had been confiscated by Argentan all those years ago when Marian's father had been murdered. Dragging his focus from the sharp edge at Marian's neck, Robin saw Guy of Gisborne flanking the sheriff, his sword at the ready.

Smiling triumphantly, Guy declared, "Today, I will have my revenge and send you to hell where you will be reunited with your father." He then charged at Robin while the sheriff muffled Marian's scream.

Robin, fatigued from the battle and shaking from dehydration, somehow found the stamina to bring his weapon up and block Gisborne's swing. Recalling his previous encounters with the tall knight, Robin knew that he was an emotional and reckless combatant. It was an Achilles' heel which the exhausted Robin hoped to use to his advantage. He sneered, "Did you learn to swordfight from a local butcher?"

Guy furiously lunged at Robin, who jumped to the side as Guy slipped on a piece of rubble, falling forward and embedding his sword into the wooden table instead of Robin.

Guy's blade was stuck, and Robin raised his weapon over his head to strike Guy, pausing to determine how to incapacitate his opponent without killing him. That hesitation was all the opening Gisborne needed. He let go of his sword, leaving it in the table, as he buried his fist into Robin's stomach. Robin, with his arms extended overhead, had not been prepared for the punch. With a loud exhalation, he tottered and lost his balance, tumbling backwards and landing heavily on his seat. While Robin regained his feet, Gisborne tugged on his weapon, finally dislodging it.

Much and Allan had awakened, but Guy and Argentan had disarmed them, so they were reduced to helplessly watching. Argentan warned them, "Stay back, or Maid Marian dies."

Robin and Guy began circling, each seeking an opportunity to attack while trying to avoid tripping on the rocks and debris scattered about. Robin worried that the slight tremor of his blade would reveal that he was on the verge of collapsing from exhaustion. Every beat of his heart created a tortuous echo thudding in his head. His mouth felt as though it were full of gritty sand, and his muscles were vociferously protesting. His weapon was growing heavier with each passing moment. A fleeting memory darted into his mind of the first time his father had handed him a full-size sword, and the mortification he had suffered when he dropped it. Robin was no longer sweating, and an odd shiver sped throughout his body. Why did he feel cold when the air was thick with the heat of the desert sun? A stark realization washed over him: he was going to lose this duel unless he could end it quickly.

Guy had calmed down, so Robin decided to provoke him into an impetuous move by asserting, "Marian loves *me*, and she will *never* belong to you." Robin's mouth was so dry that his words emerged in a hoarse rasp that sounded strange, even to him.

"No!" thundered Guy, as he impulsively slashed at Robin. "She will marry me."

Robin checked Guy's swing as Marian stridently affirmed, "I despise you with all my heart, Gisborne. I love only Robin, forever and ever! I will *never* love you. You *disgust* me. I would rather *die* than wed you!"

Robin witnessed Guy's expression darken into a red-faced humiliation shaded by black fury in response to Marian's harsh, unequivocal denunciation.

Argentan was snickering as he offered, "Gisborne, if you covet this woman, kill Huntingdon, and I will give her to you. She will learn to love you."

"Never!" Marian shrieked. She struggled against the sheriff's iron grip, squirming until the edge of his blade pierced her skin, and blood trickled down her slender neck.

An infuriated Gisborne aggressively swung his weapon, nearly overwhelming Robin, who stumbled backwards into the wall behind him. Robin was scarcely able to thwart Guy's rampageous assault.

Argentan excitedly screeched, "It is time to avenge Hugh of Gisborne!"

Robin was pinned against the wall, and he observed Guy's wrath intensify at Argentan's encouragement; evidently, Gisborne did not know the truth. Robin instantly searched his mind for what he knew of Hugh. Marshaling his waning strength, Robin defensively lifted his sword while kicking Gisborne's knee.

Guy yelped in pain and staggered back, while Much and Allan cheered.

Wheezing and doubled over as he worked to catch his breath, Robin's emotions were spiraling out of control. He snarled, "Hugh of Gisborne was a cowardly traitor who tried to poison King Henry. You must be so *proud* to bear his name." The verbal arrow flew true and found its mark.

The sound that exploded from Guy was more animal than human, and he sprang at Robin, who was so fatigued that he only partially blocked the strike as it sliced into his left side. Robin could feel warmth spread along his waist as the gash immediately started seeping blood. Marian screamed in terror as the sheriff tightened his hold on her.

Guy looked shocked that he had actually landed a blow, and he dithered, staring at Robin in disbelief. Swiftly recovering, Gisborne raised his sword. Suddenly, a rock the size of a man's fist soared through the air and smacked Guy in the side of his head. Robin glanced at Much, thankful for his friend's lifelong ability to throw stones with perfect accuracy.

Gisborne, stunned by the rock, wobbled and fell to his knees.

Robin still did not want to kill him, so he slapped Guy's wrist with the flat side of his blade, causing the dazed knight to drop his weapon. Robin kicked the sword out of reach and then shallowly cut his opponent's upper right arm, intending to disable him without mortally injuring him. Guy fainted as blood stained the sleeve of his tunic.

Robin spun towards the sheriff, raising his weapon and insisting, "Release Lady Marian. Now." He clutched his side with his other hand, compressing the laceration in hopes of staunching the flow of blood. Much scrambled to retrieve Gisborne's sword, and he joined Robin in confronting the sheriff.

Argentan freed Marian, sheathing Robin's old dagger and lifting his hands in surrender.

Marian ran to Robin, embracing him and sobbing in relief. The vigor of her affectionate onslaught practically knocked him off his feet.

Robin's gaze flicked to Gisborne, who was still unconscious, before he wearily questioned the sheriff. "Is it your intention to put John on the throne? John is not Richard's heir; his nephew, Arthur of Brittany, is next in line, but surely, you know this. Murdering King Richard would not elevate John to the throne; instead, it would launch a civil war that would rival the anarchy of King Stephen's reign."

Argentan's intelligent, dark eyes assessed the Earl of Huntingdon.

"You have much to learn, Robin Hood. Reality is revealed in the shadows, as the brightness of the sun blinds everyone to the truth." He then cackled wildly, and Robin was perplexed by the sheriff's nonsensical words and lack of concern. He had attempted regicide, been apprehended, and now faced execution, yet Argentan was apparently amused.

"Sire, wait," André's anxious voice unexpectedly rang out, and Robin pivoted to the door.

An ashen King Richard lurched into the courtyard and demanded, "What is going on here? Are we under attack?" Weak and light-headed from blood loss, Richard slumped to the ground.

André was close on the king's heels, but the battered knight was unsteady, and he collapsed beside Richard's recumbent form. André was gripping his sword in his left hand, as the laceration on his right arm had soaked his makeshift bandage.

"Sire," a distressed Robin exclaimed as he stepped towards Richard and André; he was still pressing one hand against the bloody gash in his side.

"Stop!" yelled Much.

Robin turned back to see Much holding Guy's sword and standing in front of Argentan. The sheriff had drawn his own weapon and was undoubtedly planning to kill the king.

Argentan rolled his eyes. "Out of my way, you dim-witted, dirty peasant."

Allan boldly stood with Much, even though he was unarmed. André shakily lifted his sword and protectively covered the king with his body.

King Richard was barely conscious, but he was gaping at Argentan in obvious confusion. He whispered, "You...I know you..."

Robin did not hear the king as he concentrated on finding the stamina to hoist his weapon. His sword was now visibly trembling, so he grasped the hilt with both hands in an effort to steady it. A darkness was creeping along the edges of his vision, and he shook his head, hoping to clear his mind.

Argentan calmly lowered his sword and stepped back.

Robin also lowered his weapon, relieved that the threat was contained. In truth, he no longer had the ability to hold it aloft. Marian gently took his sword and gave it to Allan as she implored, "Robin, we must send for a physician."

Peering down at Marian, he hugged her and realized that he needed her help to stand. "My love, are you hurt?" he tenderly asked when he noticed the blood on her neck where Argentan's dagger had nicked her delicate skin.

Marian fervently avowed, "Oh, Robin, I am all right. I was so frightened! I was so afraid that you were going to be killed. I love you, Robin!"

Argentan laughed loudly, and the two lovers scowled at him as he gleefully taunted, "How charming. Even heroes cannot resist the temptation of Eve. This viper's venom will be your death, Huntingdon."

Robin saw the sheriff's eyes shift ever so slightly, and he spun in the same direction, only to see Gisborne sneaking up behind him, his dagger raised and ready to strike. Robin frantically shoved Marian away and extended his hands in self-defense as he faced his enemy.

With a savage cry of rage and loathing, Sir Guy of Gisborne plunged the dagger into Robin's chest while Robin grabbed Guy's forearm in a vain struggle to keep the blade at bay. Instinctively, Guy wrapped his left arm around him while Robin continued to push against his assailant's arm. Both men were surprised to find themselves so close together, locked in a lethal embrace and illuminated by the crimson sunlight of a dying day.

Robin felt white-hot pain shoot through his upper body, and his heart pounded in sickening thuds as he endeavored to endure the torment without howling in agony. Every breath was more excruciating than the previous one.

His eyes blazing with hatred, Guy proclaimed in a ragged, yet triumphal, voice, "My father is finally avenged."

Robin beheld the pale blue eyes of his murderer, and an image of Duncan flashed in his mind. He channeled his remaining strength into stopping the blade from descending any further into his chest as he whispered, "You are wrong. Your father was Duncan Fitzooth, and we are…brothers."

Guy's eyes grew impossibly wide as he huffed, "What? That is absurd!"

Robin hissed, "It's true; I was told by–" Dizziness made Robin's head swim, and when he tried to take a deep breath, a new wave of acute pain engulfed him.

Guy's equally hushed voice countered, "I don't believe you. That is a lie."

Two pairs of identical pale blue eyes glared at each other. Robin was remarkably composed as he spoke to his half-brother; the man who had murdered him. "Look at my eyes…They are the same as yours and the same as our father's. You have the Fitzooth eyes."

Guy blanched, and he released his hold on Robin, pulling the dagger from Robin's chest and stepping away from him as he dropped the small knife. Guy was shuddering in horror at Robin's assertions—words that were sharper and more menacing to him than any double-edged sword. Robin sank to his knees and fell backwards, as searing pain tore through his body.

Marian, Much, and Allan rushed towards Robin's supine form, while Gisborne stood absolutely motionless as he stared in open-mouthed shock at Robin.

André crawled away from the king and tried to stand, hoping to attack Guy, but Argentan lunged at Richard, who was still lying on the ground. A panicked André threw himself between the king and Argentan, and a cold fear seized him: he was too weak to defeat either Guy or Argentan, and the king was in mortal danger.

The sound of horses and the beat of running feet heralded the arrival of men-at-arms from the palace, and Argentan blew out an exasperated breath. "Gisborne, we must leave, now!"

Guy snapped to attention and reclaimed his sword, which Much had tossed into the dirt before he hastened to Robin's side. Guy hurriedly followed the sheriff as they exited the courtyard via a side gate. Their horses were tethered there, and they mounted and rode away.

André was desperate to chase them, but he did not have the strength. The king was mumbling something about King Philippe when a crowd of knights burst into the courtyard. André ordered several of the men to pursue Argentan and Gisborne, giving them a brief description of the two men.

⋞

On his back, Robin felt the earth vibrating underneath him, and then he heard shouting. He gazed up at Marian, Much, and Allan as they hovered over him. "Marian?" he gasped. "Are you all right?"

Marian could not suppress an anguished sob, while Much and Allan looked horrified to the depths of their souls.

Robin was ghastly pale, and the red Crusader cross emblazoned on his white surcoat was becoming obscured by an ever-expanding blood stain. Much urgently pressed against Robin's chest in an attempt to stop the bleeding.

As Sir Baldwin de Béthune led his men into the courtyard, he was greeted by a dreadful sight. Not only was the king injured, but Robin Fitzooth, the brilliant and courageous Earl of Huntingdon, the beloved champion of the poor and downtrodden, the heroic and incomparable Robin Hood, was lying on the cluttered ground and bleeding from an apparently fatal wound.

CHAPTER 17
INTO THE SHADOWS

22 February 1192, City of Acre

The day was dying as the sun journeyed towards its inevitable demise along the western horizon. In an abandoned courtyard near the harbor of Acre, the sun's rays slanted across cluttered debris and illuminated a wounded hero, bathing him in a fiery halo of red-orange light.

It was an eerie spectacle, and Allan shivered with dread. He was standing a short distance from Robin, politely offering Marian and Much some privacy.

The previously deserted patch of ground was swarming with men as knights and soldiers invaded the space. The minstrel observed several men who were crowded around the king, giving him something to drink and checking his injuries. Allan scowled. The king wasn't as badly hurt as Robin. Meanwhile, André staggered over to him and sat on the old weather-beaten table as he gulped generous swigs from a canteen. His arm was swathed in a fresh bandage.

Motivated by his desperate concern for Robin, Allan boldly approached this imposing man who was the king's cousin. "Who are those men attending to the king?" he demanded. "Don't they realize that Lord Robin needs help?"

André scrutinized Allan as he responded, "The man wearing ecclesiastical robes is Hubert Walter, the Bishop of Salisbury. The younger man is Ranulphus Besace, the king's physician."

Allan was stunned that these two youthful men held such lofty positions. The bishop was the same age as the king, while the doctor was probably in his mid-twenties.

King Richard was much improved after drinking his fill from the bishop's proffered canteen. His voice boomed as he commanded, "Ranulphus, go tend to the Earl of Huntingdon. My scratches are nothing. I order you to heal him!"

Allan felt relief; surely, the king's physician would be able to save Robin. The young doctor and the bishop hastened to the king's favorite knight, and Allan watched as Much retreated to give them more room. When Allan saw the color drain from the physician's face, his hope plummeted. Bishop Walter was trying to persuade Marian to move away as well, but she stubbornly refused to leave Robin's side.

Ranulphus slightly lifted Robin as he took an exotic, curved bow that had been slung over Robin's shoulder and laid it aside. He then grabbed a nearby dagger; ironically, it was the very one which Guy had used in his attack, and he cut open the front of Robin's surcoat and tunic, exposing his pierced chest and the slash in his left side. Allan noticed the doctor remove a chain from around Robin's neck prior to conducting a detailed examination of his injuries.

The physician had a leather bag suspended from his shoulder, and he quickly lowered it, dropping Robin's necklace into it while retrieving an earthenware jar from within its depths. He ruptured the seal and poured sticky, golden honey onto Robin's wounds. Next, Ranulphus barked at a few soldiers, "Go into this building, and collect as many cobwebs as you can find. Roll them into balls, and bring them here."

The men practically collided with each other as they rushed to obey.

Moving closer, Allan saw Ranulphus glance up at the bishop and deliver a small shake of his head. Allan trembled in fear at the sight of that ominous gesture.

The bishop knelt and raised Robin's head as he helped him drink from a canteen. Robin eagerly swallowed until he had to stop and catch his breath. The bishop gently inquired, "My son, are you ready to confess your sins and receive your last rites?"

"No!" Marian shrieked in denial, even though she could see that Robin was growing exceedingly pale. She could hear Much weeping behind her, and she bit her lip to repress her own sobs. Robin was dying, and everyone knew it.

Hoarsely, Robin replied, "No, Your Grace, not yet. First, I must ask this fair lady a question." He hesitated and marshaled his strength. "Marian, we don't have much time–"

"Don't say that," cried Marian.

Ignoring her, Robin resumed, "Marian, will you be my wife? I want to bequeath my name and my properties to you, so that you will have wealth and security for the future."

"But, Robin–" Marian started to explain what Edmund had told her: they were already married in the eyes of the Lord *and* the law. When they exchanged promises to marry in that Nottingham church in the presence of a priest, and those vows were followed by consummation, they had entered into a clandestine marriage, and canon law considered them legally wed. But as she observed Robin's pain-filled eyes, Marian recognized that nothing really mattered except granting Robin whatever he desired. "Yes, I will marry you," she answered in a voice thick with the intensity of her sorrow.

Just then, several men carrying handfuls of sticky cobwebs hurried forward. Ranulphus pushed the webs into Robin's wounds alongside the smears of honey. Robin moaned in agony, and Marian whimpered to see him vulnerable and hurting.

As soon as the physician had finished, he withdrew, so that the king and Robin's friends could come near and bear witness to Robin and Marian's wedding. Richard appeared poised and regal, but beneath his façade of calmness there was an unfathomable, raw ache, for the prospect of losing Robin was devastating to him.

The Bishop of Salisbury pronounced them husband and wife, and the assembled onlookers, together with the king, bowed respectfully to the newlywed couple. The bishop then administered the rites that prepared Robin's soul for its final journey. Bishop Walter had endeavored to keep both ceremonies brief, and he promptly stepped back in order to permit Robin to say his farewells.

Despite the murky fog that was beginning to cloud his consciousness, Robin gazed adoringly at his wife, and Marian smiled softly in return, but her spirit was shattering into an infinite number of pieces, like tiny pinpoints of light scattered across a midnight sky.

A shadow fell over them, and Robin looked up into the somber face of his king. Richard hid his distress as he conveyed his appreciation for his beloved friend. "Robin, I am alive because you saved my life today. England and I are forever in your debt." Richard chuckled half-heartedly and conceded, "You have saved my life many times. Without you, I would have been dead long ago."

Robin soberly countered, "There is no debt, Sire." Emphasizing every word with gritty determination, he proclaimed, "I am honored to sacrifice my life for my wife, for England, and for my king."

Marian gasped in surprise. In the past, Robin's unconditional loyalty and deference to King Richard had rendered her dejected and seething with jealousy. But Robin's statement had indisputably announced that he valued her above all else, including the king. She yearned to feel exultant, but the black veil of impending widowhood precluded any joy or satisfaction which she might have otherwise experienced.

The king also noticed the sequence of Robin's priorities, and he almost scolded his faithful subject. In a rare suppression of his pride, Richard quietly withdrew, awarding Robin the last word without argument.

As the king retreated, Much advanced and slumped heavily to his knees next to Robin. He clasped Robin's hand, clinging to it as if it were a raft drifting upon a sea of angst, and he wept, "Robin, don't die!"

"My friend, don't cry for me," implored a solemn Robin.

Much fought to regain his composure, but he could not. Choking back another sob, he groaned, "What will I do without you?"

With a wan grin, Robin attempted to soothe his friend's torment. He asserted emphatically, "Much, always remember that I love you."

"Robin, I love you as well," affirmed Much, his voice quivering. "You are my best friend, and I would do anything for you."

"I know," Robin acknowledged, "and I need you to do something very important for me."

Much squeezed Robin's hand tighter, averring, "Tell me, and I will do it, Lord Robin."

"Please take care of Marian."

"I will," Much pledged. Although his vision was blurred by tears, he could see Robin's farewell smile—a treasured parting gift from his life-long companion. Hoping to give Marian and Robin privacy, Much rose to his feet, wobbling somewhat, and departed to stand with Allan.

Robin dragged a deep, excruciating inhalation. He winced as a stab of pain tore through his chest. He had to rally all his strength to speak as he focused his attention on his wife. "Marian, promise me that you will stay away from England and Nottingham until the king's return."

Marian protested, "Robin, I can't agree to—"

"Marian, you have to live for both of us," he persevered. Robin tried to smirk playfully as he repeated her words from that fateful night in the hunting lodge all those years ago. "You must be careful and not do anything reckless or dangerous."

"I promise," Marian woodenly responded, her voice sounding insincere even to her own ears, for she planned to do exactly the opposite; she would renew the fight against tyranny in the name of Robin Hood with unwavering vigor and fortitude. And she vowed to avenge his murder.

Robin sighed gratefully. "I will rest in peace, if I know that you are safe."

Marian traced the outline of his features with her finger as tears rolled down her cheeks. "Robin, I don't want to be separated from you again. Please, don't go; I need you."

Robin tenderly mused, "Marian, we were like Odysseus and Penelope, estranged because of my duty to my king and his war. I am just sorry that we will not have a happy ending on earth."

Anger at God stirred in Marian's heart. How could a righteous and benevolent God take Robin away from her while allowing a monster like Gisborne to live? She tempered her blasphemous thoughts, for Marian desperately needed to have faith that she would be reunited with Robin in heaven. "Nothing will destroy our love," she firmly declared, "not distance, or time, or...or..." She could not utter the word that would signify the end of Robin's existence.

Robin grimaced and shuddered as he began to cough. Marian offered him another drink from the bishop's canteen, which was still lying nearby. After swallowing as much as he could, Robin watched her with an unguarded adoration. There was no attempt to shield his emotions as he laid bare his heart and placed it solely in her custody. He admitted, "I did not think it possible, but I love you more than ever, my wife."

She bestowed upon him a slow, pensive smile. "I love you, my husband, my gallant and brave Odysseus."

A portentous silence settled over the married couple. In the thrall of despair and imminent doom, Robin contemplated his life.

He had courageously confronted danger and fearlessly defended his wife, his king, and his men without hesitation. On his last day, Robin had valiantly saved not only King Richard but also Marian from Argentan and Gisborne. It was a glorious death, and the troubadours would laud him as a hero. He might perish, but Robin Hood would be admired and praised for generations.

At that moment, he realized that he didn't want to be a hero and a legend; he wanted to be a husband and father. If only he could go back in time and select a different path. He would choose Marian over glory. He begged God to let him survive and be with his wife. His only solace was that the Lord had granted him the opportunity to wed Marian before dying. He would always be thankful for that; now Marian would have security and live in comfort as his widow.

More disheartening thoughts invaded his mind. He had battled tirelessly for his beliefs and principles, for justice and peace, for king and country, and ultimately for Marian. Yet, on the threshold of oblivion and preparing to enter into a gaping, bottomless abyss, he finally understood that there can never be universal peace or justice as long as men like Argentan and Gisborne existed. And such men were more numerous than those willing to fight for what was right. His struggle had been futile—destined to fail from the start. As this awareness penetrated his consciousness, a poignant hollowness curled up inside him, and Robin became a young man disillusioned by war and disenchanted by a cruel and unfair world. In the intimate presence of eternity, his life seemed so meaningless, filled with lost opportunities and thwarted dreams, and the most devastating insight was that he had squandered his chance for happiness with Marian.

His disappointment in himself and his choices was so immense that it was bounded only by the sky. Prior to going on Crusade, he had believed that his sacred mission was to liberate Jerusalem from the heathens. But now, all the slaughter he had committed in the name of God and his king was a crushing, relentless weight upon his soul. The Holy Land was a consecrated place, and yet, it was also the land where his youthful innocence had drowned in a deluge of blood. Maybe his demise in this place where he had killed so many people was his punishment for the atrocities that he had perpetrated.

A spasm of pain pulled him out of his short reverie. Looking into Marian's eyes, Robin affectionately murmured, "My Marian... My wife..."

"My husband," she whispered through tears.

She was gripping his hand, and Robin entwined their fingers as a symbol of their union. His strength was fading, but his expression was hopeful. "Can you forgive me for breaking my promise and leaving you?"

"Yes, of course, I forgive you." She suppressed another sob, attempting to be brave in front of Robin.

"Then I can die in peace."

Marian's conscience was buffeted by shame, unease, and the urge to make a complete confession to her husband. She had hidden the truth from him, and she opened her mouth, ready to divulge everything. Dithering, she was apprehensive that the shock might hasten his passing. Would she have enough time to fully explain? And did she want their remaining moments together to be filled with acrimony and strife? With resignation, she endeavored to conceal her guilt as she realized that Robin would succumb to his injuries without learning her secret.

Despondent, she implored, "Please forgive me, Robin."

"You have done nothing wrong," he replied, his brow creasing with confusion that morphed into remorse. "But I have done things which I regret."

She frowned at him, sharply asking, "What do you mean?"

Robin heaved a weary sigh. "Regardless of what you hear about me in the future, you must never doubt that you are the only woman I have ever loved." It was the only thing he could say to her because there was no time to disclose his own secrets.

Bewilderment at his cryptic words briefly troubled her, but she decided to focus on the present. In a subdued tone, she hummed, "My love, my Robin…"

He huskily entreated, "Kiss me."

Marian cupped Robin's face and gazed at him with the immeasurable devotion that pervaded her heart, seeking to forever imprint his handsome appearance in her memory. She could see tears in Robin's eyes, and he beamed at her with his majestic smile; the one she cherished most. Her tears fell upon Robin's cheek and merged with his, like the tenebrous waters of the River Styx.

Robin was so heartbroken that he could have composed a mournful dirge about their tragic love, but there was no time. He labored to maintain a calm demeanor, for he didn't want to distress Marian even more. Mortality was already fluttering between them like brittle autumn leaves dancing across a windswept forest clearing before crumbling into dust.

With noticeable effort, Robin raised his head slightly and captured her mouth, savoring the moment as his lips caressed hers slowly and achingly. A sigh of spellbound pleasure tumbled from her and mingled with the breath of doom. Each of them felt the fire of passion, but their fervency was tinged with a hue of impending bereavement.

Robin ended the kiss. "My Marian, I love you." His eyes glistening with wistful yearning, he vowed, "I will wait for you in heaven."

Marian's blood ran cold with dread at those words.

Robin beheld Marian for what he thought was the last time, as lyrical and ineluctable rhythms of ruin were spreading throughout his body. The throbbing in his chest and side intensified, and dizziness overwhelmed him as a vast cloak of night began to obscure his vision. Like a bird of prey, the Angel of Death was opening his wings and extending his covetous talons towards Robin who suddenly experienced serenity, as if he were wandering in the primeval wilderness of his beloved Sherwood Forest.

"Robin?" There was no response. Marian's heart hammered inside her ribcage so forcefully that she became light-headed. She called to him again, her eyes full of fright, her voice soft and pleading, but he didn't stir.

Ranulphus rushed forward and crouched next to Robin. He placed his fingers on Robin's neck, searching for a pulse.

Marian anxiously peered at the physician. He could not meet her eyes, and he simply shook his head. At first, Marian didn't react, refusing to acknowledge the meaning of his gesture. Finally, he lifted his gaze to her. "I'm sorry, my lady, but I cannot detect his heartbeat. Please accept my sincere condolences, Lady Huntingdon." The doctor climbed to his feet and cast a solemn glance at the young widow; he then rejoined the others standing nearby.

Marian was still kneeling beside Robin, and she slid her hands under his neck and shoulders, cradling him in her arms. A forlorn keening echoed in the courtyard, and Marian realized that it was the sound of anguish leaking out of her fractured heart, like ale seeping from a cracked ewer. A grief-stricken Marian gently lowered Robin back to the ground. She stared at him, her tearful eyes shimmering with a dismal luster. Robin looked so peaceful, as though the weight of the world had been removed from him. There was even a ghost of a smile on his face.

An ethereal voice faintly summoned her. *I will wait for you in heaven.*

Marian gasped in shock as the awful truth revealed itself with an acute fierceness. *Robin is dead!*

She wished to imagine that she had been ensnared in the throes of a nightmare, but Robin's motionless form was an inescapable fact. She beseeched God to restore Robin's life, but the mocking voice in her mind sneered that she was lost in a fantasy.

Marian raised her eyes towards the brilliant red-gold canvas of a sky at sunset, tears streaming down her cheeks. The earth seemed to be holding its breath in trepidation as its source of light and warmth drowned in the azure water off the coast of an ancient land. The sky around the dying sun was aflame with reflected glory, and its crimson color was merely another reminder of Robin's spilled blood.

That voice, which was both familiar and alien, again whispered: *Robin is dead!*

Marian recognized that it was her soul murmuring to her and enveloping her in an ebony pall of grief. Her devastated spirit perceived a new reality—a world bereft of Robin. She would never again see beauty in a sunset; now the setting sun would forever symbolize the death of hope and love in her life. With boundless contempt, Marian believed that the events in Acre were illustrative of the absolute unfairness of the world.

She rested her forehead on Robin's shoulder and wept. She had always endeavored to be courageous and steadfast, but Robin's passing was too much for her to bear, and she could no longer control her emotions. At that moment, her existence narrowed until it was reduced to a desolate wail of torment and brokenness. The feeling of Robin's warm hand was so precious to her that she wanted to preserve the sensation for all eternity.

Once more, she lifted Robin's upper body and gathered him into a loving embrace. Cradling her husband in her arms, she was sinking into an ocean of despair, engulfed by her inconsolable misery. The light of her life was gone, and she plunged into a dark world, ominous and scented with the poisonous inevitability of a future where she would be compelled to live without Robin, suffering and waiting to be reunited with him in heaven.

Hugging Robin close to her, she looked beyond his shoulder and was distracted by a blade gleaming in the diminishing rays of the sun. Sickening memories took Marian out of her trance as she viewed Gisborne's dagger, which Ranulphus had heedlessly left nearby.

She quietly hissed Guy's name with venom, her countenance a perfect cameo of fathomless disgust and implacable hatred. It was a startling realization that she was capable of despising someone with such a burning, endless abhorrence. A fog of revulsion clouded Marian's mind, and loathing clawed at her heart as she remembered how Guy had murdered her husband.

Returning Robin to the ground, Marian noticed that there was fresh blood on his cheek, and for an irrational moment, she feared that she had somehow injured him. She abruptly recalled the cut on her neck, and she skimmed her hand over her throat. She was still bleeding, and her fingers were now wet with blood. Impassively, she observed as a drop rolled languorously towards her palm. Shifting her gaze back to Robin, she was strangely entranced by the sight of a similar trickle of blood sliding down his chest. Impulsively, she reached out and touched it, and Robin's blood instantly blended with her own. In her traumatized mind, she saw this mingling of their blood as the last way in which they could ever be joined on this side of heaven. She examined the blood staining her fingers. It was impossible to discern which blood was hers and which was Robin's.

Behind her, one of the most powerful monarchs in the known world was openly grieving for her husband, but he meant nothing to Marian. Instead, her world was now governed by her ruthless resolve to ensure that the monster responsible for Robin's demise would be punished. Gisborne deserved to suffer the most horrific torture she could invent. In a hushed voice, she vowed, "With God as my witness, I swear by your sacred blood that Gisborne will pay for what he did to you. I will make his life a living hell." She drew a small cross in their combined blood near his chest wound. Then, with her clean hand, she tugged at the neck of her loose Saracen gown, lowering the front as she traced another bloody cross over her heart. Having completed her blood oath, she sealed it with a kiss, touching her lips to his before she made one more promise to

Robin. "Then I will follow you, my love. You will not have to wait for me for too long."

The mourners had bowed their heads, and they were oblivious to Marian's macabre actions. In truth, no one had the heart to watch Marian lament her tragically deceased husband, so they respectfully averted their eyes. The lethal silence in the courtyard was interrupted as Much fell to his knees, covered his face with his hands, and sobbed freely and without shame. His sincere sorrow was contagious, and a number of the men who had served Lord Huntingdon started weeping. Allan's sensitive soul was especially aggrieved, and the minstrel also dissolved into tears. King Richard, André, and Baldwin somberly struggled to restrain their emotions and accept the heart-rending death of their heroic comrade.

Anguish shrouded the gathering like a heavy mantle of perpetual woe. Robin Fitzooth, the Earl of Huntingdon, the quintessence of honor, nobility, and bravery, was no longer a part of the world, but his name would be immortalized in ballads about Robin Hood and his merry men.

CHAPTER 18
DAMNATION

n the waning light of a setting sun, the newly widowed Countess of Huntingdon was sitting on the ground and vacantly staring at the body of her beloved husband. Unfathomable sorrow, confused disbelief, and furious denial all fought for supremacy within the mausoleum where her heart was entombed. Ultimately, she surrendered to a dazed numbness that temporarily brought some clarity to her soul. In that moment, she began to direct her warring emotions at those around her. She pledged to dedicate the rest of her life to a quest for vengeance.

"My lady?"

The accented voice of a stranger resurrected unwelcome thoughts of Argentan, and Marian ignored him.

Sir Baldwin de Béthune cleared his throat and awkwardly resumed, "I am...I was a friend of Lord Huntingdon's. I am very sorry for your loss."

The silence stretched uncomfortably, and Baldwin hesitantly stood there, a lifelong bachelor unaccustomed to interacting with crying women. When Marian finally looked up at him, he recoiled somewhat from the sight of her eyes, for they appeared both infinitely distraught and utterly lifeless.

"Thank you," Marian hoarsely replied.

Baldwin averted his eyes, finding himself unable to behold this shattered, disconsolate woman sitting next to his deceased friend.

Marian was mute for a handful of heartbeats before coldly demanding, "What do you want from me?"

The knight lifted his gaze to her and was alarmed to see that her face was now set in a fierce determination, like that of a merciless goddess bathing in a sea of darkness.

"King Richard was wounded in the battle," he informed her.

"How sad for him," she sarcastically retorted as she raised a mocking brow. "And?"

Baldwin flinched at the sound of her chilly voice, and his words tumbled out in an uncharacteristically nervous rush. "The king, his cousin, and several other knights need further medical care. The sun is setting, and night will soon be upon us. We must return to the palace; the safety of the king requires it."

Marian's scrutiny veered to Richard who was quietly conversing with André on the other side of the courtyard. The setting sun illuminated the king in a golden glow that seemed to glorify and celebrate his survival. Marian rose and studied Richard as a sense of outraged betrayal emerged from the ashes of what had been her heart. Red-hot wrath stirred within her at the sight of the King of England, a man so full of life, while Robin lay dead at her feet. The scandalous idea that it would have been better if Richard had died instead of Robin festered and simmered in her tormented mind.

The king intercepted Marian's glare and gave her a solemn, compassionate nod.

"I want to talk to the king," Marian declared to Baldwin, her voice distant and strained.

"King Richard requested to speak to you as well," apprised Baldwin.

Without responding, Marian stalked towards the king. The king's men respectfully sank to one knee as she walked by, but she didn't seem to notice their sincere deference. All the men were profoundly moved by her appearance: her clothes and hands were stained with Robin's blood, and there were smears of blood on her face and a minor slash on her neck. It was a spectacle that was equally disturbing and heart-rending.

Marian stopped in front of Richard who bowed to her slightly, an uncommon gesture for the king; André briefly dropped to one knee. The tension in the air was palpable as Marian and the king stared at each other in silence.

"Lady Huntingdon," greeted André, hailing her as Robin's wife.

Steeling herself against swirling emotions of despair, emptiness, and fury, Marian acknowledged André with a dip of her head. Addressing the Lion, the civility of her words was belied by her haughty manner. "My liege, you sent for me?"

Even though Marian had endeavored to hide her mounting hostility, the king could see blatant resentment in her eyes. He cautiously offered, "There are no words to describe my grief. Robin's loss is devastating, especially for you, Lady Huntingdon."

Abandoning any attempt to control her seething anger, Marian indignantly cried, "Sire, before the feast, you accused Robin of disloyalty because he bravely spoke the truth. You threatened to cast him into the ranks of the infantry. And now you allege that you valued his life?"

As a member of one of the most powerful families in all of Christendom, Richard was not in the habit of justifying himself to others, but he bore a strong debt of gratitude to Robin, and by extension, Robin's widow. Richard asserted, "Robin knew me well; if he were here, he would tell you that I sometimes allow my temper to overwhelm my tongue. I wouldn't have endangered Robin in such a way. That is a ridiculous notion."

Marian narrowed her eyes and bitterly challenged the king,

"From a young age Robin worshipped you. He enthusiastically followed you on Crusade rather than honor his commitment to me." She gathered her thoughts. "Sire, of all your men, it was Robin who served you best. And yet, I heard you make these threats against him. Since Robin is no longer here to defend you and explain your cruel and intemperate words, what am I to believe?"

André intervened, a sharp reproach in his voice. "Lady Huntingdon, your sorrow is prompting you to speak indecorously, for surely you do not mean to insult the king."

"Lady Huntingdon means exactly what she says, and she has my permission to speak freely," King Richard decreed. His expression remained impassive, but his eyes were full of pain. "I have never doubted Robin's allegiance, and I am asking *you*, Lady Huntingdon, to stop doubting my devotion to him. I will say this only once, and then this debate is settled: I was angry and did not mean what I said. Robin knew this, which is why he did not react fearfully to my threats. I will apologize to you for causing you distress, since you mistakenly judge me capable of abusing Robin."

The king lapsed into a fleeting hush while Marian gaped at him in surprise; she had not expected an admission of imperfection from the narcissistic Lionheart. Marian felt vaguely vindicated, although there was nothing that could truly bring her any comfort in a world without Robin. She choked out a mirthless laugh—a poisonous hiss full of scorn. "Sire, I will accept your apology for all the *distress* you have caused me."

André bristled at her contemptuous tone.

She persisted, her tirade harsh and unforgiving. "Perhaps if you had only listened to Robin's wise counsel, then the war would be over, and Robin would still be alive. I can find some solace in knowing that Robin wanted to end the war and return home to me. He displayed more genuine concern for the people of England than—"

"My lady, please, you cannot say such things." André was frantic to prevent her from offending the king.

Richard interposed. "André, there is no need to rebuke Lady Huntingdon. I do not begrudge her opinions, and I have already repented for my hasty comments."

Marian heaved a sigh of regret. "I should have done many things differently too."

"If only I had killed Gisborne before he attacked Robin," lamented André.

The king consoled his favorite cousin. "You were wounded, André, and you were protecting me."

Marian did not wish André dead, but she wasn't particularly interested in his remorse or injuries, as her own anguish was all-consuming. Her eyes wandered to Robin, and tears blurred her vision again. Much was kneeling next to Robin, clinging to his friend's hand with a desperation that she understood all too well. Allan stood behind Much, frequently wiping away the dampness on his face with his sleeve.

King Richard was also contemplating Robin's body, and an all-absorbing, tart feeling of grief gained possession of his spirit. "Robin," he murmured in an unusually tender voice. "From our first meeting at the court in Poitou, I experienced a unique kinship with him. I once told him that he was the brother of my heart. I was honored to know him and call him friend."

"I treasured his friendship," grieved André. He surveyed the other knights in the courtyard. They were all somber, and some were openly weeping. He concluded, "Robin was admired by everyone who knew him."

Marian contended, "It was impossible not to love Robin."

Richard decisively proclaimed, "I will make peace with Saladin as soon as possible and depart for England. I must put an end to John's treacherous ambitions, and then certain traitors will be held accountable for their crimes."

Marian swung her gaze back to Robin, and flames of loathing

scorched her soul. "Gisborne," she spat, "deserves death more than anyone else."

"Baron de Argentan will be executed, but Gisborne—" André's voice faltered with the potency of his hatred. "He must endure a slow and agonizing death."

The Lion growled, "These traitors will be executed for the regicide attempt and for Robin's murder." Touching a gold cross hanging from a chain around his neck, he solemnly vowed, "They will suffer for taking Robin from us."

Marian eyed the famed Lionheart. While she was gratified that Richard shared her thirst for vengeance, she would never understand Robin's devotion to this man. She had no intention of fighting for the king upon her return to England. Instead, she would fight for the people in her husband's name as Robin Hood's widow.

She was abruptly reminded of an issue that she urgently needed to broach. "Sire, I require your help with something…confidential," she began, striving to maintain a steady voice and avoid revealing the depth of her apprehension. As the Countess of Huntingdon, she had obligations to fulfill, and she sought the king's assistance.

Richard was intrigued by her mysterious entreaty, so he waved dismissively at André, who reluctantly walked away to stand with Baldwin.

Baldwin inquired, "What are they discussing? Robin's funeral?"

Shrugging, André replied, "It's a private matter between the king and Lady Huntingdon."

The two knights observed Marian and Richard, and they were puzzled as they witnessed the changing emotions on the king's face. Richard seemed shocked and troubled by whatever Marian was telling him, but then his expression softened benevolently. André and Baldwin's curiosity was building to an unbearable crescendo, and they subtly shifted closer, straining to catch a snippet of the conversation.

Fortunately, Richard had a voice that carried, and they heard him pledge, "Be at ease; I will settle everything when I return to England, but in the meantime, you must keep this a secret."

"Thank you, my liege," she responded with evident relief.

"You are welcome, my lady," Richard assured her. He then beckoned to André, announcing, "We will withdraw to the palace at once."

"The Templars arrived a short time ago, and they have offered us the use of a small wagon to transport Robin's body," divulged André in a tight voice. He cast an apologetic glance at Marian.

The king gently explained, "Lady Huntingdon, we must leave as darkness is descending upon the streets of Acre. Tomorrow we will give Robin a proper burial befitting his high station."

After a tense silence, she granted stiffly, "Very well." Her gaze drifted to Robin again. "But I cannot attend his...funeral...I just cannot..." Her voice quavered as tears filled her eyes and ran down her cheeks. "I cannot watch him being...put into the ground." A forlorn sob escaped her.

Richard sympathetically promised, "I will organize everything. Do not worry, my lady."

She earnestly disclosed, "I want to go home. Now that Robin is..." Her voice faded as she found herself unable to speak the word. Exhaling deeply, she implored, "Please permit Much to return to England with me."

"His vassalage is to the Earldom of Huntingdon. I release him to you." The royal brow creased in concern. "My lady, you cannot return to England. These criminals, Argentan and Gisborne, might pose a danger to you. For now, you will reside at the Queen Mother's court in Aquitaine. You will be safe there until my return."

Without waiting for a response from Marian, Richard ordered Baldwin to arrange for passage on a boat captained by a man whom the king personally knew and trusted. It was decided that Marian, Allan, and Much would spend the night on this vessel, and that it would depart at first light the following morning.

❧

Marian slowly approached Robin, preparing for her final farewell. Much was still there, but he was no longer sobbing. She sank to the ground, feeling her heart collapse in anguish as hot tears of sorrow flowed from her eyes. Struggling to regain her composure, she notified Much, "The king has given permission for you to return home with me and Allan."

A grateful Much raised his tear-stained face to her and effused, "My lady, thank you. I want to leave this place and go home."

Marian's eyes darted to the king, who was talking with Baldwin. She lowered her voice conspiratorially, "The king plans to send me to Aquitaine, but I promise you, we are going home to Nottinghamshire. No king, or queen, not even God Himself, will thwart me in my quest to avenge Robin's murder. We will explain everything to Allan later."

Much bobbed his head in concurrence. He then asked, "What will we do with Robin's weapons?" He pointed to a nearby sword and a distinctive bow.

"I will take them. They are mine now." Marian reverently lifted the bow and hugged it.

Gesturing at the exotic weapon, Much informed her, "This is a Saracen re-curve bow. An envoy of Saladin brought gifts for King Richard, and among them was this bow. The king was very pleased to present it to Robin."

Marian examined it and declared, "Robin's bow is sacred to me. From this day forward, I will keep it with me for protection and… revenge."

Much agreed. "You deserve to have it, Lady Marian."

Retrieving Guy's dagger, she shuddered in revulsion. "Much, take this too. I will need it, along with Robin's weapons, when I take my vengeance," she hissed. Trying to banish her increasingly dark and disturbed thoughts, Marian stared at Robin, who looked as if he were sleeping peacefully.

"I can't believe that he is gone," bemoaned Much. "From the time when we were boys, I always felt it was my duty to watch over Lord Robin. I would have gladly died for him, but today, I failed him."

Marian put a soothing hand on Much's shoulder. "Robin wouldn't want you to blame yourself." Much was so absorbed in his despair that he didn't see the ruthless and unhealthy glint in Marian's slightly narrowed eyes as she snarled, "Only Gisborne is guilty."

"I hate Gisborne; I want him dead," seethed Much.

Marian's voice was edged with loathing. "Much, I swear that Gisborne will suffer."

Much's eyes glittered with purpose and tenacity. "I will kill Gisborne when we return to England," he pledged.

"There is something worse than death for this fiend," she averred.

A befuddled Much nodded. He didn't comprehend her meaning, but he trusted her judgment.

"I need a few moments alone with Robin," requested Marian, and Much obediently rose and went to join Allan.

Marian took Robin's hand in hers, kissing it tenderly. Her warm lips caressed his face, his mouth, his cheeks, and his eyes, while she was chanting his name over and over. Robin Hood's widow murmured, "I will love you forever…My hero…My husband… My Robin…"

22 February 1192, Harbor of Acre

Guy wrapped a clean cloth around the shallow cut on his right arm, shifting his weight back and forth as he endeavored to counter the swaying of the boat beneath his feet. He then pulled on his tunic and firmly grabbed the railing. The small ship was exiting the harbor and entering rougher seas as they traveled north to Tyre, where he and the sheriff would board a larger vessel and begin their journey home.

They passed the Tower of Flies, which stood guard at the western outskirts of Acre's waterfront, and then glided alongside the shoreline of the ancient city as the imposing walls of the Templar compound loomed above them. The sun was low in the sky, and the ship's captain had heatedly complained about Argentan's insistence that they sail for Tyre so late in the day.

Standing at the stern, Guy squinted at the bustling port as it shrank and blurred until it disappeared from sight; just like all his hopes for the future. A future that was now crumbling into dust because of the sheriff's failure to slay the Lion.

He gingerly massaged his temple where it was swollen from the strike of a well-aimed rock. He still felt a bit woozy and perplexed. He briefly considered the possibility that he had merely dreamt the events of this dreadful day, but the throbbing of his head and the ache in his arm assured him that it was all real.

Guy had been stunned by the unanticipated arrival of Marian. She was supposed to be in London, yet she had suddenly materialized, seemingly out of nowhere, in the midst of the attack on the king. The day had instantly assumed a dreamlike quality. Marian often appeared in his dreams; pleasant nighttime visits to his bed where the pure, innocent Marian morphed into a seductive siren who always left him panting with desire.

There had been no opportunity to ask for an explanation; Guy had quickly incapacitated the peasants with her, and he would have obeyed the sheriff's demands to kill the two men, but for the tearful, beseeching gaze of his beloved Marian. To impress her, he had ignored the sheriff, but his efforts were all for naught.

Any prospect of a future with Marian had been stolen by Huntingdon. Naturally, she would choose Robin. He was a wealthy earl and a favorite of the king. Guy castigated himself for his naiveté in believing that Marian could ever fall in love with a knight whose only property was Locksley, an insignificant estate which he held due to the generosity of the sheriff and Prince John.

He struck the railing in frustrated annoyance. He needed to feel happy. He *should* be overjoyed. He had won! Maybe the sheriff's scheme had gone awry, but Sir Guy of Gisborne had finally tasted his first victory against Robin Fitzooth.

A wicked notion occurred to him and provided a measure of satisfaction; perhaps he would never have Marian, but Robin would never have her either, for the wound which Guy had inflicted was surely fatal. The renowned former outlaw was most likely already dead. Even that idea did not lift his spirits, because he kept picturing Marian weeping uncontrollably next to Robin's corpse. He sighed regretfully, for he had never wanted to cause her pain.

No matter how hard he tried, he could not find a way to savor his triumph. He frowned as he replayed the duel in his mind. His victory over Robin had come after a disgraceful attempt to sneak up behind the man. If Huntingdon had not turned, Guy would have dishonorably stabbed him in the back, and he felt shame for this. What had he been thinking? He acknowledged that he hadn't really been thinking at all—he had only been reacting to Marian's loud declarations of love. Declarations that should have been for him.

Robin's voice intruded into his thoughts: *Your father was Duncan Fitzooth, and we are brothers.*

Guy gripped the railing and bellowed, "Stop lying!" to the swiftly passing coastline.

Two nearby sailors paused at his peculiar outburst and gawked at him curiously before shrugging their shoulders and resuming their duties.

Guy pondered those moments when he had been holding Robin in his arms. Why would Robin lie to him like that? What would be the purpose of these outrageous allegations? It made no sense.

Unless Robin was telling the truth.

Guy shook his head in repudiation of these mental whisperings and closed his eyes. But an image of pale blue eyes filled with agony surfaced in his mind, and Guy could not deny that looking into Robin's eyes had been like viewing a reflection of his own. Even though Guy's angular features and dark hair bore no resemblance to the boyish, fair-haired Robin, there was no disputing the uncanny similarity of their eyes.

"Why are you yelling at the water?" criticized a furious Argentan. The sheriff had been standing at the bow, and Guy realized that he had inadvertently attracted his notice.

Guy did not answer; he gave the sheriff proper obeisance by dropping to one knee before rising and bracing himself for the coming storm.

Argentan was livid, and he commenced humiliating Guy with a torrent of vicious epithets, sadistic threats, and withering insults. Long ago, Guy had grown accustomed to such treatment, and he found himself dispassionately watching his master's face redden as spittle collected in the corners of the sheriff's mouth. Guy's neutral response only fueled Argentan's rage, and he began slapping the tall knight so forcefully that his head swam.

Tolerating the abuse, Guy knew that the sheriff would either grow weary from the physical exertion or regain his self-control after satisfying his need to punish his favorite victim. He concentrated his mind on his loathing for the sheriff, and he tried to forget how utterly hopeless he felt to be chained to this man.

The sheriff seized the front of Guy's tunic and shook him, shrieking, "The Lion was within my grasp! I was so close to victory, and I have spent so much money, and now...*you* caused this disaster. This is all *your* fault."

Guy was tempted to point out that it had been the sheriff's plot that had failed and the sheriff's mercenaries who had been trounced, but he did not wish to be tossed over the side of the boat, so he meekly offered his excuse. "My lord, I was unconscious when the king arrived."

Argentan released him and narrowed his eyes suspiciously. "Gisborne, you look rather gloomy for someone who has finally achieved his lifelong goal. Be of good cheer. Perhaps my plans have been reduced to ashes, but *you* have defeated Robin Fitzooth, the heroic Earl of Huntingdon and the intrepid Robin Hood. How happy you must be."

"My lord, I don't want to talk about that," Guy bluntly rebuffed, his voice serious, yet shaded with anxiety.

The sheriff launched another verbal assault. "What, exactly, was your strategy when you attacked Robin Hood instead of the king? The Lion was *right there*—helpless on the ground and guarded by an injured knight whom even *you* could have overpowered." Argentan paused to catch his breath prior to continuing. "As usual, you were not thinking at all, were you? You don't care about *my* needs and *my* plans, and without me, you'd have nothing. You incompetent, use-less, sack of shit!" Argentan's dark eyes were blazing with demonic fire, burning Guy with their ever-penetrating, accusing, and simul-taneously mocking glare.

"I, uh, had to disable Huntingdon before I could kill the king," suggested Guy.

"Liar!" Argentan howled derisively. "Let me guess; did Robin's little love chat with the fetching Maid Marian provoke you?" The sheriff angrily insisted, "Answer my question, Gisborne."

Still striving to curb his own ire, Guy clenched his fists and replied in a surprisingly even tone, "My lord, why are you asking me this when you already know the answer?"

The sheriff sneered malevolently. "Because I want to hear you say it, you pathetic idiot."

Although he was aware that the sheriff was manipulating him, Guy could no longer restrain himself, and he exploded, "I killed him because he had stolen Marian from me, and it wasn't fair. Besides, his father murdered my father, and it was my right to seek retribution."

The sheriff studied him curiously. "Robin could hardly steal something from you which you never truly possessed," he observed. "Gisborne, I have always known that Maid Marian loved only Robin Hood. But apparently, your wits were so addled by lust for this daughter of Eve that you couldn't see the truth that was obvious to anyone with eyes to see and ears to hear."

His face an ugly grimace, Guy whined, "How could I compete with an earl? If only he had left her alone, she would have loved me instead. I would have devoted my life to making her happy. She would have realized that I loved her more."

"Poor Gisborne," taunted the sheriff. "First, Duncan Fitzooth stole your inheritance, and then his son stole your woman. You are a wretched creature." The sheriff feigned compassion, but his eyes were full of malice. "So many times I have explained to you that women take and take, yet they are never content. But if a man has power and wealth, then he has everything he needs for a happy, successful life."

"Maybe you are right, my lord."

"Of course, I am right, Gisborne. In fact, I am never wrong."

"Yes, my lord," Guy answered woodenly.

The sheriff scrutinized Guy, recognizing traces of uncertainty and guilt in the depths of his pale blue eyes. "Did Huntingdon tell you something when the two of you were holding each other in such a tender, *brotherly* embrace?"

The blood drained from his face as Guy hastily swore, "No, it was nothing; he was mumbling gibberish. It was ridiculous."

Argentan snickered perceptively. "Ah, now I understand why you are not yourself. Did he reveal to you some...delicate family secrets?"

Guy scowled. "He told me something, but it was a lie."

"What did he say?" Argentan eagerly prodded.

"He was lying to me, but I know the truth."

The sheriff's lips stretched into a brutish smile, but his eyes glinted like the steel of a sword. "The truth about history is that it is shaped by the living; therefore, history is a set of agreed-upon deceits. The purpose of these deceits is to provide succor and absolution for the living, and the most cherished and beloved of all deceptions are the ones we tell ourselves."

Gisborne hated the sheriff's riddles, and he reluctantly admitted, "My lord, I don't understand."

Argentan smirked. "Did Robin tell you that he was your brother?"

A panicked Guy alleged, "Yes, but I think he lied to confuse me."

The sheriff threw his head back and guffawed. "Your charming mother invented a lovely history for you. She hoped her deceptions would conceal her sins, but it was terribly embarrassing for her to be faced with the proof of her wickedness every time she saw you. The truth was hidden from you, Gisborne. Robin did not lie."

Guy vehemently argued, "It is impossible."

"It is true," affirmed Argentan. "Your mother was little more than a whore going from man to man. While she was married to Hugh of Gisborne, she committed adultery with Duncan Fitzooth. She evidently preferred an earl to a mere baron. As a widow, she willingly became the mistress of the wealthiest and highest ranking man in the county of Montlhéry. Even though you were only a boy, surely you understood the shamefulness of her behavior. Are you really so naïve?"

"No," moaned a shaken Guy.

"Yes!" the sheriff countered spitefully. "Your mother bartered her soul to secure a comfortable life for herself and an excellent education for you. She made a full confession: you were conceived when Hugh of Gisborne was far away serving King Henry on the continent. Duncan seduced her and then cast her aside when he tired of her. You are Duncan Fitzooth's bastard son. Although your father—your *real* father—diligently sent money to Lucienne for eight years, he abandoned the two of you as soon as he determined that his *legitimate* son was hale and hearty."

An all-pervading sense of dread overwhelmed Guy, and he stood utterly confounded and visibly trembling. Robin's last whispers to him, *you have the Fitzooth eyes,* echoed in his mind. His heart plummeted, and bile rose in his throat; he could not refute that he was Duncan Fitzooth's son.

Argentan grinned as he beheld Guy's shocked expression. "Gisborne, does the truth please you? Or does it trouble your conscience?" His cruel laughter drifted across the waves and faded into the darkening sky. "You murdered your own brother."

"No!" screamed a horrified Guy before he urgently spun around and emptied his gut over the railing. Slumping to the deck, he covered his face with his hands. He yearned to weep, but no tears came.

"Gisborne, you are beyond pathetic."

"Please..." begged Guy. His voice failed him; he just wanted the sheriff to stop tormenting him.

Argentan growled in disgust as he observed Guy huddled on the deck like a small child. "This is another unfortunate legacy of your dear mother. Her efforts to nurture your conscience and teach you morals have ruined you. Listen to me: you should be celebrating your triumph because you have vanquished Duncan Fitzooth in every possible way—you killed his treasured legitimate son, his precious Robin, his only heir and hope for the future. Your revenge is perfect. Duncan must be spinning in his grave."

Guy didn't reply. For some time, he remained in the same position, kneeling on the deck with his face buried in his hands. He was devastated by what he had done. Destroying Robin had been one of his most prized ambitions, but he would have never intentionally slain his own brother. Robin's demise was Guy's damnation; he would never find peace now.

"Gisborne, enough of your hysterics. Be a man, and stand up."
Guy struggled to his feet and looked dazedly at his master.

"Gisborne, do you understand the consequences of killing Robin Hood?" Argentan soberly queried.

A baffled Guy responded, "My lord?"

Argentan explained, "You murdered the king's favorite in front of him." Pausing for effect, he dramatically declared, "Robin is now a martyr in the king's eyes."

Guy stared at the sheriff helplessly as he tried to comprehend the significance of his words.

The sheriff rolled his eyes at Guy's obtuseness. "I failed to slay the Lion, and Prince John will be furious; King Philippe will be quite displeased as well." He pointed a finger at him. "But you, Gisborne, condemned yourself to death."

The younger man bitterly retorted, "*You* planned this regicide attempt; if I am condemned, then so are you."

Argentan admonished him with a scathing rebuke. "Wrong, you asinine dimwit. Prince John will not be deterred. I will have to devise a new scheme to kill the Lionheart, but I am confident that I will retain John's favor. Placating King Philippe will be even simpler; he trusts me completely, and he will protect me. But you, Gisborne, are doomed."

Guy was torn between anger and bewilderment. "What do you mean, my lord?"

The sheriff cackled nastily. "I am sure that the king's men already know that their courageous commander died at *your* hand. King Richard will most definitely glorify Robin Hood as a hero and a martyr." He gleefully elaborated, "Huntingdon will be mourned by every knight and foot soldier serving the Lionheart. They will worship Robin Hood more in death than in life."

Gisborne's eyes widened as a terrifying realization dawned.

"Heed my words," insisted Argentan. "You are in great danger.

The king's men will hunt you down like a dog, and when you are captured, they will butcher you slowly and savagely."

His trap was set, and the sheriff easily ensnared the distraught knight as he laid a hand on his shoulder and adopted a fatherly tone. "Gisborne, I am prepared to bear the burden of shielding you from the consequences of your reckless actions. You know that I am fond of you, despite your incompetence and stupidity. I will keep you alive, as long as you obey me and serve me well."

"My lord…I thank you. I will not disappoint you again," vowed a profoundly relieved Guy. "Do you have a new plan?"

"I need to think," replied the sheriff with a crafty smile. "This time, my strategy must be flawless. Of the two remaining Plantagenets, I always knew that Richard would be the most difficult to eliminate."

Guy's brow creased in confusion as he asked, "I thought the plan was to put John on the throne. Are you intending to kill him too? Who will rule if both Richard and John are dead? What is the plan?"

There was an awkward pause as the sheriff blanched, an uncharacteristic alarm shining in his eyes. As soon as Argentan recovered his poise, he scoffed, "I said nothing about killing John. But I have told you in the past that you do not possess the intelligence to understand the specifics of my plan."

"Yes, my lord," Guy sighed in resignation. In truth, he was beyond caring about anything at the moment.

Argentan burst into a ringing, sadistic laugh. "I am a genius, and I already have a brilliant idea. I will design the perfect snare for the Lion." Practically vibrating in anticipation, he started chanting, "Death to the king. Death in captivity. We will demand a ransom, and that will offset the expenses I incurred during this disastrous scheme."

"Oh," Guy exhaled, uncertain of the sheriff's meaning and assuming that he was speaking in riddles again.

"We are nearly to Tyre. Do not worry about the plan," instructed Argentan.

"As you wish, my lord." Guy respectfully genuflected as his master walked away.

⚜

In the harbor of Tyre, Guy stood on the deck of a large ship that was scheduled to depart the next morning. It would be the beginning of an arduous journey that would take them to Paris prior to their arrival in London and ultimately, Nottingham.

Moonlight reflected on the water in shimmering dapples that playfully danced below him. Above him, a boundless black canvas stretched across the firmament, and it was impossible to detect where the sky ended and the sea began. The ship was enveloped in an eerie silence broken only by the creaking of the wooden deck and the lapping of waves against its sides. The sheriff was attending a meeting with Hugh of Burgundy, and he would return soon.

Guy peered into the darkness, wallowing in self-indulgent misery. He was exhausted, yet he could not sleep. His soul was beleaguered by a writhing morass of chaotic and conflicted emotions illuminated by a single, indisputable, and inconvenient truth: Robin was his brother.

Robin Hood's murderer glowered at the ebony sky with its countless sparkles of light and grumbled to his brother in heaven in a resentful rant. "I finally defeated you, but you still triumphed."

Guy felt the weight of the world crushing him; a cruel and unfair world filled with people who had misled and mistreated him—his mother, Duncan, Montlhéry, Robin, and even Marian. The very people who should have loved, nurtured, and protected him. He petulantly wondered why he was forced to endure such suffering and woe.

And now, every knight and soldier under King Richard's command would be vying for the privilege of torturing and killing him in order to earn fame and fortune in avenging Robin Hood's death. Guy might still be breathing, but his life was over.

He raised his fist and angrily shook it at the heavens, accusing his half-brother, "Your death damned me. Because of you, I will never find peace and happiness. This is all *your* fault."

CHAPTER 19
THE MIRACLE OF ACRE

23 February 1192, the Royal Palace, City of Acre

Exhausted from hours of grieving and praying, André wearily rubbed his face. He was seated on a bench in the great hall of the royal palace along with dozens of the king's most senior and trusted knights, and they had spent the night in mourning and prayer for Robin's soul. King Richard had presided over the solemn vigil, and he had just requested that his beloved minstrel, Blondel de Nesle, perform the *Planctus Karol,* a lament on the death of Charlemagne, as a tribute to Robin.

The warm smoke from torches mingled with the pungent odor of the men crowded into the hall and created a stifling air that intensified the crushing anguish oppressing their spirits. Despite their fatigue and discomfort, the men remained fervent as they beseeched God to grant Robin immediate entry into heaven.

Through a narrow window, André detected a brightening of the sky, and he was relieved that this night of sorrow was concluding. He did not want to insult the talented Blondel, but he needed to ensure that everything was ready for Robin's funeral. Leaning forward, he signaled to Baldwin de Béthune and William de l'Etang, and the three men quietly rose and exited the hall.

"It is time to bid *adieu* to our dear friend," intoned a somber André.

"I cannot accept that he is gone," William bemoaned. "If only I had been there."

His emotions as brittle and fragile as a dry autumn leaf, André seized the front of William's surcoat and snarled, "Are you blaming me for Robin's death? I loved Robin and would have gladly sacrificed my life for his."

Baldwin quickly intervened and pushed the two apart. "My friends, quarreling does not honor Robin's memory." Gazing at André, he endeavored to explain, "I have the same yearnings; I also wish that I had been there to protect Robin. Despair and remorse fill my heart, but that does not mean that I blame you."

William earnestly entreated, "Sir André, do not take offense, for none was intended."

André recognized their sincerity and regretted his outburst. He asserted, "I would have given my life to save Robin, but I failed."

Baldwin declared, "We must focus on the traitors: Argentan and Gisborne. They alone bear the responsibility for Robin's murder."

"God damn those fiendish traitors," William cursed, the normally reserved knight spitting out words that would have shocked his friends on any other day. "I pray that God will grant me the privilege of sending them to eternal hellfire."

Agreeing whole-heartedly, Baldwin secretly prayed that *he* would be the one to bring the two criminals to justice. He queried André, "Who were those men? I am unfamiliar with them."

André clenched and unclenched his fists as a wave of black rage swept over him. "They are Alaric de Montabard, Baron de Argentan, and Sir Guy of Gisborne. They deserve a slow and agonizing death."

"Argentan?" Frowning, Baldwin recalled, "Although I am from Artois, I have traveled extensively in Normandy. The Barony of Argentan is insignificant and poor."

William recollected, "I remember that the Baron of Argentan was elderly; his sons died in battle without issue, but he also had a daughter. Maybe Alaric de Montabard was a distant relative who inherited the barony."

Scoffing, André alleged, "The Barony of Argentan is so small that a man can piss over it without watering its crops. But I suspect that Baldwin is correct; the de Montabard lineage must be kin."

"What do we know of Gisborne?" probed Baldwin, as he was impatient to begin planning the man's torture and eventual demise.

André shrugged his shoulders. "The village of Gisborne is in Huntingdonshire. Robin once mentioned that this man's father tried to kill King Henry many years ago."

A stunned hush fleetingly reigned before William growled, "Gisborne is both a traitor and the son of a traitor. He must be captured and executed for his crimes."

"He is a traitor and a coward," insisted André. "Robin had prevailed in an honest fight, and Gisborne, this damned murderer, crept up behind Robin, intending to stab him in the back. It is the only way such a worthless mongrel could defeat a warrior like Robin. I personally witnessed this."

Another silence arose, this one fueled by each man's distraught fury over the injustice of Robin's death.

Baldwin nervously asked a question that had been plaguing him. "I am confused; when did Robin become betrothed to Lady Marian of Lenton? After that incident in Poitou with the de Châteauneuf sisters, I thought he was avoiding all entanglements with women."

Baldwin and William eagerly awaited André's answer since he had been acquainted with Robin the longest. Robin had always been reticent, never wearing his heart on his sleeve and never boastful or gossipy. They had learned more about his adventures as Robin Hood from popular ballads than from Robin himself.

André paused. He had no desire to divulge Robin's private affairs to anyone, especially considering the acute heartbreak Robin had endured after receiving that letter from Lady Marian. However, he also felt compelled to offer some explanation. "Robin's betrothal to Lady Marian ended with his decision to join Richard on Crusade."

As Baldwin and William pressured André for additional information, the older knight firmly stated, "I will say no more on the subject. Baldwin, you were there. You know that Robin married without hesitation or coercion."

Baldwin conceded that Robin had willingly sought the marriage as he lay mortally wounded, and the three men lapsed into subdued reflection as the plaintive melody and poignant stanzas of Blondel's song drifted from the great hall into the passageway where they stood.

Tears stung André's eyes, for the lyrics lamenting Charlemagne's death reminded him that Robin was irreplaceable.

Baldwin articulated their sorrow. "Robin was a remarkable man. There will never be another like him."

William brushed away a fat tear trickling down his cheek, unashamed to weep for his friend and unable to find words to convey his immeasurable sense of loss.

André disclosed, "The king is also grieving. He has been profoundly affected by Robin's passing." He then announced that the time had come to make ready the final preparations, and the three men reluctantly trudged in the direction of the nearby chapel where Robin was lying in repose.

Unexpectedly, their somber march was interrupted by an urgent, high-pitched voice yelling, "Sir André! Sir Baldwin! Sir William!" A young guard was running towards them, scrambling awkwardly and slumping to his knees at their feet, pale and panting.

André glowered and irritably barked at the youth, "We are in mourning, and the king has commanded that everyone comport themselves in a dignified manner. If King Richard complains about your noise, do not beg me to rescue you from his wrath."

Baldwin and William murmured their concurrence as the frightened guard shakily implored, "My lords, please forgive me. But...but...I saw...I touched..." he stammered.

André dragged a deep inhalation to reclaim his composure. He attempted to speak in a more conciliatory tone, but his words still sounded sharp. "What is the problem?"

"There is...something wrong...with Lord Huntingdon," stuttered the guard.

"Of course, there's something wrong with Lord Huntingdon, you idiot. He's dead," André sneered. He ominously suggested, "Perhaps I will dispatch you to him where you can apologize in person for showing him such disrespect."

André's threat terrified the young man, but he persisted and bravely delivered his strange news to the king's men. "Lord Huntingdon is...not cold."

"What?" the three men chorused.

"I was standing watch with another man," the guard hastily described. "He said that he saw Lord Huntingdon move, and I told him that he imagined it. But when I put my hand on his body, his skin was hot, and it appeared as though he was sweating too." The youth's voice rose an octave. "We didn't know what to do; I thought bodies always became cold after death. Please, you must come."

A startled silence stretched between the three knights as they gaped at the guard, utterly and completely dumbfounded.

William was the first to regain his ability to talk. "Do you mean that he might be alive?"

Baldwin shook his head resolutely, declaring, "That's impossible."

"I watched Robin die in Lady Marian's arms," reminisced André despondently.

The guard was afraid and befuddled. "All I know is that he is not cold."

André, Baldwin, and William shared uneasy glances while endeavoring to assume circumspect expressions. The seasoned knights had seen enough death to know that corpses inevitably grew cold and stiff. They definitely did not sweat. And the chapel would have been quite chilly during the night. Robin should be cold.

With pronounced effort, André kept his voice calm and detached. "We were just on our way there. I'm sure you are mistaken."

Baldwin's gaze slid to André as he speculated, "Two young guards, alone all night with a dead body…it is not unusual for their minds to wander."

The guard boldly countered, "How could my hands imagine warmth? Please, you must come and see for yourself."

"Very well," André consented in an increasingly tremulous voice.

"I will fetch the king's physician," proposed William, who turned on his heel and re-entered the great hall, searching for Ranulphus.

André and Baldwin trailed the guard, leaving the keep and walking across the bailey to the chapel. The crisp morning air was a welcome respite from the smoky great hall. The two knights simultaneously lifted their eyes to the heavens, where the first rays of the sun were chasing away the melancholy dreariness of night. Foreboding filled them; although both were convinced that the guard was mistaken, a cruel hope had invaded their hearts, and they felt doomed to suffer the disappointment of Robin's death a second time.

Reverently, André and Baldwin approached the stone bier on which their beloved friend was lying. Robin's body had been washed and wrapped in a white linen shroud of the finest weave. His head remained uncovered in order to permit his friends to bid farewell before the funeral.

Initially, nothing seemed out of place, and the nascent optimism in their hearts perished. But when they drew near, alarming and amazing details became evident. The white linen was faintly stained where it touched Robin's chest and side. Instead of the ashen skin of a corpse, Robin's face was flushed. Then, they observed a drop of sweat roll down from his forehead and across his temple before it vanished into wavy strands of wheat-colored hair, and this was followed by a nearly imperceptible twitch of Robin's brow.

In that astonishing moment, it was André and Baldwin who ceased breathing, as their minds desperately struggled to reconcile what they were witnessing with the certainty of Robin's demise. After a pause that felt like a lifetime, yet was shorter than the beat of wings taking flight, the two men rushed forward and put their hands on Robin, determining for themselves that his body was indeed burning with the fire of deadly wound fever.

Behind them, William and Ranulphus dashed into the chapel, and the young doctor cried, "My God!" Ranulphus was so disturbed that he rudely pushed the king's own cousin out of his way. The men anxiously yanked on the linen shroud, revealing that Robin's injuries were swollen and seeping a small amount of blood, the skin a bright red.

"Is he…alive?" inquired a breathless Baldwin.

Without looking up, the physician snapped, "Dead men don't bleed or suffer from fever. Lend me your dagger."

"He's sweating too," André helpfully interjected as he offered his dagger to Ranulphus.

The doctor positioned the blade under Robin's nose, and everyone else held their breath as they leaned closer and watched the shiny metal become fogged.

"He's alive!" cheered Baldwin. The others were too stunned to speak.

Ranulphus gave the dagger back to André. The physician's nimble fingers began to dance across the wound on Robin's chest, massaging and manipulating the swollen skin until a mixture of blood and watery puss oozed out, and Robin moaned feebly. The three knights audibly gasped, and the doctor grabbed the leather bag that was slung over his shoulder and emptied it on the floor next to the bier, frantically rummaging through its contents. He snatched a sealed container before targeting his glare at the nervous guards huddled nearby and screaming at them, "You! Go to the kitchens; I need wine and vinegar. And you! Go to the great hall, and find the king's apothecary. Tell him I require more wormwood."

As the soldiers promptly scurried from the chapel, André could not suppress his elation. "Robin is alive! I can scarcely believe it."

Ranulphus sighed as he regarded the king's cousin. "He is barely alive. Help me tear this shroud into strips that we can use to wash and wrap his wounds."

André, William, and Baldwin dutifully helped until the guards returned with the requisite items. Ranulphus meticulously cleaned Robin's injuries with wine and vinegar. He then dressed the wounds with a poultice comprised of wormwood and other ingredients prior to wrapping the linen around Robin. His shroud of bereavement had become a cocoon of hope.

Abruptly, the chapel doors were shoved open with a force that nearly splintered the aging wood. "What is going on here?" the Lionheart's booming voice echoed in the space. "Why are you still preparing Robin's body for the funeral?"

The giddy laughter from his three most senior knights rendered Richard speechless.

André hurried to the king. "Sire, it is a miracle. Robin is not dead."

William jubilantly exclaimed, "God has smiled upon us. Robin is alive."

Richard scowled, and he demanded answers. "Ranulphus, what are they talking about?"

The doctor nodded in confirmation. "It is true, Sire. Lord Huntingdon is alive."

The king opened his mouth to say something, but no sound

came out, and the color drained from his face. Clearing his throat, he questioned in a hushed voice, "How can this be true?"

Ranulphus enlightened, "Sometimes, when a man is gravely injured, it can be difficult to detect his heartbeat, and his breathing can become weak."

There was a deep rumbling noise in Richard's broad chest, and the laugh that emerged was both exhilarated and flustered. "This is a miracle from God. Robin is alive! Our glorious bird did not fly away to heaven after all."

"Lord Huntingdon is more dead than alive; he is suffering from wound fever," Ranulphus clarified as he labored to appear poised. The doctor was besieged by conflicting waves of joy, dread, and mortification. "Sire, forgive me; I have made a terrible mistake, and I will take responsibility for it."

The king beamed. "Robin is alive, and that's all that matters to me at this moment." A note of apprehension crept into his voice. "Can you save him?"

In the stillness that ensued, it seemed as though the weight of the world was pressing upon the shoulders of Ranulphus, and the weary young man desperately wanted to cast his burdens away. He was standing at the edge of a precipice and balancing the hopes of his king against the grievous nature of Robin's injuries. In the end, only God Himself would tip the scales. "I cannot guarantee that Lord Huntingdon will survive, my liege," the physician responded honestly. "It is a miracle that he is alive." He hesitated. "I am very worried; wound fever is frequently fatal."

"Can you save him?" repeated the monarch, his urgent voice tinged with unease.

Richard and his knights intently scrutinized the doctor, and the naked fear on his face told them more than any words he could have spoken. A grim veil of reality descended upon them, obscuring and quelling the optimism and euphoria in which they had been basking since the discovery that Robin was alive.

They might still lose Robin. Nothing was certain.

Ranulphus closed his eyes briefly, and his distress was unmistakable. In a voice layered with regret and trepidation, he admitted, "Sire, my knowledge might not be enough to save his life, but by the grace of God, I will try."

❦

Preparations were soon underway to carefully move Robin to a chamber in the palace. While Baldwin and William coordinated the arrangements, Ranulphus was on his knees, gathering the scattered contents of his leather pouch and bemoaning the breakage of one of his vials. André kindly knelt to assist him; the older knight was so grateful to the doctor that he would have happily done any task at that moment.

It was then that a glimmer at the base of the bier caught André's eye. He scooped it up and ascertained that it was a silver chain with something brown suspended from it.

"That belongs to Lord Huntingdon," Ranulphus explained. "It was around his neck and had been pushed into his chest wound."

André was horrified to realize that the object was brown because it was caked with dried blood.

Ranulphus reached for it and requested, "My lord, may I see that please?"

In fascination, André observed Ranulphus grab a discarded strip of soiled linen which he then used to clean the necklace. To his utter amazement, he recognized the ring that Lady Marian had returned to Robin after ending their betrothal. Only now the ring was bent and misshapen. André sternly warned, "That ring is special to Robin; he will want it restored to him."

The color rose slightly in the doctor's face; he was embarrassed that André thought he might pilfer it. "Of course, my lord. I merely wanted to examine it. Notice how it is no longer a circle."

André mused, "It looks as though it has been flattened."

Ranulphus excitedly proclaimed, "It saved his life. He must have been wearing the ring over his heart. When the other man stabbed him in the chest, the blade of the dagger was obstructed and diverted from Lord Huntingdon's heart."

André contemplated the physician's theory, and he was astounded by the extraordinary likelihood that Robin had been saved by this ring that he obviously cherished. André could hardly wait to tell the king and Lady Marian.

André froze. *Lady Marian...Oh, my God!*

Without another word to Ranulphus, André leapt to his feet and ran to the king, who had returned to the great hall to announce that Robin was alive. He burst into the hall just as Bishop Walter was leading the men in prayers of thanksgiving, and he was obliged to linger with increasing agitation as the bishop droned on and on.

When an emphatic "Amen" echoed in the hall, André sprinted forward.

Richard paled. "What is it? Is Robin...?"

"No, not that, Sire," André hastened to reassure. "But we must send for Lady Huntingdon before she sails. The sun has risen and mid-morning is upon us."

Understanding flashed in the king's eyes, and he summoned Baldwin. As soon as Baldwin arrived, Richard ordered, "Go to the harbor. You must locate Lady Huntingdon and bring her to the palace."

Baldwin frowned. "Sire, the ship left at first light. You know this captain; he is as reliable as the sunrise. They will be well on their way to Cyprus by now. Shall I launch a swift boat to intercept her there?"

"Yes," Richard immediately approved, but then the royal brow creased in concern. "No, wait. Robin might die while she is returning to Acre. She would suffer his loss twice."

André and Baldwin nodded in agreement while the king pondered the situation.

The Lion decreed, "Let us delay until Robin's condition is more stable. Lady Huntingdon is traveling to my mother's court in Aquitaine, and I will send word to her when we are certain whether Robin will survive."

Baldwin offered, "Tuck could accompany her if she decides to return here to be with Robin while he is convalescing."

"Tuck?" inquired a puzzled André.

Richard divulged, "I have sent a Templar knight by the name of Tuck to watch over Lady Huntingdon as she travels to Aquitaine. She does not know, of course. But I could not risk anything happening to her during her journey."

4 March 1192, the Royal Palace, City of Acre

Robin was imprisoned in an ebony darkness, and the boundaries of his cell were defined by misery. Within this dungeon, his reality was inextricably tied to his physical agony, and his pain seemed to exist as a separate creature.

Perhaps it was a dragon. Robin had never seen a dragon, and he had always doubted the existence of such monsters. Yet, something was sitting upon his chest and crushing him, as if he were grain beneath a millstone. This dragon exhaled fire as hot as the forge of a blacksmith, for Robin could feel his body burning in the flames of its breath.

Sometimes the dark curtain lifted, and the murkiness enveloping him receded like the ocean's tide. During these moments, Robin inhabited a peculiar world that was both familiar and foreign.

He was standing on a hill outside of Acre, peering at the sky. Churning, leaden clouds and a clap of thunder heralded a violent tempest, and he was suddenly bombarded with a hailstorm of decapitated heads. Raising his shield, he shuddered in horror.

The steady rhythm of marching feet replaced the storm, and Robin was on the road to Arsuf, except that the defensive wall of

Crusader infantry protecting him crumbled into dust, and he was left alone on the battlefield to confront Saladin's army. An ominous shadow above him became a deluge of deadly arrows.

He ran from the arrows and dove into the nearby sea, but then he began to sputter and choke as warm, bitter liquid filled his mouth. He gulped rapidly and groggily found himself in a darkened chamber. Murmurs of comfort would vibrate in his ears—soothing, yet insistent encouragement to keep fighting and to swallow more.

Despite its unpleasant taste, the foul potion was a key that liberated him from his prison of pain and delivered him into the cool shade of Sherwood Forest, where the verdant foliage would morph into green eyes full of tenderness. Robin would sigh in profound relief; he was with Marian, and everything would be all right. Serenity would engulf him, her smile would captivate him, and Robin felt as though he were cloaked in contentment.

These happy feelings would slowly fade, and the dragon of his torment would return and incinerate him in a blast of fire and pain. The safety of Sherwood would dissolve, and Marian would vanish. Her loving gaze would be supplanted by either the mocking, cruel eyes of his half-brother or the aloof, unfathomable eyes of his father—each pair of pale blue eyes so different, yet the same.

He was vaguely aware that he was alive and in the haze of a delirium, and at times he begged God to end his sufferings. However, no matter how much he told himself that he wished to die, in reality, he was desperately clinging to life and battling the Angel of Death with a single-minded vehemence.

He raised his bow, nocked an arrow, and took aim at Death as it came for him in the guise of a fire-breathing, winged dragon of doom, its sharp claws dripping blood, and the air surrounding it heavy with the scent of decay.

Hands were grabbing him, pulling on him, and lifting his shoulders.

"My lord, please, you must drink this; otherwise, you will

perish from hunger. I am not saving you from wound fever only to lose you to starvation."

The words were jumbled in his mind at first—nonsensical and far away. Robin opened his eyes, and gradually the blurred form in front of him came into focus. A man was holding a cup to his lips. Recalling the bitterness of the brew, Robin tried to jerk away. He was distressed to discover that he did not have the strength to move, and warm liquid flooded his mouth. Robin realized that it was not the sour drink, but a hearty meat broth. He took several deep swallows.

"That's much better, my lord," the man commended with marked enthusiasm.

"Who?" Robin could scarcely recognize his own rough voice.

"I am Ranulphus, the king's physician," he replied simply.

"Where?" Speaking was such an effort that Robin's head started spinning.

"You are in the royal palace of Acre. You were injured in an attack. Don't you remember?"

Robin's memories were seized by thoughts of Argentan and Gisborne, but before his wrath could be roused, Marian's beautiful face surfaced in his mind, except that it was ashen and tear-stained, and her eyes were devastated by grief.

The physician was pouring more soup into his mouth, and he greedily consumed it. When he next paused to catch his breath, he hoarsely asked, "Is Marian safe?"

A smile tugged at the corners of Ranulphus' mouth. "Lady Huntingdon is safe. But if you wish to be reunited with her, you must rest."

Once more, the doctor pressed a cup to Robin's lips, only this time it was the bitter remedy. He bravely drank his medicine and returned to his battle against the dragon.

8 March 1192, the Royal Palace, City of Acre

It was almost daybreak as André dutifully escorted King Richard along a dimly lit corridor. Approaching a closed door, Richard waited while André briskly tapped on it. The squeal of ancient hinges reverberated in the narrow hall, and the men winced at the disagreeable sound.

"My lord?" Ranulphus blinked at the light from André's torch. The chamber behind him was shrouded in darkness. As soon as the doctor saw the king he exclaimed, "Sire, I did not know that you had returned from Ascalon."

Richard huffed in annoyance. "I received word that Robin had recovered. I came to see for myself."

"Recovered?" Ranulphus' brow knitted in confusion.

"Well?" scowled André. Like the king, he was anxious to see Robin.

The physician dropped to one knee to give his king proper obeisance and welcomed them into the chamber. The only illumination in the space was a candle flickering on an adjacent table and the torch that André was carrying. The aroma of herbs and vinegar mingled with those odors typically found in a sickroom, and it required a moment for André to adjust to the smell.

There were two beds: a smaller one where Ranulphus evidently slept, ready to care for his most important patient night and day, and a larger bed for Robin, who was lying very still, ghostly pale and emaciated.

"Sire," Ranulphus drew their attention from Robin. "The message I sent was that Lord Huntingdon's fever had broken, and that I was more hopeful. I did not mean to imply that he was well again. He will need time to regain his strength and for his injuries to fully heal."

André sighed in disappointment. He had been so excited to receive the good news of Robin's recovery.

Richard's temper flared, and he was visibly struggling to subdue it. In a taut, exasperated voice, he growled, "When will you know whether he will live?"

Even in the faint light of the chamber, André could see the physician's broad grin. "There has been a change since I dispatched that letter. Lord Huntingdon no longer suffers from wound fever. He will live."

For several heartbeats, André and Richard stood there, staring at Ranulphus and replaying his words in their minds, fearful that they might not have heard him correctly.

"He will live? How can you be so confident?" asked Richard.

Ranulphus answered judiciously, "I must give all glory and praise to God, of course. But I also confess that I received invaluable assistance from the apothecary generously sent by Sultan Saladin. He brought me poppy flowers and showed me how to brew a special remedy that gave Lord Huntingdon respite from his pain. The medicine allowed him to sleep while his body healed."

"He has slept all this time?" André was credulous. No one could survive sleeping for a fortnight.

"No, my lord," Ranulphus clarified, "He slept most of the time, but I woke him periodically to give him nourishment. Therefore, he has become very thin. Rebuilding his strength will be imperative to his eventual recovery."

"Thanks be to God," proclaimed Richard, and the three men reverently crossed themselves. The king continued, "I am humbled by His mercy, for this is truly the Miracle of Acre."

Shadowed by the other men, Richard walked to the bed and quietly called to Robin.

Robin stirred, and his eyes opened, although they were unfocused. "Sire?" His voice was rasping and frail.

Richard's gaze flitted to André and Ranulphus, and all three men beamed, their eyes lit by joy. The king reached down and gently placed his hand on Robin's shoulder in a comforting gesture.

To his immense relief, Robin's body was no longer feverish. "My friend," the king tenderly declared, "we are pleased that you are still with us."

Robin shifted his head slightly; perhaps it had been a nod. "Sire...tell Marian..."

The king understood at once. "Robin, you must concentrate on regaining your strength. I will notify your wife that you are much improved."

A blissful smile spread across Robin's face as he closed his eyes and breathed, "My wife..." He then slipped back into the arms of Morpheus.

Praising Ranulphus for his service to Robin, King Richard led André out of the chamber, and they strode in ecstatic silence until they arrived at the king's own quarters. Richard signaled for his cousin to join him on a balcony adjoining his solar.

Richard had formulated his plan, and he commanded, "André, make arrangements for Sir Juan of Navarre to travel to Poitiers next month. My mother is acquainted with him, and she will trust him. I will compose a poem commemorating the Miracle of Acre and announcing that Robin lives, and I want him to deliver it to Countess Huntingdon. However, I insist that she remain at court; it would not be prudent for her to risk the dangers of another journey here."

"Yes, Sire," agreed André, "that is a wise decision."

Richard resumed, "Send word to Sultan Saladin, thanking him for the assistance of his apothecary and inviting his brother for another round of peace negotiations. I will stay here in Acre until the end of this month, but at that time I must return to Ascalon and celebrate Easter with my men."

André again dipped his head in respectful concurrence.

The two men were exuberantly optimistic as they inhaled the fresh, early morning air. The sun was just peeking above the horizon, its soft rosy glow conquering the gloom of night. André was filled with wonder at Robin's survival. He reminisced how Robin had seemingly died at sunset, yet his life had now been miraculously restored to him.

It was the dawn of a new day for Robin Hood.

End of Part I

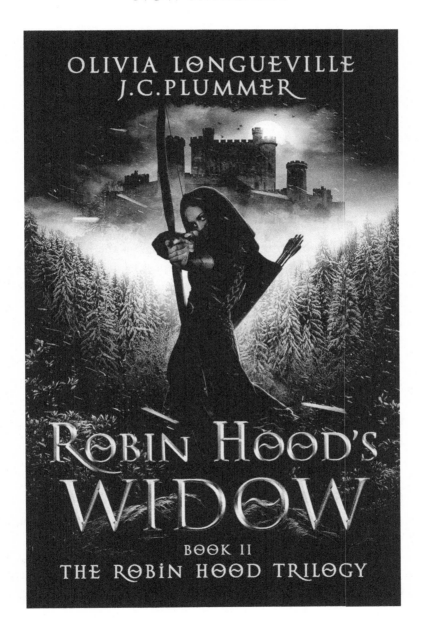

THE ROBIN HOOD
TRILOGY, PART II:
ROBIN HOOD'S
WIDOW

Robin's duty to his king sends him on an odyssey that will unfold from the streets of Paris to the banks of the Danube. From incredible triumphs on the battlefields of the Crusade, to harrowing sea voyages, to a desperate dash across the frozen landscape of Central Europe, Robin Hood must ensure that King Richard safely returns to England.

Meanwhile, the outlaws of Sherwood Forest rise again under a new leader—and she is unwavering in her pursuit of justice against the tyranny of Sheriff de Argentan. Marian endures the heartbreak of widowhood only to find strength and purpose as she leads a small band of devoted men in her quest for vengeance while she protects Robin's legacy.

Sir Guy of Gisborne, tormented by his conscience and enslaved by the sheriff, faces the wraith-like fury of the woman he once loved. How do you find forgiveness when you have committed an unforgivable crime? He must attempt a daunting journey of redemption, while finding inspiration from an unexpected source.

And through it all, Robin, Marian, and Guy are entangled in a web of treachery spun by the King of France and his sinister advisor, Montlhéry, as the plot to dismantle the Angevin Empire and take the throne of England from the Plantagenets boldly continues.

Visit our website to learn more about the Robin Hood Trilogy. You will find bonus materials relating to this book and articles about this fascinating, exciting time in history.

www.AngevinWorld.com

GLOSSARY

Achilles' heel

In Greek mythology, a small, but fatal, weakness; a vulnerability in an otherwise invincible opponent which will lead to the opponent's downfall. It can refer to any type of weakness—not just a physical vulnerability.

Angevin

Originating from or belonging to the County of Anjou in France. Henry II's father had been Count of Anjou, and Henry ruled both England and vast continental territories, including Anjou. For this reason, Henry II, Richard the Lionheart, and John are referred to as the Angevin Kings of England, and their holdings are called the Angevin Empire. John lost control of these continental lands; thus, he is considered the last Angevin King of England. These three rulers are also referred to as the first Plantagenet kings.

antechamber

A chamber that serves as a waiting room and entrance to a larger room.

apothecary

A person with specialized knowledge of herbs, spices, and medicines. An apothecary would also be knowledgeable about poisons.

bailey

The courtyard of a castle. It's an open area enclosed by the castle wall.

berm

The area between the castle wall and the moat.

bliaut

A long outer tunic worn by both men and women. The bliaut had a full skirt, a fitted bodice, and sleeves which were fitted along the upper arm while flaring between the elbow and wrist. The lower part of the sleeve sometimes flared into a trumpet shape. The length of the men's version varied, but the women's bliaut would have been full-length. Women's tunics were also called gowns or kirtles.

bodkin

A long, narrow arrowhead designed to pierce chainmail.

bow *(bōh)*

A weapon that propels projectiles (arrows).

bow *(rhymes with how)*

1) Bending at the waist towards another person as a formal greeting. Typically performed between men of equal rank.

2) The front of a ship.

brace

In addition to the usual architectural meanings, a brace also refers to a pair. The phrase, "a brace of coneys," refers to two wild rabbits.

bracer

A bracer is wrapped around the forearm of an archer in order to protect the arm from the bowstring. Bracers were made from leather or horn.

braies

An undergarment that was made of linen and worn by men. Although underwear as we know it today was not worn, these would have been similar in that they were worn under other clothing.

brocade

A heavy fabric woven with an elaborate, raised design or pattern. During this time period, brocade fabric was the height of luxury and very expensive.

brooch

A clasp or ornament with a hinged pin and a catch to secure the point of the pin on the back. In the 12th century, there were no buttons or zippers, so a brooch was an indispensable piece of jewelry for securing clothing, especially cloaks. Elaborate, jeweled brooches were a sign of wealth and status. Brooches were popular gifts.

Carentune

A town east of Nottingham which was mentioned in the Domesday Book of 1086. Today, the town is a suburb of Nottingham, and it is called Carlton.

causeway

A road or path that is raised in order to cross a moat, marshland, sand, or similar impediments to travel.

chausses

Leggings or stockings. They could be made of either cloth or chainmail.

Circe

In Greek mythology, Circe was a witch who turned men into pigs by giving them a drink from her cup of enchantment. With the help of Hermes, Odysseus was able to defeat her magic and force her to restore his men to human form.

clandestine marriages

Before 1215, a couple could declare their intention to marry in front of witnesses, and if these vows were followed by consummation, canon law considered the couple to be legally wed.

coney

An older term referring to wild rabbits or hares.

courtesan

A woman who seeks financial support and security from noblemen and men of wealth in return for companionship and sexual favors.

courtier

An attendant at court, especially a person who spends a great deal of time attending the court of a king or other royal personage.

cross guard

For swords and daggers, this is positioned crosswise to the blade and between the grip and the blade. It protects the user's hand. See also: hilt, pommel, and grip.

curtain

Another name for the castle's outer wall surrounding the bailey.

curtsy

A formal gesture of greeting and respect made by women and girls consisting of bending the knees to lower the body while slightly bowing the head.

destrier

A large, strong war horse. Only wealthy lords and knights could afford them.

dowager

A widow whose title was obtained from her deceased husband. Adding this modifier to a title distinguishes the widow from the wife of the man who currently holds the title.

dowry

Money or land given by the bride's family at the time of her marriage. If the girl entered a convent instead of marrying, the dowry would be given to the convent.

drawbridge

A bridge that can be raised to prevent access or lowered to allow passage of vehicles or pedestrians.

empyreal

Heavenly; pertaining to the highest heaven.

Ernehale

A town northeast of Nottingham which was mentioned in the Domesday Book of 1086. Today, the town is a suburb of Nottingham, and it is called Arnold.

ewer

A large earthenware jug or pitcher with a wide mouth.

fallow field

A field that has been left unseeded for one or more growing seasons in order to restore its fertility.

fealty

Loyalty that a vassal owes to his lord. This often refers to the actual loyalty oath, as in "an oath of fealty."

Feast of St. Andrew

This was celebrated on November 30th. It was considered a major feast that was observed as a holiday and required fasting on the previous day.

Feast of St. John the Baptist

Also known as Midsummer; it was celebrated on June 24th. It was considered a major feast that was observed as a holiday and required fasting on the previous day.

Feudal System

This land-based economic and social system determined the rights and obligations of men. See also: fief, vassal, lord, liege, homage, and fealty.

fief

Land granted to a vassal for his use. In return, the vassal provided loyalty and service to the owner of the land. A fief could also be a payment instead of land.

fiefdom

Land owned by a noble or knight.

field

In heraldry, the background color of a coat of arms is called the field.

fleur-de-lis

In heraldry, a stylized representation of an iris, consisting of three petals. This heraldry represents the royal family of France.

forthwith

An old word that actually dates to the 13th century. It means immediately, at once, without delay.

fortnight

A period of two weeks, or fourteen days.

gatehouse

A complex system of gates and towers which protected the entrance to a castle. See also: causeway, drawbridge, and portcullis.

genuflect

Briefly dropping to the right knee before rising. This was a formal greeting performed when in the presence of a man who is of superior rank. It is also performed towards the altar when in church.

great hall

Known as the heart of the living space in a castle, it was the location of feasts, and it was often the area where business was conducted. In earlier times, it was also where people slept.

grip

The part of sword or dagger that is gripped by the hand. See also: hilt, cross guard, and pommel.

Hades

1) In Greek mythology, the god of the underworld where the dead lived.

2) A name for hell. This use is not capitalized.

hauberk

A chainmail shirt or tunic that protected the upper body, especially the neck and chest.

heathen

1) A person who does not worship the triune God of the Bible.

2) An irreligious, uncultured, or uncivilized person.

high table

An elevated table in the great hall where the lord, his family, and important guests were seated during feasts.

hilt

The handle of a sword or dagger. It is comprised of the cross guard, grip, and pommel (see the entries for these words for additional information). Hilt is often used interchangeably with grip.

homage

A declaration of loyalty from one man to another. The man declaring his loyalty would typically receive a fief in return. The first step in becoming a vassal is to pay homage to the lord.

homily

A sermon, usually on a Biblical topic.

Hospitaller

See: Knight Hospitaller.

humors

The fluids in the body. In ancient Greece, Rome, and the medieval period, humors were thought to be closely tied to health. Balancing your humors was vital to good health.

infidel

For Christians, a person who is not a Christian. For Muslims, a person who is not a Muslim.

jousting

A tournament competition where two mounted knights rode towards each other with the goal of unhorsing their opponent using blunted lances. This contest was conducted in a highly formalized manner, but it was still very dangerous.

keep

The living area inside of a castle complex. It was a heavily guarded and fortified building or tower. The great hall would be located in the keep.

Knight Hospitaller

A member of the "Order of Knights of the Hospital of Saint John of Jerusalem." A religious charitable organization founded circa 1096 to provide aid to Christian pilgrims traveling in the Holy Land. In the last half of the 12th century, they became more militaristic. Plural is Knights Hospitaller. Also spelled Hospitaler.

Knight Templar

A member of the "Poor Fellow-Soldiers of Christ and of the Temple of Solomon" (simplified to "The Order of the Temple of Solomon" in this book). A religious military order founded by Crusaders in Jerusalem around 1118 to defend the Holy Sepulcher and Christian pilgrims. Plural is Knights Templar.

Lent

A Christian season of fasting and penitence in preparation for Easter, beginning on Ash Wednesday and lasting 40 weekdays to Easter, observed annually.

leprosy

A devastating illness that destroys skin, flesh, and bones. During the Middle Ages, it was considered divine judgment for a sinful life.

liege lord

A feudal lord who is entitled to allegiance and service from his vassals.

lord

A landholder, typically a noble or the king, who granted fiefs (the use of land) to vassals (who were often knights, or even other nobles).

lute

A stringed musical instrument that is plucked to produce sound. It has a long, fretted neck and a hollow, pear-shaped body.

Mass

A Catholic Church service which includes Holy Communion.

men-at-arms

A general term for trained soldiers. Typically, they were trained like knights, but not all men-at-arms were knights.

Michaelmas

The Feast of St. Michael was celebrated on September 29th. It also marked the end of the harvest season. It was considered a major feast that was observed as a holiday and required fasting on the previous day.

Midsummer

Also known as the Feast of St. John the Baptist; it was celebrated on June 24th. It was considered a major feast that was observed as a holiday and required fasting on the previous day.

millstone

A heavy disc-shaped stone. Grain was placed between two millstones, and they were rotated against one another in order to grind the grain into flour.

minstrel

An entertainer. Minstrels were primarily performers. Although some wrote their own songs, they often sang songs composed by others, notably the troubadours. Minstrels also performed acrobatics, juggled, told jokes, and recited poems.

Moor

The name given to the Muslim people who invaded Spain in the 8th century. The Moors were from northwest Africa, and they were of mixed Arab and Berber heritage.

Morpheus

In Greek mythology, Morpheus was the god of sleep and dreams. The phrase, "in the arms of Morpheus" simply means that the person is asleep. Today, the narcotic morphine can trace its name to Morpheus.

Mount Olympus

In Greek mythology, the location where the gods lived.

obeisance

Giving proper respect and deference to someone of superior rank. Typically this would require kneeling (see genuflect), bowing, or curtsying.

Odysseus

In Greek mythology, Odysseus was the King of Ithaca, who was called by his High King, Agamemnon, to wage war against Troy. Known as "Odysseus the Resourceful," it was his strategy of the Trojan horse that resulted in the victory of the Greeks over Troy. Odysseus was anxious to return to his wife, Penelope, but his voyage home was fraught with fantastical dangers and adventures. His story is known as the Odyssey. He was gone from Ithaca for twenty years, and many believed that he was dead. He returned in disguise and defeated the men who were pursuing his wife by winning an archery contest where he demonstrated his amazing skills with a bow that only he could string.

Orpheus

In Greek mythology, Orpheus was a talented musician and poet. While still living, he descended to the underworld in hopes of rescuing his dead wife, Eurydice, from Hades. He was given permission to lead her back to earth, as long as he did not turn around to look at her. At the last moment he looked, and she was lost to him forever.

Outremer

A French word meaning, "overseas." Used as a name for the Crusader States, especially the Kingdom of Jerusalem, after the First Crusade.

page

A boy in training to become a knight. He would progress from page to squire to knight.

palfrey

A horse used for everyday riding. These smaller horses were often ridden by women.

parchment

Animal skin that has been processed to use as a writing surface. It was typically sheepskin, and it was also used to cover windows before the widespread use of glass.

passant

In heraldry, a beast walking, with the right foreleg raised.

Penelope

In Greek mythology, the wife of Odysseus. She faithfully waited for her husband and refused to remarry when everyone else was convinced that Odysseus had died and would not return. Pursued relentlessly by a band of unwanted suitors, she delayed any decision to remarry by weaving a shroud for her father-in-law by day, only to unravel her work at night. When her ruse was discovered, she devised an archery contest that only Odysseus could win. He returned just before the contest and won it before slaying the unwanted suitors.

physician

A university educated doctor.

pilgrimage

A religious journey to a holy place.

Plantagenet

This became the family name of Geoffrey V, Count of Anjou. Reputedly this name was given to him due to his habit of wearing a sprig of yellow broom blossoms (in Latin: *planta genista*) in his hair. Geoffrey's descendants would rule England from 1154 to 1485 as the Plantagenet dynasty.

Poitevin

Originating from or belonging to the County of Poitou in France.

pommel

1) A knob attached to the end of the grip in swords and daggers. It provided a counter balance to the blade, and it helped the user maintain a better hold on the weapon because it prevented the hand from sliding off the grip. See also: hilt, cross guard, and grip.

2) A knob at the front of a saddle.

portcullis

A heavy gate that was raised and lowered to control entry into the grounds of a castle. It was part of the gatehouse. A portcullis was composed of crossed bars, forming a grate or grille. The bottom edge consisted of spikes.

postern gate

A small door hidden in the castle wall that allowed soldiers to enter and exit the castle grounds without using the main gate. This was useful during sieges. Typically, a postern gate was only large enough to allow the passage of one man at a time.

rampant

In heraldry, a beast standing on its hind legs, the right foreleg raised above the left.

relics

Sacred objects which were associated with a saint or holy person. It was believed that relics could work miracles. Relics included objects that the saint might have owned or touched. Physical remains of a saint, including blood and bones, were also considered relics.

Saint George and the Dragon

This legend was very popular during the 12th century. A dragon had nested in a village, and he would not let the people draw water from a nearby spring unless they gave him one person to eat each day. The victims were chosen using a lottery, and one day the town's princess drew the unlucky lot. Saint George was traveling through the town and heard about the princess' plight. He slew the dragon, saving her and all the people of the town.

Saracen

During this time period, Muslims, particularly Arab Muslims, were called Saracens.

scabbard

A rigid sheath made of wood, metal, or hardened leather. It is used to enclose and carry the blade of sword or dagger, both to protect the wearer and to keep the blade clean and sound.

scythe

A farming tool with a sharp, curved blade affixed to a long wooden handle. It was used to cut grass for hay.

sennight

A period of one week, or seven days.

shire

A county in England, typically combined with the name of the shire to form a single word: Nottinghamshire.

sickle

A farming tool with a sharp, curved blade affixed to a short wooden handle. It was used for cutting grain, corn, grass, and similar crops.

Sire

The form of direct address used for royalty prior to the 16th century. "Your Grace" was also used for royalty and high-ranking clergy.

solar

Inside a castle tower, this room (or suite of rooms) was the primary living area for a lord and his family, and it provided them with some measure of privacy.

squire

A boy in training to be a knight. He would progress from page to squire to knight.

staff

A traditional pole-shaped weapon popular in England during the Middle Ages. It was made of hardwood and was typically 6 to 9 feet (1.8 to 2.7 m) long. It was also called a quarterstaff or a short staff.

stern

The back end of a ship.

Styx

In Greek mythology, a river in the underworld over which the souls of the dead were ferried by Charon.

surcoat

This sleeveless cloth tunic was worn over chainmail. Heraldry symbols were often sewn onto the chest of the surcoat. For example, Crusaders often wore white surcoats with a red cross emblazoned on the chest.

tack

Saddles, stirrups, bridles, halters, reins, bits, harnesses, and so forth. The equipment and accessories needed for horseback riding and for hitching horses to wagons and carts.

tallage

A tax that a lord could demand at any time without giving a reason.

Templar

See: Knight Templar.

tournament

A sporting event that allowed knights to demonstrate and hone their skills. Tournaments also provided an opportunity for knights to build wealth from winnings.

trestle table

A table composed of a removable top supported by trestles (A-frame supports with horizontal beams at the top). This type of table could be easily moved around or stored when not needed.

troubadour

A poet and songwriter. Troubadours sometimes performed, but they were primarily seen as composers. They were sometimes from noble families.

vassal

When a man swore loyalty to a noble landowner in return for use of that land (a fief), he became a vassal of the lord. A vassal was expected to provide services to the lord whenever needed. A vassal might be required to go to war and fight for his lord. If the vassal could not go to war, he would have to provide a substitute to fulfill his vassalage. Although it is often thought of in terms of lower ranking men, such as knights, anyone could be a vassal. Henry II was King of England, but he was also Duke of Normandy (and many other noble titles). As Duke of Normandy, Henry paid homage to King Louis VII of France; thus, he was also Louis' vassal. The same was true for King Richard; as Duke of Normandy, he was King Philippe's vassal.

vestry

A small room in a church used for storage of items such as vestments, sacred vessels, and other worship-related supplies and accessories.

waning

When the illumination of the moon is decreasing; the time between a full moon and a new moon.

ward

A person who has been placed under the control and protection of a guardian. In 12th century England, if the child of a noble family became an orphan, the child automatically became a ward of the king. This would include unmarried daughters, regardless of their age.

waxing

When the illumination of the moon is increasing; the time between a new moon and a full moon.

wheelwright

A craftsman who builds and repairs wooden wheels.

wound fever

An infection.